TREACHEROUS IS
THE NIGHT

Center Point
Large Print

Also by Anna Lee Huber and available from Center Point Large Print:

This Side of Murder

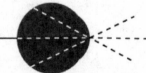

This Large Print Book carries the Seal of Approval of N.A.V.H.

TREACHEROUS IS THE NIGHT

A Verity Kent Mystery

Anna Lee Huber

CENTER POINT LARGE PRINT
THORNDIKE, MAINE

This Center Point Large Print edition
is published in the year 2018 by arrangement with
Kensington Publishing Corp.

The text of this Large Print edition is unabridged.
In other aspects, this book may vary
from the original edition.
Printed in the United States of America
on permanent paper.
Set in 16-point Times New Roman type.

ISBN: 978-1-68324-982-5

Library of Congress Cataloging-in-Publication Data

The Library of Congress has cataloged record
under LCCN: 2018041773

I dedicate this book to the so-often overlooked victims of every war and conflict—the refugees and beleaguered citizens of territories occupied or bombarded by the enemy. In particular, the people of brave little Belgium during 1914-1918, whose country might have been small, but whose hearts and courage were immense.

And I would also like to dedicate it to the women throughout history who have always done their parts, in matters both big and small, at home and on the broader stage of conflicts. Often underappreciated and dismissed, and sometimes derided, still they soldiered on for the greater good.

You have my undying gratitude.

ACKNOWLEDGMENTS

As all authors know, there are books that are relatively straightforward to write, and then there are those that are not. They run through your house like a toddler freed from their clothes, refusing to follow your plot, forcing you to give chase, and laughing all the while at your frustrated folly. Like those sweet, impish little cherubs, it is books like these that in the end are often the most rewarding to produce, but during the process cause you no end of exasperation, pain, and self-doubt.

Treacherous Is the Night definitely fell into the latter category. And as such, I have many people to thank.

Loads of gratitude to my mother, who took care of my flesh-and-blood sweet, impish little cherubs while I wrote, and helped keep our home from dissolving into a trash heap.

Immense thankfulness to my husband for all his love and support, and for helping to work out the tangle of Sidney's motivations, and the struggles and joys of marriage. Also, thanks for diving down the research rabbit hole of 1914 airplanes, ordnance, and detonators with me. (But probably the less said about that, the better.) Love you, babe!

Thank you to my children for their sticky kisses and silly dances, and for making my life more wonderful than I ever could have imagined.

Thank you to my agent, Kevan Lyon, for all of her confidence and wisdom.

Thank you to my editor, Wendy McCurdy, and the entire Kensington team for all their stellar efforts and expertise.

Much thanks to the real-life members of the British Secret Service and the intelligence-gathering networks throughout the former occupied territories of Belgium and France, and in particular to those who survived to write about their experiences.

Thank you to all my friends and family for their love and support, be it in dropping me a note to tell me they enjoyed my book, or in answering my telephone call to talk me down from my panic, or in responding to a message to ask for some random bit of research I think they might know.

And last, but definitely not least, thank you to my readers for embracing this new heroine, Verity Kent, and for feverishly debating which direction she should take next, and which fella should ultimately win her heart. I hope you enjoy this next stage of her journey.

TREACHEROUS IS
THE NIGHT

CHAPTER 1

Oh, treacherous night!
Thou lend'st thy ready veil to ev'ry
   treason,
And teeming mischiefs thrive beneath thy
   shade.
   —Aaron Hill, from his adaptation
      of Voltaire's *The Tragedy of Zara*

July 1919
London, England

"I've a favor to ask of you," Daphne declared as she plopped down on the emeraldine cushions of the sofa in my drawing room. "Now, hear me out before you say anything," she added, removing her gloves.

I gazed at her in wary amusement. Her enthusiasm was boundless, as was her penchant for stumbling into bizarre circumstances. I could only guess what predicament she'd found herself in this time.

She inhaled swiftly and then leaned toward me. "I want you to attend a séance with me."

11

My eyebrows arched in surprise before lowering in displeasure.

She held up a hand to forestall me even though I hadn't uttered a word. "I know you don't believe in them. That you think they're poor form."

"I've never said that."

"No, but it's plain to see. Anytime anyone mentions them, your mouth gets all tight. Like it is now."

I relaxed the muscles pursing my lips, taking her point.

"I'm not saying you aren't right. There are a lot of fraudulent mediums about these days shamelessly swindling the bereaved."

This was sadly too true, and what lay at the heart of my objection to such things. It seemed all of England had gone mad for Spiritualism, desperate to speak to their loved ones who had died before their time, lost to the senseless carnage of the war. This made them all too easy prey for the unscrupulous.

"But I have an appointment with one of the most gifted and attuned Spiritualists in all of London," she hastened to say. "She comes very highly recommended. Surely you don't object to all such things? Only the shams?"

Rather than answer her, I asked a question of my own. "Who recommended her?"

She sat back, plucking at a loose string on her pale pink frock. "Well, my sister for one."

"Your sister?" I couldn't withhold my disdain, for Melanie was not the most astute judge of character.

"Yes, but not just her. Several other ladies have told me how wonderful her manifestations are. I've even been told the Queen Mother and Princess Louise have consulted her."

This did not sway me, for I'd spent enough time with royals to recognize they were as fallible as the rest of us.

I tilted my head, studying her fretful expression. "Why is this so important to you?" I asked more gently. "Who is it you want to make contact with?" I could guess, but I wanted to hear it from her.

Her eyes slid to the side, staring at the pomegranate damask wallpaper. "Gil's birthday would be tomorrow." She swallowed. "His twenty-fifth. And mine is next month, and I can't stop thinking about how I'll be the same age he was when he was killed." Her stark gaze lifted to meet mine. "I . . . I just want to know he's well."

I wanted to reassure her. To quote the same assurances I'd been told time and time again by clergymen, by my parents, by friends, and even by strangers over the long years of the war. They readily sprang to my lips, but I did not let them pass. I was as tired of repeating them as I was of hearing them. Daphne already knew them, and my reiterating them yet again would not help.

What she really wanted was a connection, a way to reclaim that which war had severed, and I could not give her that.

I grimaced in understanding, allowing her a moment to compose herself again as she dabbed at her eyes. I was finding it very difficult to say no to her. Not only because she was my dearest friend, but also because her petite stature, golden tresses, and limpid blue eyes aroused a protective instinct within one. She might have been just another bland blond beauty, but for the pronounced hook in her nose. She was forever cursing her imperfect beak, never recognizing it saved her from being a cliché, and instead elevated her into the stratum of arresting.

It wasn't that I didn't sympathize with her desire to contact her brother. Many times, I'd contemplated what it would be like to be able to speak to one of the dozens of loved ones and friends I'd cared for—who had become casualties of the war and the outbreaks of Spanish influenza that followed. But for my part, I was having more than enough trouble dealing with the living.

As if summoned by my thoughts, my husband strode into the drawing room of our Berkeley Square flat. As always of late, my heart beat a little faster at the sight of him. Until a month ago, I'd believed Sidney was dead, killed in France during the Germans' brutal final push in the spring of 1918. But although he'd been

14

critically injured, he'd managed to survive, using his reported death to clandestinely search for evidence that would uncover the traitor working amidst the fellow officers in his battalion. The same man who had shot Sidney and left him for dead.

Although we had worked together to unravel the nest of traitors, I was still coming to grips with his return. Still trying to reconcile myself to the fact that he'd allowed me to believe him dead for fifteen months. Still trying to bridge the distance four and a half years of war had built between us. Our five-year wedding anniversary would be in October, and yet these four weeks since his reappearance were the longest we'd ever spent together.

Correctly sensing that my conversation with Daphne was somewhat delicate, he nodded a greeting to my friend and then settled in a chair on the opposite side of the room, screening himself from our view with his newspaper.

"Can't you take George?" I asked Daphne, feeling only a small twinge of guilt for suggesting she plague our mutual friend with her request.

Daphne's mouth pursed. "He's even more against it than you are. Thinks it's all hogwash, you know that. And he's twice as vocal." She crossed her arms over her chest. "He'd probably tell Madame Zozza to her face."

I well knew George's thoughts on the matter.

A brilliant cryptologist and mathematician, George's mind worked along strictly logical lines, and Spiritualism did not fit those. He and Daphne seemed the unlikeliest of friends. He with his stoic logic and calm precision, and she with her wide-eyed naïveté and vibrant enthusiasm. But though Daphne might be a bit thick at times, she was unfailingly, unflinchingly loyal, and George and I both valued that quality almost above all others. As for Daphne, I'd long suspected she'd taken to George because he reminded her of her older brother, Gil, lost early to the war. The same brother she hoped to contact.

"Madame Zozza?" I queried.

"Yes! Quite dramatic, isn't it? I'm sure it's merely her stage name, so to speak."

"You think?"

Her brow lowered. "Yes, but don't let that dissuade you. After all, one hardly wants to visit a medium named Betty Smith."

Perhaps she didn't, but I would feel better about her consulting a woman without such pretensions. Sadly, I knew I was in the minority. After all, the number of séances being conducted across London was nearly as abundant as the number of dances. Those mediums who were most popular performed sessions that were often more spectacular than they were accurate, and consequently were able to book as far in advance as the tickets for a popular revue at one of the theaters.

I had only ever attended one séance—an amateur bit of table-turning at a country house party—and I hadn't found it to be the least entertaining or enlightening. It had all seemed like nothing more than a ridiculous bit of theatrics, even before the ladies involved decided it would be capital fun to channel my still-believed-dead husband. Now that I knew my husband was very much alive, their cruel trick did not bother me over much. But the memory of that night still made my jaw tight with anger and my skin prickle with unease.

To Daphne's credit, she didn't know about what I'd endured at that house party. Otherwise, she would never have asked me to attend this séance with her. And if I told her now, she would be horrified. So I kept the matter to myself.

Torn between my desire to protect Daphne from her own gullibility that would make her an easy mark and my own revulsion at the practice, I tapped my fingers against the arm of my bergère chair. "When is this séance?"

She pressed her lips together, hesitating before she admitted, "Tonight."

I narrowed my eyes in suspicion. "If this Madame Zozza is as gifted as you claim she is, how long have you had this session booked?"

"Three weeks."

"Daphne!"

"I know, I know. I should have asked you sooner. But . . . I was afraid you'd say no."

I scowled, furious at this bit of manipulation. "It would serve you right if I did. Let the woman bilk you of all your money. See if I care."

I folded my arms over my chest and turned to stare out the tall Georgian-style windows where a light summer rain fell. Sidney's newspaper rattled, and I was certain he'd heard at least this outburst. That is, if he wasn't already remorselessly listening to the entire conversation.

Daphne's eyes flicked toward him before she shifted forward on the sofa, leaning across the distance toward me. "You have every right to be furious with me. I would be cross, too, if I were in your shoes. I know how you feel about these sorts of things. Which is precisely why I need you to be the one who comes with me." She pressed a hand to the powder blue serge of my skirt. "Please, Ver. I wouldn't ask you if it wasn't *extremely* important. You know I can't go alone."

She was right about that, and I was relieved to hear her admit it. A good con woman would recognize how much she'd loved her brother, how terribly she missed him. And she would also quickly realize how naïve and trusting she was. After all, the success of her scams depended upon that knowledge. She would twist that to her advantage if someone wasn't there to shield her.

I turned to look at her and then wished I hadn't. Then I wouldn't have seen that cursed gleam of hope shining in her eyes. Or watched it dim as I remained silent.

She heaved a sigh. "I suppose I shall just have to take my sister then. Though she'll make the entire session about her. Who knows if I'll even be able to slide in a word edgewise?" She frowned. "She'll probably wish to summon Humphrey, and you know how tiresome her husband was in life. Well, to hear Melanie talk, he's even more so in death."

I couldn't help but crack a smile. Not that I believed a medium had actually ever summoned Humphrey. But if she was skilled enough, she would read Melanie's clues and respond appropriately.

However, I sobered quickly at the preposterous idea of Melanie being trusted to protect Daphne. Melanie was enough of a spendthrift that no matter how deeply she was taken in by a medium, such a person would never be able to defraud her of all her money. But Daphne was much more impressionable, and her heart bruised easily. I'd seen it often enough. The walls I'd been able to erect around myself during the war, to shield me from the full impact of hearing of yet another death, seemed non-existent for her. She felt it all. Perhaps in the end, that meant she was better off than the stilted, jumbled mess

I'd become, but it also meant she was vulnerable.

I swallowed my affront, reaching across to clutch her hand. "You're determined to see this medium? I can't sway you to let it go?"

She shook her head. "I know you mean well, Ver, but I'm going, no matter what you say." Her mouth set with stubborn determination.

I glanced up at the ceiling, just knowing I would regret this. "Then, I'll go."

Her eyes widened. "Truly?"

"Yes."

She gasped in delight and sprung forward to embrace me, enveloping me in the scent of lavender. "Oh, thank you, thank you! You'll see. There won't be any shenanigans."

I smiled tightly, wishing I could believe that.

She gathered up her hat and gloves, and hurried toward the door, lest I change my mind.

Sidney lowered his newspaper as she approached. "Good morning, Miss Merrick."

"Hullo, Sidney. And remember, I told you to call me Daphne. I'm not about to stand on ceremony with my dearest friend's long-lost husband." She grinned at me over her shoulder, though the wattage was a shade too bright. I could tell she was somewhat unnerved by Sidney. Since his return, he was more reserved, more intense, and combined with his brooding, dark good looks, it was difficult not to feel off-balance. But nonetheless, I appreciated the concerted effort she was making to befriend him. Even if it was a tad too relentless in its cheer.

His answering smile was polite. "Of course. Shall I ring down to ask the doorman to hail you a cab?"

"No, I've brought my umbrella, so I think I shall walk," she replied breezily, already bustling out into our entry hall. "Goodbye!"

At the click of the door to our flat closing, Sidney dropped all pretense of reading the newspaper. "What was all that about?"

I crossed the room to the matching sofa closest to his chair, folding my legs underneath me as I leaned against the arm. He was turned out quite impeccably today in a crisp white shirt and deep blue suit that offset his eyes. His dark hair was once again cut neat and trim, the curls smoothed flat, save for that one stubborn lock that insisted on falling over his brow—as if to tip off unwary strangers that his interior was not quite so ruthlessly set in order.

"She wants me to attend a séance with her tonight after our dinner at the Langham's."

"Well, I suppose she at least shows some sense in taking you along with her." He dropped the newspaper on the table and reached over to remove one of the Turkish cigarettes he preferred from its silver box. "I suspect if you sent her off to sell a cow, she'd return with a handful of beans."

I sighed at his derisive tone of voice. He'd yet to warm to Daphne. He thought her flighty and ingenuous, both counts I couldn't entirely dispute. His wit was darker, more sardonic since his return, but on this matter he usually kept his opinions to himself. Especially after I'd explained what a boon she'd been to me during the war.

"She's not quite so foolish as that," I retorted.

His expression as he lit his fag was doubtful. "I still have difficulty imagining her working for the Secret Service." He exhaled a stream of smoke, tilting his head in consideration. "Unless it's all a charade."

"I told you she worked for counterespionage, managing the Registry." A massive filing system that kept track of every foreigner or suspicious person on British soil. "And artless as Daphne might seem, she's not stupid, and very good at minding her tongue."

I still found it odd to be sharing such information with him after I'd spent the entire war hiding it. I'd been forbidden to reveal my part in the Secret Service to anyone. Very few people even knew of the agency's existence, particularly the branch in which I worked, handling the military intelligence from overseas. Later in the war, Sidney had grown suspicious about the true nature of my war work, and uncovered the truth by getting a colleague of mine drunk, a man who also happened to be an old school chum of his.

However, he'd not revealed to me that he knew what my real war work was until after he returned from the dead.

It still irked me that he wouldn't tell me who had betrayed me. Loose lips were extremely dangerous in that line of work. I could only hope the fellow hadn't shared sensitive information with someone less honorable than Sidney.

"Regardless, she doesn't work there anymore," I added, uncomfortable with this turn in our conversation. Just as I had been let go a few months after the armistice, my services no longer needed, what with the men returning from overseas.

I still didn't know what Sidney thought of my having worked for the Secret Service, and part of me was afraid to ask. After all, there were many who thought of spies, particularly women ones, as sordid, licentious, and untrustworthy. The manner in which they were portrayed in books and in films at the cinema did not help, for they usually fit the mold of the infamous Mata Hari rather than the more realistic portrait of the vast majority of the women I had known in the service.

I resisted the urge to squirm under his regard, uncertain what he was thinking. Whatever it was, it wasn't light or frivolous.

He exhaled again. "So you're attending a séance at this . . . Madame Zozza's."

So he had been listening, at least to part of our

conversation. I rested my chin on my hands. "It appears so. What of you?" A sudden thought occurred to me. "Will you be all right?"

I hadn't ventured far from his side in the past four weeks, and the few times I had gone out in the evening without him, I'd returned home to find him staring morosely into the fire while he nursed a glass of whiskey.

His mouth twisted in mockery. "Better hide the key so I don't wander about the corridors in my dressing gown, shooting imaginary Bosche."

I flushed. "I was not suggesting you would do any such thing."

"Perhaps not, but it's always possible, right?" he challenged lightly.

The unsettling reality of his nightmares lay heavy between us. He had yet to pass a night without having at least one. And the more tired he was, the more quickly they seemed to come. The worst were so frightening I had to wake him, lest he disturb the entire building with his shouting. Once he'd lashed out at me before coming to his senses, to realize he was in bed with his wife, and not struggling with a German in the trenches.

He lifted his hand to smooth back his wayward lock of hair, little good it did, for it fell right back over his brow. "I believe I'll meet some friends for drinks. Perhaps go to the club." His lips curled into the semblance of a smile. "I'm sure I'll find something to amuse myself."

I nodded, not knowing what to say. I never seemed to know what to say. Not anymore. Perhaps I should have asked more questions. Perhaps I should have made him talk. But then that might mean I would also have to share what troubled me, what kept me awake at night. And I wasn't sure I was ready for that. Not yet.

He ground his cigarette out in the ashtray on the table and rose from his chair to come sit next to me on the sofa. "I wanted to discuss our retiring to the cottage."

It took all my self-possession not to react to his statement, but even so I wasn't certain he hadn't seen apprehension flicker in my eyes as I lowered my feet to face him.

He took hold of my hands. "Now that the initial furor over my return and the recent events at Umbersea Island has diminished somewhat, I thought it might be a good time for us to get away for a while. Just the two of us." His eyes gleamed with an intensity I felt in the center of my chest. "The cottage in Sussex seems the natural choice."

It was true. Once word of his survival and our part in unmasking a small band of traitors became known, we'd had little peace. I'd always received numerous invitations, but the torrent that arrived in the post had overwhelmed even me. Add to that the journalists and photographers dogging our steps and snapping pictures of us, and it was all a bit jarring, particularly for Sidney. His fortunes had swung from facing the very real fear of a court-martial for desertion—a trial that likely would have resulted in imprisonment and public condemnation if he'd failed to prove sufficient evidence of the treasonous plot—to suddenly being lauded and courted by everyone, from the man seated next to him on the underground who had seen his picture in the newspapers, to the very king himself.

As such, we'd had little time to begin mending the damage war and separation had wrought upon our marriage. In many ways we felt like strangers, for neither of us was the same person we'd been when we married in the autumn of 1914, just days before he marched off to the trenches. The snatches of time we'd had together during his short leaves from the front had been but interludes, fever dreams. This was reality. One I'd not been prepared to face given his reported death.

He was right. If we were ever to make a go of it, to patch this rift between us, then we would have to do so in private. But that also meant giving up our fears, our insecurities, and revealing those things we might rather remain hidden. In that sense, the cottage was a risk. One I was as terrified of taking as not.

"All right," I replied placidly, though I felt anything but. "However, we've already accepted the invitation to the Duchess of Northumberland's ball."

There was no real reason we needed to attend. This was but a paltry attempt to delay the inevitable. One Sidney must recognize. Even so, he did not push.

"After, then," he said. Perhaps he needed a reprieve as well. "Just so long as we're gone before the bloody Peace Day celebrations they all seem so determined I attend."

I knew Sidney wasn't the only former soldier dreading the festivities, but most of the others were not being pressed to be put on display.

I had no more desire to attend than Sidney, even if my abhorrence wasn't so pronounced, so I readily agreed. "I'll write to the Froggets and ask them to air out the cottage and hire any additional staff needed for the rest of the summer."

"Tell them to be sure the cellars are restocked. Oh, and ask them to clean out the carriage house as well. I'll need some place to store the Pierce-Arrow," he remarked, rattling off what appeared to be his most pressing concerns—booze and his prized motorcar.

"I trust you don't plan on indulging in those simultaneously."

"What? And risk my motorcar? Not a chance."

"I'm more concerned with your noggin."

He draped his arm across the back of the settee, his eyes twinkling with amusement. "Don't worry, darling. I don't plan on making you a widow again so soon."

"See that you don't," I replied, rising to my feet. "I don't relish being forced to wear black." I crossed toward the door but paused to offer one last parting jest over my shoulder. "It's simply not my color."

CHAPTER 2

Daphne grinned at me in anticipation as I climbed into the idling taxicab. In the dim light of the streetlamps, I could see she was wearing her royal blue gown. It was one of my favorites for it complimented her coloring so well.

"I hope you didn't put on those glad rags simply for the sake of this séance," I remarked, feeling rather dowdy seated next to her in my modest willow green evening gown.

"No, I had dinner with Stephen Powell at the Savoy."

I arched my eyebrows. "And you sacrificed his company to attend this farce?"

Her smile turned long-suffering. "It's not a farce. And in any case, he was well acquainted with Gil. He understood."

Perhaps. But regardless of his thoughts on Spiritualism, somehow, I doubted he was pleased to be discarded in favor of the possibility of her speaking with her dead brother. In any case, Stephen was not my concern. Besides, if he'd remained at the Savoy, I was sure he'd meet plenty of young women willing to dance with him and help him forget his disappointment.

I studied Daphne's profile in the light and shadow of the passing streetlamps as they flickered through the motorcar's window. She almost seemed to vibrate with nervous energy.

"You could have asked Stephen to attend with you," I remarked.

She shook her head. "I don't know him well enough. It would have been much too awkward. That's why I refuse to attend the stage shows. To be singled out in such a large crowd." She shivered. "No, thank you. Victoria Revel's deceased fiancé once contacted her through a medium at the theater. She said it was both mortifying and thrilling."

"Yes, well, Victoria Revel couldn't hold her tongue if her life depended on it. She likely beat her gums to anyone in that theater who would listen. The medium's assistants probably heard everything she said and then reported it to the medium to use in her show."

Daphne gasped. "That's perfectly dreadful." She frowned. "But surely, they're not all that way. After all, there must be *something* to them if so many people are attending."

I opened my mouth to refute that, having a far lower opinion of people's gullibility than she did. After all, they'd swallowed down all the war propaganda nice and neat. But she cut me off.

"*Please,* promise me you'll keep an open mind." She reached down to clasp my hand where it rested against the seat. "I admit most mediums are likely frauds, but that doesn't mean they all are." Her brow furrowed. "You're very clever, Verity, but one day you're going to experience something you can't explain."

I wanted to scoff at this suggestion, but I knew doing so would only make her more intractable. After all, if I wished to convince Daphne of the medium's trickery after the fact, then I would have to at least pretend to be receptive to the possibility she was genuine.

"You're right," I relented. "I'll try to be more objective."

"Thank you." She squeezed my fingers and then released them. "Who knows? Perhaps she'll even be able to make contact with Rob for you."

"Don't," I snapped, unwilling to broach the subject of my second brother's passing. Especially not in such a context.

Daphne's face blanched, her own features crumpling in response to the pain she heard in my taut reply. I felt an answering lump rise in my throat and turned away.

Rob had been dead for four years, his aeroplane shot down over France in July 1915. And yet I struggled every day to push him from my thoughts. With Sidney's return, my brother's specter now loomed even larger.

31

Swallowing hard, I focused my thoughts on the damp streets and buildings passing outside the window. We'd entered Chelsea, I realized—that enclave of so many artists, poets, and writers. I wondered if this Madame Zozza saw herself similarly.

The taxicab turned into a small side street off Cheyne Walk, and drew to a stop before a warm redbrick town house on the corner with black wrought-iron railings and a black door. It was rather inconspicuous in appearance. Not even a swath of exotic curtains to liven up the bow windows, only a solid, dark color drawn tight.

I glanced at Daphne, curious whether we were in the right place, but she said not a word as she climbed from the cab. Fortunately, the rain had ceased, so there was no need to make a mad dash to the door. The fringe of my dress brushed my legs as I followed her out of the cab and up the short flight of stairs.

The door opened swiftly to Daphne's knock, and we were ushered inside by a young woman of about twenty-five. Her hair was pulled back severely from her face, and her stark clothing did nothing for her coloring or her shape. I presumed she was an assistant of some kind to the medium, for she greeted us coolly and took our wraps. Though she strove to feign disinterest, I caught her sneaking glances at me. I presumed, like so many others, she'd seen my photograph in the papers. She directed us into a sitting room, which would not have been out of place in any British middle-class home, where we were supposed to order our thoughts in preparation for the session. In all honesty, I didn't hear much of what she said in her crisp French accent once we crossed the threshold into the room, for something else had caught my eye. Or rather someone.

Max Westfield, the Earl of Ryde, stood conversing with an older woman seated in a Queen Anne chair next to him. Apparently, he'd been spending a great deal of time in the sun since last I saw him, for there were pale streaks running through his dark blond hair, and his skin had taken on a bronzed glow, which looked very well next to his dark evening kit. He smiled gently at whatever the woman said next and then lifted his head to glance toward the door.

Our eyes met, and I felt warmth spread through me as his smile widened. In the face of such a reception, I was helpless not to grin in return.

He excused himself from the woman and crossed to meet me. "Mrs. Kent, what a pleasant surprise."

My lips quirked. "Mrs. Kent, is it? After all we've been through, I should think you've earned the right to use my given name permanently."

Some of the brilliance faded from his eyes. "Yes, well, that was before."

My own good humor dimmed. "Yes, I know."

Only a short time ago, we had worked together to solve a deadly mystery, not yet knowing that mystery involved treason. Or that my husband was still alive and intent on uncovering the murderous traitors himself. During those short days before Sidney revealed himself to me, Max and I had developed an affinity for one another. One that, in time, might have developed into something more.

As a result, though our investigation had been resolved, my emotions could not be untangled so easily. I still loved Sidney. There was no doubt of that. And with him being my husband, I had made the decision that we should try to make a go of it. However, I would be lying if I said Max had not been in my thoughts.

His soft gray eyes searched my face. "How are you?"

"I'm well," I replied, knowing I couldn't very well tell him otherwise. "What of you? I didn't know you were in London. You were supposed to pay us a call if ever you were in town."

"I only just arrived yesterday." His brow furrowed briefly before smoothing. "I must admit, I'm surprised to see you here."

My cheeks flushed. Max had witnessed how I reacted after that sham séance I'd endured. He'd seen how distraught I'd become. "Yes, well, Daphne can be rather persuasive." My gaze slid to her as she joined us. "Daphne, are you acquainted with Lord Ryde?"

Her eyes widened, recognizing his name from the few details about the events on Umbersea Island I'd relayed to her. "I don't believe I've had the pleasure."

"Max, this is my dearest friend, Daphne Merrick."

He took her proffered hand. "Charmed, Miss Merrick. Do I have you to thank for this fortuitous reunion?"

"Yes, Verity isn't a great believer in Spiritualism. But she's willing to humor me," Daphne jested, tilting her head coyly in the manner she did when she found a gentleman attractive.

"I can't claim that I am, either." He glanced over his shoulder toward the older woman he'd been standing next to when we arrived. "But my aunt wished to attend, so I thought it my duty to accompany her."

Before I could respond, the medium's assistant returned to the room. "Please, if you'll all follow me, we can begin the evening."

Max excused himself to return to his aunt's side, and I sidled closer to Daphne, linking my arm with hers. My chest tightened with something akin to dread, and I couldn't resist one last attempt to dissuade her. "Are you certain you wish to do this?"

"Yes." She flashed me a grin and trapped my

arm against her side as she towed me toward the door. "Don't be such a wet blanket, Ver."

I scowled at this assessment of my conduct, but obediently trailed along.

We filed into a large room across the hall where the lights had been dimmed. Heavy, dark drapes covered the windows, and a large rug spanned much the length of the floor. But for a round table covered in a black cloth and the chairs surrounding it, the room was empty. I wrinkled my nose at the cloying scent of sandalwood that filled the air—an odor which I had never liked.

A middle-aged gentleman with a receding hairline and a thin mouth rushed past us to claim the seat to the left of where the assistant stood, grasping the back of a chair. Presumably, this was to be Madame Zozza's place.

"Please, be seated," the woman intoned somewhat belatedly.

Daphne's eyes twinkled with amusement. She settled into the chair next to the overeager gentleman and I sat beside her. There were eight chairs in all, and the other clients quickly filled these spaces.

A genteel woman of about forty chose the seat to the right of Madame Zozza. Silver streaked her dark hair and she clutched a locket dangling from a chain at her neck. The man next to her clasped his hands in his lap and did his best not to meet anyone's eyes. I suspected they were husband and wife, and it didn't require any otherworldly gifts to deduce from their taut expressions they had lost at least one son to the war. Facing their stark grief, my apprehension turned to anger that this medium should prey upon such people. But recalling my promise to Daphne that I would keep an open mind, I held my tongue.

Max helped his aunt into the chair next to the gentleman and then slid into the last chair on my left. He smirked and leaned toward me to make some remark, but the assistant cut him off before he could speak.

"Madame Zozza asks that you remove any gloves and place them in your lap. She also asks that you remain silent and order your thoughts. The spirits do not like distraction."

My gaze slid sideways toward him and I arched one eyebrow cynically as I plucked the gloves from my fingers one by one. A smile lurked at the corners of his mouth and he bowed his head to hide it. Unfortunately, his aunt had not missed this exchange. She glared at me, and I felt as if I'd been scolded for making one of my siblings laugh during church service. Though given the nature of this gathering, perhaps such a comparison was sacrilegious. I'd yet to be introduced to his aunt, but she appeared familiar to me somehow, though I couldn't recall how.

The assistant backed away from the chair,

sweeping her arm toward the door. "And now, Madame Zozza."

We all turned as one to see the woman who entered the room, pausing for dramatic effect. Whatever the truth about her gifts, I could well understand why high-ranking members of society and even royalty had flocked to her parlor. Attired in a loose-fitting black dress that swayed when she moved, and a matching head wrap affixed with a brooch of black jet, she appeared precisely as one thought a medium should, yet in an understated way. She clearly understood the power of subtlety.

Dressed as she was, it was difficult to accurately predict how old she was. There were few lines on her face and she walked with such grace of movement, I rather suspected she was no older than thirty. But the look in her dark eyes when she lifted them to examine each of us in turn, the depth and solemnity, made me wonder if perhaps she was nearer to fifty.

Other than the brooch on her headdress, she wore no jewelry or cosmetics. I had expected her eyes to be lined in dark kohl, but she did not affect such a gypsy-like artifice. She didn't need to. Her gaze was unsettling enough without it. I had to resist the urge to squirm whenever it fastened on me.

"Good evening," she declared in a well-modulated voice. "We are gathered here tonight to commune with those who have passed beyond the veil. To make contact with those who should wish to speak with us." Her eyes continued to scour our forms and faces, and I got the distinct impression she missed nothing. "I cannot guarantee that those people you wish to speak with will be receptive to our request. There are those who have moved beyond who, for reasons of their own, do not wish to converse with the living. But the fact that you are here, calling them to mind, may influence them to do so."

A gleam flared to life beyond Madame Zozza's shoulder, and I realized the assistant was lighting a candle. She silently slid it into place at the center of the table.

"In a few minutes, the lights will be turned off leaving but this single candle. These conditions make it easier for the spirits to manifest." She nodded toward the man on her left, urging him to take the object the assistant held out to him. "I will ask the spirits to ring this bell to notify us of their presence. And to ensure no trickery is involved, we will place it in plain sight of all here."

The gentleman examined the bell carefully before passing it to Daphne, who did no more than a cursory inspection. Then the assistant reached between them to set the bell on the table and place a glass bell jar over top of it.

I scrutinized each of her movements with

care while at the same time trying to keep tabs on the medium's actions. However, Madame Zozza continued to sit very still. Perhaps she was manipulating items beneath the table, but I doubted it, for the muscles in her shoulders and upper arms never shifted or bunched.

As if sensing my distrust, her gaze swung to meet mine. "In a few moments, I will ask you to join hands, to channel our energy, and to confine the spirits to the space between us. Do not be alarmed if I should seem unresponsive. I will return to my right self once the spirits depart, but I may not recall everything that has occurred." Her voice sharpened. "It is very important that you do not break the spirit circle. If there is any cause for concern, my assistant will step in to end the session. Do not break the connection until she directs you to do so."

I straightened and glanced at Daphne, curious how she had accepted this pronouncement. But rather than appearing unnerved, her attention only seemed more rapt, eager for the session to start.

Madame Zozza inhaled deeply and closed her eyes. "Let us begin."

The lights were switched off so that only the single flickering gleam of the candle remained. I blinked, trying to adjust my eyes. The grieving faces of the husband and wife seated across from me distorted in the yellow glow, taking on an even grimmer cast.

"Let us join hands," she directed us.

Daphne's palm was slightly damp, indicating she felt more anxious than she wished me to know. However, Max's hand felt warm and dry. A frisson of awareness ran up my arm. Different than what I felt with Sidney, but no less arresting.

"Now breathe in and out, slow and steady," the medium intoned in a soothing voice. "Focus your thoughts on the person you wish to contact. Recall their smile, the sound of their voice. Imagine them beside you, holding your hand, touching your face."

I had no wish to summon anyone, so instead I focused on studying those around me. Most of the others at the table appeared to be following Madame Zozza's instructions with varying degrees of success. The middle-aged gentleman on her left breathed rather too rapidly for someone who was supposed to be relaxing. If I had been the medium, I would have found his inhalations most distracting, but she seemed to pay him no heed.

Daphne's hand trembled in my grasp, and I glanced up to see that her face had crumpled. Whatever she was envisioning about her brother was causing her grief. Had I not known she would be furious with me for doing so, I would have called an end to our part in the séance right then.

Madame Zozza suddenly drew herself up taller.

"Spirit, this is a safe place. Give us a sign of your presence."

The skin along my arms prickled as cool air blew across the back of my neck. I searched the darkness behind the others at the table, but I could not tell where the assistant had gone. I was suspicious that it was she who had created the breeze, by waving a fan or opening some strategically placed vent.

Then the bell jangled. It was a muted ring, as it should be if it truly issued from beneath the bell jar. And hard as I concentrated, I could not deny that was where it sounded like it was coming from. The woman on the medium's right gasped in astonishment, and the others glanced about the table at each other before riveting on Madame Zozza's face.

Shockingly, her features seemed to sag and dissolve before our very eyes until one side of her face drooped lower than the other. I had never seen the like before. That a person should be able to manipulate such a thing and maintain it as she did for the next several minutes unnerved me. Especially when she began to mumble in a low, ravaged voice.

"Mother, is that you?"

The woman to the medium's right hiccupped on a sob. "Yes. Yes, it's me. Your father is here, too," she added, though she never took her eyes from Madame Zozza's distorted features. She seemed to scour them, searching for her son's resemblance.

But far from welcoming, the medium's slurred words crackled with anger. "Why are you here? I told you not to come!"

The mother blinked in shock.

Madame Zozza lowered her face. "I didn't want you to see me like this."

Tears slipped down the mother's cheeks as she leaned toward the medium. "Oh, darling, I wish I *had* come. If I'd but known . . . But your letter said your injuries weren't life-threatening, that you would be with us soon." She sniffled. "I . . . I wish you hadn't lied."

She tried to pull her hand from her husband's grasp, but he held firm as the medium had directed us. Her gaze darted to his in surprise and then registered comprehension.

She sniffed harder, even as tears continued to trail down her face. "Are you . . . in a better place now?" she asked hesitantly when Madame Zozza did not respond to her earlier statements.

The still active side of her face crumpled in confusion. "I . . . I don't know." The medium turned her head as if to look over her shoulder. "I think so."

Witnessing this exchange, I gripped Daphne's hand harder. If this medium truly was capable of summoning spirits—and I still held strong doubts that she could—but if she could, then it seemed she was pulling them from wherever they rested, and back into the torment they had felt in their earthly bounds. I couldn't bear to think of her brother being subjected to such a thing, or witness what effect that would have on Daphne.

Like my brother Rob, Gil had been a pilot. But unlike Rob, he had survived his injuries for a short time after his aeroplane was shot down. I had never told Daphne, but I had seen reports of the incident. As was often the case, his aeroplane had burst into flames, and before the men could pull him from the cockpit, Gil had been badly burned. It would have been far kinder had he died a swifter death.

I couldn't repress a shudder at the thought of forcing him back into such a corporeal form. It was beyond cruel. It was torture. I could only cling to my hope this was all a terrible hoax. For surely the medium would never attempt to perpetuate such a scene for her clients. It would frighten them all away.

My distress must have communicated through my hands for both Max and Daphne glanced at me in concern. I shook my head slightly to allay their concerns, hoping they would attribute my shivering to the cool temperature of the room. I wished now that I'd kept my wrap. The skin along my bare shoulders and arms prickled with gooseflesh.

"I should go now," Madame Zozza mumbled, her voice still soft with uncertainty.

"No, wait," the woman on her right cried, pulling at the medium's hand. "Not yet. Please . . ."

"Goodbye, Mother."

"Davy," she whimpered.

Madame Zozza's eyes returned to her. "Tell Father I couldn't help who I was. That I'm sorry he was ashamed of me." She paused. "I suppose at least I died honorably enough for him."

At this, his presence, be it feigned or not, seemed to depart, for the air felt lighter somehow. As if I could breathe more easily. Davy's father's face seemed to cave in on itself, and his shoulders shook as he bowed his head against his chest, and wept silent tears. I turned away, unable to stand the sight of their grief. It was too raw. And I still believed it had been exploited as part of this medium's deception.

Her face resumed its previous smooth, somber appearance, but for a furrow running between her eyes that had not been there before. She closed her eyes, inhaling deeply, and I tensed, praying she would not cause Daphne pain.

"Spirit, this is a safe place," Madame Zozza repeated. "Give us a sign of your presence."

Several moments passed in which Davy's parents' muffled sniffles were the only sound. I could tell Daphne was concentrating hard. As was the man on her other side, though in a different way. While Daphne's eyes were squeezed shut tight, his sunken eyes seemed to be cataloging the medium's every feature. Perhaps he thought that by doing so, he could impose his will and force her to summon the person he wished, but I couldn't help but wonder if there was more to it than that. Especially when his gaze shifted as if to do the same with everyone at the table.

Then suddenly something that felt like a hand seemed to trail up my spine even though I was seated firmly against the back of my chair. I jerked forward, glancing over my shoulder to try to discern what sort of trickery was at work. My head snapped back around as the bell began to ring, just in time to see Madame Zozza suck in a harsh breath.

Whether it was my own imagination or real, the stench of smoke filled my nostrils, and I braced for whatever she would say next, expecting her voice to dip into a lower register. But the expression that settled over her countenance, the complexity of it, somehow communicated that whoever she was pretending to channel was a female. My shoulders relaxed even as her eyes darted anxiously around the table. However, my relief was short-lived.

"Verity, *ma compatriote*, where are you?"

CHAPTER 3

I stiffened at her use of my name and the French accent with which it was done.

Madame Zozza's dark eyes finally fell on me, sharp with expectation. "Do not look at me so. Do you not recognize me?"

I stared at her, not knowing what to say, or if I even wished to say anything at all.

"Ah, well, that would be the fault of the filthy Bosche," she fairly spat the word. "I do not think I looked much like myself when they were done."

A heavy blanket of dread settled over me, for I had a strong suspicion now who this was supposed to be. She shook her head, "tsking" me. "It's Emilie, *ma chère*. Do not look so shocked. It was only a matter of time before I was caught, no? Even though I delivered their paramour's *bébés*."

I could feel the others' eyes boring into me, their curiosity rampant, but I had no attention to spare for them. Because Madame Zozza was correct. I was shocked. But not for the reason she wished.

Emilie had been a member of La Dame Blanche, an intelligence-gathering network that had been active in German-occupied Belgium and France during the last years of the war. As a midwife, she'd had the ability to travel about without arousing suspicion under the tight restrictions of the Germans. As such, she'd acted as a courier for the network, as well as gathering information while about her duties. Upon occasion, in my role with the Secret Service, I'd been required to penetrate into Belgium and France, behind enemy lines. Several of those missions had put me into contact with Emilie.

However, although I admitted to one disquieting second of doubt, I now faced the medium with certainty she was playing false. One could perhaps overlook the faultiness of her accent, being much more Parisian than Belgian. Maybe the pronunciation was lost in transmission, so to speak. But Emilie hadn't known my real name, just as I hadn't known hers. It was safer that way. And even had she discovered it, the quick-witted, pragmatic woman I had known would *never* have called me "*ma chère*." "*Petite imbécile*" was more likely.

Which begged the question, how had Madame Zozza known about her and my connection to her? Such information was highly classified, even now, after the treaty had been signed. For her to know any part of it meant someone from the Secret Service, or an ally we'd relied upon, had had a slip of the tongue.

I glared at the medium, letting her know she'd made a grave miscalculation. I was not going to be duped, so she had best conclude this nonsense before I concluded it for her.

Not by the batting of a lash did she seem intimidated by my expression. But I supposed this wasn't the first time she'd faced a hostile client.

"Let us forget that for now, *oui*?" she persisted. "I have more important things to tell you." She inhaled as if bracing herself. "I need you to unearth my secrets, *comprenez-vous*? I need you to reveal them." She shook her head sadly. "I know it will be difficult for you. But it is what I want. What I need."

My fury turned to bafflement, for I hadn't the slightest idea what she was talking about.

Madame Zozza nodded serenely, seeming content to pass this burden from her shoulders on to mine. "You will do what is right. And now I must go. *Au revoir, ma petite*." Her expression wavered and then she spoke once more. "But beware the man hiding behind a mask. He does not mean me well."

Then the candle flickered as Emilie's part in this mockery was over.

I continued to glare at the medium, though she kept her eyes shut as she feigned concentration to summon yet another spirit. Why on earth would she pretend Emilie wanted me to unearth some secret? And exactly what secret was that supposed to be?

In her work with La Dame Blanche, she must have kept many secrets, chief among them her involvement in the intelligence-gathering network. But by now that was known, for the leaders of La Dame Blanche had written a history of their network in order that they all might be recognized and compensated for their contributions and sacrifices to Belgium, France, and the Allied cause. My part had likely also been recorded in their annals, though the only people with access to that report or my real name were intelligence officials. The members of La Dame Blanche had only ever known me as Gabrielle Thys or Honoria Dupont, depending on which persona had been needed for a particular assignment.

I had to believe there was more to her decision to feign channeling Emilie. After all, I had lost friends and loved ones who would be much easier to gather information on than a clandestine contact in the depths of Belgium during the war. Surely any of them would be a better choice than Emilie.

Which meant someone had wanted Madame Zozza to "summon" Emilie for me. But who? And why?

The medium proceeded to summon the spirit of

Max's cousin for his aunt, a soldier who had died at Ypres. The aunt kept peppering the medium with rapid-fire questions, many of them about a cemetery at Boeschèpe where I gathered the son was buried. The medium ignored most of them, to the aunt's mounting frustration, and I swiftly lost interest in the back-and-forth of their struggle.

My thoughts were preoccupied by the more pressing puzzle before me. I struggled to control my impatience, biding my time until this phony séance was brought to an end so I could confront the medium. Infuriatingly, she seemed to have anticipated this very thing.

Her appearance had grown progressively more haggard throughout the session, so that by the time she contrived the departure of this third spirit, she slumped heavily in her chair. Her head lolled on her neck, and the people on either side of her seemed to strain to keep her upright.

"Be at peace," she whispered in a hoarse voice and then a gust of wind suddenly blew out the candle at the center of the table.

It was quite an affecting piece of theatrics, but I was not taken in. The same could not be said for Daphne and many of the others at the table, who gasped and began to mutter in hushed voices.

"Do you think she's all right?" Daphne leaned toward me to say.

"Somehow I suspect she'll survive," I muttered wryly as the assistant turned on the lights and

51

hurried over to where Madame Zozza drooped over the table. Her eyes stared blankly before her.

"There's no cause for alarm," she assured us as she pulled the medium's arm over her shoulder to help her to her feet. "This happens sometimes when her psychic energy becomes too drained. Some food and some rest, and all will be well again." She glanced around at us still holding hands, and it might have been my imagination, but her harried gaze seemed to linger longer on me. "You can sever the connection now," she instructed before she staggered toward the door, supporting some of her employer's weight.

Max rounded the table to assist her, but she demurred.

"Please, it's best for a stranger not to touch her just now. But if you could get the door."

He hastened to comply.

"You can show yourselves out," she called over her shoulder as they left the room.

The others rose slowly from their chairs and made their way toward the entry hall to gather their things from the racks hanging there. Some were silent and stiff while others conferred with each other in hushed voices. But no one dared raise their voice above a whisper.

I followed suit, though I didn't bother to hide the anger smoldering in my gaze, even when Max glanced at me in concern as he helped his aunt from her chair. Having witnessed her snide questioning of the medium, I'd recalled why she seemed familiar. I had never met Lady Swaffham, but I knew of her by reputation. More determined to win acclaim for herself than to do any real good, she had opened her own private hospital on Arlington Street when the war began, and resorted to what amounted to body snatching— seizing invalided officers whenever and wherever she could and transporting them to her hospital. She had also been one of the most notorious recruiters, competing with other gentlewomen to see who could compel the most young men to enlist, and publicly shaming those she saw as not properly doing their bit for the war effort.

At one point, her viper's tongue had briefly sharpened itself at the expense of my cryptographer friend George. That is, until Sir Alfred Ewing of the Royal Admiralty warned her that just because she was not aware of a gentleman's particular contribution to the war effort, did not mean it did not exist, and that her uninformed opinions were unwelcome. I'd even heard it rumored that privately he'd threatened to have her added to MI5's Registry for unpatriotic activities. Both George and I had wished we could have witnessed her response to that.

So her contemptuous treatment of the medium was not indicative of her disbelief, but rather of her own nature. That she was Max's aunt was as unfortunate as it was difficult to believe. When she followed his gaze toward me and pursed her lips in distaste, I found it difficult not to vent my anger on her with some snide remark. However, for Max's sake, I merely turned away. Not forcefully enough to be considered a snub, but sharp enough to make it clear I had no care for her opinion.

Daphne and I were the last to leave the table, though for my part, I was tempted to remain, refusing to be budged until Madame Zozza, or whatever her real name was, answered my questions. But one look at Daphne's face, the bewilderment and stark disappointment, convinced me it would be best if I confronted the charlatan on my own later. I located our wraps and hustled her out to the street and the cab we had paid to wait for us.

As we drove away, I turned my head one last time to see Max descending the stairs with his aunt. Whether or not he could see my gaze through the reflection of the glass I didn't know, but the light above the door clearly illuminated his face. I suspected if he had not needed to escort Lady Swaffham, he would have come after me, but perhaps it was all for the better that he could not. After all, his appearance at our flat at such an hour would require some awkward explaining to my husband.

I waited until the cab had turned east toward Westminster and Mayfair before speaking to

Daphne. "I know you're disappointed," I began as gently as I could. "But that woman was a fraud. If she had summoned your brother, you can be certain it would not have been real."

"How can you say that?" she protested. "What of the woman she channeled for you? You seemed genuinely shocked."

"I was shocked that she knew the code name of a member of one of our intelligence networks inside Belgium. That she had access to such classified information. But that was nothing like the real Emilie. She was faking it."

"You're certain?"

"Yes."

She blinked at me in the darkness. Perhaps I'd snapped at her, but she needed to grasp the seriousness of what I was telling her.

"How did the medium know I was going to be there?"

Her lips parted as if she was surprised by this question.

"Daphne, did you tell her I was coming?"

"I . . ." She shook her head. "No. I actually never spoke with her or her assistant. Melanie made the appointment."

"Your *sister* made the appointment?"

She nodded slowly. "Yes. She gifted it to me as an early birthday present."

I arched a single eyebrow skeptically. "Has she ever given you a birthday present before?"

"Well, no." She frowned. "I thought with Gil, and Humphrey, and so many of our friends gone, she might be making a better effort . . ."

Hearing the disillusionment in her voice, I reached over to take her hand. I liked that Daphne always tried to see the good in people, even when they didn't deserve it. But Melanie was as rotten and selfish as they came. I highly doubted anything would change that. And it infuriated me when she toyed with her kindhearted sister's affections.

"Did she suggest taking me along?"

"Well, yes, actually. She said you might like to contact your brother or a friend."

I sank back against the leather seat, ruminating on Melanie and just how involved she was in this scheme. A visit to her town house tomorrow morning seemed in order. But only after I spoke with the medium.

Daphne squeezed my fingers. "You're not cross with me, are you? I had no idea the medium would—"

I cut off her distressed words. "Of course not, darling. I'm well aware none of this is your fault."

She exhaled audibly in relief. "Oh, good." She sat beside me, tilting her head sideways to lay it on my shoulder. "I've already got George cross at me for even contemplating the idea that he might consider attending a séance with me.

I should hate for you to be angry at me, too."

I nudged her. "You told me you hadn't asked him."

"Yes, well, I hadn't. Not as of this morning anyway. I went to see him after I left your flat. But he reacted just as I'd predicted he would."

I smiled down at Daphne's golden curls. So she had tried to spare me. "Well, I shouldn't fret too much. He'll come around in a day or two. He always does. Remember when we made him crash that party at the Cheshire Cheese with us?"

Daphne giggled. "I wonder why he puts up with us."

I knew, but I wasn't about to say.

When I returned to the flat, I discovered Sidney was still out. This should have relieved me. After all, it was better than finding him sitting alone in the dark. But it did not. Not when it meant I had no distraction from my own troubled thoughts.

The irony of the situation was not lost on me when Sidney returned home to find me perched on the deep ledge before the open window in our drawing room, drinking a gin rickey. The rain had begun to fall again, pattering softly against the grass and the pavement outside. A cool breeze rustled the leaves of the trees in the square and brushed against my cheeks. All in all, it was a pleasant, peaceful evening, save for the roar and whoosh of an occasional passing motorcar.

And yet this glass was not my first. Perhaps because rain seemed to accompany all of my most unpleasant memories of the war. Even the telegram informing me of Sidney's death had been delivered in the rain.

The last time I'd seen Emilie it had also been raining, and it had not been a gentle shower either, but fat raindrops capable of soaking you to the bone in the matter of a few minutes. She had guided me across the heavily guarded frontier Belgium shared with France. Though she had undertaken just such a task many times before, this incident had proved particularly hazardous, for the Germans had increased security all along the border. There had been rumors the Kaiser had taken up residence at the Château de Merode in Trélon, one of the German Army's Headquarters, and the stepped-up patrols seemed to confirm this.

However, the Kaiser had not been my objective. The timing of his visit was simply poor.

Emilie and I had narrowly evaded two patrols, both of us conscious of what would happen if we were caught. The second time we had only escaped detection by the slimmest of margins, diving into the sodden undergrowth of the forest. She was the one who'd recognized the danger seconds before I would have blundered into the two sentries standing against the trees at the edge of the wood. It was not the first time her finely tuned senses and intuition had saved me.

I'm not sure how long Sidney stood watching me, but I looked up to find him hovering in the doorway. I hadn't bothered to switch on any other lamps than the one closest to the sideboard, so I sat mostly in shadow, providing me the advantage for once. His expression was vexedly impassive, as it so often was, so I couldn't tell if he was startled, disgusted, or concerned. Either way, I couldn't hide my behavior from him now.

I took another drink and turned back toward the open window, lowering my glass so that it rested against my bent knee. I suddenly felt very conscious of my bare feet, having kicked off my pumps and removed my stockings the moment I found the flat empty. Sidney had yet to hire a new valet, and the maid-of-all-work I'd employed a little over a year earlier, returned home to her own lodgings at the end of the day. I'd preferred it that way. Particularly given the fact that my previous lady's maid had been a disapproving stick who was spying on me for my mother. But I supposed that would have to change now that my husband was returned.

I expected him to voice his disapproval of my indecorous behavior—seated on a window ledge with my dress nearly ruched up to my knees while nursing a glass of spirits alone in the dark—but he merely crossed to the sideboard and began to pour himself a drink. Knowing Sidney's penchant for straight whiskey or brandy, I was surprised to hear the clink of ice being added to a glass. If he wondered at my proficiency with cocktails, or at least this particular one, he chose not to ask. When he'd departed for the front three days after our wedding, he'd left behind an eighteen-year-old bride who'd imbibed little more than the occasional glass of wine at a dinner party. I cringed to think how he would react if he knew how much I'd put away on an average night at the end of the war.

He leaned against the opposite side of the window frame, staring out into the night as he drank from his glass. I'd always found Sidney frightfully attractive in his dark evening kit. It suited him, even now, when the years of war had cast a harder edge over his features. Looking over at him, I had to steel myself lest I melt into a pliable puddle of goo.

"Did you have a pleasant evening?" I remarked offhandedly.

"Yes. Crispin and I went to the club. Played a few hands of brag with some of the other fellows." He shrugged one shoulder. "Nothing very thrilling."

"I hear Crispin's been stepping out with Phoebe Wrexham," I said after a beat of silence. We might be incapable as of late at discussing anything of importance, but as well-educated upper-class Brits, we could always rely upon our proficiency at inane small talk. After all, we'd been drilled in it since the cradle.

"Yes. Seems to fancy her."

"She's a good sort." I rubbed my thumb against the cool condensation on the outside of my glass, wondering if I would be risking too much if I mixed another one.

But then Sidney's eyes landed squarely on me for the first time since he'd crossed the room, glinting with sardonic humor. "So, are you going to tell me what's wrong?" He nodded his head toward my glass. "Or do I just need to wait until a few more of those do the trick?"

CHAPTER 4

I frowned, tempted to freeze him out, as he'd been doing to me. But the truth was, I did wish to talk to someone.

There had been a time when Sidney would have been my first choice. If we were ever to return to that, if we were really to make a go of repairing this marriage, we would have to start sharing things with each other. Otherwise, we were doomed to fail. In any case, this would be easier to discuss than some of the other matters looming between us.

"Your evening might have been uneventful, but mine was not." I lifted my glass, gesturing toward the window with it. "This . . . *charlatan* Daphne dragged me to pretended to summon one of my contacts during the war." I tipped my glass back, draining it of all but ice.

Sidney spoke without inflection. "A contact? From the Secret Service?"

I nodded. "A midwife named Emilie. Well, that was her code name anyway. She gathered intelligence and worked as a courier for La Dame Blanche, a spy ring operating in German-occupied Belgium and France that passed information to Britain during the war."

He sank down onto the ledge by my feet. "La Dame Blanche. After the legend of the White Lady whose appearance was supposed to herald the downfall of the Hohenzollern dynasty?"

I shouldn't have been surprised he would recognize it immediately.

"Appropriate given their goal of helping to defeat the German Army."

"Yes, well, Madame Zozza shouldn't have had any knowledge of the woman, let alone my activities during the war. So the very fact that she did suggests that *someone* has been sharing sensitive information."

"Unless she was also an agent," he suggested, speaking into his glass.

I turned to look at him as he drank, not having considered such a possibility.

"Surely you don't know everyone who worked for the service during the war?"

I rested my head back against the window frame behind me. "Then if that's the case, she's using confidential information in order to further her cons. I suspect C would want to know about that." I hadn't spoken to the chief since I was released from the service months earlier. But having spent four years on his staff—first as a typist and secretary, and then in various other roles, from translator to field agent—I knew him

63

well enough to apprehend he would not find such a breach of the Official Secrets Act amusing.

I frowned and Sidney arched his eyebrows in expectation, waiting for me to share my thoughts.

"Your suggestion has merit, but . . . I find it difficult to believe this woman worked for us in any capacity. She didn't work in the London or Rotterdam offices, I can tell you that. So for her to have access to Emilie's name and the fact that I was in contact with her, she would have had to be either an agent within the occupied territories or stationed at Folkestone."

"So lodge your complaint with C, or whoever you intend to get in contact with, and leave the matter for them to sort out."

There must have been something in my eyes that gave me away, for he paused in raising his glass again. "Or don't you intend to leave the matter to anyone?"

I resented his long-suffering tone. "I don't think you appreciate how serious this is. Someone divulged classified information to a Spiritualist, information that pertains to *me,* and I want to know why. Was it intentional? Were they merely desperate for money? Or do they have a careless tongue like your chum from Oxford who revealed my role in the service after a few drinks?" I narrowed my eyes in challenge. "Perhaps he's the culprit. Now might be a good time to tell me who he is."

He ignored this pointed query. "Maybe Madame Zozza learned of your involvement from Emilie herself. Or from someone Emilie told."

I shook my head. "She never knew my real name."

He lowered his hand to gently grasp my bare foot where it rested against the ledge next to him. "Darling, our pictures have been in all the newspapers over the past few weeks. Even overseas. It would not have been difficult for her to discover who you really are."

I half suspected he was intentionally trying to distract me, for I found it difficult to ignore the frisson of awareness that swept through me at his touch. Nevertheless, it would take much more than that to divert me from my concerns. "You don't know Emilie. Her role in La Dame Blanche may now be known, but she's hardly one to beat her gums about it. Not to mention the fact that the medium implied she'd been caught by the Germans and killed. To my knowledge, that never happened. The last time I saw her was in August 1918, so if she'd been apprehended after that, she almost certainly would have still been awaiting trial when the armistice occurred in November. There wouldn't have been time for her to be transported to Siegburg or executed." My brow furrowed. "Unless she was killed while being captured." I shook my head. "No. It simply doesn't make any sense."

But Sidney had latched on to something else I'd mentioned. "Siegburg? Isn't that a German prison?"

"Yes. That's where most of the women convicted of espionage were sent, and some of the men."

He stared down at the ice melting in his glass. "Is that where they would have sent you had you been caught?"

I chuckled mirthlessly. "No, as a British citizen I'm sure the Germans would have been only too happy to execute me." The fact no longer troubled me. I'd made my peace with it long ago. And in any case, the war was over. I was no longer in danger of facing a German firing squad.

But Sidney had clearly not confronted such a possibility. He didn't flinch or protest. In fact, he barely seemed to react at all. But apparently, I still knew him well enough to be able to tell I'd shocked him. When he lifted his gaze to meet mine his jaw was tight and his pupils dilated.

The air between us was heavy with unspoken things, chief among them the reality of our lives during the years of war. I was more familiar than most with the conditions Sidney had contended with while in the trenches. I'd been close enough upon occasion to see them in the distance, to smell them, even if I'd never set foot inside. So, while I might not know the details of each day, each battle, I had a general idea of the hell he'd been through.

But Sidney had no concept what my war had been like. He'd spent most of it believing me safe in London, tied to a clerical job, and assisting at the canteens. Gathering chestnuts for acetone, packing socks with cigarettes and peppermints to be shipped to the front, and crumpling tissue papers until they were so soft they no longer crackled when packed into the lining of sleeping bags—tasks that many women had undertaken for the war effort. Even after he'd discovered I worked for the Secret Service, it was evident he hadn't truly comprehended what that involved.

In truth, I was glad he hadn't known, for then he would have worried when there were far more important things demanding his attention. It also meant he hadn't been able to forbid me from doing my bit in the manner I wished.

Regardless, we were treading on dangerous ground, at least for tonight. There would come a time when I would have to stop avoiding the subject, but not now. Not while my nerves were still taut from that farce of a séance, and my wits were dulled with drink.

I reached out to pull the window shut. "I'm going to pay Madame Zozza a visit tomorrow morning, and find out just what she knows, and who told it to her."

"What if she won't tell you?"

I swung my feet down to the floor, but remained seated as the world tilted a little. "Oh, I suspect she will." My voice was hard with determination. "If a bribe won't work, then my threatening to inform the Secret Service should do the trick."

"Is that necessary?" he grumbled.

I looked up at him sharply.

"I mean, so she pretended to summon a woman from a now-defunct intelligence network. Does it really matter? The war is over. No one is going to go after her."

"Should I have argued the same thing when you feigned death for fifteen months and dragged me into danger, all to catch the man who betrayed your battalion?" I asked.

He scowled. "That was different. That was treason. We don't even *know* what this is."

"Precisely. We don't know."

He sighed, conceding my point.

"And I will not let it go until we do."

I glared at him a moment longer to be certain he understood before turning away. The floor was cold beneath my feet and I wanted nothing so much as to retire to bed and warm them beneath the covers. However, I wasn't certain how steady I would be on my feet. Oh, I wasn't so primed that I couldn't walk a straight line, but even a wobble might tip Sidney off to the true depth of my inebriation.

But then he surprised me.

"Would you like some assistance? I mean, you helped me solve my investigation. It seems only right I should return the favor."

I drummed the fingers of my left hand against the ledge beneath me, considering his proposal. Part of me was suspicious of his offer, especially after he'd tried to convince me to forget the matter entirely. But another part of me recognized he could be quite helpful. It would also give us a chance to interact with one another without our marriage being the focus. Of course, given the nature of the questions we would be asking, I would likely be required to share things about my time in German-occupied Belgium and France that might shock him, but I was willing to risk it. So long as my time in Brussels didn't come under scrutiny, and I couldn't see how it would. Emilie had not operated anywhere near there.

I allowed my gaze to travel over him as if examining him critically. Not that there was anything to physically criticize. Far from it. "I suppose you might prove useful."

A glint I well-remembered entered his eye, one that reassured me even as it made my breath quicken. One that made me believe the distance that separated us might not be so insurmountable after all.

"Ah, well, I do so long to be useful," he leaned closer to drawl in my ear.

The gust of his breath against my neck raised

gooseflesh along my skin. Gooseflesh I was certain he could see and feel with his fingertips as he slid his hand up my back into my auburn castle-bobbed tresses. I turned my head, allowing his lips to find mine, and fell into his kiss.

At least this firestorm of attraction was something I could be certain of. Neither time nor war nor separation had dimmed it. Since Sidney's return, I'd alternately craved and feared the intensity of our joining, for in many ways it was the only thing that seemed right between us. And yet, even in this, something was still lacking.

But for now I didn't fight it, I leaned into it. Wanting to forget, at least for a little while, that part of us was broken. And I had no idea how to fix it.

"You should have let Sadie answer it."

I glanced up from where I sat fuming in the passenger seat of Sidney's Pierce-Arrow the following morning to glare at him. "You sound just like my mother."

"Well, if you had, you wouldn't have had to hear that from either of us," he pointed out with irrefutable logic.

I exhaled an aggrieved sigh. I'd rather gotten into the habit of answering the telephone myself while the war was on. So naturally I'd picked it up when it rang while I was standing next to it before we departed for Chelsea. This action

70

never failed to set my mother's teeth on edge.

"I do so wish you'd let the servants answer your telephone like any proper British woman of means," she groused upon hearing my voice.

"Good morning to you, too, Mother." I rolled my eyes at Sidney.

His lips quirked. "It's good she can't see you," he murmured, placing his hat on his head.

"Is that Sidney, I hear?"

"Yes."

"Oh, good. He's still there."

I couldn't keep the mischievous twinkle from my eye. "Did you wish to speak with him?"

He shook his head vehemently and I was forced to suppress a laugh. Though my amusement didn't last.

"Not just now, dear. But I worried his learning about all of your carrying on during the war might have run him off."

"Why would you say such a thing?" I gasped.

"Because husbands don't want their wives gallivanting about town while they're away, dear," she delivered with cutting precision, as always casting my actions in the worst possible light. I could practically see her patting her hair as she examined herself in the reflection of the mirror positioned over the table where the telephone stood in my parents' entry hall, thoroughly unremorseful. "Besides you were raised better than that."

71

"He was away at war, Mother. And then dead. Not visiting Norfolk."

Sidney's eyebrows arched at this pronouncement and I turned away.

"Oh, but he wasn't really dead now, dear. That makes all the difference."

I closed my eyes and inhaled deeply, holding on to my temper by the thinnest of threads. Upon learning Sidney was alive, my mother, like most of Britain, completely ignored the fact that he'd allowed his reported death to go uncorrected for fifteen months. Fifteen months which I'd spent grieving. The only thing that mattered was that he'd returned.

I'd fielded an endless number of remarks about how delighted I must be. And I was. Though "delighted" wasn't the immediate word that came to mind. Relieved, pleased, and grateful were more accurate. But it was all much more complicated than that.

It wasn't that I wasn't conscious of how fortunate I was. I knew there were thousands upon thousands of women in Britain who wished they were in my shoes, welcoming their newly resurrected husbands home. Nor was I unhappy about his return. But all those people failed to consider the ramifications of his absence.

I'd tried pointing this out to my mother, but she seemed to think the fact that he'd been pursuing a traitor wiped the slate clean. At least, on his part. She much preferred to focus on my behavior while I believed he was dead.

"Did you want something, Mother?" Other than to criticize me.

"Your brother will be traveling to London on Wednesday. He wants to have dinner with you and Sidney."

Why my mother had called to tell me this and not Freddy, I didn't know. Being a decorated surgeon, my oldest brother was perfectly capable of operating a telephone. Of course, she could be referring to Tim. Just seventeen months younger than I, he'd always been happy to take the path of least resistance and let Mother do as she would. But somehow, I knew it must be Freddy making the trip.

"Of course, we'd be delighted to."

"Good. He'll ring when he arrives. He's staying at the Savoy, as usual," she added as an afterthought.

Definitely Freddy then.

She rang off rather quickly, and I stared down at the ear piece, suddenly having the sneaking suspicion I'd been taken in. If I had still been a gambling woman, I would have bet a tidy sum that my mother was about to telephone Freddy and tell him *I'd* asked *him* to dinner. Not that I minded seeing my brother, and I knew Sidney would be pleased to chat with his old friend, but I very much resented my mother's machinations. I knew my mother loved me in her own disapproving, domineering way, but I often wished she was not so very difficult.

That being said, I vastly preferred her to the almost stoic indifference exhibited by Sidney's parents. I'd spoken to them but a handful of times during the war and after their son's reported death. His father hadn't even traveled to London to manage the business of Sidney's death. Everything had been coordinated through his solicitors—even notifying me of the stipulations of Sidney's will and that they would handle the payment of the death duties.

Upon Sidney's miraculous return, they'd taken the train up from their estate in northern Devon to see him, but they'd only stayed two nights. His sister had dashed up to London for just an afternoon. I rather thought they would wish to spend more time with him. And although he never said so, I could tell from Sidney's expression that he had, too. But apparently, pressing business was waiting for them in Devon. More pressing than spending time with their resurrected son and brother.

Determinedly pushing my mother's criticisms from my mind, I turned to stare out the windows of Sidney's motorcar at the passing buildings along King's Street. "It will be good to see Freddy."

"It will." He darted a glance at me as he sped

74

around a lumbering omnibus, barely missing the fender of a Hudson. "Though, didn't you say his wife just gave birth to their first child?"

Sidney had never been what one would call a careful driver, and his time at the front certainly hadn't cured him of his devil-may-care attitude when he was behind the wheel. I gripped the seat, trying to stop myself from sliding toward Sidney as we zipped back into traffic.

"In May."

His gaze flicked toward me again, and I continued.

"But what you're really asking me is whether this trip is at the instigation of Freddy or my mother. And the answer is, I suspect, a little of both. I've no doubt Mother encouraged the trip, but Freddy would never have agreed had there not been some real reason for him to make it." I turned my head to peer under my lashes at him in cynicism. "The dinner, however, is almost certainly Mother's concoction." Seeing the smile curling his lips, my sarcasm turned to puzzlement. "What?"

He shook his head. "Nothing. It's only . . . I've missed this."

"Missed what?"

His deep blue eyes met mine. "Your reading my mind."

A warmth filled me. It *was* nice. This easy camaraderie. During our whirlwind courtship that last glorious summer before the war, it had come so naturally almost from the start, and I'd taken it for granted it would always be there. But war and time and separation had slowly chipped away at it, so that now it seemed almost a rare occurrence. Which made it all the more affecting when it did happen. So much so that, for a moment, I couldn't form a response.

Fortunately, Sidney wasn't expecting one. "So we're to be spied upon, is that it? What's the standard procedure when facing an enemy inter-rogation?" he jested. "Do we feign ignorance and canoodle, or do we call him on it?"

I laughed. "Given the fact that Freddy would see through our canoodling ruse in an instant, I suggest . . ."

Sidney slammed on the brakes, cutting off my thoughts as I tried to stop myself from flying into the dashboard. His arm shot out to right me as we came to a stop inches from the rear of the motor-car in front of us. Any outrage I might have felt at the actions of the driver was swiftly eclipsed by the shock of the sight before us.

"Good heavens!" I exclaimed upon seeing the flames engulfing the house on the corner across from us. "I hope they all got out safely."

My chest tightened as I suddenly recognized our surroundings, glancing left and right to be sure. "That's Madame Zozza's!"

CHAPTER 5

I didn't wait for Sidney to reply before I opened the motorcar door and clambered out. I weaved my way closer along the pavement, trying to see beyond the onlookers who had gathered to watch the fire brigade try to extinguish the blaze before it spread to the neighboring homes. This was no small matter. Smoke billowed skyward and the roar and crackle of the flames was intense even from this distance. Anyone still inside could not have survived.

Rising up onto my tiptoes to see over the people in front of me, I swept my gaze along the streets in all directions.

"Darling, what are you looking for?" Sidney asked, catching up with me. Being a foot taller than I, he had no need to strain to see beyond the people blocking our path.

"Madame Zozza." I stilled as I caught sight of a familiar figure across the street staring forlornly at the conflagration. "Or her assistant."

I glanced in both directions before dashing across the street, forcing my husband to follow once again. "Miss . . ." I realized I'd never learned the assistant's name. "Miss!"

She shifted her bleak gaze to meet mine, and for a second I could have sworn her eyes sharpened with wariness before being suppressed.

"What happened?" I gasped, searching beyond her toward where a few members of the fire brigade were gathered. "Did Madame Zozza make it out?"

She shook her head, tears filling her eyes. "I tried to get to her, but the smoke and the fire . . ." She sobbed. "It was already filling the house."

"I'm terribly sorry," I replied. It seemed impossible that the woman should be killed just as I was coming to question her. Killed in a manner in which one couldn't immediately verify the truthfulness of the assistant's assertions. Oh, the fire was definitely real. But as to her employer's death, that was highly suspicious.

As was the assistant's distress. In some sense it seemed sincere. I well believed she was genuinely shaken, but there was also a wariness, a calculation in her eyes that I couldn't comprehend. She seemed to gauge both my and then Sidney's reactions. But why?

"Did you live there as well?" I asked.

She sniffed and nodded. "And now I've lost everything."

Sidney offered her his handkerchief and she

dabbed at her eyes before pressing it in front of her mouth in a show of great despair.

"Oh, what am I going to do?"

One glance at my husband's face told me he suspected the same note of falsity as I did.

"What is your name?" I asked. "I didn't catch it last night."

She hesitated before replying, and whether she gave us her real name was up for some debate. "Pauline Laurent."

"Miss Laurent, perhaps we can help," I offered.

She blinked up at us hopefully. "Really?! You would do that? But I am just a stranger."

"Nonsense," I replied as Sidney removed his wallet and extracted a ten pound note.

"I . . . I couldn't," she protested even as she reached for it.

But before she could wrap her fingers around it, I snatched it from Sidney's hand. "Of course, you could." I arched a single eyebrow at her. "Especially as you're going to give us information in exchange."

It was a testament to her skills as an actress that she maintained her façade of shock and anguish for several moments longer, a space long enough for a small sliver of doubt to form within me. But then she quickly dropped the act, her eyes losing their soft glisten to turn sharp with cynicism, though the guardedness remained.

"What do you want to know?" she demanded in

her French accent. I'd half expected it to disappear as well, but it seemed to be unaffected.

"Who supplied Madame Zozza, if that's her real name, with her information?"

She wrung her hands, as if considering what to say, and I began to pass the bank note back to Sidney. Until she lifted her hand in a staying gesture. She swallowed. "It depends." Her eyes darted warily around her. "She got her information from several sources."

"Society women?" I guessed, not having difficulty deducing how the medium uncovered her miraculously accurate details.

"Yes. She paid a few . . . *ladies* . . ." Her mouth twisted in derision ". . . to pass along information from time to time about the deceased—physical descriptions, characteristics, particulars about their deaths, that sort of thing. As well as to praise her talents to their friends and acquaintances."

"So essentially they were informants. Part of your employer's scam," Sidney stated bluntly.

She shrugged. Clearly this did not trouble her.

Sidney scowled, but I cut him off before he could utter whatever sharp retort was forming on his lips. After all, we weren't here to debate ethics.

"Who did she pay to inform on me? I want a name," I added sharply when I could tell she was about to dither.

She shook her head. "I do not know. I wasn't

privy to all of her conversations. Not by a long shot."

I glared at her.

"It's true. I swear. I could give you a name. I could give you several. But I have no idea if they were the ones to tell her about you."

She was good. Very good. However, there was something in her face, a flicker of her eyelashes that told me she wasn't being entirely honest. "But you *do* know something. Maybe not a name. But you have a suspicion."

Her eyes darted back and forth between us before relenting. "There . . . was a man. He came to the house a few weeks ago. I remember him because he insisted on keeping his hat low and his collar turned up."

I glanced at Sidney. Definitely suspicious. "Go on."

"He asked to speak with Madame. Normally under such circumstances, with a strange man, she asks me to remain close by. Just *in case* she should require assistance."

I nodded my understanding.

"But after he murmured only a few words to her, she sent me away. This wasn't entirely out of character," she hastened to add. "She did send me away from time to time. But there was something . . . odd about it all."

"Did she seem frightened of the man?" Sidney asked.

"No. If anything, she seemed excited."

I frowned. "Did you ever see the man again?"

She shook her head. "No. But . . ." Her complexion paled. "She sent me away again this morning."

"You think she was meeting with him?"

"I . . . I don't know. But I was headed to the greengrocer and I'd forgotten my bag, so I returned for it, thinking to just sneak in through the mews and snatch it from the kitchen table where I'd laid it. When I turned in to the mews, I saw a man hurrying away from the house in the opposite direction. I didn't see him leave the house, but . . ."

But he very well could have.

"Was the house already on fire?" I asked.

She nodded. "I smelled the smoke as soon as I entered. It . . . it spread so quickly. By the time I reached the top of the stairs, it had filled the upper story. Mona. I could hear her. She . . . she was screaming . . . and . . ." She stopped and turned away, trembling.

I pressed a hand to her arm in comfort. Her display of emotion earlier might have been suspicious, but this was genuine. It also effectively answered my questions about whether the fire had been set in order to stage the death of Madame Zozza, or Mona, as her assistant had called her. The fire might have been intentionally set, but not by the medium.

"Do you have any idea what the man looked like or who he might have been? Any inkling of what he and Mona . . ." I trailed away, hoping she would supply me with a surname.

"Kertle."

I nodded. "Any idea what they discussed?" I pressed gently. It seemed we both needed answers.

Her throat worked as she struggled to speak. "I . . . I wish I did. But I never got a good look at his face. I'm fairly certain his hair was dark blond or maybe light brown. And he was average height." She sighed, realizing this was not very helpful. "But I do know Mona kept meticulous records about her clients. She said the surest way to be marked a fraud was by being careless. She always consulted her notes before she met with a client." Her dark eyes lifted to meet mine. "I do know she wasn't satisfied with the amount of information she'd been able to get on you. And she was flustered after the séance last night."

"Probably because she realized I hadn't been even remotely taken in by her performance."

She scoffed. "I could tell that just from the expression on your face when you arrived. And I *told* her that. Said it would be better if she targeted your friend. But she deviated from the script. She would not listen."

I didn't understand exactly what she meant,

but it seemed less important than another matter. "These notes," I said, harking back to what she'd been explaining earlier. "Where are they?"

She nodded toward the crackling inferno behind her. "Inside the house."

Just then, the roof at the back of the building collapsed with a great roar, sending a plume of smoke and ash high into the sky. Sidney grabbed both of our arms, backing us further away from the street.

I thanked her and gave her the money we'd promised, but not before asking her to contact me if she thought of anything else. She appeared to be on the verge of saying something more, but then hesitated, thinking better of it. Whatever it had been brought a deeply troubled look into her eyes. I hoped she might decide later to trust me with it. Whatever she'd actually felt about her employer, it was evident she was distraught her home and livelihood had, quite literally, gone up in flames.

Sidney guided me back to his motorcar and I sat silently as he maneuvered around the other vehicles and turned us back toward Mayfair. Though apparently my quiet pondering went on too long, for my husband grew suspicious.

"What are you thinking in that clever brain of yours, dear wife?" he drawled as he braked behind a lorry and then swerved around it.

I straightened the skirt of my mauve dress. "Just contemplating the identity of that suspicious man, and wondering if he has anything to do with me or that fire."

"I agree it does seem indicative of something. The question is what?"

"The fact is *someone* gave Madame Zozza sensitive information about me. I just wish I knew whether it was that man or someone else."

"Miss Laurent didn't give us much to work with by way of a description, did she?"

"No," I groused, gripping the seat below me as much in frustration as in an effort to keep myself from careening from side to side as Sidney made a series of sharp turns. I suspected at least eighty percent of my male colleagues at the Secret Service matched the vague account she'd been able to give us.

I turned to study my husband's profile. "What about your chum? The one who was so easily persuaded to share what he knew about me. Does he fit the description?"

He shook his head, gallingly determined to keep the man's identity secret. "I'm afraid not. He nearly lost a leg and still walks with a rather pronounced limp. Given her stock-in-trade, I doubt she would have missed that."

I sat taller. "You're right. I didn't factor any of that into account. I would say close to half the men in military intelligence had been invalided home, unable to serve at the front because of various injuries. So that would rule them out, as well as my female colleagues."

"Assuming this man is the person who informed on you?" he reminded me.

"Of course." I frowned at the distinctive façade of Harrods as we sped by. "This entire matter is both vexing and unsettling. First, to discover someone has either been sharing or using classified information for their own benefit. Information that happens to involve me. And then, to find out that the woman who might have supplied me with answers has been killed in a suspicious fire, her notes burned to ash." I exhaled heavily. "That's simply too incredible to be a coincidence."

He flicked a glance at me. "So, what do you plan to do?"

I contemplated this question. "First, I'm going to speak with Daphne's sister, Melanie Tuberow." I narrowed my eyes. "I want to know why she did something so out of character as to gift Daphne last night's session with Madame Zozza. And why she suggested her sister invite me."

"Then you'll have to excuse me. I've just remembered I have an appointment."

I couldn't suppress a smirk, for this was obviously a lie. "Oh, really? And what appointment is that?"

"It's of a . . . rather personal nature."

"One so personal you can't share it with your wife?"

His eyes creased with humor, catching on to my game. "Especially not my wife."

"You know," I remarked, fiddling with the button closure on my cream kid leather gloves. "I could postpone my visit until later." I raised my gaze just in time to see him cringe before he smoothed his expression out again.

"No, please, don't do so on my account."

I shook my head at his antics. "Sidney, I wasn't aware that you were acquainted with Mrs. Tuberow."

"Through her late husband. What a bore."

I giggled at his unconscious echo of Daphne's sentiments the day before.

"What? Did you never meet the chap?"

I waved his protest aside. "I know what you mean. Melanie is nearly as tedious." If for a different reason.

He shook his head. "It's a wonder they ever had children. Between his droning and her spiteful soliloquies, I would have thought they'd render each other catatonic."

"Sidney!"

He cast an impatient look my way. "Tell me you never wondered how they endured each other."

"Well, yes . . ."

"There you go."

I sighed. "You're very provoking, you know that?"

"It's one of my lesser charms." He flashed me a grin, one that was calculated to melt any residual irritation. "Shall I deliver you to Mrs. Tuberow's door?"

"Please."

Melanie Tuberow lived in tidy little home in Belgravia. Close enough to hear voices from the various parties and receptions held in Buckingham Palace gardens. Or so she claimed. Judging from the sharp glint that entered her eyes whenever she mentioned this, I suspected it was meant to imply that she overheard *things*. Important things. But in all honesty, I could have cared less what vicious *on-dit* she intended to spread. Until today.

Melanie received me in her overstuffed drawing room. I'd only had occasion to visit here once and it appeared much the same as before. Bric-a-brac covered the surfaces until one was afraid to move, lest some poor china shepherdess meet her untimely end. The rug was fashioned of some shaggy material she said some member of royalty had claimed was all the rage, while the chairs and sofas were packed with needlepoint pillows of every shape and size. This forced one to either endure Melanie's pointed glare for daring to remove them or perch at the very edge of the cushion.

Having never cared for Melanie's good opinion, I quickly dispensed with three pillows as well as the pleasantries. "I understand Daphne and I have you to thank for our session with Madame Zozza yesterday evening."

At first, Melanie seemed torn between maintaining her displeasure at my ill treatment of her bolsters and gossiping about the medium. Her enthusiasm for Spiritualism swiftly won the day. "Isn't she grand? Such immense talent."

"I have to wonder at your willingness to give up a session with a woman of such abilities to your sister."

She simpered, completely missing my sarcastic undertone. "Yes, well, that's simply the kind of person I am. One must be generous to those less fortunate. And Daphne, poor darling, is still quite balled up over our dear brother's death. She'll never catch a husband if she can't bear up better under the strain."

I ran my eyes over her where she lounged in a gamboge yellow satin gown, smoothing her hands over the silken fabric of the pillows on either side of her, her face plump and flush with health. Given the recent rationing in England, there were many who would find her appearance enviable. But having spent time in German-occupied Belgium and France during the war—where the food situation had been nothing short of desperate, even given the aid being spearheaded by the once-neutral Americans and the Spanish that the Germans had agreed to allow through—I found myself biting back an even sharper retort.

"Yes, you seem to be bearing up remarkably well."

This time she seemed to sense my words weren't quite the compliment they seemed. That or she was showing her claws. "Well, we can't all be so fortunate as you and have our husbands return from the grave, now can we?" Her mouth formed into a tiny moue which I presumed was supposed to encourage me to share, but merely looked pettish.

Tired of trading thinly veiled barbs, I elected to be blunt. "Why did you really give Daphne the session with Madame Zozza?"

Her brow furrowed in displeasure. "I told you, it was a gift."

"So you say, but did someone put you up to it? Were you promised something in return?"

She arched her chin in affront. "I'm not sure I like what you're implying. I don't need to be bribed in order to give Daphne a gift. I've given her many things over the years."

I was tempted to ask her to name one, but that would not get me the answers I sought. So instead I switched tactics. "I'm not sure if you're aware yet, but Madame Zozza is dead."

This captured her attention. "Dead? How is that possible?"

"There was an unfortunate fire this morning and she was trapped inside," I replied soberly.

Melanie turned away, seeming to struggle with some strong emotion. For a moment, I thought I'd misjudged her. Perhaps she had cared for the medium in some way. Perhaps she considered her a friend. I began to lean forward to offer her my sympathy when she spoke.

"Well, that was a waste."

CHAPTER 6

I was taken aback by the anger that flashed in Melanie's eyes.

She tossed aside one of the pillows cradled in her lap in a huff and glared at me. "*She* asked me to give Daphne the session. Promised me three sittings in exchange." She sniffed. "Well, she offered two, but I insisted upon three."

I stared at her, finding it difficult to believe she'd coughed up this information so quickly after denying it. Almost as difficult as I found it to believe how selfish and insensitive she was.

"I suppose now I shall have to find a new medium. And I tell you, it will not be easy. There are *far* too many charlatans in this city, eager to cheat you."

Ignoring the fact that Madame Zozza had been one such woman, I returned to the matter at hand. "What of me? Whose idea was it to suggest Daphne invite me?"

Melanie twirled the tassel on one of the pillows, answering me distractedly. "Hers, I believe." She sighed as if my question was tedious. "That assistant of hers said Madame Zozza had received a message she wished to deliver to you. One from beyond the grave."

I frowned. "Her assistant told you this?"

"Well, yes. She always arranged such things." Melanie huffed. "You don't think someone of Madame Zozza's prestige would concern herself with such trivial matters, do you?"

I took her point. "Did you not wonder why?"

She stared at me blankly.

"Why she wanted you to give last night's session to Daphne and me?"

"I assumed she wanted to prove her worth." She shook her head as if I were a simpleton. "Genuine mediums are always looking for respectable, new clients. I imagine they encounter far too much of the riffraff."

Somehow, I was surprised to find she hadn't lumped me into the latter category.

I allowed her to rant several minutes longer without truly listening.

So Madame Zozza, through her assistant, Miss Laurent, had made the arrangements so that I would attend. But I still didn't understand why? Had she been attempting to con me of her own accord? With insufficient information?

From everything her assistant had told us, this seemed to be out of character. She kept careful notes and did thorough research on all of her clients. She must have had more than enough data to use on Daphne, so why instead had she chosen to "summon" Emilie?

Unless she'd been convinced to do so by someone else. Someone who would not have been pleased if she neglected to try solely because of inadequate research. Whether they'd used threats or merely the allure of money to persuade her was unclear, but everything seemed to point to the existence of a third party. Perhaps even the suspicious man who'd evidently wished to remain unidentifiable.

There was only one thing for it. If I was going to get answers, I would have to approach my former colleagues at the Secret Service. And I knew just where to start.

Deciding I'd remained long enough, I made my excuses. But rather than ask Melanie's footman to hail me a cab, I set off down Chapel Street. George was currently staying nearby, occupying his aunt and uncle's town house while they spent the summer at their country estate. The rest of the year he kept to his set of rooms at the Albany on Piccadilly.

The footman tried to lead me into the drawing room, as would be proper, but I breezed past him, telling him George and I never stood on such ceremony. At least, not since the night we sat huddled together in a cold cellar during a Zeppelin raid. I expected to find him ensconced in the library, and there he sat beside a window, puffing away at a cigarette.

"It's a glorious day, and yet here I find you with your nose stuck in a book."

He glanced up with a smile. "Hullo, Ver."

"Move a little closer to that window," I urged him as I dropped my handbag onto the settee cushions and began to remove my gloves. "That way you'll at least get some fresh air and indirect sunlight."

His expression turned puzzled. "I didn't forget we'd made plans, did I?" He stubbed out his fag and flicked open his pocket watch. "Were we supposed to meet for tea?"

"No, no. But I wouldn't refuse a cup."

He nodded to the footman still standing in the doorway behind me. "Send some up."

"Yes, sir."

The door shut behind him and I collapsed into the chair across from George's in a rather unladylike sprawl. His brown eyes warmed with humor. By any standards, my friend would be considered attractive, if not quite to the degree of Sidney or Max. His height was slightly above average and he possessed a wide pair of shoulders and a sturdy frame.

Enviably, his skin remained a lovely shade of caramel, courtesy of his Indian grandmother, even though he rarely spent time outdoors. The top of his head was covered in rich black hair which curled into tight whorls that defied being straightened, even with the aid of copious amounts of pomade.

"So what brings you to my uncle's humble abode?" His fingers tapped the spine of the book he'd been reading. "Still avoiding Sidney?"

I scowled at him, hating how perceptive he was. It was true. When trouble was brewing, my preferred method of dealing with it was either avoidance or distraction. Both tactics which had served me surprisingly well as a field agent. I avoided most people and situations I'd sensed might cause me trouble and learned to distract those I could not. But in confronting my own emotions, as well as the strains in my intimate relationships, these strategies had proved to be less than effective.

"You can't sidestep him forever," he reminded me not ungently.

I sighed in exasperation, not wishing to discuss it further. "Yes, I know. But actually, that's not the most pressing issue at the moment."

His eyebrows arched doubtfully.

"I allowed Daphne to drag me along to that séance yesterday evening," I hastened to say, knowing this would distract him.

His brow lowered in displeasure. "Such utter nonsense!" he began. "Why, it defies explanation why so many people allow themselves to be taken in by such charlatans." His eyes flicked over my face. "Why on earth did you agree to go? I told her it was all hogwash."

I held up my hands, forestalling him before he could descend into a full-fledged rant. "I told her the same thing. But you know Daphne. She was determined to attend and if I didn't go, she was going to take her sister."

George's face tightened in disfavor.

"But that is neither here nor there. The real issue is what happened during the séance." I relayed the details of how Madame Zozza had pretended to summon Emilie. His face puckered like he'd bitten into a sour grape. Until I informed him of this morning's fire and everything her assistant had to say. Then his expression turned troubled.

I paused as the footman returned with the tea tray. As soon as the door closed behind him, I leaned forward. "Is it possible?" I asked, having shared Sidney's theory. "Could Madame Zozza have worked for the Secret Service in some capacity?" I lifted the teapot, automatically preparing his tea how he liked it while he ruminated over my question.

"I suppose it's possible," he acceded. "Heaven knows the service employed any number of strange characters." He scoffed. "Knox had to have his own private bathtub to soak in while he deciphered codes. It was undoubtedly effective but dashed awkward to confer with the sap."

I sat back to sip my tea. "Mmm, yes. I heard he and Miss Roddam are to be wed." When Miss Roddam lost her fiancé early in the war, her parents had used their connections to find her a clerical position they hoped would help her overcome her grief. They'd believed, erroneously, that their gently bred daughter would remain sheltered in such a place as the Admiralty, where the codebreaking department was housed in the Old Admiralty Building, Room 40. Hence its code name, 40 OB. Little did they know she would become secretary to the brilliant, but eccentric, Dilly Knox, with his penchant for bathing.

George snorted. "Well, that's not surprising. But back to this Madame Zozza." He paused. "That *cannot* be her real name."

"Mona Kertle."

"That's more like it." He took a drink of his tea, his mind processing the name and searching for any possible connections or permutations. At this point, I knew how his brain worked. "Never heard of her," he declared, setting his teacup back in its saucer. "But I was mostly holed up in 40 OB. Daphne's the one who was friendly with half the workers on Whitehall. She's more likely to know than I."

"Yes, but you still work for Military Intelligence," I pointed out. "We don't."

There were some women still employed by

98

the departments of the Secret Service, but large swathes had already been demobilized, including Daphne and me.

He set his teacup on the table next to him, the careful attention to his movements telling me how conflicted he was inside. "It's only a matter of time before I'll be cut loose as well."

"But surely they'll wish to keep a staff of cryptologists. And you're the best," I protested, surprised by this bit of news.

He shrugged. "They didn't before the war. And I suspect it will go back to being much the same as before."

I doubted that. Not if C, my former chief, and Kell, the head of MI5, had anything to say about it. But I didn't argue.

"I'd planned to ask Daphne now that I know the medium's real name. But can you sniff around among your colleagues, see what you can uncover?"

He turned to stare down his nose at me.

"I'm not asking you to betray your country," I retorted impatiently. "But I need to know how Mona Kertle came to possess such classified information." I leaned forward, ticking items off on my fingers. "If *she* wasn't an agent, then she learned about it from someone who either did or still does have access to that knowledge. I want to know who, and why they shared it with a fraudulent medium. And whether they've been sharing their information with anyone else."

He rubbed his chin as he considered my request and then nodded. "I'll see what I can find out."

I sank back. "Thank you." I glanced out the window where a pair of sparrows hopped along the branches of a holly tree. "I'm certain the report on La Dame Blanche has been filed by now, but it hasn't been declassified, has it?"

His expression told me what a foolish question he thought that was. "They would never willingly declassify something they don't have to. And given the fact that only about a dozen people in all of Britain even know it existed, I highly doubt it."

I nodded.

"But that should be easy enough to verify," he added. "For the sake of thoroughness."

I took another sip of tea, wondering where Emilie was now, whether she had any inkling that something unsettling was going on. She'd always had such a keen instinct. It was one of the things that made her such a good courier. Her work as a midwife had given her an excuse to travel at odd hours, but her instinct had been what told her when to leave the road rather than risk being questioned by a German patrol. Or when to lie and when to try to brazen out the truth.

Because she was often so much more familiar with the territory and the people involved than I was, I usually followed her lead, for good reason.

One night, when we were traveling further outside of the area where Emilie normally practiced her midwifery, we were stopped at the edge of a village by a pair of German sentries. They demanded to see our papers, which we swiftly handed over. When I accompanied her, our normal story was that I was her young niece, who she was training as her apprentice. But this time, for whatever reason, Emilie varied from this bit of fiction.

Instead, she told them she believed that the woman she was on her way to care for would not survive the childbirth. That she was too ill and worn down by grief over the loss of her husband. So Emilie had begged her neighbor to allow me, his daughter, to come with her, so that should the worst happen, she would have help in bringing the woman's four young motherless children back to the village.

At the time I had been horrified by this deviation from our plan, especially after hearing her concoct, what seemed to me, a rather convoluted story. But then the German soldier admitted to us that they'd had instructions to stop two women traveling together as midwives. That they were wanted for questioning. And apparently satisfied with Emilie's explanation, they let us pass.

Her sharp instincts had likely saved my life that day. And I had never forgotten it.

"Verity."

I glanced up to find George studying me intently.

"I'm not certain there's actually cause for concern, but . . . be careful."

Given my ruminations, the seriousness of his tone made my insides turn cold. "Aren't I always?" I quipped, forcing a jovial tone.

"No," he answered bluntly. "You're not."

I frowned, resenting his saying so, even if he was right.

"You may have made it through the war unscathed, at least physically, but if you keep placing yourself in dangerous situations, your luck won't last forever."

"Then I suppose all I can promise is that I'll try."

"I wouldn't count on it," he muttered into his cup.

I pushed up from my chair. "Go get some fresh air," I leaned over to murmur before giving him a swift buss on the cheek. "The sun does produce this little thing called light. So you can read your books out there just as well as in here."

"Yes, but the books are already here," he replied dryly, not appreciating my wit.

I bent to retrieve my things. "Hopeless. You're simply hopeless." I smiled over my shoulder.

Though I trusted George had been honest with me and would do his best to uncover what he could,

I had no intention of leaving the matter entirely in his hands. Not when my former employment in the Secret Service should afford me some access to the information I sought, particularly as it pertained to me. As such, I decided a visit to C was in order. I hadn't seen him since I'd been released from the service some months before, but I felt certain he would agree to talk to me.

But first, I needed to change into something a bit more subdued than my mauve taffeta summer frock. So, I directed the taxicab to take me back to our flat.

We passed a group of young children playing under the cool shade of the tall trees at the middle of the square, as the cab swung around to the north side, where our building dozed in the sun. Formerly a fashionable hotel, it had been converted into a six-story block of luxury flats at the turn of the century. Fashioned with Portland stone elevations, Neo-Grec detailing, and Parisian-style ironwork, it was quite a desirable address for those not wishing to take on all the hassles and expenses of a town house. And since the war, the number of upper-class people capable of affording such expenditures was rapidly dwindling.

Upon entering our fourth-floor flat, I thought I heard a voice coming from the drawing room. "Is that you, Sidney?" I called, dropping my things on the bureau in the entry hall. "Back from your 'appointment' so soon?"

My teasing smile froze on my lips at the sight of Max standing next to my husband.

CHAPTER 7

They flanked the console table where our photographs were displayed. The image captured on our wedding day stood in pride of place at the center, with me in my lace-edged dress and Sidney looking impossibly handsome in his uniform. We both appeared young and happy. And oblivious to what was to come.

"I see you decided to finally pay us a call?" I jested, recovering with what I thought was admirable speed. Especially given the look Sidney had cast my way. To any casual observer, it would have appeared perfectly amiable and indifferent, but there was a sharp glint in his eyes that told me he wasn't pleased. And I could guess why.

I pressed a kiss to Sidney's cheek before bussing Max's.

"I told you I intended to," Max replied. "And after last night's debacle, I decided I'd best do so sooner rather than later." His gaze flicked over my appearance. "But you look as if you've suffered no ill effects."

"Yes, well, as you know, I don't take kindly to

someone pretending to conjure someone who's not dead."

Sidney paused with his drink lifted partway to his lips. I remembered too late that I hadn't yet told him about that cruel bit of amateur table-turning that had been done just hours before he revealed he was alive to me.

I fanned myself, finding the drawing room to be quite stuffy despite the windows being open. "I take it neither of you wants tea," I remarked, staring pointedly at the beverages in their glasses. "But how about some sandwiches," I suggested as I crossed to pull the cord to summon Sadie from the kitchen. "I don't know about you, but I'm simply famished."

"Your husband was telling me you plan to retire to the country after the Duchess of Northumberland's ball, and just in time, it seems," Max said, as I moved to the sideboard to mix myself a drink heavily iced. "I'd forgotten how stifling the city can feel during the summer."

I flicked a glance over my shoulder to find Sidney's lips quirked in amused challenge. He'd warned me that, while he liked Max well enough, he wasn't about to give me up without a fight. But given the fact that Max was hardly here to stake a claim, it was wholly unnecessary.

"What brings you to London then?" Sidney asked casually enough, draping one arm across the back of the sofa he sank into.

Max dropped into the chair across from him, forcing me to sit next to my husband with his fingers brushing my shoulder. Not that I normally would have minded such a thing, but I resented being made to feel as if this was some move on an invisible chessboard.

"My aunt," Max said. "She lost her son to the war, so I feel it's my responsibility to look after her. And when her daughter telephoned to tell me she was consulting a Spiritualist, I thought it best to intervene." He paused as Sadie slipped in quietly to set a tray of sandwiches and other tidbits on the table, but his eyes were troubled. "She's also insisting on taking one of these guided tours of the battlefields. Have you heard of them?"

I nodded, too horrified to respond. I'd seen the advertisements in the newspapers for package trips to the "devastated areas." The first time I'd read about these ghoulish holidays to Belgium and northern France, I'd thought they must be a terrible joke. But then I'd overheard women discussing their intentions to go, and I'd seen for myself the stacks of the Michelin Tyre Company's illustrated guidebooks to the battlefields in bookshops.

I didn't need to tell Max or Sidney what a terrible idea this was. They knew far better than I what a foul and desperate place the trenches had been, and still were. Tens of thousands of laborers were at work on the monumental task of tidying up the battlefields, but it would take years to set things to right. To gather up the barbed wire, the twisted scraps of wood and metal, the spent shell casings. To remove the empty ammunition boxes and rifles, the heaps of overturned tanks, and the stumps of shattered trees. To extract the unexploded shells and corpses. To fill in the trenches and cratered landscape of shell holes.

But sadly, many men had marched off to war hale and whole, simply never to return. Their families were told they were dead, but there was no body for them to weep over, no grave for them to visit, making it difficult to accept. People wanted to stand over the places where their loved ones had breathed their last, to see the soil where underneath they were buried. I didn't know whether this truly brought them any comfort, especially given the incomprehensible devastation of the battlefields. But I comprehended their motivation, even if I didn't endorse it.

Max's gaze fastened on the Aubusson rug at my feet. "I've begged her not to go, but she won't be swayed. So I must go with her."

Not truly. He didn't *have* to return to those places that likely populated his nightmares as much as Sidney's. But I understood what he meant. He wouldn't let her go alone.

Sidney turned his head to the side so that I couldn't see his expression, but I could see the tension in his profile.

"When do you leave?" I asked as my husband stood to collect a cigarette from the silver box across the room. I nibbled at the cucumber sandwich I'd taken, but the macabre turn in our conversation had soured my appetite.

Max smiled grimly. "The day after the Northumberland ball. Three days in Calais and then on to Lille, where the tour departs."

Sidney inhaled a deep drag of his fag and exhaled. "At least, it won't be the dead of winter." He stared down at the tip of his cigarette. "Though, in this heat, the smell . . ." He broke off, shaking his head.

I watched my husband in concern as he downed the rest of his drink and went to refill it.

"But back to this medium." Max leaned forward. "I gathered you were infuriated by what she was implying. Was this Emilie woman your relation or some such thing?"

In the course of our previous investigation together, he'd become aware of the part I'd played during the war, though to an even more limited extent than Sidney. As such, I was hesitant to say too much, but I also knew Max could be trusted. And in fact, might prove useful.

"She was an intelligence operative inside the German-occupied territories. I had collaborated with her on occasion. Are you familiar with the name La Dame Blanche?"

His brow furrowed. "The legend, yes. But I take it that's not what you're referring to."

I flicked a glance at Sidney as he returned to the sofa, trying to decipher his expression, but it was once again carefully controlled. "La Dame Blanche was an intelligence network at work behind enemy lines in occupied Belgium and France. Truth be told, the information they gathered was indispensable to the Allies during the last years of the war. Particularly the data they collected from their train-watching posts, which made note of all the German troop movements up and down the Western Front."

"And you were their . . . liaison?"

I could tell he was trying to understand exactly what role I had played, but I wasn't willing to share those details. "At times. You have connections at the War Office, do you not?"

This question was merely a formality, for we all knew he did. As the Earl of Ryde and a former staff officer during the war, he received more dispensation than most. Add to that the connections groomed by his late father, who had been a powerful politician, and I suspected Max would be granted access to just about anything he wanted.

"Yes."

"I need to know what reports have been filed on

them. Requests for recompense for the services they rendered, that sort of thing. And does the Crown have any plans to confer honors on them or is the matter still being debated? Among all that paperwork, there should be an official list of La Dame Blanche's members, and Emilie should be on it."

"I thought you said Emilie was her code name?" Sidney interjected.

"It is, but I'm hoping the list will also make note of their duties and exact locations. If so, I might be able to figure out who she is."

Max swirled the dregs of his drink in his glass. "I take it you believe she's alive and may be in some sort of trouble."

I pushed my bobbed curls back from my face in aggravation. "Truthfully, I don't know what to think. But Madame Zozza learned about my connection to her somehow and sought to exploit it. I need to understand why."

"Why don't you simply ask her?"

Sidney and I shared a glance. I'd forgotten Max didn't know yet.

"I tried to. This morning. But she's dead."

Max's eyes widened. "You're jesting."

"I wish I was. Her entire home went up in flames. She was trapped inside."

"Amazing how bodies seem to drop around her," Sidney remarked offhandedly.

I turned to glower at him, curious how many

drinks he'd imbibed before I arrived, but his eyes were clear.

"What about the secret she mentioned?" Max suggested. "The one Emilie supposedly wants you to unearth?"

I sighed. "If I knew that, I might have the key to the entire matter."

"And the masked man you should beware of?"

I shook my head in ignorance. "Though that does beg the question, was she being literal or figurative?"

After all, London wasn't exactly short on men wearing masks these days. Those soldiers who had come home with horrific facial injuries often had to settle for concealing their disfigurements with galvanized copper masks painted with their former likeness, or that of another person. Repair was not always possible, and those surgeons capable of such advanced feats of medicine were few.

It had been alarming at first to see men walking around London in such masks, the expression never changing. But now, it was almost common-place.

"I see your dilemma." Max shifted forward in his seat. "Well, I'll see what I can uncover. But for now, I'm afraid I must beg your apologies. I have an appointment I must keep."

I shot Sidney a teasing glance. "Of course. There seem to be a great deal of those today."

Max's gaze turned quizzical and I shook my head as we rose to our feet to see him off.

Once the door shut behind our guest, Sidney wrapped his arm around my waist, preventing me from escaping. "I'm glad to see I'm not the only one you fob off with vague answers," he drawled, as he guided me back toward the drawing room.

"I don't know what you're talking about," I replied breezily, picking up another sandwich and settling back on the sofa. When facing an interrogation, it was always good to have something to distract the interrogator's attention, in addition to offering a ready excuse for any failure to immediately respond to a question.

Sidney leaned against the arm of the chair Max had vacated, sliding his hands into his pockets and watching me while he brooded. He sat that way for so long, his eyes flicking between my eyes and my mouth, that I felt the intense urge to fidget. Whether this was intentional on his part or he didn't know how to say what he wished, I didn't know, but I was almost provoked into speech.

"You conveniently forgot to mention Ryde's presence at the séance last night," he finally taunted.

I frowned. "There was nothing convenient about it. It quite honestly slipped my mind." I glared at him. "I had more troubling things to occupy my thoughts, you'll recall."

"Wouldn't Ryde be heartbroken to hear that."

"Don't be nasty."

He slid off the arm of the chair into the seat as I reached for another sandwich. His fingers drummed against the chintz fabric. "What of this other séance you referred to? The one where they summoned someone who was not actually dead?"

I stilled, wishing I'd minded my tongue more.

"Was it me?"

I pulled out a sliver of thinly sliced cucumber peeking from between the pieces of rye and popped it in my mouth. "Some of the ladies at the Umbersea house party decided it would be good fun to do a bit of table-turning, and one of them made the rather rude choice to pretend to conjure you."

His brow crinkled.

"I wasn't so silly as to fall for the trick, of course." I forced a laugh. "Though, for a moment, when you appeared in my room later that same night, I admit I wondered if perhaps somehow we *had* summoned your spirit."

From the look in his eyes, I could tell he wasn't fooled for a moment by my lighthearted manner. "Why didn't you tell me?" His voice had softened, making me feel absurdly guilty both for not doing so and for unnecessarily worrying him.

I stared down at the remnants of my sandwich. "Because . . . because at the time it was irrelevant." I sat forward to drop the bread onto the tray. "You had just returned from the dead, for heaven's sake, and there was a traitor to catch."

"But what about later? After we'd returned to London."

I turned to the side, crossing my arms over my chest and cradling my elbows in my palms. "I . . . I don't know. I suppose it never came up."

Sidney's face tightened with cynicism. "Then, by that standard, *nothing* ever comes up. I've been home for four weeks and yet you've shared almost nothing with me about your life while I was away."

I scoffed, shaking my head to deny the truth, even to myself. "Don't be so dramatic."

"If I want to know anything, I practically have to drag it out of you."

"And what of you? You don't share many details about the past four and a half years either."

"That's because I was at war! I'm not going to tell you about the mud, and the trenches, and the death . . ." He broke off, cursing under his breath. His chest rose and fell rapidly. "Trust me, you don't want to know."

"And what if I do?" I challenged.

He looked up into my defiant glare.

"What if the price for information about my war years is information about yours?"

We sat staring at each other, the tea table seeming to form a barrier between us, a no-man's-land where neither of us dared to tread.

There were simply too many hazards, both seen and unseen, littering our years apart. My chest tightened with the knowledge that if we were ever to repair this rift between us, then one of us had to take that first step. And yet, I didn't want it to be me.

And so, it seemed, neither did Sidney.

"Then we seem to be at a standoff," he murmured.

I blinked, surprised to feel the sting of tears at the back of my eyes, and nodded. I couldn't speak. Not past the lump at the back of my throat.

Sidney pushed to his feet and left the room. I stared forlornly at the space he'd vacated, forcing breath into my lungs. But the sound of the outer door closing with such finality nearly shattered my hard-fought composure.

By the time I'd regained my self-possession, the afternoon was too far advanced for me to visit Whitehall. So instead I set about making preparations for the dinner party we were to attend that night. I considered cancelling, but if I remained at home there would be nothing to distract me from the very thoughts I wished to avoid.

I pulled my new Chinese blue chiffon gown from the closet and draped a pearl necklace around my throat. I'd just finished adding a dusting of rouge to my cheeks, fearing they looked too wan, when Sidney appeared in the bedroom doorway. Part of me had worried he wouldn't return, while the other part of me knew that he would.

"I'll be ready in ten minutes," he said, pulling at his tie.

I nodded, forbidding myself to watch in the mirror as he disrobed. However, just the sound of his movements behind me were enough to set my traitorous heart fluttering. Passion had never been the problem between us. Even with our marriage so strained, I still wanted to be close to him. I simply didn't want to talk.

After pressing a dab of perfume to the side of my neck, I retreated to the drawing room to wait for him. My feet instinctively crossed to the sideboard, but then I hesitated. I could feel my stomach quavering, and I wanted badly to settle my nerves with a stiff cocktail. But there would be no time to hide such an action from Sidney. I couldn't decide whether I wanted to risk his censure.

He found me still standing there in indecision a few moments later. I'm not sure what exactly was written on my face, but his steps slowed to a stop. His eyes searched mine and then dropped to the assortment of bottles before me.

"Darling, if you're worried I disapprove of your drinking, I don't," he assured me as he adjusted his cufflinks. He had always been remarkably perceptive when he chose to be. "It's only natural you should have a cocktail or two."

I pushed away from the sideboard, licking my lips. "Yes, well, I'm afraid I've drunk far more than one or two cocktails of an evening in the past." I was still second-guessing the wisdom of making such a remark even as I let it slip off my tongue.

Sidney's hands stilled and he raised his gaze to mine, though it took a moment for me to gather the courage to make my eyes meet his. I braced for the flash of disgust or disappointment, but I saw nothing reflected there but dawning comprehension.

He lowered his hands to his sides. "I suspect many of us are guilty of the same thing." His gaze shifted slightly to the right, as if seeing something beyond me. "It is rather easier to forget when one's senses are dulled."

I inhaled a shaky breath, wondering what he most wanted to forget. "Yes."

His eyes locked with mine again and his mouth flattened into a humorless smile. "Come on, darling. Or else we'll miss dinner altogether." His arm slid around my waist and I allowed myself to be led from our flat, pushing darker reflections from my mind for the moment.

CHAPTER 8

It had been four months since I'd last walked through the doors at Two Whitehall Court. Four months since I'd been dismayed, and a little angry, to receive my demobilization papers and sent packing. There was no shock. All of us women knew the day would come, that they would replace us with returning soldiers in need of a job. But that didn't stop us from feeling a bit miffed to be told, "Thank you for your service. Now go back to your homes and stay there."

The adjustment had been startling. One minute I was useful, necessary, bustling here and there, reading intelligence reports with classified information from across the globe, and consulted about my opinion. The next I was redundant, dispensable, horribly idle, and absolutely at loose ends. For idleness gave one time to think, to remember, and that was to be avoided at all cost.

In that four months, little about Whitehall Court had changed. The French château-style palaces of flats that lined the road still stood grandly, their towers and gables forming a distinctive skyline visible from the Thames. The street had always been a rather quiet one, with few reasons for motorcars and omnibuses to traverse down it. The lobby still hummed with the sound of the electric lift. But once I passed through the glass-canopied doorway into the large flat occupied by the foreign intelligence section of the Secret Service, I noticed the transformation immediately.

There was no flurry of activity as people rushed to and fro; no sharp staccato chorus of typewriters; no odor of the lemon juice and ammonia used to unveil invisible ink lingering in the air, mingling with the stench of the onion Lieutenant Wallace's wife packed him in his lunch every day. And rather than the smiling face of Mary seated at the desk nearest to the door, I was greeted by the disconcerted gaze of a young officer. He glanced about him, as if hoping someone else from the empty room would step forward to deal with me.

"May I help you, miss?" he murmured somewhat timidly as he rose to his feet.

I recognized at once the best manner in which to handle the lad. "It's missus," I informed him with a melting smile as I crossed the room toward the opposite door. "And, yes, I'm here to speak with C. I'll just show myself to his office, shall I? Is Miss Silvernickel still his secretary?"

"Miss! Er . . . missus!" He stumbled around his desk to follow me. "You can't go back there."

Noting his pronounced limp, I felt rather bad

for steamrolling past him, but I had no intention of being fobbed off. Men at various desks and stations glanced up in startlement as I strode down the corridor and through the various rooms on the way to my destination. I waved a hand, greeting one officer who had worked with me with a disarming smile, but some of the other men were unfamiliar. One of those strangers leapt up as if to intercept me, but another man I knew stopped him with a hand to his arm. I was grateful to my former colleague for running interference for me. But the good deed proved to be in vain.

Kathleen Silvernickel lowered the paper she was reading, her eyes blinking wide as I charged into her office. "Verity? What are you doing here?"

"I'm here to see C. Is he in?"

"No."

This softly spoken response quite effectively took the wind out of my sails when none of the young officers' shouts had. I stumbled to a stop. "Truly?"

She nodded.

My shoulders fell and I silently cursed. I'd felt certain I could get some answers from C, that he would even find my efforts to gain access to him amusing. But his second-in-command? Not so much.

I turned to see Major Davis scowling at me in

121

that supercilious way of his from the doorway on the opposite side of the room. "Mrs. Kent, may I have a word?"

I barely managed to suppress a sigh of frustration, for there were few people in the world I detested more than Major Davis. Kathleen cast me a look of empathy, and even the young officer seemed to cringe in compassion.

There was no doubt Major Davis possessed some redeemable qualities and his fair share of intelligence, otherwise C would never have tolerated him for so long as his second-in-command. But in my estimation, he was naught but an officious pig, no offense to the swine. Not that he had any higher opinion of any of the women in the Secret Service. He believed we were ruled purely by our passions, and just as likely to betray Britain for love or revenge as to serve it. However, he'd taken a particular dislike of me almost from the beginning. I liked to think this was because he knew I was cleverer than he, but I'm not sure he was that insightful.

Whatever the reason, our relationship was contentious. So, it was with great reluctance that I turned to follow him into his office. "Oh, dear. Am I in trouble?" I mocked in a lilting voice.

He shut the door with a sharp click, shaking his head at me as if he was scolding a child. "Mrs. Kent, this is unacceptable. You were released from the service . . ." He glanced at his calendar as if he didn't know the precise date I'd been demobilized. "Over four months ago. Do I need to have you escorted from the building?"

It had not failed my notice that he'd not offered me a seat, but I sank into one of the chairs across from his desk anyway, prompting a glare from behind his monocle. I was certain he'd taken the affectation as a ploy to exploit C's vanity, for the chief also wore one.

"I'm quite aware of when I was given my papers, thank you. But I need to speak with C. It's come to my attention that someone who was part of the service, and perhaps still is employed here, is in violation of the Official Secrets Act."

"Yes, we know." The dry tone of this voice and the censorious gleam in his eyes left me in no doubt as to whom he was accusing.

I'd wondered if anyone at the Secret Service would question whether I'd shared confidential information with my husband. Whether they would think I'd gone rogue, joining forces with Sidney from the very beginning to catch the traitors we'd finally unmasked a few weeks prior. This meant that I would have been cognizant of his feigned death and desertion following his life-threatening injury. The idea was preposterous. But in Major Davis's prejudiced mind, this must seem vindication of his belief that, as a woman, I was a slave to my emotions.

Ignoring his vague indictment, I arched my eye-

123

brows. "Then you are aware of the person who's been selling classified information to a medium who calls herself Madame Zozza."

His expression shifted from disapproving to dubious.

"That is, unless Mona Kertle was directly employed by the Secret Service?"

Rather than answer my question, he flicked his gaze scornfully up and down my form. "Why am I not surprised you consult a mystic?"

"I do not consult mystics," I retorted sharply, glad I'd decided to be vague about how I'd discovered my information. "The woman is a fraud, but she was also in possession of sensitive information. Information that pertains to our intelligence networks in the German-occupied areas."

He sat back, narrowing his eyes as he considered me. I recognized this tactic for what it was. He was stalling. What I didn't know, was whether this was because he knew something, or if he was simply struggling to think of a cutting comeback.

"Perhaps because of that . . . *little matter* you and your husband managed to clear up for us on Umbersea Island, you believe that gives you the right to . . . dabble in other matters of intelligence-gathering." He waved his fingers as if I was embroidering a sampler. "But it does not."

My cheeks flushed with anger and I was forced to bite my tongue on the scathing retort I wanted to give. *Little matter?* Since when was treason a "little matter"?

But in this instance, the incident on Umbersea Island was of no consequence. Except to underscore my capability. Of course, I was sure he completely attributed our success to the fact that Sidney had been there.

"I'm not 'dabbling' in anything," I replied with a clenched jaw. "I am informing you of information I happened to discover. Information that clearly demonstrates someone is in breach of the Official Secrets Act. So that perhaps this agency can do something about it, lest the damage be even more serious."

He huffed an exasperated breath. "How do you know this information is particularly sensitive?"

"Because it happens to involve me and some of the other agents I liaisoned with in Belgium and France. This Madame Zozza knew one of the agent's code names."

"How do you know it wasn't declassified?"

I arched a single eyebrow derisively, not bothering to hide what a stupid question I thought that was. He knew as well as I did that nothing was ever declassified unless it had to be.

He tapped his fingers against the blotter on his desk. "You said it involves agents in Belgium and France? One of them probably bragged about their experiences. They're not like us, you know. The partnership was merely expedient."

I scowled at his cool dismissal of the dangerous work those in La Dame Blanche and other intelligence-gathering networks like it had undertaken. They'd risked their lives daily to report on German troop movements, and hunt down rumors of the enemy's plans.

I shook my head. "La Dame Blanche took an oath of allegiance . . ."

"Not officially."

I opened my mouth to protest, but he was already rising to his feet. Their oath had been as serious to them as anything we had sworn, and more immediate. For they had known if they broke it, it could mean death for them and their comrades. La Dame Blanche was not some patchwork of loosely connected spies, it was a structured, militarized network of agents.

"Regardless, we'll look into the matter." His voice conveyed he thought this a waste of time. "So you needn't concern yourself with it."

Refusing to have him stand over me, I rose to my feet. "Then you should know that Mona Kertle is dead."

His brow furrowed. "Dead?"

"Yes. She was killed when her house went up in flames yesterday morning."

"Well, then, the matter is closed."

"No," I replied, no longer able to keep the contempt from my voice. "That fire was extremely suspicious. And we still don't know who shared that classified information with her."

"There is no 'we' about it," he snapped. "*You* are no longer with the service. Anything that needs to be done will be handled out of this office." He lifted his chin, staring down his weaselly nose at me. "Is that clear?"

"And what of C—"

"*I* shall inform him of your visit and your . . . concerns."

I clenched my fists at my side. Of the former I was certain, but I doubted he would deliver the information I'd shared with any resolve, if he shared any part of it at all.

"Now, can you show yourself out, or do I need to send for Lieutenant Ross?"

"I know the way." I yanked open the door, but before I could depart, Major Davis offered one last remark.

"Oh, and Mrs. Kent, I am ordering you to stay out of this matter. Should I discover you disregarded this warning or should you attempt to visit us here again, I will not hesitate to contact Scotland Yard." His eyes gleamed with the pleasure it would give him to see me arrested. "Is that clear?"

"Except I'm no longer a member of the service, as you so helpfully reminded me. So you have no authority to *order* me to do anything," I replied as I closed the door. Perhaps it would have been wiser to hold my tongue and allow Major Davis to believe he'd won, but once the words were out of my mouth, I couldn't call them back.

However, one thing was for sure, he didn't want me anywhere near this. It was true Major Davis had always held me in disdain, but he'd never overtly threatened me. Not when he knew C would countermand whatever his intentions were. For him to do so now must mean he really didn't want me to investigate, or to share what I'd discovered with C. I had to wonder why? Was he just being an interfering bounder, or was he genuinely worried?

Kathleen glanced up at me as I exited, her gaze sympathetic.

I inhaled a deep, calming breath, and projected a lighthearted voice. "Good to see you," I told her, forming the letter "C" with my hand, and shielding it from the view of any who might be watching through the open doorway with my handbag.

Her eyes dipped to see it, but did not react. "Take care, Ver."

I strode away, tossing greetings to the men I cared to, and ignoring the rest. None of my former colleagues would be surprised Major Davis and I had argued. After all, during the latter years of the war, it had occurred on an almost weekly basis.

As I strolled through the entry, I made certain to flash a winning smile toward the man I'd charged past, presumably the estimable Lieutenant Ross. He didn't return my grin, but his brow cleared of some of its displeasure.

"Good day!" I called with a jaunty wave before sailing out the door.

A short time later, Kathleen came striding down Whitehall Place from Whitehall Court. She walked swiftly, but steadily, her handbag clutched under her arm, and her face tilted up to catch the rays of the sun that had penetrated through the blanket of clouds. From my vantage at the corner of Northumberland, I had a clear view of her progress. So when she veered left toward Charing Cross, I could tell that no one from the service was tailing her.

I hurried up the smaller lanes which veered north toward the Strand and into the forecourt of Charing Cross Station. I reached the base of the gothic Queen Eleanor Memorial Cross, a replica of the medieval Eleanor Cross, just as Kathleen approached from Trafalgar Square.

"Was I followed?" she asked.

I shook my head. "I see Major Davis is as odious as ever."

She screwed up her nose. "Worse." She glanced over her shoulder. "Though, I suppose some of his suspicious nature is slipping." She exhaled, crossing her arms in front of her chest. "But you didn't ask me here to discuss that puffed-up peacock. What's going on, Verity?" Her dark head tilted to the side. "I heard about your husband."

"Yes. But this isn't about him," I hastened to say, not wanting to discuss Sidney. "I must speak with C. Where is he?"

Her eyes followed a man whose gaze lingered on us overlong as he strolled toward the entrance to the train station. "You know I can't tell you that." Her gaze searched mine. "Even though I know you must have good reason to ask."

"Then can you tell me when he returns? Surely that's not sensitive information."

She frowned. "You're not going to like the answer. He's gone for almost another fortnight. I don't expect to see him until at least the twenty-first, and that's assuming he returns early. You know what a workhorse he is."

I closed my eyes, fighting disappointment and frustration.

"What is it? Why are you so desperate to talk to him?"

I laced my arm with hers and guided our steps around the monument, feeling we'd stood immobile too long. We were attracting attention. "Because I think there's been a security breach."

Her eyes registered alarm. "What do you mean?"

I wanted to tell her more, to enlist her help,

but doing so might constitute a security breach itself. It was true what I'd said. Since I was no longer a member of the Secret Service, Major Davis couldn't order me about. But I had signed the Official Secrets Act, and that did not lose effect simply because one was demobilized. I'd already risked much by speaking to George about it, even though he was part of 40 OB. But at least I'd spoken to him before Major Davis had made his threats. With Max being an earl with contacts at the War Office, and Sidney a war hero, Major Davis wouldn't dare to touch either of them or me for sharing information with them.

In any case, there was little Kathleen could do to help me. It was more important that she remain at her position close to C, so that should I have need of her later she would still be there. However, I decided to risk one question.

"I can't reveal the details. Not like this. But I do need to know one thing if possible. Have you ever seen or heard the name Madame Zozza or Mona Kertle mentioned?"

Kathleen had a mind like a steel trap. She never forgot a name. It was how she'd first come to C's attention during the war and been promoted to one of his assistants.

She shook her head slowly. "I don't think . . . wait! Isn't she that famous medium? I've seen her name mentioned in the papers."

"Yes."

Her brow furrowed and she hesitated before saying more. My nerves tautened, realizing this meant she'd thought of something.

"I've never heard either name mentioned in the office, but . . . I overheard some talk of a Spiritualist a few weeks back. Something about someone paying her a visit. I'm afraid I didn't listen very closely."

I patted her arm where it still lay clasped with mine. "I understand." Sometimes listening to others' conversations at the service only got you in trouble for hearing things you shouldn't have. "Thank you for telling me. I won't ask anything more of you. Except, will you let C know I came to see him? Davis promised he would, but I don't trust him."

She nodded. "Of course."

We ceased our stroll and I gazed into her brilliant green eyes. Her cheeks had regained some much-needed color and fullness. I'm not sure I'd ever seen her looking better. Particularly given how wan and drawn she'd been at the end of the war, the loss of her fiancé and father having taken a terrible toll on her. "It *is* good to see you," I remarked.

She smiled. "You, too." Then she leaned in to buss my cheek. "One of these days we shall find time to truly catch up." Her eyes glinted. "And you can tell me all about the reappearance of that dashing husband of yours."

I gave a little laugh. "Yes. Let's."

I crossed the street toward St. Martin-in-the-Fields, and then paused to watch Kathleen's retreating form until it disappeared around the corner. When no one moved to follow her, I strolled on past the church and up toward Trafalgar Square. I could have easily hailed a taxicab, but I wanted time to puzzle out the morning's developments.

It was true. Major Davis and I had always had a contentious relationship. His high-handed treatment was business as usual, but his outright dismissal of my concerns was unusual. In the past, he had always been keen to catch security violators, and almost eager to prove others untrustworthy. Perhaps he'd already been aware of the matter I'd brought to his attention. I supposed that could explain my swift removal. But even if that was correct, I would have expected him to mine me for more information. He'd never shown any qualms before about claiming the ideas and evidence I'd given him as his own. But this time it seemed he had been more interested in silencing me.

Kathleen said she'd overheard discussion of a Spiritualist, but that did not necessarily point toward Madame Zozza. With the rampant popularity of Mysticism, there were hundreds of mediums operating throughout the city. However, I was not a fan of coincidences. The fact that

133

it had been mentioned at all made my instincts stand up and take notice.

It seemed to me that the Secret Service had at least some level of awareness of the matter. The question was how much? And had Major Davis discouraged me from making further inquiries because there were secrets to keep hidden, or simply because he'd missed ordering me about? Was there cause for concern or not?

Whatever the truth, I was not going to receive assistance from my former colleagues in the London office. At least, not until C returned. I could only hope George and Max were able to uncover something of use. Because someone had certainly wanted me to believe Emilie was dead, and to unearth this secret of hers, whatever it was. I only wished I knew what they'd been referring to.

I'd started to ruminate on the medium's particular choice of the word "unearth" when suddenly the back of my neck began to tingle. During the war, I'd learned quickly never to dismiss such a sensation. I scanned the street around me, never breaking my stride as I searched the faces of passersby. I couldn't help but note the two men wearing copper masks, though neither of them seemed to pay me the slightest attention. Another man fiddled with a camera, but he didn't seem to be pursuing me for a photograph.

When the feeling did not abate, I paused before

a shop with large glass windows. The Pall Mall store sold leather goods for men, and I feigned interest in a pair of shoes all the while scanning the reflection for the sight of a suspicious or familiar face.

In the far corner, I saw a man swerve almost erratically toward the doorway to a pub and disappear inside. I couldn't tell whether this meant this would not be his first drink of the day, or he had been following me. Regardless, I made note of what little I'd seen of his appearance and his dull gray suit in the glass's reflection.

CHAPTER 9

"Y ou are looking much too staid and respectable," I told my older brother as I leaned up to buss his cheek after surveying him from head to toe.

Freddy grinned. "Yes, well, I suppose war and marriage will do that to a fellow."

"I suspect it's more the marriage bit," I replied as Sidney pushed my chair in for me.

Freddy had secured us a table at the edge of the Savoy dining room near a column. The light from the chandeliers sparkled off the crystal and silver and glinted on the jewels adorning the fashionably dressed patrons. As usual at this hour, the restaurant was crowded, though the band had not yet begun to play any music to dance to, only a soft melody to accompany the din of voices and clink of silverware.

"Has it made me respectable?" Sidney asked me as he settled into his seat.

"Not in the least, darling."

The twinkle in his eye told me he'd been expecting me to say just that.

Ignoring him, I leaned toward Freddy. "How is

Rachel and, of course, your darling baby girl?" His hazel eyes softened with affection. "Rachel is doing well. Not sleeping much. Finds it impossible to let the nanny do her job. But Miss Pettigrew assures me that's normal. Says all new mothers are the same."

I nodded to the waiter as he offered me wine. "And Ruth?"

"Ruthie is sweet as can be. Takes after her mother, fortunately. Though don't tell Mother that. She insists the baby is the spitting image of me as an infant." He shook his head. "No one else sees it."

I shook my head after we placed our orders, marveling at the changes in my brother. "I never would have believed it. All those years of your incorrigible antics, of dashing about the country. But you really have become a family man."

Freddy flushed, trying to laugh off my comments. "Well, we all must grow up sometime."

From his pointed stare, I wondered if this was supposed to be a jibe at me and Sidney, but I wasn't about to let him make me feel guilty for not towing the traditional mark. "Mother must be pleased as punch. A decorated medical man and a doting father. What more could she wish for?"

I knew my voice had become snide, and I lifted my glass to drink, angry at myself for allowing my own frustrations with our mother to color my interaction with Freddy. The truth was, I couldn't help feeling a bit betrayed. Freddy had always been even wilder than I was, though as a man he was given a great deal more leeway. Boys would be boys, after all. But now that he'd turned reputable, my high-spirited lifestyle and tumultuous marriage must seem all the more scandalous.

"I'm sorry," I said into the silence that had descended as I set my glass back on the table. "That was uncalled for. I'm happy for you. I truly am." I sighed, pressing a hand to my temple. "I'm just a bit out of sorts today."

Freddy continued to scowl, his eyes scouring my face. "Are you certain you simply haven't overindulged?"

I narrowed my eyes at his obvious disapproval. "Actually, no. But perhaps I should be sipping tepid water instead. Would that be more suitable?"

Sidney stepped in then to ask about my brother's medical practice, as well as some mutual friends of theirs from their days before the war. I should have been grateful he'd distracted Freddy before we started a row in the middle of the Savoy, and I was, but I was also irked he hadn't defended me. My headache, bleary eyes, and irritability were courtesy of the hours I'd spent in the library poring over Belgian and French newspapers from the past three months, and Sidney well knew this for I'd just told him.

None of the papers had mentioned La Dame Blanche, or a midwife, or anything else connected with the intelligence network. But I had found several articles about my and Sidney's exploits on Umbersea Island, which each included a photograph reporters had snapped of us about London following the incident. Which could have explained how Emilie or any of the others might know my identity, though I was still certain Emilie was not dead.

I sipped my wine and studied the people around us as my temper cooled, only half-listening to the men's conversation. Five years ago, when Sidney had been courting me, I would have listened with rabid interest, devouring and memorizing everything they said. My how things changed.

However, my attention immediately shifted after a lull in the conversation when Sidney drawled, "So, what has Mrs. Townsend sent you to find out?"

Freddy nearly choked on his drink. "She hasn't sent me," he managed to splutter.

Sidney's gaze met mine before fastening on him with skeptical amusement. "Come now. We know why you're here. My mother-in-law certainly didn't take great pains to hide it by arranging the dinner herself."

If it wouldn't have been unseemly, I would have launched myself across the table and kissed my husband then and there. For Freddy would handle being interrogated by his old school chum far better than by his little sister.

"Don't tell us she didn't harangue you into coming," he added when Freddy still held his tongue.

He lifted his eyes heavenward. "I told her to let me handle matters." He exhaled resignedly. "I'm not here purely at her bidding. I am meeting with some medical colleagues, and I had planned to ring you up and invite you to dinner. But . . ." He grimaced. "She did ask me to speak with you."

"More like she wants the scoop on me and Sidney. After all, she's so certain I'll botch things up."

Sidney glanced at me in surprise. I'd not shared that lovely bit of criticism.

Freddy fidgeted with his serviette. "Yes, well, she's concerned about you, Pip," he murmured, using the shortened form of Pipsqueak, the nickname my older brothers and their friends had always called me.

"She has a funny way of showing it," I muttered dryly.

"Perhaps. But you make it difficult for her to show it any other way." His brow creased in worry and his voice softened. "You haven't been home since almost the beginning of the war. Not even after Rob died."

I looked away, unwilling to continue to meet his gaze. It was easier to feign indifference, even if I wasn't completely convincing. "You know how it was. The shortages and delays." Most of

140

the trains were being used to transport troops and supplies back and forth from the coast, so travelling north as far as Yorkshire could take days if your luck was rotten. "And there was my war work."

"Surely your position in that shipping office and at the canteen wasn't so important they couldn't give you leave for a few days," Freddy protested, not unkindly. It was evident he was trying to understand.

Except he didn't know the true nature of my war work. None of my family did.

My husband sat silently through this exchange, leaning back in his chair at ease. But I could see the shrewdness in his eyes as he considered the ramifications of all he was learning. We'd not broached the subject of Rob or my family at large. Just as I'd not asked him how he felt about his parents rushing back home to Devon after only two days.

"You would think," I answered Freddy, being purposely vague. "But it wasn't that simple."

He frowned and lowered his voice even further. "You should have at least come home after Rob died. For Mother's sake."

I felt a pinch in my chest, a throb of pain and guilt. "Yes, you're probably right." I inhaled past it and shifted my gaze to scan the other diners, lest the emotion inside me find its way out.

It had been rather rotten of me. But much as I'd

accepted Rob was dead, there was still this black veil between myself and the stark reality of that truth. It was the same veil I'd drawn between myself and the loss of Sidney when I'd still believed him dead. Going home would mean I would have to face that.

I knew I couldn't avoid it forever. But just a little longer. At least until I knew whether Sidney and I were going to make a go of this marriage or not.

"Go easy on her, Freddy," Sidney murmured. "The war was hard on everyone, not just those of us at the front."

I looked up into his eyes to see them glistening with a compassion I wasn't certain I deserved. Especially when he learned all of the truth.

"Yes, that's true," my brother replied falteringly, and then with more confidence. "I just know Mother has been concerned with some of the things she reads in the newspapers . . ."

"You can't believe everything they print in the papers." Sidney's hand stole across the table to clasp mine. "Half of it is sensational rubbish."

I couldn't tear my shocked gaze away from his, feeling utterly foolish. I'd thought with Sidney overseas hunting down a traitor during the months after his supposed death that he hadn't seen our London newspapers. In the weeks since his return, he hadn't once mentioned the gossip surrounding me and the society pages in which

I'd appeared from time to time—as attending this party or that nightclub, sometimes on the arm of one gentleman or another with whom I'd been linked. Dolt that I was, I'd never even considered that my husband might already be aware of some of the high jinks I'd been up to.

"And the other half . . ." Sidney shrugged. "How do you think you would have behaved if you'd believed you lost Rachel?"

Freddy's mouth curled into a humorless smile. "Given my rather . . . boisterous past, I suspect you already know. But I take your point."

Sidney stared down at his thumb where it brushed across the back of my hand. "Try as they might, I don't believe our parents can truly appreciate our circumstances."

For all that they shared in our grief, the older generations couldn't understand what it was like to have one's youth ripped apart by war. Not when it had been a hundred years since a conflict of even close to this magnitude had occurred. To watch our friends, brothers, fiancés, and husbands march off to battle, and return shadows of their former selves—broken in body and mind. Or worse, never to return at all. Leaving gaping holes in our lives where our loved ones should have been.

Instead of spending our time at dinner parties, picnics, and afternoon teas, we young women were sent off to work in hospitals, and offices, and factories. To bind ghastly wounds, and type morose correspondence, and build guns and bombs. Just when our lives seemed to start, they were snatched from us—all for the sake of a cause we believed in less and less with each passing year, and each roll of casualties, until the reality of what a cruel joke had been played upon us had sunk in. And then when it was finally coming to an end, to have tens of thousands more snatched away from us by the Spanish influenza.

Was it any wonder we scrambled to find respite and pleasure wherever we could? That we'd chosen to drown ourselves in gin and dance a frenzied tarantella to blot out the pain of the present. Just for a moment to forget our black, yawning future.

On this gloomy note of pondering, our dinners arrived. As the only female at the table, I rallied myself and shifted the topic of conversation to something far lighter. In time, the stiltedness of our interaction faded, as I'd known it would. After all, Freddy was my brother. We'd seen each other knee-deep in mud, and screamed at each other for one slight or another more times than I could count. I'd lied to keep Freddy out of trouble for canoodling with a neighbor girl in the barn, and he'd bloodied more than one boy's nose for teasing or trifling with me. And Freddy and Sidney had been friends since their days at

Eton, long before I'd ever met the roguish boy Freddy had spoken of at dinner.

Before long we were laughing together as we reminisced about old times, and chuckled about our younger brother, Tim and his foibles, and about Grace, the baby of the family, and her struggles with Mother. I cringed hearing about some of the rows my sixteen-year-old sister and Mother got into. I couldn't help feeling I should be there to help mediate, but I was also glad I was far away from the confrontations. It was frustrating enough to contend with Mother's disapproval from such a distance. I knew full well how much worse it would be if I lived closer.

It seemed the evening would end on a happy note until I noticed the expression on Sidney's face. Something, or rather someone, across the room had arrested his attention, and much of the light and frivolity had drained from his features leaving him pale. I tried to follow his gaze, but in such a crowded room it was difficult to tell who he was looking at.

"If you'll excuse me for a minute," he said stiffly, before pushing back from his chair to cross the room.

I followed his progress, watching as he stopped next to a table near the middle of the floor. He bent over to speak with the man seated there, whose eyes stared vacantly toward the dance floor now filled with couples. The fellow looked up at Sidney, almost in startlement before extending his hand for him to shake. It wasn't until Sidney dropped into the chair next to his that I realized the other man was in a wheelchair.

I turned away, seeing that Freddy had observed the exchange as well.

"Are you truly all right, Pip?" he asked, his voice soft with concern.

"Of course. Why shouldn't I be?" I replied with forced insouciance.

His eyes searched mine. "You do know you can tell me anything. I might understand better than you think."

I studied him in return, wondering more at his troubles than truly considering taking him up at his offer to be my confidant. Perhaps his marriage to Rachel was not as content as it would seem. Perhaps they had their own troubles. Perhaps all the couples whose husbands had been caught up in the war were struggling to adapt to one another.

I lifted my glass of golden wine, studying its amber depths. "The war is over, my husband is returned from the dead, and I no longer have to toil my days away. What more could I wish for?"

Freddy didn't reply, but I could tell he wasn't fooled. Just as I wasn't when Sidney returned to our table and pretended he wasn't troubled. Whoever the fellow was he'd spoken to, his presence had upset him in some way. And I couldn't help but remark on it when we climbed into a taxicab to return home.

"Who was that man you went to speak to? The one in the wheelchair?"

He sank into the dark corner of the seat, turning his head to stare out the window. "A young corporal from my company. He was invalided out in the autumn of '15."

That Sidney remembered when the man was injured said much. Though he didn't speak of it often, I'd swiftly realized he seemed to be able to recall every soldier, from private to lieutenant, who had served under him, who had been injured or killed. The names of hundreds of maimed or slain men were trapped in his brain. Whether he had done this by choice or he simply couldn't forget, I didn't know. I hadn't asked.

"Was this the first time you've seen him since he left for Blighty?" I prodded gently.

He glanced up, perhaps surprised by my choice of words. I'd spent a large portion of the war surrounded by soldiers, in the canteens and nightclubs, as well as those at work in the Secret Service who had been invalided out of the trenches. I'd heard my fair share of trench talk.

"Yes."

I nodded, trying to appear only marginally interested lest he notice the importance of his sharing this with me and fall silent again. "Was he surprised to see you?"

"He read about my return from the dead in the newspapers. Said he had little better to do," he muttered almost under his breath as he turned away again.

"Where does . . ."

But before I could finish my question, he cut me off. "I forgot to tell you. I spoke with another former soldier of mine who happens to work for Scotland Yard."

He had known this would distract me, and I let it. "Oh?" I asked, sitting taller.

"Rawdon confirmed that the fire set at Madame Zozza's house was, indeed, suspicious. Said the fire had burned so hot on the upper floors where the bedrooms were that they believe some sort of accelerant was used."

I pressed a hand to my mouth, feeling ill. I prayed the medium was overcome by the smoke and fumes before the fire ever reached her. "I suppose there wasn't much left to say for certain whether Madame Zozza had been intentionally trapped?"

He reached out to take my hand. "I'm afraid not. But based on the evidence available, it appears so."

Though I'd alleged as much, having my suspicions all but confirmed rattled me more than I wished to admit. Someone had ruthlessly gone about ensuring she would remain silent. While I had no proof it was because of the information shared with her, so that she could pretend to channel Emilie—I couldn't help feeling deep in my gut, in my bones that I was right. There were too many unsettling coincidences for it not to be so.

Even Sidney seemed to accept it. "He also mentioned that while they've had reports of mediums being threatened and blackmailed, as it seems to go hand in hand with the shady nature of their business, no Mystics or Spiritualists have been killed for it. Until now." He frowned. "So let's hope your friend Bentnick has some answers for you."

I nodded in agreement. "I'm meeting George tomorrow."

I elected not to remind him that Max might be the one who uncovered the truth for me, for I doubted he'd forgotten the information I'd asked Max to find out. He simply preferred to keep the shadow of his presence from between us, though I could still see it in his eyes as he turned away to gaze out the window once more.

CHAPTER 10

I wasn't sure what woke me. I rarely was. The flat was dark and quiet, the drapes drawn to block out light and sound. But when I rolled over, it was to find the other side of the bed empty. Stretching out my hand, I could feel the sheets were cold.

I stared at the depression on the other pillow where Sidney's dark head had lain. Though I had initially resisted taking him back into my bed, once the traitors he'd been pursuing had been caught and he was able to resume his old life, that hadn't lasted long. After all, he was still my husband, and I'd never stopped loving him despite the tangled mess we'd made of our marriage. He'd tried to be patient, to restrain himself, and to give me the time and space I needed, but I could tell he wanted me. And when he pulled me into his arms, it's what I wanted, too.

The truth was, we'd always been well-matched physically. When words had failed us—during those few nights after our wedding we'd had together before he departed for the front, and during the too-short days of his leaves—at least we'd always been able to depend on that connection. The feverish heights of our couplings and the glow in his eyes had said more than any pretty speech, and had left a far greater impression through the long, lonely nights that followed. So it only made sense that we should fall back on our passion to help us find our way back to each other again.

Except this time was different.

Perhaps it was the finality, the realization that he would not be leaving again after just a few short days. Or maybe it was the anger I still felt at him for allowing me to believe him dead for fifteen agonizing months. Or the secrets we both protected, the fears that made us draw back into ourselves, lest the other one discover the truth. Whatever the case, there was a barrier between us that kept us apart, even when we were as intimately close as two humans could be. And the more desperately we tried to forge the connection, the more evident the chasm became.

When we'd returned from the Savoy, I'd wanted nothing more than to retire. But the look in Sidney's eyes had told me how urgently he'd needed me. Something had been stirred up inside him by seeing that invalided corporal, and I'd been helpless to say no.

After all of his pleasurable efforts, I should have been exhausted, as should he. But here I was lying awake in the wee hours of the morning, while he was somewhere else.

Unable to sleep without knowing what had become of him, I pulled my dressing gown over myself and padded softly through the flat. I expected to find him in the drawing room, pacing before the windows or seated on the sofa. And there he was, alone in the dark, his head sunk back against the cushions. He might have been asleep but for the extreme watchfulness of his demeanor, the tension in every line of his body. It was as if he was still on sentry duty, waiting for the enemy to show itself by sight, or sound, or creeping mist.

I stood in the doorway, careful not to make a noise, wretchedly torn about what I should do. Should I go to him or walk away? Would he welcome my presence, or be furious I'd seen him this way? Would he even know it was me and not some German creeping up on him out of the shadows?

My chest ached, wanting nothing more than to wrap my arms around him. But another part of me urged caution. That I was not welcome here.

So in the end, I turned away, wondering what it meant for our marriage that I could not comfort him in the depths of the night. Wondering if I was a coward for not trying to do so despite the risks.

· · ·

During the war, George, Daphne, and I had often haunted St. James's Park, sometimes desperate to escape the confines of our mutual departments of Military Intelligence and the Secret Service, the weight of all we knew heavy upon us. Other times, the distraction of a stroll under the trees and around the lake, whatever the season, helped to clear our heads. Countless were the number of times I'd silently promenaded beside George as he worked out a code and I contemplated the ramifications of a troubling report, neither of us speaking except in greeting and parting. Nearly as many times as I'd listened abstractly to Daphne's exuberant chatter, finding her inconsequential prattle soothing in the midst of all the critical matters I confronted day-to-day in Whitehall Court or while off on assignment.

Of course, not all of her burbling on was insignificant. Sometimes the gossip she passed along proved to be useful intelligence, whether she was conscious of it or not.

Which was one of several reasons I'd asked her to meet me and George that day. As well as the fact that her presence would make my stroll with George seem less conspicuous should someone from the service happen to be watching either of us after my visit to Whitehall the day before. I felt almost certain I wasn't being tailed, and I knew George would also be conscientious of such a thing given the sensitive nature of the information I was seeking. But even the best agent can be foiled. The moment you believed yourself infallible was the moment you were at most risk of being caught.

The sun was hot that day, blazing down on us from a crystalline blue sky. So we kept to the paths under the trees, seeking the cool shade. Daphne attempted to cajole George into attending some play with her and her friends that evening.

"It's hot as Hades. Why would I wish to go sit in some broiling theater?"

She giggled. "Oh, it'll cool off by this evening. And besides, I want you to meet my friend Daisy."

George gave a long-suffering sigh. "I knew this was about some deb of yours. Daphne, I've told you before. I'm content as I am."

"Oh, piffle! You may be content, but there are a whole slew of single gals who are not." She scowled, clearly thinking of her own unwed state and the shortage of young, marriageable men created by the war. "It's your duty to wed one. Don't you think, Ver?"

I kept my eyes forward. "I think George knows his own mind."

This was a common argument between them, and one in which I was not going to intervene. Though I did wish Daphne would stop being so thick. At this point, George was a confirmed bachelor, and likely to remain that way.

She harrumphed, crossing her arms over her chest. There were few things less attractive than Daphne in the midst of a sulk, so I thought to stave it off.

"Did you hear about Madame Zozza?" I asked as we paused to watch the ducklings. They seemed to be making a game of diving below the water and then resurfacing under each other. A bead of sweat trickled down my back, making me wish I could join them.

"Oh, yes," she gasped, turning to grip my arm. "That poor woman! And to think, we'd been with her just the evening before."

"I don't believe they've spoken about it publicly yet, but Scotland Yard is fairly certain the fire was set on purpose."

Daphne's eyes blinked wide in shock.

"So your suspicions were correct?" George remarked.

"It seems so."

Daphne's eyes darted between us. "You think someone set fire to her house because she was a fraud?"

It was too hot to stand here explaining the entire matter to her, so I let her believe what she wished. "That or there's another reason someone wanted Mona Kertle dead," I said, mentioning the woman's real name and my main motivation in asking Daphne to join us.

At first the name seemed to mean nothing to her, but then a tiny furrow formed between her brows. "Wait. Was that the medium's given name?"

"Yes. I learned it from her assistant."

I waited for her to say more, but she turned away, staring across the expanse of the lake. George's eyes caught mine where he stood on the opposite side of her and I subtly shook my head. If Daphne knew what exactly I was investigating, she would be less likely to tell me what she knew. During her time with counterintelligence, she'd forever lived in fear of getting in trouble, and sharing information with someone outside MI5—even someone in the foreign intelligence division—was definitely forbidden without authorization.

However, I knew her. I knew her tender heart. If she knew something that might lead to the medium's killer, she wouldn't keep it to herself.

I'd shifted my feet to begin walking again when she whirled around to face me.

"You have a friend in Scotland Yard?" Her eyes searched mine fretfully. "Someone who's making inquiries about the fire?"

"Yes."

She pressed her lips together a moment and then spoke quickly, before she changed her mind. "Then they should know that Mona Kertle was on the Registry."

A jolt of excitement shot through me. "The one at MI5?"

She nodded. "I remember because . . ." She broke off as a couple strolled past, waiting until they'd moved out of hearing before leaning closer to speak in a hushed voice. "I remember because one of the other gals used to make up funny rhymes to help us pass the time. 'Mona Kertle wears a girdle made of myrtle.' It was such a funny name."

I pressed a hand to her arm to reassure her and slow her frantic flow of words. "I understand. Sometimes when there's naught but tedious work to be done, you have to break up the monotony with something or else go mad."

She squeezed my arm back. "Exactly."

"Do you remember why she was on the list? Was she a foreigner?"

"Maybe." She worried her lip between her teeth. "Or maybe a suspected German sympathizer." She shook her head. "I can't recall the specifics."

I nodded, puzzling over the implications of what she'd told me. If Mona Kertle was on the Registry, then it was because of one of two main reasons. Either she was of foreign birth or the wife of a foreigner, which automatically flagged a person as being of interest because of their overseas connections and uncertain sympathies. Or, she had done something or met with someone that made her particularly suspicious. Whatever

157

the truth, this meant she was definitely not a British Secret Service agent.

"Maybe whatever got her put on the Registry also got her killed?" Daphne suggested hesitantly. "Will you tell your friend at Scotland Yard? But don't tell him *I* told you," she hastened to add.

"Of course not. All of this information came from an anonymous source."

"Yes. Precisely." She offered me a tight smile.

"Thank you for telling me," I said, and, indeed, I meant it. I knew it hadn't been easy for her.

She waved it aside, as we resumed our stroll around the lake. From the abstract look in George's eye, I knew he was contemplating something, but I didn't attempt to question him about it while Daphne was with us. Instead I prodded her with questions about how she'd found out about the fire, and whether anyone she'd encountered since had anything relevant to say about Madame Zozza.

We had almost completed the entire circuit of the lake, and yet no opportunity had arisen for me and George to speak alone. I was wilting in the heat, even in the light summery gauze of my sap green crepe dress. My hairline was sweat-soaked under my wide-brimmed hat, which meant my softly curled tresses would have to be washed and restyled before the ball that evening. I could only imagine how uncomfortable George was in his sack suit and straw boater hat.

As such, I opened my mouth to call an end to our promenade and ask George to escort me home. A meeting in plain sight was always less suspicious than one done in private, but given the fact that we didn't know whether Major Davis or anyone else was actually scrutinizing us, I was willing to risk it in favor of heatstroke. But then Daphne caught sight of a friend she declared she simply must say hullo to. Another bead of sweat rolled down my torso just watching her prance across the lawn, her arm raised to hail her friend.

"Well, Daphne answered my question about whether Madame Zozza could have been a British agent," I declared, shielding my eyes to gaze over the water at the imposing edifice of Buckingham Palace.

George seemed to rouse himself from wherever his thoughts had gone. "Hmm, yes. I told you she could tell you better than I."

"Then what have you been puzzling over so intently?"

"Just contemplating the possibility that she could have been a German agent. Someone who'd been convinced to sell information to our enemies."

"I wondered the same thing," I admitted.

He turned to look at me, hearing the clear frustration in my voice. "It could explain how she knew about you and this Emilie woman from

La Dame Blanche. Perhaps it was a ruse by the service to draw her out."

"And then they trapped her in her house and set fire to it?" I shook my head. "She would have been arrested, not executed."

"Yes, but what if the Germans realized she'd betrayed them and got to her first?"

A pair of older ladies stood up from a bench nearby under the shade of a plane tree and I crossed to it to sit down, giving consideration to his words. Such a scenario was possible. If the Secret Service had been attempting to entrap her, that might explain why Major Davis's reaction had been so strident. But capturing a foreign agent on British soil would have been a matter for MI5, and I'd never heard of the Secret Service using such methods before. Under the Defense of the Realm Act, such extreme measures weren't necessary to arrest her.

I also questioned the suggestion that the Germans would have gone to such trouble to silence her. Germany was in extreme disarray, struggling to right itself and find food and basic necessities for its people, after living for years under the choking British blockade. The likelihood that they had the time or inclination to worry over one stray operative was doubtful. Maybe the Russians would have used such methods, for the Bolsheviks had shown how ruthless they could be, but the information Madame Zozza had shared with me had no bearing on them.

George sank down on the bench beside me, and I pushed the questions to the back of my mind to be considered later. We only had moments before Daphne returned, and I had more to ask him.

"What of the report on La Dame Blanche? Were you able to find out if it was declassified?"

The fingers of his right hand tapped restlessly against his leg. "None of the people I spoke to knew anything about it, or at least they professed not to. So, I suspect there's our answer."

I nodded. We'd expected as much, but it was always good to have confirmation, of a sort. But sometimes that was the best you could hope for in the Secret Service.

"I also had a colleague share with me an interesting incident that happened during the war."

Something in the tone of his voice indicated to me this might be important.

"Apparently, there was a Spiritualist who purported to summon the sailor from a certain British ship that had been sunk by a German U-boat—before that news was ever made public. The government had decided to withhold the information about the sinking for morale purposes until a later date."

"So this has happened before?"

He dipped his head to the side noncommittally. "Granted, there are similarities, but the medium in that situation was detained by MI5. After some strenuous questioning, she admitted that an informant had told her that the mother of that sailor had dreamt her son came to her in her sleep after his ship was sunk. That she'd been having the same nightmare since he deployed."

I scoffed in disgust. "So this 'psychic' didn't, in fact, know the sailor was dead or that the ship had been sunk. She was purely exploiting her client's fears to make money."

"Precisely." The sour expression on George's face said he was even less impressed than I was. "And as a result, those mystics who drew the most clientele, particularly those of foreign or unknown origin, were consequently monitored closely during the remainder of the war. Lest they, advertently or not, reveal any sensitive information that could reach the Germans and ruin the element of surprise."

"I suppose they were less worried about the women who traded their Cockney accent for an exotic lilt." I frowned. "But I wasn't aware of any of this."

"It was a matter for the War Office and MI5, not the foreign division. Yet another example of stellar interdepartmental cooperation," he remarked wryly.

I wasn't about to comment on that. I'd heard more than my fair share of C's remarks on the matter. "So in theory, this might not be the first time Madame Zozza had come in contact with military intelligence."

He nodded, lowering his voice as Daphne approached with a striking brunette in tow. "Not that I'm certain it has anything to do with your current situation, but I thought you should know."

We pasted smiles on our faces and pushed to our feet to greet them as Daphne introduced us to her friend. Though it was really to George that Daphne was presenting the girl. I had to give her credit. She was persistent. I turned my head to the side, hiding my amusement at her enthusiastic endorsement of George and his dazed response.

And that's when I saw him. The middle-aged man from the séance. The one who had been so eager to claim the chair next to Madame Zozza.

He was seated a short distance from us on another bench. For a moment, I thought I might be mistaken, for there was nothing remarkable about the fellow except his sharply receding hairline of muddy brown hair, and that was currently hidden by his hat. However, when he snuck a glance at us over his newspaper, I recognized his face.

Our eyes collided for a moment and I could have sworn his flared wide in alarm, but from such a distance it was difficult to tell. Whatever the case, he recovered quickly, tipping his head to me in polite acknowledgment. Then he leisurely folded his paper and tucked it under his arm as he rose to saunter off in the other direction.

I didn't know what to make of him. Was it purely coincidence that he happened to be here in St. James's Park, or was he following me?

My mind flashed back to the day before when I'd felt I was being followed after leaving Charing Cross. Could this man be the same one I'd seen darting into a pub through the reflection in the shop window?

It was possible, though I hadn't much to go on. Not enough to say for certain either way. But I would certainly be paying attention now. If he showed up again, I would have my answer.

CHAPTER 11

"The duchess must be pleased," Sidney remarked as we stood along the edge of the ballroom, watching the dancers as they castle walked across the floor.

I sipped from the cool glass of champagne he'd handed me. "Yes. It's an absolute crush."

As if to emphasize this point, someone jostled me from behind. Sidney's arm snaked around my waist and pulled me closer to his side. Not that I minded being so close to my husband, who looked strikingly handsome in his dark evening kit, but with so many people crowded into the room, the air was stuffy and sickly sweet with the scent of too many perfumes.

"She seemed happy to see *you*," he leaned close to my ear to say in order to be heard over the orchestra and the dull roar of voices.

I laughed. "I think she was happy to see both of us. After all, we are quite the celebrities at the moment."

We'd already been stopped by no fewer than a dozen people, some of whom were unknown to either of us, to ask about Sidney's return from the dead and the traitors we'd unmasked. But our notoriety was being overshadowed by today's events at Wimbledon. Everyone was abuzz with discussion over Suzanne Lenglen's tennis dress. Apparently, the nineteen-year-old French athlete had won the women's singles title while wearing a sleeveless dress with a skirt so short the hem barely reached her ankles.

"Did you and the duchess volunteer together?" Sidney asked.

"Mmm, a few times," I replied imprecisely. The truth was I was more familiar with her husband. While serving with the Grenadier Guards, he'd provided intelligence reports of his first-hand accounts of the battles and the state of the trenches. I'd read those dossiers, and even liaised with the man himself at one point as he was preparing to go up the line before a major battle.

Sidney sipped from his own glass, before remarking. "I shared a drink with His Grace a time or two in one of the estaminets while at rest behind the lines. He's a decent fellow."

I glanced up at him, wondering if he'd read my mind, but his gaze remained trained on the people across the room. Sometimes I wondered if Sidney should have been the spy.

Scanning the room, I spotted my friend Ada, who had quite recently become the second wife to the Marquess of Rockham, looking lovely in a rather scandalous gown of vermilion. It quite made my jade green tunic-style fringed dress seem downright demure. I was about to make my way over to her, when Sidney spoke again.

"I had Rufus give the Pierce-Arrow a complete tune-up today so that she'll be ready for our trip down to Sussex."

"Oh?" I replied evasively, while my heart kicked in my chest.

It wasn't that I'd forgotten our plans to retire to our cottage. In fact, they'd been ever present at the back of my thoughts. But I'd been trying not to give them much deliberation, lest the panic that seemed to lurk hand in hand with those intentions rise up and grip me. My investigation into who had shared classified information with Madame Zozza, and then possibly killed her to keep her quiet, had occupied much of my thoughts, making it far easier to ignore the dates on the calendar.

Another couple squeezed past us, nearly driving an elbow into my ribs. I turned to press closer to Sidney, feeling as if I was practically plastered to his side.

His deep blue eyes met mine, their depths shimmering with heat. My breath caught as a tingle raced down my spine, one of both longing and alarm.

"Dance with me." His lips curled upward at one corner. "At least then we'll have room to move."

"All right," I murmured.

He took my champagne flute into the same hand as his own, and somehow managed to pass them off to a waiter as he escorted me toward the dance floor. The notes of a more traditional waltz floated through the room as he pulled me into his arms, and soon we were twirling about the floor.

For the first two minutes I was too overcome to speak. Too awash in the sensation of being in Sidney's arms. Too lost in the memory of the first time he'd danced with me this way.

In the spring of 1914, he had come home with Freddy to Upper Wensleydale for what was supposed to be a short visit. I hadn't seen him in nearly six years, though I'd been harboring a girlish crush on him ever since. Sixteen-year-old Sidney had been kind to the gangly eleven-year-old girl I'd been. More kind than Freddy. Though I'd been able to tell how amused he was by my determined efforts to earn his attention and favor. But upon his return, I was a mature seventeen with a bevy of admirers of my own, and I was resolved not to make a cake of myself.

As such, I'd contrived to ready myself at a friend's house for the soirée a neighbor of ours happened to be hosting the evening of his arrival. It had been a rather traditional affair, no rag music or cocktails like tonight, but there had been dancing. I'd forbidden myself to watch the door, so I was taken by surprise when Sidney suddenly stood before me. He'd bowed ever so politely and teasingly called me Pip, the nickname my older brothers and all their friends had used for me. But there was a gleam in his eyes I'd never seen before, so rather than remain determinedly aloof, I'd allowed him to lead me onto the dance floor for a waltz.

By the end, I'd known I was a goner. And it wasn't long before I knew Sidney was, too.

That same gleam was in his eyes now. I wished I could say it only brought me joy as it had before, but it also drove a dagger through my heart. Especially knowing the things I was keeping from him. Things he might come to hate me for.

Whether Sidney could sense the turmoil inside me or not, the light in his eyes never dimmed.

I inhaled a shaky breath, grateful for his strong hand pressed to the small of my back, the warmth of his skin tangible through the silk of my gown. "Do you ever think about the Lucas's spring soirée? About our first dance?"

His lips curled into a soft smile. "All the time."

"Did . . . did you think about it while you were away?"

His smile faded to an expression more earnest. "Yes."

"What else did you think about?"

He inhaled, his breath hitching briefly. "Well, I thought about our wedding day. And night." His eyes flashed wickedly. "I thought about that picnic on Hardraw Beck, and how delightfully you turn pink wherever you're kissed." His gaze trailed over my flushed face. "Or think about being kissed, apparently."

"Sidney," I warned.

"I thought about the apple trees that grow at the edge of Barbrook Abbey that I used to climb as a boy, and the apple tarts the cook used to make from them. Though not often," he amended. "Not when all I had to look forward to were bully and hard biscuits." He spun me in a tighter turn, guiding us around another couple. "I thought about the wind blowing through the pines outside our cottage, and the beaches at Seaford." He chuckled. "And I thought of that colorful Bavarian your parents employed as a gardener."

My grin widened. "Fashugel?"

"That's the one. The tales he used to tell, and the colorful language he used. I'm relatively certain your mother would have sacked him on the spot if she'd known the curses and stories he was exposing her sons to. You as well, given the riotous impression you used to do of him."

"Oh, I'm sure he toned it down whenever I was within hearing, but I still learned my fair share of expletives, in English *and* German." I tilted my head, picturing the bluff older man. "There were a number of phrases I heard during the war that I might not have comprehended had it not been for the education he provided. And in one instance, I had the information he shared about his home village to thank for helping me to charm one particularly cantankerous Bavarian border guard."

The look in Sidney's eyes recalled me to myself, and I fell silent, wishing I'd guarded my tongue. We'd been having such a pleasant time until I'd forgotten myself.

As if sensing my withdrawal, his hand on my back shifted, drawing me closer. "Whatever happened to Fashugel? Is he still employed by your parents?"

"A few months after the war began, they sent him back to Germany. To my great-aunt's home in Westphalia. Like everyone else, they wanted to put as much distance as possible between them and our German connections, including family." It had happened all over Britain, this fear and scorn of all things German. It was still happening. I was perhaps one of the few who felt some gratitude for my paternal grandmother's Germanic roots, for otherwise I would not have spoken the language so fluently.

"When my great-aunt's letters were able to get through to me again after the war, I discovered he'd died." My voice dipped. "She said his heart simply gave out."

Sidney didn't reply. Perhaps he realized there was nothing to say.

We finished the dance in silence on that somber note, and then I excused myself to visit the lady's retiring room. I needed some time to set myself to rights, both physically and mentally. Once I'd freshened my lipstick and put aside my maudlin emotions, I went in search of my husband again, expecting to find him in the parlor, which had been set aside for gambling. But someone else found me first.

I turned at the sound of my name and smiled as Max finished climbing the stairs toward me.

"You look lovely," he said by way of greeting, his eyes trailing over me appreciatively.

I returned the favor. His dark blond hair gleamed in the light of the chandelier, a stark contrast with his black dinner jacket. "You clean up remarkably well yourself."

He drew me to the side, away from the head of the grand staircase where others streamed past. "I have some information for you."

I immediately sobered, stepping into the relative hush of a small alcove. Here we could see and be seen, but we were at least separated from the crush of guests. "From the War Office?" I prodded.

He nodded. "Popular opinion is that La Dame Blanche will receive their honors, though there is still some debate whether it will be from the military or civilian division. Some of the upper brass are balking at presenting military medals to women, regardless of their contributions."

I grimaced. "I expected as much. So they haven't been granted yet?"

"No. And I wasn't able to find out much about the report you mentioned, other than to confirm its existence."

I nodded, glancing over my shoulder at the stairs in disappointment.

"However, I contrived to see a list of all the citizens employed by British Intelligence in the occupied areas who were either captured or killed during the conflict."

My head snapped back around.

His mouth briefly curled into a grin at my apparent eagerness. "There were notations designating the networks and areas they'd belonged to, as well as notes on family members to receive compensation for their loved ones' services, and in many cases, code names," he delivered the last words fully knowing I would instantly leap at this bit of intelligence.

I leaned toward him. "Was Emilie on it?"

He shook his head. "She was not."

"So I was right. She *is* alive. And she was never caught by the Germans as Madame Zozza portrayed."

"It certainly seems that way. But that's not all." He reached up to touch my arm, drawing me even deeper into the alcove as his voice dipped even lower. "I spoke with a Captain Xavier."

I stiffened, unprepared to hear that name. Especially not here. Not now.

Max hesitated, sensing my alarm. "What is it?"

I shook my head, forcing myself to relax. "It's nothing." But I could tell he would not let me leave it at that. "I . . . worked with Captain Xavier a number of times while I was in Belgium. Our last . . . assignment was not so pleasant." I forced a tight smile, for that was a lie if ever I'd told one.

His gaze was quizzical, but he allowed the matter to drop for the sake of expediency. "Captain Xavier has been in and out of Belgium a number of times since the armistice, and he said there's some concern because a number of Britain's former intelligence contacts have received threats."

"Threats?"

"Yes, that's rather vague, isn't it? But he wouldn't be more specific."

Not with Max. But he might with me.

I bit my lip, considering the implications. "Is he regularly stationed at the War Office?"

Max followed my line of thinking without further explanation. "I gather he does a great deal of traveling for military intelligence. He was headed off to somewhere again when I spoke with him this afternoon. I . . . suggested he might pay you a call, but he said he was already late to catch a train."

So he had already known about Captain Xavier's and my connection. I couldn't help but wonder what else Captain Xavier had told him. But Max didn't seem about to volunteer that information, and I wasn't going to ask.

"So Emilie, as well as others, might legitimately be in danger," I remarked, returning to the more pertinent matter.

"But the intelligence staff in Belgium are aware of the situation. I'm sure they're monitoring it closely."

He had more faith than I did, but then again, he was not as well acquainted with the workings of the Secret Service as I was. The staff in Brussels was a skeleton crew at best, stationed there to liquidate the intelligence service's assets; assess claims; and make recommendations for pensions, compensations, and decorations to be awarded. They weren't exactly equipped to investigate threats to former agents.

"I highly doubt they're doing much monitoring at all," I replied, the vague sense of anxiety I'd been suppressing for days now stirring in my gut. Something was wrong. And Emilie, and perhaps I, were somehow at the center of it.

"Verity, what are you thinking of doing?" Max asked, his voice taut with misgiving.

I scowled, disliking his tone. "I'm not thinking of doing anything. Yet. I'm simply concerned."

His expression said he didn't believe me,

and he pulled me closer with the hand that still gripped my arm. "Promise me you'll tell Kent before you do anything rash."

If not for the genuine concern I saw reflected in his eyes, I might have snapped at him to mind his own business. But I held my tongue, realizing he only wished to protect me.

"I leave with my aunt for France tomorrow, and I don't want you getting into trouble by yourself while I'm away."

I narrowed my eyes. And then he had to go and ruin it by saying something so high-handed and typically male.

But it turned out I should have been grateful to him for doing so, because my bristling anger might have been the only thing that prevented Sidney from resorting to violence when he happened upon us a moment later.

"Attempting to make off with my wife, are you, Ryde?" he drawled acerbically. His deep blue eyes were hard chips.

Max immediately released my arm and stepped back, as if we had something to feel guilty for. "My apologies, Kent," he replied, his demeanor stilted. "I had something important to relay to her."

"I'm sure you did."

His gaze flicked toward mine for the first time, and I could tell just how furious he was. It halted the scathing retort I had for both of them on my lips. Unless I wanted to create a scene, it would be best if I saved it for when we were in private.

"Shall we?" He crooked his arm, expecting me to comply.

For a moment I considered striding off without either of them, but then I could appreciate how things must look. Had Sidney stood so close to a woman, whispering with her in an alcove, I would have been displeased, too. Especially if I knew they had formed a sort of attachment, unacted upon though it might be.

So I threaded my arm through his and allowed him to lead me away. I could feel Max's gaze on the back of my neck following us, but I didn't dare turn to look.

Sidney led me down the grand staircase, but rather than turn to rejoin the crush in the ballroom, he instead guided me out the door. We stood stiffly under the portico, waiting for his Pierce-Arrow to be brought around. The warm day had cooled, and I welcomed the chill of the breeze across my flushed cheeks. I thought he might say something, but he merely stared straight ahead, his arm rigid beneath mine.

"He truly did have important information to tell me," I murmured when I could bear the silence no longer.

"Had you arranged to meet him?" he bit out. And I realized what he was maddest about.

"No," I protested. "I would never . . ." I broke

off as another couple passed through the portico. I turned to stare out over the drive, refusing to defend myself so stridently against the insinuation behind his question. I'd done *nothing* wrong.

I inhaled a steadying breath and began again in a lower voice. "I knew he would likely be here tonight, and I'd hoped to find out from him if he'd uncovered anything at the War Office. He happened upon me as I was about to descend the stairs and pulled me aside. It's as simple as that."

"It's never that simple," he muttered.

"Well, this time it is," I snapped, pulling my arm from his grip and striding out toward his motorcar as it came to a stop. The footman had to scramble around the vehicle to open the door for me.

Sidney climbed in behind the wheel and slammed his door before accelerating at a spanking pace. I didn't attempt to speak with him, instead preferring he focus on the road if he was going to drive at such reckless speeds. Which gave me more than enough time to stew over my own grievances.

How dare he accuse me of carrying on with Max behind his back? It was his fault I'd met his former commanding officer in the first place. Had he not feigned his death and drawn me to that house party, I never would have allowed myself to develop any sort of feelings for the man. Perhaps the attraction would still have been there, but I would have drawn the lines clearer around our friendship. In any case, we had never acted on those feelings. So for Sidney to imply I'd been playing him false was beyond unfair. It was hypocritical.

And so I told him when we returned to our flat. "You're a bloody hypocrite," I snapped, throwing my reticule down onto the bureau in the entry hall. I couldn't recall the last time I'd been in such a rip-roaring fury. And the fact that we were prodding so closely to the worst secret I'd been keeping from Sidney only fueled my ire, desperate to block out my conscience.

I yanked off each of my evening gloves and tossed them aside as I rounded on him. "You accuse *me* of deceit when *you're* the one who deceived me for fifteen bloody months, letting me mourn because I believed you to be dead!"

His eyes flashed with answering fire. "You're still angry about that? You know it was for good reason."

"Yes, yes, because you were intent on catching a band of bloody traitors. I don't need to be reminded of that by you. Everyone else does it often enough," I muttered under my breath as I strode into the drawing room. This was one time I was glad we didn't have live-in servants, for neither of us appeared to be willing to placate the other, and we certainly didn't need an audience.

I made straight for the sideboard, not caring for once if Sidney saw me drink.

"Then, what do you want me to say?" he growled from the doorway. His hands fisted at his sides. "I've already apologized. Shall I do it again?"

I held up my hand cutting him off. "What I want is for you to stop assuming that absolute forgiveness happens overnight. It's a process. *And* I want you to stop bristling at Max whenever he's in my company. He has behaved honorably through all of this."

He scoffed.

"More honorably than you or I have," I charged, but then I paused. "I can appreciate how finding us in that alcove together might have looked, but he wasn't making overtures. Nothing of the kind. In fact, from the first, he has encouraged our reconciliation." I didn't add that he'd suggested he would be waiting for me should that reconciliation fail. No need to share that. Not when it was obvious Sidney already suspected it. "So you can stop treating him like he's the serpent in our Garden of Eden. We created our own problems quite without his help."

I poured myself a whiskey neat, too impatient to go to the kitchen in search of ice to mix a cool cocktail. I downed it in one swallow, welcoming the burn as it slid down my throat, before pouring myself another two fingers.

"What was this important information Ryde so urgently needed to relay to you?" To his credit, he had at least lost the sarcastic edge to his voice, though it was still taut with resentment.

"Several things." I crossed toward the sofa, leaning against the arm as Sidney poured himself a drink. "He confirmed the existence of that report on La Dame Blanche, though not much else about it. And he also saw a list of all the citizens employed by British Intelligence in the occupied areas who were either captured or killed during the conflict. A list that included code names."

Sidney arched his eyebrows as he sipped, not missing the significance.

"Emilie's wasn't on it."

"So the medium lied. Not that there was any real doubt. As far as anyone knows, Emilie is alive. That must be of some relief."

My eyes dipped to the amber liquid in my glass. "That's not all."

He stilled, clearly sensing the apprehension coursing through me.

"It seems a number of our former intelligence contacts throughout the occupied territories have received threats. And I can only presume Emilie is one of them."

He searched my gaze, waiting for me to continue, for it must have been evident there was more. Why else would my hand be gripping my cut crystal glass so tightly my knuckles turned white?

I inhaled past the constriction in my chest, forcing myself to inform him of the decision I'd made almost within seconds of hearing everything Max had discovered. "There are no answers to this in London. I have to go to Belgium. I have to find her."

CHAPTER 12

I expected him to erupt in anger. To yell, or glare at me with icy disdain, or hurl his glass into the fireplace. Anything but the blank stare he leveled at me, his face wiped clean of all emotion. It made my heart shrivel inside me and my conscience scream.

His silence prodded me into speech. "If someone is sharing classified information about Emilie, about me, if someone is threatening her and some of the other agents, then I need to find out why. I need to know if she's in danger." My voice turned to pleading. "I know this must be difficult to understand . . ."

"Then make me." His voice was clipped, and I realized he'd been furious all along. He'd just been restraining it. "Make me understand," he demanded, his voice dripping with contempt. "Because I can't see it. You're not in the Secret Service anymore, Verity. It's not your job to look after their agents."

"In theory, yes," I replied stiffly. "But the staff has already been reduced, and now that the treaty has been signed, it's only a matter of time before it's slashed again. The lives of a few foreigners who passed on intelligence during the war will mean little to the bureaucrats. And even though they might matter to the chief man on the ground in Belgium, I doubt he has the time or the resources to do any significant investigating."

"But that's not your problem."

I slammed my glass down on the table next to me and stood tall. "Yes, it is! They've dragged me into this by sharing information about me with that medium. They've implicated me. And I can't walk away without knowing why."

"But it doesn't make any sense, Ver."

"I know it doesn't!" I inhaled a shaky breath. "And that's precisely why I have to go. To make heads or tails of this madness and why I'm linked to it."

His eyes scoured my face, as if searching for something, something I didn't know how to give him. "And you must go now? Just when we're supposed to retire to our cottage?"

Some of my vehemence drained out of me in the face of his disillusionment. "I realize the timing isn't opportune . . ."

"I can appreciate why you want answers. But is it really more important than fixing this, fixing us?"

I blinked at him, stricken with pain and guilt.

He turned away, raking a hand through his dark

hair. "Dash it all, Ver. When are we to have time for us? I just returned to you, and now you want to run off to Belgium."

"So come with me," I murmured before I had time to reconsider the words.

Sidney glanced up at me, perhaps wondering if I was serious or not. His eyes grew haunted, their depths stark with shadows I could only guess at, and he shook his head. "I spent four and a half years in war-torn France and those blasted trenches," he swore, using far stronger language. The words were torn from deep inside him. "I don't want to go back."

I swallowed the lump in my throat that had risen at the evidence of his distress. My gaze dipped to the arm of the sofa as I ran my fingers along the rough fabric, knowing that my next words would hurt him. "This is something I have to do. I . . . I won't be able to rest until I know that Emilie is safe. Not after everything." I clenched my hand into a fist, firming my resolve. "She would do the same for me."

I glanced up at Sidney, seeing that blank look had returned to his eyes, though now I could sense the brittleness behind it.

"At Umbersea Island you asked me to trust you. To understand why you were so determined to find the traitors who betrayed your battalion. That you couldn't let it go until you knew the truth, for you and your men."

His jaw clenched, holding back words, evidently guessing where I was going with this.

"Well, I'm asking you to trust me now." I pressed my hands over my chest. "Now I'm the one who needs answers, for me, for Emilie, and for the others. Perhaps we weren't fighting in the trenches, but that didn't mean our work wasn't dangerous. That our lives weren't in each other's hands."

For a moment he merely stared at me as if in an agony of indecision, and I waited for him to say something, anything.

Then he turned on his heel. "Do as you must," he bit out.

Each word lodged like shards of glass in my chest.

Near the door, he paused and turned his head to speak over his shoulder, not even bothering to look at me. "I only wish you were as intent on fighting for us as you are for your friends."

With that parting shot, he was gone. The door to the flat clicked shut behind him.

I stood in the middle of the drawing room and listened to the echoing silence of the flat, while my world crumbled around me. With the end of the war, with the coming of peace, things were supposed to be better. But I still felt the same yawning emptiness, the same unbearable pain I'd experienced whenever I heard of the death of yet another friend or loved one. When I'd received the telegram that informed me of Sidney's passing, the blackness inside me had already been so deep I thought I might drown in it.

I felt it again now, rising up to drag me under.

My eyes strayed toward the sideboard, toward the glittering bottles of forgetfulness. My mouth dried, urging me to taste them. My nerves begged for release from their tightly wound state.

I inhaled a shaky breath and forced my feet to move toward the bedchamber. If I was to make the early morning train toward the coast, I had packing to do.

The wind whipped against my cheeks as the ship slipped out of Folkestone Harbour on steel blue waves and headed west toward Ostend, Belgium. It was a familiar enough sight, since I'd sailed from here several times during the war, though more often I'd embarked from Harwich on the east coast. I also felt the same flutter of nerves in my stomach as I'd felt then. Though at least this time, there was no need to fear being torpedoed by a German U-boat.

A heavy blanket of clouds covered the midday sun, making the sea breeze all the more biting, though not nearly as frigid as it was in the depths of winter. I rested my hands on the cold metal rail, welcoming the sting. Anything to distract me from the churning in my stomach. Though I tried to tell myself it was because the only thing I'd managed to consume that day was a cup of tepid tea in a café at the quay as I waited for the ship, I knew better. For one, I'd never suffered from seasickness in all my life, even traveling through a torrential gale which had threatened to swamp the boat with its heaving waves. And for another, my nausea was accompanied by a sharp ache in the vicinity of my chest where my heart should be.

I'd been on the move since daybreak, leaving the flat with only a valise and small portmanteau. Given my uncertainty about the conditions in Belgium and how I would arrange travel, I thought it best to pack light. I hadn't even needed to creep, for Sidney wasn't there.

I'd tried to pretend I hadn't cared, but the truth was I'd started at every noise, every creek in the flat, until falling into a fitful slumber sometime in the wee hours of the morning. Given that fact, I was fairly certain he'd never returned. And I hadn't the slightest idea where he might have gone.

I left him a short note, informing him of my plans, and ended it with another apology. Though heaven knew when he would read it. If he chose to read it at all.

My heart grew heavier as the distance increased between the boat and the shore, between Sidney and me, until it seemed I might suffocate from the weight. I couldn't stop the feeling that I'd just rashly thrown something precious away. After all those months of wishing Sidney were still alive, of begging God to turn back the clock, only to end it by walking away like this.

But what could I do? It was too late to turn back now. And in any case, Emilie still needed to be found.

I closed my eyes, fighting back tears.

Well, I'd made my bed, and now I would just have to lie in it.

After I'd ensured Emilie and the others were safe and all was set to rights, I would return to London, to Sidney, to see if our marriage was still salvageable. I would finally tell him the truth about what I was hiding and let the chips fall where they may. My hopes weren't high, but I only had myself to blame for that.

A tear slipped down my cheek and I gripped the railing tighter, trying to swallow my pain back down deep inside me, as someone moved forward to stand beside me to look out over the water. They shifted and I felt something brush my shoulder.

"Handkerchief?"

My heart surged in my chest at the sound of the familiar deep voice and I blinked open my eyes to see the white fabric fluttering before me.

"Thank you," I managed to stammer, taking it from his fingertips to dab at my eyes. "This . . . this dashed wind. It's dreadful on the eyes," I murmured in a feeble attempt to salvage my pride.

"Of course."

I turned to look at him then. His expression was guarded. His deep blue eyes wary beneath the brim of his hat he'd pulled low against the wind.

"You came." It was an inane statement, but profound for all that, given the manner in which we'd parted.

"Yes, well, I couldn't let you go alone." Sidney's lips quirked upward at one corner. "I may be a terrible husband, but I'm not as bad as all that."

The jest fell flat.

"You're not a terrible husband," I contradicted, turning back toward the sea. "You've barely had a chance to be one. The war stole that from you. From me."

He joined me at the rail, standing close enough that I could feel the heat of his body. "I wasn't anticipating the ship to be so crowded. Belgium hardly seems the ideal tourist destination at the moment."

Though the number of people on the deck was fairly sparse, allowing us a degree of privacy, the interior cabins were jam-packed with passengers. "I suspect many of them are embarking on one of those guided tours of the battlefield. The ones Max was telling us about."

Consternation furrowed his brow. "But so many of them?"

I also had been surprised by the macabre flood of passengers boarding the ship, many in fashionable, albeit somber-colored attire that would hardly be fitting to the mud and rubble and ghastly sights they would soon encounter. "I suppose there are more people than one realizes struggling to deal with the loss of their loved ones."

"That or some dashed-fool matriarch declared it an illuminating experience and they're all flocking to follow her advice," he scoffed, pulling his battered, silver cigarette case from his inner coat pocket. I could just make out the faint outline of his initials in the dented cover.

The case had been a wedding present from me, engraved with the inscription "Love always, Verity" on the interior. Somehow it had survived four years of war and another six months of his searching for evidence of treason, and though I'd offered to order him a new one, he'd insisted this one would do. Just now, it seemed an odd metaphor for our marriage.

I watched as he lit one of his Turkish cigarettes, shielding it from the wind with his cupped hands. "I'm not sure I have any better opinion of the intelligence of society at large than you do, but in this instance, I think these people are genuinely desperate to visit the battlefields where their loved ones breathed their last, imprudent as that may be."

He didn't reply, but his square jaw was tight with disapproval.

We stood companionably side by side, Sidney smoking his fag as the shores of Britain faded further into the distance. Much of the shock of his sudden appearance had faded, leaving a pleasant hum of gratitude he'd followed me when he could so easily have walked away. I knew full well this was not going to be easy for him, and I hoped our search for Emilie would keep us as far from the front as possible. Seeing the trampled countryside, the devastation of the shelled towns behind the trenches would be difficult enough, without actually venturing into the waste that stretched for miles behind the battle lines.

"You saw the trenches?" he asked carefully, his gaze fastened on the glowing tip of his cigarette.

I answered with just as much restraint, understanding what he was really asking. "Not the front line. But the rear, the clearing stations and such, yes."

Upon hearing that I knew something of the conditions he and the other soldiers on the Western Front had endured for over four long years—the sights, and sounds, and, perhaps most disturbingly, the smells—he merely nodded. For there wasn't anything *to* say. Words could never truly capture the horrifying reality of it all anyway.

He inhaled a deep drag of his cigarette, blowing the smoke out to sea. "You never told me, how did you come by your post at the Secret Service? A friend?" The words were spoken lightly, but I could sense his genuine interest.

I nodded. "Do you remember how, when the war began, we all thought it would be over by Christmas?"

He snorted. "Oh, how naïve we'd been."

"Well, when the holidays came and went, with no end in sight to the conflict, I began to feel at loose ends. I volunteered where I could, but it was never enough to fill my time or, more importantly, my thoughts." I laughed self-consciously. "I thought I would go mad with the waiting and worrying. I mentioned this to several friends, and one of them told me she had a situation she thought I would be perfect for. Most of the positions at the service were filled that way, by word of mouth to men and women from good families who knew how to keep their mouths shut."

"The 'old boy' network."

"Yes. In most instances, it worked remarkably well since discretion was the utmost skill requirement." I adjusted my leaf green cloche hat. "They asked me to take a few language proficiency exams to test my fluency in German and French, and even Italian, and then I was sent in for an interview with C. He seemed to take a liking to me almost immediately, for whatever reason."

Sidney chuckled. "I can guess why." His gaze traveled over my features almost like a caress. "And you're also quick and clever. It doesn't take long for one to apprehend that."

I flushed under his praise. "In any case, I was hired as one of the secretaries. I also did a bit of translation."

He pitched the end of his fag into the water. "So how did you come to be an agent out in the field?"

We'd never discussed any of this, and I'd lived under the strain of believing we never would until a month ago. Since then Sidney had asked few questions. Perhaps he'd been waiting for me to broach the subject myself. But years of enforced silence—knowing it could mean life or death for me, or my colleagues, or the soldiers overseas— were difficult to overcome. Even now, I found the details hard to relay.

"For a while I was content, pleased to know I was doing my part and perhaps making a differ- ence to the war effort. But as the months stretched on and the casualties continued to mount, it became harder and harder to push it all out of my head." I stared down at the railing gripped beneath my hands. "Work no longer exhausted me as it had before. At least, not enough to bring sleep easily. And sitting at home through the long nights, fretting over everything we'd learned started to become unbearable."

I braced myself, uncertain how Sidney would take the next. "So Daphne, and I, and a few of the other girls, would go out to parties, and restaurants, and nightclubs, ignoring the curfew set for women. We weren't the only ones. There were plenty of other upper-class girls doing the same thing. Dashing out between their nursing shifts, like Lady Diana Cooper, or simply intent on escaping their parents, like Nancy Cunard. There were always soldiers home from the front, eager to be entertained, desperate to forget, for a short time at least, all the horrors they'd witnessed before they had to return."

I could feel Sidney's eyes on me, weighing, wondering.

"I . . . I danced and I flirted, but mostly I listened. It was sometimes astonishing the things I could learn just from letting the men and some of the women ramble, many of them too deep in their cups to properly mind their tongues. A lot of times it was just a vague remark here or there, which without context would mean little. But with all the things I learned day-to-day in the office, I already had the framework to string it into. I took this information to C, and he began to take notice."

I exhaled, relieved to be past that part of my

explanation. "Then the man in charge of the military section at our Rotterdam station cabled, needing assistance. He'd been sent there to reestablish connections with our agents inside the German-occupied territories who had been cut off for some months by a series of arrests by the Germans' Secret Police. He was attempting to resuscitate or re-create some of the old intelligence gathering networks at work earlier in the war. And C asked me to go."

"Because you'd already proven yourself capable of gathering intelligence?"

"That, and because I'd been handling most of the reports coming out of Holland with the information our contacts in Belgium and north-eastern France had been able to gather. So I was already familiar with the situation there." I shrugged one shoulder. "And I spoke a little Dutch."

Sidney's expression was infuriatingly impassive, telling me nothing about what he was thinking. Only the manner in which he leaned forward to rest his elbows on the rail told me he was not seething or disgusted, though inside he might have been churning with resentment.

"I'm surprised they didn't send a man," he remarked evenly. "Or was there not one capable enough to send?"

"It's true a number of our male staff had been invalided home from the front because of various injuries, but not all. There were plenty of colleagues still whole in body. However, many of them didn't speak the necessary languages. And in these instances, being a female actually worked to one's benefit. The Germans were far more suspicious of men in general, especially young, hearty ones. But a young woman who dirtied her hair and skin with dirt and soot to mask her health and make herself look ordinary could pass by relatively unnoticed."

He looked up at me at this revelation, his eyes registering some alarm. "I suppose beauty wouldn't be an advantage."

I shook my head. "It was best to be unexceptional. Not smart. Not stupid. Not tall. Not short. And certainly not beautiful. Or ugly," I added. "That invited too much interest. And you did not want to draw interest," I muttered under my breath, suppressing one particularly unpleasant memory.

Too late, I remembered who I was talking to. His expression was nothing short of forbidding, his mouth clamped in a thin line. And even though I didn't think it was directed at me, I couldn't be sure. So, I decided a change of subject was in order.

"And that's how I came to be sent into the field, so to speak," I announced with aplomb, affecting a lighter tone. "I certainly wasn't the first female to undertake such work, nor the last."

"Dangerous work," he protested. From the glint in his eyes I could tell he wasn't pleased.

"Yes, well, someone had to do it," I replied, trying to keep the defensiveness out of my tone. "Many of our agents at work early in the war had been caught by the German Secret Police as their methods improved. Our posts had broken down completely and nothing was getting through. Yet the Allies were relying on us to get as much accurate intelligence from behind enemy lines as possible. It was absolutely essential to know the German troop movements; when and where they were massing troops and moving armaments and supplies; and if they'd developed any new weapons with which to attack.

"I couldn't exactly say no, could I?" I rounded on him to ask. "Thanks, but I'll stay here in my cozy bed while our men overseas are killed by the tens of thousands. You forget, I'd already made brief trips to northern France behind our lines to relay reports or gather additional information for C. I saw what was happening."

"I suppose not," he conceded.

I turned to scowl out to sea. "Besides, my job wasn't nearly as dangerous as it was for those in Belgium and France who had to live under the Germans' thumb and never leave. They couldn't let their guards down for one minute, for when an agent was caught, it was more often than not their own fault. At least I got to leave. And as long as I knew what I was doing while I was there, as long as I followed my training, I was relatively safe."

The last was a lie. The Germans were a rather predictable lot, but all it took was one instance where they deviated from routine for you to be found out. I knew this well, for I'd had a number of near misses.

"Wasn't the border between Holland and Belgium blocked by an electric fence?" Though his movements were calm and steady as he pulled his cigarette case from his pocket again, I could hear the tension crackling behind his voice.

"Yes, but rubber gloves and socks took care of that. The sentries and searchlights were harder to circumvent."

This, it seemed, had finally served to unnerve him when all the rest had not. His hands froze in the act of extracting another cigarette, his eyes riveting to my face. "How can you be so dashed sangfroid about it all?" He snapped the case shut, turning away as if he couldn't look at me. "All this was going on. You . . . crawling . . ."—he almost couldn't get the word out—". . . through electric wire and trudging through a countryside swarming with Jerrys, who may or may not have pestered you." He glared at me, letting me know he hadn't missed the implications of my oblique statement about not drawing interest. "And I hadn't the faintest idea. I foolishly believed you were safe in your bed, just as you said."

"Do you know how many times I wanted to tell you about it, how many times I wanted to ask your advice?" I pleaded, trying to make him understand. "But the Official Secrets Act prevented me from being able to do so." I scowled. "I saw what the war was doing to you, to all the men I cared about, and yet you wouldn't share that burden. And I couldn't share mine."

I inhaled a shaky breath of salty sea air, trying to compose myself. The couple next to us was now staring at us.

"I knew the assignment was dangerous," I continued in a softer voice. "But I decided that if it would end the war sooner, if it would bring you home from that hell, then I would do it." I paused, gazing into the haze where the shores of Britain had disappeared, leaving our ship floating alone in the endless sea. "And then you died, and it didn't matter anymore what happened to me."

CHAPTER 13

I hadn't planned to say that, but I realized if he was to really understand, then he had to know it all. Even the sordid bits I would rather hide.

He didn't speak for a moment, the weight of my revelation heavy between us, and I began to wonder if he meant to gloss over it, to ignore it as many men would have done. But then I felt his hand on my back as he gathered me closer to his side. His warmth and scent assaulted my senses, making me fight back the tears I'd only recently stifled.

"No wonder you're still furious at me," he murmured into my temple, his lips brushing my skin there. "I never thought beyond what I had to do. I never imagined it would affect you so. I'm sorry, Ver." His words were anguished. "If something had happened to you . . . because of me, because you believed me dead . . ." He breathed in sharply. "I would never have forgiven myself."

I pressed a hand to the dark wool of his coat. "Well, nothing did. At least, nothing insurmountable."

I lifted my face to look up at him and his fingers

gently touched my cheek. His eyes darkened, and I could tell he wanted to kiss me, even though doing so would be terribly indecorous. Despite that, I thought he might shock the other passengers anyway, but he restrained himself. I'm not sure I didn't feel more breathless from longing him to do so than I would have had he actually done as he wished.

"Your cheeks are cool. Perhaps we should go inside."

I swallowed. "In a moment."

He nodded, and I rested my head against his chest.

We stood silently side by side as the ferry sliced through the water, the choppy waves of the channel slapping against its hull. Sidney widened his stance to steady us as the boat dropped over a rolling wave.

"What's the plan once we reach Belgium?" he asked. "Where are we going?"

"Brussels first, I think. Then perhaps Liège. We'll have to see what my former colleague can tell us." I lifted my head as he flicked open the cigarette case he still clutched in his hand. "Another?" I was hesitant to pester him, but something had to be said. "Don't you think perhaps you smoke too much?"

He grimaced. "Probably. I got used to doing so in the trenches. It was the only thing that dampened the smells." He exhaled a long breath and closed the case before sliding it back into his pocket. "Ready to get out of this wind now?"

"If you can find us a place to sit in that crush." I nodded over my shoulder toward the packed cabins.

That's when I saw the gentleman standing a few feet to our right along the rail. His hat was pulled low over his eyes, but that did not conceal the fact that he was wearing a copper mask. As if sensing my notice, he pushed away from the rail and retreated toward the cabins.

Though he'd done nothing more suspicious than walk away, the hairs on the back of my neck tingled in alarm. Madame Zozza's warning echoed in my head, and whether it was nonsense or not, I'd decided to heed it.

"Excuse me, sir," I called after him, swiveling to follow.

But rather than pause to address me, he lengthened his stride.

"Excuse me," I tried again, lifting my hand.

However, he never turned to look, merely disappeared around the side of the cabin.

"Darling?" Sidney inquired in confusion.

By the time I rounded the corner after the man, there was no one there but a pair of older ladies in dark hats covered in a profusion of netting. I clenched my hands in frustration, wondering where he could have gone, and if I should continue to pursue him.

"What is it?" Sidney asked, catching up to me.

"There was a man. He seemed to be listening to us. And when he realized I'd noticed him, he darted around this corner."

"The fellow in the mask?"

I nodded.

His eyes surveyed the deck. "You're thinking of Madame Zozza's caution to beware a man in a mask." He frowned. "And you think that was him?"

"I have no idea. But it could be."

"Maybe this fellow was just embarrassed to be caught looking," he suggested, though I could tell he wasn't convinced of that himself. "After all, most of those poor chaps who have to visit the Tin Noses Shop simply want to blend in, not be noticed."

"Maybe," I conceded. "But there was another incident yesterday. A man who was at the séance in Madame Zozza's parlor—I never learned his name—was seated nearby on a bench in St. James's Park while I conferred with George. And I swear he was following me away from Charing Cross the day before that after I'd spoken to another former colleague."

He nodded toward the empty deck. "Was this the same man?"

I shook my head. "I don't think it could have been. This man was taller, and he moved differently." I narrowed my eyes. Except there had been something about this fellow that seemed familiar. Something I couldn't quite place.

"Well, then, I doubt they're connected." He arched his eyebrows. "Unless you think your admirer hired an assistant."

"That does seem rather farfetched." Except I felt certain that whatever about the man was tugging at my memory, it had something to do with my time spent in German-occupied Belgium.

Maybe it had been a German officer I recalled who lurked in much the same manner. I'd assisted Emilie in delivering the baby of a local woman the officer had taken up with. Or forced himself upon. The line between such distinctions was very thin during the war. Many times, the women who had been raped had no choice but to welcome the attentions of their aggressors, especially if they already had hungry little mouths to feed.

It was nothing but a fleeting impression. With the man on the boat wearing a mask, I hadn't seen enough of him to know if he was that German officer or someone else. But it unsettled me nonetheless.

"Come on," Sidney urged me. "I could do with a warm cup of tea."

"Yes, that does sound lovely," I replied, allowing him to lead me away. Perhaps we'd find the man in the mask doing the same, though I doubted it. I suspected he would remain hidden until we docked. Regardless, I vowed to keep my eyes peeled. For if a former German officer was following me, one who had a connection to both Emilie and me during the war, he could hold the answer to this mystery.

Before the war, Ostend had been a popular holiday destination, chiefly during the summer months when tourists flocked to its beaches, and filled its casino and theaters to capacity every night. However, it had been heavily shelled by the Allies during the war as they attempted to drive out the German invaders, reducing many of its buildings to rubble. Now eight months after the armistice, the work of restoration and rebuilding had begun.

As such, though most of the debris had been cleared away, the various construction projects blocked streets and created a maze of roadways. I had thought to avoid this by traveling to Brussels via the canals and rivers that ran through Belgium, but Sidney had other plans.

I'd been surprised to discover his prized Pierce-Arrow in the belly of the boat and had warned him the thoroughfares would still be in a state of disrepair. He'd brushed this off, unconcerned, so I'd happily settled into the passenger seat as he navigated his way out of the harbor town onto the road that would take us through Ghent to Brussels. In truth, it would be easier to have our own mode of transportation, particularly when we left Brussels and headed into the countryside. The number of private vehicles had been scarce during the war, confiscated by the Germans, and the country was still struggling to replace such motorcars. As such, there was no guarantee we would have been able to find one to borrow.

I glanced behind us as we made a sharp right turn to avoid a blockade. The motorcar would also make it more difficult for anyone to follow us, if in fact someone was.

Irrespective of the advantages, I was relieved to see he'd elected not to take any chances with the limited provisions Belgium might have to offer. Several extra petrol tanks were strapped to the car, as well as a spare tire.

"Is that where you were all night? Outfitting the motorcar?" I raised my voice to be heard over the roar of the engine, as we gathered speed when the road began to widen and the old buildings in various states of disrepair began to fall away.

"Once my temper cooled and I could view things a little more objectively, yes."

I hesitated to ask, but I was curious what exactly had changed his mind. "Objectively?"

He sighed, reclining further back in his seat. "I realized you were right. That this situation isn't so very different from the one we faced on

Umbersea Island." His brow furrowed. "When you discovered I was alive and that I'd lied, luring you there under false pretenses, you could have told me to go to the devil. But you didn't. You leapt right in to help me. Partly because I asked, and partly because it's in your nature." He flicked a glance at me. "I know you. You have to uncover the truth, in everything. I believe I even said as much. And if it was true then, then it's still true now. I can't expect that to change simply because it's not convenient."

I felt a little stunned to hear him state it so succinctly. I wanted to argue that my motives were not so simplistic, but in essence, they were.

Sidney yawned and blinked his eyes wide several times.

"Then did you get any rest at all last night?" I asked in concern.

Having only snatched a few hours myself, I felt fatigue dragging at my bones. I could only imagine how tired he must feel, dashing about all night and then motoring south from London to Folkestone.

"I'll be all right. It's just a few hours to Brussels. Why do you wish to go there first?"

"Don't try to distract me," I chided. "You look as if you're about to fall asleep at the wheel. Why don't you pull over and let me drive?"

He smiled as if he found my surly tone amusing. "Truly, Ver. I'm fine. I survived many a battle on less sleep than this. I can get us to Brussels in one piece. Just . . . keep me talking."

I rolled my eyes at the foolish obstinacy of men. The soft green hills of the Flemish countryside now opened before us and I was relieved to see that many of the fields that had lain fallow were now sown with crops. Stalks of wheat, barley, and hops swayed in the summer breeze, separated here and there by narrow canals. Rustic farms dotted the landscape, with their traditional red roof tiles and pale clay-finished Kalei brick walls. Further to the west stood the remains of an old windmill, its roof and sails damaged by a shell.

I shifted in the seat to see Sidney better, casting another glance over my shoulder at the road behind us. Far in the distance I could see the shiny fender of another motorcar cresting a hill, but nothing close enough to suggest we were being tailed.

"I've been watching to make sure we weren't followed since we left the boat," my husband said. His eyes flicked toward the wing mirror. "If we are, they're either being extremely cautious about it or they've got a hayburner of a car." A smug smile stretched his mouth. "Though there's few that can keep up with the engine in this beauty."

A thought occurred to me as he was singing his Pierce-Arrow's praises. "If you knew you were going to join me, why didn't you intercept me before I left the flat this morning? I could have driven down to the coast with you." I tilted my head to the side. "Or were you still hoping I might change my mind?"

My husband was not the sort of person prone to fidgeting. His normal state was cool and collected, sometimes infuriatingly so. But there was a difference between composed and rigid.

"I didn't return to the flat until after you left," he replied smoothly enough, but there had been too long a pause before his answer.

I narrowed my eyes, sensing there was something he wasn't telling me. "Lucky the boat didn't leave earlier."

"Hmm, yes."

"Or that I didn't take the one bound for Calais which departed earlier."

He pressed a fist over his mouth, stifling a yawn. "Yes. Now tell me, why are we headed to Brussels? Do you think this Emilie will be there?"

I wasn't fooled for a moment that he'd told me everything, but I allowed the matter to drop. For now.

"I doubt she's in Brussels." I turned to gaze out over the passing scenery. It seemed surreal to think of how not so long ago, the guns had roared in the distance and whistling shells had shattered the tranquility of this peaceful setting.

The very scent of the damp soil and the air rich with grass and wildflowers stirred memories of this landscape.

I studied Sidney's profile, wondering if it evoked memories for him, too. Though he had been stationed along the Somme for much of the war, not in Flanders, and the terrain and soil composition there were different.

"But I know Captain Landau is there," I continued. "He was the man I mentioned who was in charge of the military section of our Rotterdam Station. I worked closely with him in the latter years of the war. And I know he's been assigned to Brussels since the armistice, working to liquidate the British intelligence networks in Belgium and northeastern France."

"You think he might know where she is?"

"If we're lucky, she's still living in the same place she was during the war. The place I'm familiar with." I sighed. "But somehow I don't think it's that simple. I'm *hoping* Landau may know where she is. But if not, maybe he'll know how to find her."

"And what of these threats Ryde told you an old colleague mentioned?"

"Yes, I'm hoping Landau has some more information he can share with me about that as well."

Sidney must have sensed I was holding something back, "You think he won't?" He darted a swift glance at me before returning his eyes to the road. "Or you don't know if he'll share it with you?"

I should have known he would guess. After all, he'd spent four and a half years in the trenches as first a lieutenant and then a captain, being forced to blindly follow the orders of officers far behind the front. Officers who often didn't share the information they possessed, and who weren't required to explain their decisions to subordinates.

I grimaced. "When I visited my colleagues at Whitehall Court, they were less than forthcoming."

"But you said you worked closely with this Captain Landau?"

I nodded.

"And you said he's working with a limited staff. So perhaps he'll appreciate your initiative."

"He always appreciated it before. Truthfully, he was one of the least narrow-minded of the lot. He grew up on a farm in the Transvaal of South Africa, and he shared a bit with me about his mother, who I gather is a strong, resourceful, eminently capable woman, so I think that accounts for it."

"She must have been one tough dame. Particularly given the fact that for a period of her life the Boer War must have been going on."

"It was. His father was caught up in it."

Sidney's eyes met mine, perhaps comprehending for the first time just how young Captain Landau was. "I'm curious to meet this fellow."

"Yes, I always suspected the two of you would get along famously."

It being late in the day by the time we reached Brussels, we found a hotel for the night near The Grand Place, surrounded by its beautiful, Gothic buildings. Fortunately, the city stood far enough from the front to avoid the shells, which had damaged so many other cities. I'd always loved Brussels, having stayed there a number of times before the war on the way to visit my great-aunt where she lived near Münster, Germany.

As we stretched our legs, looking for a restaurant for dinner, I was relieved to see that much of the drab state of disrepair that had marked the city during the war had faded away. The shops that had sat closed or nearly empty, unable to replace their inventory, were open again. And while still not filled to their pre-war standards, it was good to see the customers bustling in and out.

There were notices about the impending celebrations for Belgian National Day, their first since the armistice, and the city displayed the country's fiercely independent spirit proudly. Who could blame them after such a long and terrible war and occupation? Streamers in Belgium's national colors and flags festooned many of the buildings, while signs announced "Vive la Belgique!" I couldn't help but smile.

The following morning, we made our way to the rue Stevin, not far from the British Embassy and the large green space of Parc du Cinquantenaire with its grand triumphal arch, built to celebrate the country's fiftieth year of independence many years earlier. The building where Captain Landau lived and worked was lined with charming stone town houses. A young clerk opened the door to our knock and ushered us inside before scurrying out on his own errand.

I breathed my first sigh of relief that the young man hadn't told us Captain Landau was out of town. I was well aware of the great deal of travel his task required, interviewing several thousand agents scattered about Belgium and northeastern France, so to find him in residence was a stroke of luck.

However, my pleasure at such fortuitous timing did not last long.

No sooner had we strolled through the door into the echoing entry hall than a familiar voice rang out. "Verity Kent, is that really you?"

I looked up into a pair of laughing eyes.

"By Jove! It is you." He crossed the room to take my hand in his. "And dash if it isn't good to see you."

I blinked up at him, feeling rather stunned.

"And this must be your long-lost husband, resurrected from the dead." He shook Sidney's hand. "Good to meet you, old chap. Any man capable of securing our girl's affection must be a dashed fine fellow."

This was spoken without a trace of irony, and nearly made me choke. Recovering myself with some effort, I gestured to the man before us. "Sidney, this is Lieutenant Alec Xavier."

"It's captain now," he corrected me good-naturedly.

I shook my head. "Yes, of course." I forced a smile. "It's good to see you, too. I hadn't expected to. Lord Ryde gave me the impression you were traveling."

He grinned that same blinding smile I remembered. The one that enabled him to gain information from just about any susceptible female in the near vicinity. "I'm always traveling. In fact, I'm off from Brussels this afternoon, so it's my great fortune to be here now to see you arrive."

"Yes, how fortunate."

If he could hear the reluctance in my voice, he didn't show it.

"But what brings you back to Belgium?" He paused to search both my and Sidney's faces. "From your expressions, I doubt this is a social call."

I glanced up at my husband, seeing the watch-fulness in his gaze. He evidently noticed my shock and discomfort, and if I didn't pull myself together quickly, it was only a matter of time before he put two and two together.

"Given your encounter with Lord Ryde at the War Office, I'm sure you're well aware that we're here for information," I replied, arching my eyebrows in gentle reproof. I might be out of practice, but I was not going to fall victim to such an obvious ploy for our confidence.

His whiskey brown eyes gleamed. He always had enjoyed sparring. "About La Dame Blanche. About the threats to its agents. Then I suppose you're really here to see Landau." He tipped his head to the right. "Come with me."

We followed him into another room, this one filled with the rapid click of typewriters, and across to a door. He rapped twice and then opened it to poke his head in.

"Oh, good. You're alone." He opened the door wider. "Guess who's here to pay us a call?"

I was gratified to see Captain Landau's face break into a smile at the sight of me. He wasn't an altogether unattractive man, though his small eyes and round face were rather dominated by a misshapen nose, and his ears that stood out from either side of his head like the handles of a Grecian urn. However, he was possessed of a sharp wit, a natural manner with people of all stripes, and an incredibly quick mind—all of which had propelled him into his position at such a young age and helped him to succeed. That, and his command of multiple languages. It was from him that I'd learned much of my Dutch.

"Mrs. Kent, what a lovely surprise! And of course, this must be your husband I've heard so much about." He shook his hand heartily. "Quite a sacrifice you made going undercover like that to capture those traitors. I admire you terribly for it."

Sidney appeared staggered by these words. "Oh, well, thank you."

"It couldn't have been easy, especially keeping it all from Mrs. Kent." He glanced at me in question. "You didn't know, did you?"

I shook my head. "Not an inkling."

His face relaxed again. "I thought not. Mrs. Kent was always remarkably cool and capable. Had to be to fool all those Germans. But for her to have feigned such grief would have to make her the greatest actress of our time." He gestured toward the chairs before his desk before rounding to resume his seat. "I worried after her, you know. Concerned she might do something imprudent and get herself caught, or worse. But she came through it all well enough."

It was maddening how people could talk of my grief over the loss of my husband as if it was some jolly jest, all forgotten for the best now that he was discovered to be alive. But as always, I swallowed my annoyance and straightened my skirt as I settled into the left chair while Sidney took the right. Xavier leaned against the wall, hovering at the edge of my field of vision.

In any case, Landau was wrong on one point. I *had* done something imprudent. It just hadn't gotten me captured or killed.

But I should have known he would sense some of my turmoil. "When I read about your survival in the newspapers, I was extraordinarily happy to hear it." He gazed at me fondly. "Couldn't have happened to a better lady."

I returned his smile with a gentle one of my own.

He clasped his hands in front of him. "But what brings you to Brussels? I suspect this isn't strictly a social call."

"I'm afraid not." I glanced at Xavier, who was eyeing me with interest.

Landau's gaze traveled over Sidney. "I suppose you've read Mr. Kent into whatever the situation is. Impossible to avoid, really."

"Yes," I replied, relieved he hadn't questioned this decision.

"But shall I ask Captain Xavier to leave?"

I considered this and then shook my head. "No, he may know something we don't." Then I inhaled a deep breath, electing to dive straight to the heart of the matter. "I need some information on the whereabouts of one of the agents I worked with from La Dame Blanche. I'm worried she may be in danger."

For a moment I thought I'd shocked him, but then he tipped his head back and laughed. "Well, by Jove, if the old darb wasn't right. C said he suspected you'd be coming to see me about just such a thing, and here you are."

CHAPTER 14

C told you I was coming?" Somehow, I felt I should have been more astonished, but having worked with the chief for four years, I couldn't say that I was.

Landau nodded and leaned back in his chair. "Had a cable from him just yesterday. Said he had a hunch you'd be headed my way. I thought he was going barmy. That you'd be cozied up with your husband somewhere, not traipsing over to the continent." He lifted his arms to gesture to us. "But here you are."

I didn't know quite how to respond to that. As it was, I was fighting a guilty flush, as if I'd failed on some point in my devotion to my husband. I certainly couldn't look at Sidney.

Fortunately, Landau continued, his face settling into more serious lines. "All right. Tell me all. This must be important."

Though curious what C's instructions to him had been, I knew better than to ask. In any case, I viewed his resolve to hear everything I'd learned as a good sign. Why else would he waste his time?

Unless he needed to know more to effectively block my efforts?

I shook that possibility aside. I felt I knew him well enough to expect more courtesy than that.

So I launched into my tale of the séance at Madame Zozza's, her conjuring of Emilie, and the things I'd discovered since then. I also made mention of the medium's real name of Mona Kertle, hoping either man would recognize it, but both protested having any knowledge of the woman. When I'd finished, his brow was scored with furrows.

"Well, that is concerning." He sighed, staring sightlessly at his desk as he gave the matter some more thought.

I was accustomed to this response, for he never did anything hastily. I was merely gratified he hadn't brushed the entire matter off as inconsequential, or told me it was none of my business, as Major Davis had. At one point, his gaze flicked to Captain Xavier, as if in question, and then back to his blotter.

For his part, Xavier still lolled against the wall, one ankle crossed over the other. Not a flicker of his real opinion showed in his eyes. But then I'd learned long ago how very good he was at concealing his thoughts. He'd had to in order to survive the assignments he'd undertaken.

By all appearances, Sidney seemed unruffled by my former superior's silence as well. He settled back in his chair, removing his cigarette case and tipping it to each of the men. Landau waved it off, but Xavier crossed to take one with a softly worded "thank you." However, I knew my husband well enough by now to realize that when he was growing tense or anxious he often chose to smoke in order to mask it. Especially when he exhaled so deeply after his first drag.

Xavier seemed to take note of this as well, watching him through half-closed eyes as he exhaled a stream of smoke. I wasn't certain I liked him taking such an interest in Sidney. But then again, he probably did such things without even thinking, having lived so many years covertly.

Landau tapped the arms of his chair, coming to a decision. "I have met this woman you speak of, this midwife who operated under the code name Emilie. I interviewed her some months ago, and she was very much alive. Her real name is Rose Moreau." My face must have registered my surprise, for he smiled. "Yes, it is difficult to imagine a woman less suited to such a name."

My lips curled in answering amusement. "Where did this interview take place?"

"In Liège, at the former secret headquarters of La Dame Blanche. She had insisted on coming to me, rather than the other way around. Which was not entirely unusual. A number of other members did the same." He frowned. "However, Emilie did ask me to convey any further correspondence or compensation from us to her former chiefs there in Liège, and they would forward it on to her. She said she'd decided to move, and she wasn't quite certain where she would settle."

"Did she say why?"

"She said the memories were too painful for her to remain in her old home, and I did not question this assertion. After all, she'd lost her husband and son to the war."

I had not known this, though I had guessed. As a general rule, the agents in La Dame Blanche did not discuss their personal lives with one another, and I had been only too happy to abide by this. The less I could recall about them, the better, in case I should be caught and subjected to the German's third-degree methods to elicit information from me. Plus, for rather more selfish reasons, I'd no desire to share my own troubles.

Landau grimaced. "Now I wonder if I should have."

"Could she have moved for another reason? Perhaps to hide from someone? She seems to have been doing her best to keep her whereabouts unknown."

He shrugged. "That I don't know. But she didn't seem unsettled or frightened. Merely worn down, as so many others were."

My mouth twisted in commiseration. After four and a quarter years of war, who of us wasn't?

But the Belgians and the people of northeastern France had also been forced to contend with a harsh foreign occupation as well. Conditions had been insufferable, the people near starvation. And those working for British intelligence had known they could be betrayed or discovered at any moment.

Landau glanced up at Xavier. "You had nothing to do with La Dame Blanche, but did you by chance have any dealings with Madame Moreau? Ever hear the Germans mention her?"

At this comment, Sidney shifted in his seat, obviously deducing Captain Xavier's wartime service had been an interesting one.

"I'm afraid not," Xavier replied.

Landau shook his head. "I'm afraid I'm at a loss."

"What of these threats Captain Xavier mentioned to Lord Ryde? Could Madame Moreau have received one?"

"Yes, we were just discussing that." His chair squeaked as he leaned back, clasping his hands over his stomach. "They're very odd, almost childish in nature. Letters scrawled in large letters on bits of paper or cardboard and left on their doorstep. I quite honestly don't know what to make of them."

"What do they say?"

"Various things. 'I know who you are.' 'I'm not fooled.' Or simply, 'Spy'!"

My eyes widened.

"Most of the recipients have not been concerned. After all, many of them wanted their wartime service to be known. So many of the young men could not escape the occupied areas to join the armies and do their duty as they wished, so they settled for doing their bit here. And for the most part, they've been lauded for it."

"But not by all?" I pressed, pouncing on his hesitation.

He shared a look with Xavier, as if debating how much to say. "The vast majority of Belgians are happy to have their country back and see the Germans sent packing. But there have been a few who are not so pleased. German loyalists who were content for things to remain as they were." His face tightened with displeasure. "Most of these German loyalists have been satisfied with making their malcontent known in small, petty ways. But in May, someone bombed the police station in Blankenberge, killing two officers and seriously injuring two more."

I gasped. "Why didn't we hear about this in London?"

Landau's mouth flattened into a thin line, giving me my answer.

"Ah, I see the government's propaganda is still at work." I sighed. "Well, were the perpetrators at least caught?"

He shook his head. "Two brothers were suspected, but there wasn't enough proof. And in the general chaos that's gripped the country, no one came forward with more information. Most everyone is consumed with just the day-to-day necessities of surviving and beginning to rebuild. The economy is sluggish, the country's coffers are empty, and half the villages and cities in the east are in ruins, not to mention those villages to the south that were burned when the Germans invaded five years ago. I'm afraid law and order are not the highest priority."

"If that's true, I'm surprised any of the members of La Dame Blanche want their service to be known," I remarked in concern. "Doesn't it put them at risk?"

"Don't mistake me. These incidents of revenge are few and far between. For the vast majority of Belgians, their service to the Allies is a badge of honor. These threats are an aberration."

"Then it's no great secret who were agents. But would they have revealed their code names?" I asked, curious how many people were aware that Madame Moreau was Emilie.

He shook his head. "Though the existence of La Dame Blanche is now publicly known, they all swore by their oath not to reveal information concerning the service without formal permission. And that has not been granted."

"Yes, but would they take such an oath seriously? Especially now that the war is over?"

Sidney asked, speaking up for the first time since we'd sat. His face betrayed no scorn, merely genuine curiosity.

"Oh, yes," Landau said, his voice growing fervent. "They organized their network as a militarized observation corps of the Allies, and they upheld that designation to the letter, fully prepared to court-martial any offenders. The entire operation was quite brilliantly constructed, each unit separated from the others as much as possible. Separate letter boxes. Separate couriers. So if one was compromised, the others would not be at risk of being apprehended, too. That's why it was such a success." It was evident he'd argued this point many times.

"So only the immediate members of Madame Moreau's platoon even knew she was an agent, and possibly the person who manned the letter box, where she delivered reports in her role as a courier," I explained to Sidney.

He leaned forward to stub his cigarette out in the crystal ashtray on the corner of Landau's desk. "Then that narrows our pool of suspects considerably, doesn't it? To the people in her platoon and those in the Secret Service who knew of her existence."

"In theory," Landau said. "But there are other ways the information could have spread. Did someone from that narrow pool break their oath and relay sensitive information to someone else?

Did Madame Moreau confide in someone herself? Did someone witness something and fit the pieces together?"

"And we also have the connection to Madame Zozza to consider," I reminded them. "How did she come by her information? Did someone put her up to performing such a trick, and then kill her to silence her? Not everyone would have the means to go to such lengths."

"For that matter, why would they draw you out like that?" Xavier ruminated, still nursing his cigarette. "What of these 'unearthed secrets' the medium mentioned? Do you know what she was referring to?"

I hesitated only a moment, still finding it difficult to relay the intelligence I'd sworn to keep even in such company. But his eyes sharpened with interest, recognizing I was withholding something.

I glanced at Landau, who nodded his permission, which unstuck my tongue from the roof of my mouth. "I can think of two possibilities. Unless she was speaking metaphorically rather than literally. The first was a map case I stole from a German aviator in Chimay." I didn't explain how that was done. How I'd seized the chance encounter with one of their crack pilots—a gregarious fellow with a professed fondness for redheads. It had only cost me an evening of pretending to drink kümmel while he swilled enough to swim in, fending off his kisses long enough for him to pass out. "It contained a handful of maps marked with all the aviation fields behind a large section of the German front."

"I doubt I need to explain how the information those maps supplied was incalculably valuable. Particularly considering the fact that marking them in such a manner was entirely against German Army regulations," Landau interjected. "God bless that aviator's folly."

I nodded, wondering again what had happened to that pilot when he'd confessed to his superior officer about his lost case. But such was the manner of war. "The maps were too large to transport in one piece, so we cut them into strips, numbered them so they could be quickly reassembled, and stitched them into the hem of my skirt for me to transport over the border. The rest of the papers we burned, but we buried the leather map case in the woods near the frontier between France and Belgium."

Landau was already aware of these specifics, and Xavier had faced far more dangerous missions to be fazed by such a common tale. Sidney, however, was not. Though he hid it well, I could tell from his tightened jawline that he was not pleased. What I couldn't tell was whether this was in reaction to hearing about the sometimes sordid assignments I'd undertaken and their inherent dangers, or because I hadn't shared any of these "unearthed secrets" with him earlier.

Quite honestly, there had been so many aspects to my life with the Secret Service, so many facets big and small, that it would be impossible to share them all. So I had been operating sort of under a code of necessity, and these details hadn't seemed to fall under that purview.

"You say you emptied the case, but could you have missed something?" Xavier asked as he stepped forward to stub out his cigarette. Rather than return to his slouch against the wall, he instead perched on the corner of Landau's desk, far too close to me for my comfort.

"It's possible," I admitted. "The entire affair was somewhat rushed. It was done in the midst of Emilie attending to a birth. I'd actually met the German aviator as he was likely leaving the mother's cottage, and he pressed me to join him for dinner. Given the fact that I suspected he was the young woman's lover, possibly even the father of her baby, the proposition was distasteful." I glanced at Sidney to gauge his reaction. "But in such situations, it was far more dangerous to decline and risk angering him. So I agreed, hoping he might let something useful slip."

"As he did," Landau confirmed.

I nodded. "So when the pilot passed out, I hurried back to the cottage where Emilie was still assisting the woman. Emilie had learned from one of the woman's neighbors that there were German patrols in the area conducting random searches and making further requisitions of materials, so we realized we had to get rid of any incriminating evidence as swiftly as possible. And in fact, I very nearly stumbled into one of those patrols on my way back from burying the case in the woods behind the cottage. So it's possible we missed something in our haste. But at the time, the maps were of chief importance. As well as discarding the proof that we'd had such materials in our possession."

He nodded. "And the other possibility?"

I frowned, staring at the wall behind Landau's desk as I thought back on it. "It was a somewhat odd occurrence, and it may mean nothing. But there was one instance when Emilie asked me to stand watch as she disappeared into the woods a short distance. When she returned, I noticed she was scrubbing dirt from her hands. She explained she'd sensed we weren't alone in the forest and had buried a report she would retrieve later. I didn't question her, having already learned to trust her instincts. And sure enough, not half a mile further along the lane, we encountered a patrol."

"Did Emilie ever retrieve the report?" Sidney surprised me by being the one to ask.

"I don't know. She was acting as a guide,

conducting me to another rendezvous. I didn't return with her."

"And you never actually saw this supposed report?" Xavier pressed.

I shook my head. "But at the time, I had no reason to doubt her assertion. I'm still not sure I do. It was just something I thought of when Madame Zozza used the word 'unearth.' "

"This isn't the first I've heard of an operative discarding compromising information on a hunch," Landau declared somewhat distractedly, his eyes seeming to peer into the distance. "Keen instincts are a powerful asset." He blinked several times, refocusing his gaze in time to catch me watching him with interest. "Of the two, I find the aviator map case a more promising lead. Do you think you could find it again?"

"Maybe. If I can find my way back to that cottage where the woman was giving birth, I should be able to locate it." But I didn't think that was what he'd really wanted to hear.

He nodded decisively and opened a drawer of his desk to extract a piece of paper. "Then I think your next step should be to speak with the chiefs of La Dame Blanche in Liège. They will be able to tell you more about Emilie and these threats than I can. I'll write you a letter of introduction, and that should smooth over any difficulties."

"I'm headed in that direction myself. I can escort them to Liège." Xavier grinned at us. "That is, so long as you don't mind another passenger in your Pierce-Arrow." From the gleam in his eyes, I knew he had seen me stiffen in alarm.

Had it been possible, I would have clubbed him. But as it was, there was nothing for me to do but smile in return. "That would be quite helpful." I turned to my husband, forcing a brighter smile at the sight of him studying us. "Sidney?"

"If you can direct us where we need to go, then it's fine by me."

"I'll just have to collect my luggage . . ." Xavier began as they rose to their feet, conferring with one another as they moved toward the door.

I remained seated, waiting on Landau to finish his letter of introduction.

Once complete, he folded it into thirds and passed it to me. "This and Xavier should convince them to talk, but if for some reason they should balk, have them telephone me directly."

"Thank you." I tucked the missive into my handbag, lowering my voice as I next spoke. "Is that all you wished to tell me?" I lifted my gaze to his pointedly.

His lips curled into a reluctant smile. "Should have known better than to think *your* instincts weren't as finely tuned as ever." His gaze flicked toward the doorway where Sidney and Xavier still stood talking. "All I can say is that some agents were forced to keep more secrets than others. Secrets that could come back to haunt them."

My chest tightened upon hearing him echo my own thoughts, as I was feeling rather hounded by my own secrets at the moment. But outwardly I scowled. "That's a rather oblique statement."

He held up his hand. "I know, and I wish I could say more. But I can't." He lowered his voice further. "Other than to tell you that C instructed me to offer you whatever assistance you needed. Off the record, of course."

"Of course," I replied, unable to hide my sarcasm. I couldn't recall the number of times I'd been told just such a thing. Though in this case, it was interesting to note that C's orders were in direct contrast to Major Davis's. Kathleen must have gotten word to him after all.

"And I will, any way I can."

"Can" being the operative word.

Xavier called out from the doorway. "All set?"

Landau's gaze did not release mine for a moment longer, but then he blinked, settling back in his chair as if our exchange had never happened.

"Yes," I replied before telling my former superior, "I'll be in touch."

He nodded minutely, and I moved to join the other men.

CHAPTER 15

Apparently Sidney had arranged for Captain Xavier to meet us at our hotel where our luggage and the Pierce-Arrow were currently stowed, for he peeled away from us with a jaunty wave as we exited the building. A light rain had fallen while we were inside, and the pavements were still damp.

"Interesting fellow," he remarked as we strolled down the street arm in arm. He projected an apathetic mien, with his hands tucked in his pockets and his hat pulled low over his eyes, but I could sense the hum of attentiveness under the surface. "I gather he had a rather remarkable assignment during the war."

I decided there was no reason not to reveal this secret. Not when he'd undoubtedly already deduced it for himself.

"He was planted in the German Army a few years before the start of the war. There were several of them fitted to that role, in fact. So he posed as a German officer for much of the war, stationed mostly on staff in Brussels. That is, until he was almost caught."

If Sidney was at all surprised by this, he didn't show it. "And I take it you had some interaction with him."

"When necessary."

His eyes dipped to mine and I cursed my choice of words. As if I found the prospect of working with Xavier distasteful.

"It was safer for someone like me to be seen fraternizing with him than the women who had to remain here," I hastened to add, scrutinizing the passersby as we talked. "In the eyes of their neighbors, they would be tarred as whores and collaborators. The Allies even compiled lists of women suspected of intimate relations with the enemy, many of whom were included entirely because of hearsay."

"Searching for your German admirer?"

I glanced up in startlement, and then realized he meant the man I had seen on the boat. "Yes, or the fellow from our séance." I noticed his eyes were also scanning our surroundings. "Why? Have you seen him?"

"No, but shall I hail a taxicab anyway?"

"Yes, let's."

I wasn't surprised this was done with minimal effort on his part, even given the general short-age of such vehicles. Once ensconced inside, I peered out the window, watching to see if any-one scrambled for their own conveyance. Though we had almost certainly lost them in Ostend,

Brussels would have been the logical place for them to pick up their search. And the British Embassy, a few blocks from rue Stevin, would have been at the top of their list of places to try first.

"Have you paused to consider that you might be playing right into this person's hands?"

I turned to find Sidney staring broodingly forward through the taxicab's windscreen. That stubborn lock of his dark hair had fallen over his brow again, and he had not pushed it back, such was the evidence of his distraction.

His gaze shifted to meet mine. "Have you considered that you might be leading them straight to Emilie?"

I smoothed out my rumpled charcoal gray skirt, trying to calm the anxieties his words had stirred inside me. "Yes, actually. After all, it's clear to me—if nothing else is—that Emilie has gone to ground, so to speak. And the likeliest solution to the riddle of Madame Zozza's involvement and suspicious death, is that someone desperately wants to find her. I suppose that's where I come in." I realized I was worrying a loose string from the saddlebag pocket of my skirt and forced my fingers to still. "Whether the culprit is a fellow Secret Service agent who already knew of my connection, or I was recognized from our photograph in the newspapers, I am relatively easy to find. So they hoped to set me on the trail to either find Emilie or unearth this secret of hers for them."

"Then why are you doing it?"

"Because what other option do I have?" I retorted, as much frustrated with myself as I was with him. "If they're so determined to find her that they're willing to commit murder to cover their tracks, then if I don't lead them to her, they'll find her another way." My hands clenched into fists. "I'm not about to let that happen. Not until I know what this is about."

I turned to gaze out the window as we passed the imposing edifice of the Palais de Justice, which had been used as barracks for the German Army during the war. Its courtyard and all the grounds of Parc du Bruxelles, stretching to the Palais du Roi at the opposite end, had housed one large army camp. A place any self-respecting Belgian woman traveled miles around to avoid, except for the older women who drove the fruit and vegetable carts in from the countryside each morning to sell their goods. I had skirted the grounds of the camp only once, a considered risk I'd felt forced to take given the haste of my objective. Fortunately, I'd emerged unscathed, but I'd met plenty of women who had not.

"Intelligence work is all a matter of calculations," I ruminated softly, trusting the driver could not hear us over the rumble of the engine. If he could understand English at all. "Taking the objectives, dividing the risks versus rewards, estimating the enemy's plans, and solving to find your course of action. Sometimes the equation balances better than others. Sometimes the odds are not in your favor, but the importance of the objective outweighs all else." I frowned. "This is a calculated risk I have to take. For Emilie."

Sidney's warm hand settled over mine where it rested on the seat. "Then we'll just have to make certain no one follows us."

I nodded, suddenly finding it hard to speak.

His fingers wove between mine, and I leaned my head to the side, resting it on his shoulder.

"She must be quite remarkable to inspire such devotion." He spoke casually, but I heard the genuine curiosity behind his words.

"She saved me several times, from death or, at the least, from some very unpleasant experiences. But beyond that, she was a comrade." I glanced up at him. "Would you not go to great lengths to protect your fellow officers, to shield the men who were under your command?"

This question was a rhetorical one, for he'd already proven what lengths he would go to to catch a traitor among their ranks.

His mouth curled wryly. "Point taken." He dropped his gaze, watching his thumb rub along mine. "I suppose that's also why you didn't tell me about the map case and the buried report. After all, I never explained every detail of how

I went about searching for proof of treason, just those that were necessary."

I was glad he'd worked that out on his own and I wouldn't have to explain this omission to him. However, it also left my heart feeling heavy.

"Yes. But sooner or later, if we're going to make this marriage work, it seems we shall have to share some of those details of our lives during the war we would rather not," I murmured, speaking as much to myself as to him.

"True."

But the silence that fell made it quite obvious neither of us was eager to start.

Though there were several personas Alec Xavier could have adopted, and indeed I'd seen him shift between these with impunity, for some reason he'd elected to affect a manner of good cheer. Whether this was truly felt was a matter of debate. I was more interested in the fact that he'd taken it upon himself to befriend my husband. I couldn't tell if this was working, for Sidney had always possessed an excellent poker face—no doubt improved by playing brag with his fellow officers at the front during the hours of monotony on rotation at the rear of the trenches. Whatever the truth, they were soon jesting and carrying on as if they'd been chums for ages. Meanwhile, I sat in the rear seat, shaking my head at their antics.

Having grown up with three brothers and scores of their friends, and later served with men in London, Holland, and the occupied territories, I was quite accustomed to their talk and traits. Though by no means were Sidney and Xavier crass or rude. I couldn't imagine my husband ever speaking of a woman in a disrespectful manner or allowing someone else to. On the other hand, I was quite certain Xavier would stoop to do so if the situation called for it.

However, their bull session rather quickly grew tiresome. Fortunately, when we encountered yet another rain shower on the outskirts of Brussels, Sidney decided to stop at a café for us to grab a bite to eat. I wanted nothing so much as a strong drink, but I settled for coffee and sandwiches. Once I'd done what little I could to salvage my hair, which kinked in the damp air, I returned to the table to find our coffee had already been delivered.

"So how did the two of you meet?" Sidney asked as he settled back in his chair. "Or is that information too classified?"

I'd known the question was coming, but I was surprised by how quickly.

"If Verity trusts you, I suspect I can, too," Alec replied, my given name tripping off his tongue. He'd insisted we call him Alec, and while I'd wanted to argue against it, not wishing to conjure that familiarity, my husband had already agreed.

241

"The first time we met she was acting as a temporary courier." He laughed suddenly. "And I don't think either of us was what the other expected."

I couldn't help but smile in agreement. "That's true enough."

"As I'm sure Verity already told you, I was fitted into the German Army before the war. Sort of a man inside, if you will. I was stationed in the Kommandantur in Brussels, and my usual letter box where I dropped my intelligence reports had been compromised. So I'd been told to watch for a person wearing a blue cornflower. Naturally I expected a man with a boutonniere. But instead, in walked Verity with the flower tucked in her hair."

"Yes, well, I was hardly expecting a German soldier to make the anticipated remark, 'Ich denke, eine Rose passender wäre.' I was told to pretend to attempt to secure a special pass to visit my ill sister, and I thought one of the Belgian clerks would approach me."

"But before she could reach the front of the line, or one of the Bosche could get to her first, I pulled her into my office."

I arched a single eyebrow. "You winked and told them I was being saucy, or rather the German equivalent."

He shrugged, taking a sip of his coffee. "Yes, well, unfortunately that's all that was required should a German officer take an interest in a girl."

And I'd been trained well. One did not exhibit disgust or refuse an officer outright. Not unless you wanted a backhand across the face and possible confinement for one trumped-up charge or another. If you were lucky, like me, they stopped at groping. It didn't bear thinking about what happened if you were less fotunate.

He chuckled. "I'll never forget. There I was apologizing for standing much too close to her in order to shield her through the glass windows of my office from the others. Had to put on some sort of show for my fellow soldiers. And what does she say?" His eyes twinkled. " 'Well, at least you're not a foul-smelling oaf. So, what have you got for me?' "

Contrary to what I'd expected, Sidney's lips actually twitched. "Yes, that sounds like Verity."

"Well, there was nothing for it but to brazen my way through," I replied in my defense.

"I understood then why she had been sent as my temporary courier," Alec said. "I admired her aplomb. And I requested her anytime I needed assistance after that."

I was arrested in bringing my cup to my lips, not having been told this before. "You did?"

He nodded. "Too many of the male agents were bloody obvious. Not you. Even with your dirt-mussed auburn hair. You pulled that coded message from under my hatband where it rested on my desk, wrapped it around your hairpin, and secured it in your tresses without missing a beat. And all while having some strange fellow breathing down your neck."

"Yes, but . . ." I halted, struggling to get the words out. "But I was the reason you were almost caught."

He brushed that aside with a shake of his head as our food was set before us. "I told you before, it wasn't. That oberst had been suspicious of me for some time. It would have happened eventually anyway. Besides, you risked your own safety to see that I was warned and extracted. So the argument is moot."

I wasn't certain I felt the same way, but I didn't argue.

"What about you?" Alec gestured between the two of us after swiping his mouth with a napkin. "I knew you existed," he told Sidney. "But I'm afraid it wasn't safe for Verity to share much beyond that with me. So how did you meet?"

I launched into the tale, expecting him to interject a comment or two himself. But it became apparent he wasn't listening, and I soon realized why. Across the café were seated two older women, fashioned after my mother's ilk, and a rather anemic-looking young woman of about eighteen. They were speaking rapidly in English, and, if I should guess, had embarked on one of those macabre tours of the battlefields. Though apparently, they had not hired a tour company, but were determined to go it alone with only the illustrated guidebook the young woman was attempting to hide behind to direct them. Given the fact that they were sixty kilometers or more from the trenches of the Western Front, they weren't doing a very good job of it thus far.

But their poor sense of direction was not my concern, nor Sidney's, but rather the insensitive nature of their exchange. We weren't the only ones bothered by it. Based on the sour looks some of the café staff sent their way, they seemed to have a good enough grasp of English to comprehend what they were saying.

The ladies' conversation started with complaints about how hard it had been to find butter during the war, comments that, while insensitive to the Belgians who had faced much more serious food shortages than anything the British experienced, were relatively harmless. Then they progressed to a sort of back-and-forth competition of the various war committees to which they'd been appointed to the board, and the number of recruits they had signed up, just doing their bit. As if *they* should be ultimately thanked for those boys' service and not the soldiers themselves. This smug, self-congratulatory prattle was vexing, but nothing I hadn't heard before.

However, their discussion devolved into a sort of callous comparison of their losses.

"Johnny received the MC, you know. So wonderful. But also sad, of course. Nearly wore myself to the bone with worry. But one must smile and carry on, knowing they died for the greater good."

"So true. They say my Davy was called up to the worst sector. Such an eager, strong boy. If only he'd had longer to earn his distinction. But, of course, I'm still so proud. By Jove, my boy wasn't a slacker. And neither was my girl." She smiled at the young woman now slumping low in her seat. "She set such a noble example. Wouldn't keep out of it. Simply had to join the VAD."

I stared down at my coffee, now grown cold, trying to stifle the anger building inside me. I hated hearing this sort of talk. Not all of the older women were like this, thank heavens. Not all of them seemed so detached and heartless, determined to prove they'd done more, sacrificed more—than even their own flesh and blood—to the cause. I empathized with all the mothers who had lost their sons and daughters to the war, but I could not reconcile myself to these women who made the war a tally for their good works, who counted their children's service and deaths as more a mark in their favor than a terrible tragedy.

And neither could Sidney, it seemed. Seeing the tension along the line of his neck, I reached out to take his hand underneath the table and found that he was shaking with fury. He gripped my fingers back, as if struggling to restrain himself. This was clearly his first encounter with their like, and I pressed my other hand gently to his arm, thinking to distract him.

"Let's talk of something happier, shall we?" I suggested. Much as I wanted to give those women a piece of my mind, I knew it would do no good. For they could not hear how cold and insensitive their words were. In their minds, they were the victims, and any attempt to explain why their attitudes were so insulting would fall on deaf ears.

"Yes," Alec agreed, catching on. "Tell me, who was the stroke during the Boat Race your final year at Oxford? I can't recall. Was it Horsfall or Pitman?"

Sidney looked up from where he had been glaring at the table. The glint in his eye made it clear he didn't give a fig for rowing—polo had always been his sport—nor did he care to be diverted. But then he relented, perhaps realizing we were only trying to help. "Horsfall," he grunted.

But before Alec could respond, one of the women's voices trilled with intensity. "Oh, if only my younger son Cecil had been old enough to serve! I should have happily given him to the cause as well."

At this last, Sidney could stand it no more. He rose from his chair, rounding on them like a tiger. "Would you? Would you happily sacrifice his youth, his sanity, his very life to gratify your vanities, without a thought to his wishes, without a care to the horrors he'll never be able to forget?" he snarled. "I suppose you would spill the blood from every last Englishman to indulge your conceits, spill enough to flood the sodding trenches." He stabbed his finger at his chest, leaning forward to hiss at them. "Well, I held the hands of those whelps you recruited, I watched the life drain from their eyes, and I can tell you they cared naught for your self-righteous patriotism. They died begging to know why you *lied.*"

He whirled away from the cowering women and stormed off through the door out into the light patter of rain. For a moment, no one moved or even dared to speak.

Then one of the women lowered her hand from where she had been clutching her bosom. "Well, I never," she exhaled in protest. "How abominably rude. And he's one of our countrymen. If it were the French, or one of these Belgians, I shouldn't be so shocked. But an *Englishman.*"

"It must be shell shock," the other woman murmured in a hushed voice, though not low enough I couldn't hear it. "My sister's son had to be confined to a hospital." She darted a glance at me before looking away. "They say it's caused by cowardice."

I closed my eyes and clenched my fists, lest I stride across the café and slap both women across the face.

But the truth was, I was also shaken by the vehemence of Sidney's outburst. Before the war, his emotions had always been so contained. He would have made some scathing quip, but he would never have allowed his anger to get the better of him.

I didn't know how to deal with this new side of him. This man whose pain was at times so raw, so exposed, and yet he refused to talk about it. Though he hadn't directly admitted, I knew he was bothered by the number of men who had died or suffered under his command. It was evident in the way he spoke of them, in the way he interacted with them, like that man at the Savoy. In the way he'd risked everything to uncover the traitor who had been responsible for at least some of the deaths of the men in his battalion.

It was also apparent how much he despised lies. It was as if he'd been fed more than one man could handle, and perhaps had been forced to dish out a fair share of his own, all in the name of the greater good, and he simply could no longer stomach them.

The thought made my own stomach churn with dread. For while I'd not directly lied to him, I also hadn't been completely honest. Not yet. And now I was even more afraid of how he would react when I was.

Not that I thought he would strike me. Sidney had never been the violent type. But then again, how did I know exactly how much war had changed him?

Still, I thought it more likely my confession might turn whatever affection he still felt for me to hatred. And whatever became of us, I didn't want it to end that way.

"Have you told him?"

I looked up into Alec's keen brown eyes, unsurprised he'd divined my thoughts. After all, he was a very good agent.

"About us?" he clarified, as if I needed it.

I inhaled an unsteady breath, sitting taller. "No. And don't you dare say anything. I'll do it in my own time."

He dipped his head once in acknowledgment. "Just . . . don't wait too long. You must be aware he already suspects. And the longer you wait, the harder it will be for him to forgive."

I wanted to take offense. I wanted to argue that it hadn't been my fault I hadn't known he wasn't really dead. But I knew none of that mattered. Not really. So I simply nodded.

CHAPTER 16

We arrived in Liège in the heat of late after-noon. Liège had been heavily damaged during the siege of the city in August 1914 as the German Army invaded Belgium and attempted to sweep rapidly on toward Paris—all part of their infamous Schlieffen Plan. But plucky little Belgium had managed to stall them just long enough for the French and British forces to arrive and mount a defense to prevent them from reaching their ultimate objective. However, during the five days in which Liège held out, it saw its city and ring of steel-capped forts pounded into submission by the Germans' Big Bertha howitzer guns.

Five years later, the evidence of this bombard-ment was still apparent, from the pockmarked and crumbling towers of the churches to the piles of masonry and rubble still waiting to be carted away. We drove south along the Meuse River, which divides the city. Crews were at work repairing the bridges the Germans had blown during their retreat to halt the advance of the Allies.

A short distance from the cobblestoned streets of the old city, Alec directed us to turn into a lane which ran between two thick hedges. The dirt track was bordered by horse chestnut trees. The prickly casings of the conkers, which had dropped to the ground before they could fully ripen, crackled and popped under the tires. This would be the first year in many, I realized, that all of the horse chestnuts in Britain would not be gathered up for acetone production.

At the end of the lane stood the Villa des Hirondelles, a cool white block of stone with a wide oak door and brick red shutters. Beyond the trees, we could see the home backed up to the River Meuse. The boat moored to its dock must have provided a clever means of escape should one have been needed.

As we stepped down into the dirt, the door opened to reveal a lanky gentleman with a sparse black beard. I had never worked directly with the chiefs of La Dame Blanche. This might have seemed odd, but even Landau had only encountered one of them once, and the other not until after the war. So this was my first time meeting them. But there was no need to tell me the man before us had been one of those chiefs. Quiet authority practically oozed from his pores.

"Welcome. Captain Landau telephoned to say that you were on your way." He reached out to take my hand, clasping it gently between his.

"You must be Madame Kent." His dark eyes were almost piercing in quality as they scrutinized me. "I have wanted to meet you for a long time. I am Walthère Dewé."

"Likewise, Monsieur Dewé. It is a funny business we have worked in, is it not? Needing to rely so much on people we've never met, having to trust them with our lives." I smiled softly. "Captain Landau speaks of you with the highest of praise."

"As he does you, Madame." His gaze shifted to look over my shoulder. "And this must be your husband." The men shook hands. "We were very happy to read of your survival, Monsieur Kent."

Sidney nodded. "Thank you for agreeing to see us."

His eyes twinkled, flicking between us. "You seem to be well-suited. At least when it comes to investigative instincts, no?"

Sidney's eyes warmed with affection. "Oh, I'm not certain I'm quite in her league."

I felt a flutter of pleasure at his compliment, as well as the touch of his hand against the small of my back. But I wasn't so distracted that I failed to note the slight stiffening of Monsieur Dewé's spine as Alec stepped forward, his hands clasped behind him.

He dipped his head once in acknowledgment. "Captain Xavier."

"Monsieur Dewé, I trust that you are well."

I couldn't tell whether the tension between the men was due to status, or because the men didn't like each other. Or, more accurately, because Monsieur Dewé didn't like Alec. As usual, Alec's thoughts were all but impossible to decipher.

Our host gestured toward the door. "Please, come inside. Allow me to introduce you to my compatriot Herman Chauvin."

Monsieur Chauvin waited for us in a wood-paneled study, which looked out upon a small garden and the river beyond. His outward appearance was such a stark contrast to the other chief's, that they seemed each other's foil. Chauvin was slight and boasted a head full of pale hair, as well as a long beard. His blue eyes perpetually seemed distracted, as if he was engaged in some abstract thought, and perhaps he was, for he was a professor at the University of Liège. And yet, I strongly suspected those eyes missed nothing.

He greeted me genially in a silvery voice and offered us drinks before we all settled into a grouping of mismatched chairs positioned near the hearth. The furniture was shabby and not altogether comfortable. I suspected it wasn't original to the house, and I couldn't help but notice the empty spaces on the walls, and along the mantel and shelves where items had previously hung.

"The villa was requisitioned by the Germans, along with much of the furnishings," Monsieur

Chauvin explained, noticing my inquisitive scrutiny. "And what wasn't taken during the war, was pillaged during their retreat." He seemed very accepting of the matter, but then, maybe this wasn't his property.

"But you have not come to talk about the Germans' ravages, I think." Monsieur Dewé crossed one long leg over the other as he sat tall in his creaky ladder-back chair. "What can we do for you?"

I briefly outlined the events and discoveries that had led me to seek them out, starting with Madame Zozza's sham séance and progressing to our meeting with Captain Landau that morning. Both men listened attentively, though they each seemed to process my words in a different way. Monsieur Dewé interrupted me from time to time, and by the nature of his questions I could tell he was attempting to neatly organize the data as if in little rows. Had I forgotten, this method would have reminded me the man had been a high-ranking administrative engineer before the war, and perhaps was once again. In contrast, Monsieur Chauvin gazed out the open window across from him, his eyes narrowed contemplatively, and his mouth clamped around an unlit pipe. Whether he'd elected not to light it out of deference to me or because he'd become accustomed to doing without during the years of deprivation, I didn't know. But Sidney and Alec felt no qualms about smoking cigarettes as I relayed my tale.

When it was done, Chauvin's gaze shifted to peer at his colleague, nodding as if giving him permission for something.

Dewé sighed before turning to me to clarify. "So you are here out of concern for the operative you knew as the code name Emilie, one Rose Moreau? You wish to verify she is safe and perhaps warn her?"

"Yes, I suppose that's the most succinct way to put it. Captain Landau said she refused to give him her new address. Do you know where she is? Has she gone into hiding?"

The two Belgians glanced at each other again. "That is the troubling thing, Madame. For we do not have an address for her either. At least, not one that is any good."

I sat taller. "What do you mean?"

"We sent her a message some weeks back to the address she had given us, but the letter came back unopened. And when we sent a young courier to investigate, her neighbors told him no one had lived there for some time. Not since the start of the war."

My eyes widened in shock and I looked toward Sidney, who had lowered his cigarette as if equally dumbfounded. "Then . . . none of you have been in contact with her since Captain Landau interviewed her some months ago?"

"I'm afraid not, Madame." A tiny furrow formed between Dewé's eyes. "And you are correct. It is concerning."

"So, it seems she *has* gone into hiding." I frowned. "Unless you think her new neighbors could be lying?"

He shook his head. "I do not think so, Madame. Our man reported that the home was in bad repair. It was obvious no one had lived there for quite some time. So unless some sort of harm befell her upon her arrival, I think they are as ignorant as we are."

I nodded, trusting his word. Monsieur Dewé was a thorough man. The coming of peace had not changed that, nor had it dimmed the responsibility he evidently still felt for the agents who had been under his command.

"What of her home village?" Sidney suggested, stubbing out his fag. "Could she have decided to remain there after all?"

"We had the same thought," Dewé replied. "But they could not tell us her direction either."

"Why did she choose to move away from her home in the first place?" I pressed. "Do you know?" We had heard the excuse she had given Landau, but I wondered if she had told these gentlemen something more.

"It is not so very uncommon," Chauvin murmured in his gentle voice. "There have been others who have chosen to relocate, finding the task of rebuilding too overwhelming. But . . . I think Madame Moreau was burdened by more than that."

Dewé stroked the scrubby beard on his chin. "We were forced to find a new courier to replace her during the last few months of the war when she informed us through her company's letter box that she feared she was being watched. She said she even suspected her home had been searched twice while she was away. Though thankfully there was nothing for them to find." He dipped his head. "As I'm sure you can appreciate, we took all such matters seriously. Even though we'd never met Madame Moreau in person until after the war, we'd been aware of her activities. We'd read her reports and knew of her tireless devotion to her courier duties. So we trusted she knew of what she was speaking."

"Her keen instincts saved me more than once," I admitted, wholeheartedly agreeing with their assessment of her. "If she thought she was being watched, then she likely was. But did you ask her about it after the war?"

Dewé began to shake his head, but then Chauvin spoke up.

"I did. Or rather I made a passing remark about it. All she said was that the Secret Police were rather dogged fellows, and something about how if they could have arrested her, they would have."

I wasn't certain how to take this remark, and it

was clear from the quizzical light in his eyes that neither did Chauvin. Had Madame Moreau meant they would have loved to have found evidence to arrest her? Or, perhaps more intriguing, had there been something that prevented the Germans from doing so? Could she have held leverage over the Germans, or rather the officers of the Secret Police in that district? Maybe because of something she'd learned pursuing her midwife duties.

"Perhaps whoever was watching her wasn't the Secret Police?" Alec suddenly interjected from where he relaxed into the saggy cushions of his chair. His eyes being at half-mast, I'd wondered if he was partially asleep until he spoke. "Perhaps it was someone else?"

"But who?" I retorted, struggling to keep my irritation from my voice.

He shrugged, as always keeping most of his thoughts to himself and only speaking up to stir the pot, so to speak. I'm not sure how I'd forgotten that about him. It was all well and good to examine something from every angle, and Alec was good at asking the questions that were not so obvious. But he rarely posited any answers to those questions, merely left you festering with frustration at the implications they raised.

Then I noticed the way the two chiefs of La Dame Blanche were looking at him, with guardedness and displeasure. I wondered if perhaps Alec was subtly trying to imply something else, something these two men did not take kindly to. It appeared Sidney had a similar notion, and less qualms about asking it.

"Could it have been someone from La Dame Blanche?" His face crinkled in puzzlement, softening the sting of such a question. "Maybe that's why she gave you a false address. Maybe she's still . . . wary."

"It's possible," Monsieur Dewé admitted. "Though unlikely. Each sector was kept as separate and isolated as possible from the others so that if one platoon or company should be compromised, the others could still operate without risk of discovery. Madame Moreau was part of a platoon made up exclusively of couriers. As such, she mostly collected reports from each of the other three platoons' letter boxes and transported them to the company letter box, adding in her own reports when she had intelligence to share. She knew who the head of her platoon was and perhaps one or two of the other couriers, but otherwise she would have been relatively isolated from the other members. And all our agents were forbidden to try to uncover the names of other agents."

"But you forget the special work Madame Moreau undertook for me." I sat forward, tucking my hair behind my ear. "She mostly operated as a guide, but in doing so, from time to time, she happened to encounter some of your other agents. She was not often privy to the information I discussed with those agents, but she was in the vicinity."

"True. But in that case, you would know better than us who these people were and whether they raise any concerns."

I sighed, worry and frustration tightening my voice. "I have been circling around and around every moment I spent with her; every time we happened upon another person; every moment of unease in our surroundings. And yet I cannot figure out why a medium would pretend to summon her and ask me to unearth her secrets."

The two Belgians gazed back at me in sympathy, but it was clear they had no real answers for me. I turned away to stare out the nearest window at the glittering ribbon of the river. A barge slipped past, weighted down by coal.

At the touch of a hand on my arm, I glanced up into Sidney's eyes. Their deep blue depths shimmered with sympathy. He squeezed my elbow in a show of solidarity before picking up the questioning himself.

"What of these threats Xavier and Landau mentioned? They said several of your members had received them. Could they be from a German loyalist who was angered by the outcome of the war?"

Dewé's expression turned grim. "Perhaps. It is

true there is a great deal of unhappiness in Belgium and elsewhere. Many are unemployed, food is still scarce, and the government is struggling to manage it all, particularly without the funds needed to rebuild. But most people properly blame the Germans for our hardship. German loyalists are few." He exhaled a heavy breath. "Even so, they are concerning. But not many have turned to outright violence. At least, not since the early days after the Germans' retreat, before the Belgian Army could return to restore order."

"One mostly hears of brawls between unemployed workers, and who can blame them." Chauvin gestured with his pipe. "The country's state of general chaos makes it ripe for such behavior. Especially when so many of our young men have differing experiences of the war. From the soldiers who spent over four years in the trenches, never able to return home to their families. To the people forced to live amongst the enemy, sometimes intimately with their soldiers billeted in their homes, never forgetting they were under the Germans' thumb. To the thousands conscripted and deported to Germany, treated as no better than slave labor in their crumbling industries. It's only a wonder things are not worse."

Hearing all of this was disheartening. For it made it clear how all too easy it would be for a person to disappear, willingly or not, in the midst of such disorder. It was no wonder whoever was looking for Madame Moreau could not find her. In some ways this was reassuring, and yet, by no means a guarantee that they wouldn't eventually. If anything, it only emphasized the difficulty of the task before me.

"All that being said, the threats have not overly concerned us." Dewé held up a hand to stay us. "Do not mistake me. We are taking them seriously. But thus far no one has followed through on these threats or shown the least inclination to."

"And you've received no word from Madame Moreau, so you could not know whether she has received any," I summarized, still staring out at the water beyond, a memory tickling at the back of my brain.

"Actually, I think she has."

We all glanced up at Chauvin in surprise, even Dewé.

"A few months ago, the man who was captain of our Chimay company mentioned that he had spoken with Madame Moreau," he explained. "This was before she disappeared."

"What did she say?" Dewé asked.

"She wanted to know the names of our agents in the Chimay area during the war." His brow puckered. "She said she was concerned about potential reprisals and wished to warn them."

"But the captain wasn't completely convinced of this," I guessed.

"He admitted that he had wondered if she wanted them for a different reason. If perhaps there was more to her interest than she claimed."

Had she received threats of her own? Was she worried for her fellow agents? Or was it more a matter of suspicion? Perhaps she didn't trust them.

Whatever the truth, I wished these men had more to tell us, but they knew no more than I did about Madame Moreau's current location. All I'd been able to confirm is that she definitely seemed to be hiding, and I couldn't imagine the strong, determined woman I had known doing so without very good reason. But the questions remained. Why? Because of the threats? And who had set me on her trail?

As if sensing my disappointment, Dewé spread his hands. "I'm sorry we could not be more helpful, Madame. But those in her old village may be able to tell you something we cannot." His eyes sharpened, as if trying to impart something important. "If I were you, the village is where I would go next."

I wasn't certain what he was trying to convey, but it was clear he wanted me to visit Macon. It also hadn't escaped my notice that he'd yet to call her village by name. I could only assume this was because of Alec.

Once again, I was puzzled by the reticence they displayed around the man. Even more so when Chauvin suddenly pushed up from his chair. "Madame Kent, I understand you have a great fondness for orchids. Come. I will show you my specimens before you go."

"Oh, how lovely," I replied, hastening to comply.

I listened attentively as he began to yammer on about crossbreeding and proper pollination, forbidding myself to look back, lest my enthusiasm prove unconvincing. We exited onto the back terrace and descended the steps to cross the lawn before I risked a glance behind me on the pretense of surveying the property.

Upon seeing we were well and truly alone, I interrupted him. "Enough of that. I have absolutely no interest in orchids or the mating rituals of honeybees, as doubtless you're not surprised to learn."

His eyes twinkled with humor.

"You have me alone. Now what did you wish to tell me?"

He opened the door to the greenhouse, allowing me to enter before him. Once inside, I could see several of the tables were indeed laden with orchids, and I moved closer to them, continuing our charade, at least in appearance.

"Dewé might disagree with me, but I believe you can be trusted. You certainly took enough risk upon yourself during the war on behalf of the Belgian people to earn it." He leaned closer, reaching out to delicately finger one of the flower stems. "In one of Emilie's . . . excuse me, Madame Moreau's . . ." He sighed, shaking his head. "It is easier still to speak in code names after so many years of doing so."

"Then do so."

He nodded. "In one of Emilie's last reports she made mention of a weapon the Germans were rumored to be developing. A wireless-controlled aeroplane. One both capable of flying the aircraft and dropping bombs on a target, all without need of a human pilot in the cockpit."

I stilled, a trickle of unease sliding down my spine.

But Chauvin misunderstood my reaction. "I know. This sounds rather farfetched, no? But your HQ showed great interest and asked specifically for more information."

Knowing much of what HQ had known, I didn't find it so very farfetched. After all, Landau had learned from two German deserters who escaped into Holland, that the enemy had developed a wireless remote-control motorboat fitted with torpedoes and guided by a seaplane which flew overhead. A fact which was confirmed by the Secret Service agent stationed at Cadzand in Holland with a powerful telescope. The Germans' base at Zeebrugge, Belgium, was only eleven kilometers distant from this point, so it was possible for him to observe much of the activity in that port.

There was no need to explain why these wireless torpedo boats would be so concerning to the British, and why action was taken immediately to counteract the new threat. How much more dangerous would a wireless-controlled aeroplane be, particularly if it could be maneuvered from a greater distance?

"What was she able to uncover?"

"Nothing." He shrugged. "The German she learned it from was killed, and she had no other contact to ask."

"Was his death suspicious?" I asked, finding such a coincidence noteworthy, if not yet alarming.

"She did not say, and we did not ask. If so, there was naught she could do without drawing unwanted attention to herself."

"But you mention it because it concerns you."

It wasn't a question, but he nodded anyway. "If Emilie is, indeed, in some sort of trouble. If she is hiding . . . this may be why."

I turned to stroll deeper into the greenhouse, contemplating everything he'd told me. If the Germans had been developing such a weapon, and she had been able to obtain more information— be it in the form of reports and specifications, or simply the name and whereabouts of the inventor—then she could be in a delicate, if not dangerous situation. If such information were to fall into the wrong hands . . . I shuddered at the thought.

But then why hadn't she come to these men for help? Did she not trust them? Or did she not trust them not to involve the British? Perhaps she feared the information even falling into the hands of supposed allies.

Or was it only one man?

I pivoted to look at Chauvin, finding him watching me, perhaps waiting for me to speak.

"Why are you and Monsieur Dewé wary of Captain Xavier? Why did you pull me aside to tell me about the wireless-controlled aeroplane?"

His eyes crinkled in approval, and I somehow felt I'd passed some test, for the tone of his voice gained a richer timbre than before. "You know of Captain Xavier's work during the war?"

I nodded.

His gaze dropped to the table beside him as his fingers reached out to swipe away some speck of stray dirt. "He did such a good job fooling the Germans for so many years, walking amongst the enemy without suspicion. It is difficult to know if one can truly trust him."

I understood what he was saying, for I had entertained similar thoughts about Alec. Even as I was forced to rely on him.

Chauvin's mouth creased into the ghost of a

smile. "But perhaps that is our failing and not his."

In other words, they had no definitive reason to suspect him, no evidence of wrongdoing, only the unsettling feelings in their guts. Ones that even they admitted might be influenced by the four years spent living under the heel of German oppressors.

But although I allowed him to dismiss the topic, I was not so quick to forget it.

CHAPTER 17

As the day was already slipping into evening, Sidney and I elected to find a hotel for the night rather than push on toward Macon. The further south and west we drove toward the desolate landscape of the Western Front, the more uncertain conditions would become, and the less likely we were to find accommodations. It was true there must be inns operating in Lille and some of the other cities, despite the devastation they'd experienced—for the tour companies were using them as the starting points for their guided excursions—but we were headed into the more rural areas of the Ardennes forests.

In any case, I wished to stay as far from the former battle zones as possible, and not just to spare my sensibilities and avoid the groups of tourists traipsing over that unholy ground. I was also worried what effect they might have on Sidney. To see the land where so many of his friends, so many of the men he'd commanded, had fought and died—some of them still interred in the shell-shattered soil.

I felt a pang of sympathy for Max, knowing he

would soon be accompanying his aunt through that quagmire of despair. I hoped there was someone else in his group with whom to empathize, and not just a lot of mourners wrapped in their own grief, unconscious of the strain his being there must cause him.

Once we reached a hotel at the center of Liège, Alec thanked us for the lift and the pleasant company, and then set off for the train station on foot, telling us he hoped to catch the late train onward to wherever his ultimate destination was. I supposed I shouldn't have been surprised by his abrupt departure, except part of me had become suspicious of him. I'd half-expected him to make some excuse as to why he wished to remain with us to continue to aid in our search. But instead, he shook Sidney's hand, bussed me on the cheek, and gave us a jaunty wave as he set off down the street with his valise in hand.

Sidney must have harbored similar qualms, for he remarked upon it later as we strolled the city streets after we'd enjoyed a pleasant meal in a café off the Place du Marché. The sun was only now sinking low on the horizon on this lengthy summer day, casting long shadows over the boulevards. A cool breeze blew down from the heights at the edge of the city, rustling the hair at my temples, and tempting others from their homes and shops to congregate in the squares.

"So we are free of *le Capitaine* Xavier, but for how long, I wonder?" he ruminated aloud as we passed a trickling fountain hidden amongst a grouping of low-hanging trees.

I glanced up, studying his guarded expression. "You don't like him."

He sighed. "I'm not sure it's a matter of like versus dislike, but more of an issue of trust. Monsieurs Dewé and Chauvin certainly did not. And I can't say I do either." His eyes slid sideways to meet mine. "I'm surprised you do."

I laughed humorlessly. "I never said I trusted him."

His brow furrowed. "Then why did you agree to let him accompany us?"

"I didn't. *You* did. I simply didn't kick up any unnecessary fuss over the matter. Besides, he'd already sat in on our conversation with Captain Landau. He knew where we were headed."

"And yet, you worked with the man during the war." Which was a leading comment if ever I'd heard one, but I was not going to explain my relationship with Alec. Not here. Not now.

"I worked with a lot of people during the war," I replied steadily. "Including a few real Germans. That doesn't mean I trusted them all. Sometimes I had to take calculated risks, and hope the bribes we paid for information and safe passage also bought their silence."

"Then you've already considered the fact that

Xavier could be the man searching for Emilie?"

"Of course. I would have to be deluding myself not to." I ticked off the points on my fingers. "He's an officer in the Secret Service. He worked in Belgium during the war. And while I'm not aware of any encounters between him and Emilie, it's possible they met. He travels about in whatever capacity he now serves, and he was in London just a few days ago. Feasibly he could have convinced Madame Zozza, by means fair or foul, to pretend to summon Emilie during a séance with me, and then killed her with that fire to keep her silent." I shook my head. "But it seems a horribly convoluted way to go about it all. Already knowing me, why wouldn't he have just asked for my assistance under false pretenses?"

"Maybe he was worried you wouldn't be fooled. The man is obviously intelligent, and he must realize how perceptive you are."

I arched my eyebrows skeptically. "Let's say you're right. That he couldn't think of a simpler way to go about the matter than enlisting the help of a medium. What's his motive? Why does he need to find Emilie?"

Sidney fell silent, ruminating on my question. He wrapped an arm around me, guiding me around a group of boys kicking a ball back and forth in the middle of the street. Their shouts echoed off the buildings around us. However, once we'd navigated around the game, he didn't release me, but instead weaved my arm through his.

"I don't know," he admitted. "Perhaps we haven't uncovered his reasons yet."

"Perhaps," I conceded. "And as such, I'm not ruling him out. But there's also far from enough evidence to name him our culprit."

My thoughts on Alec Xavier were complicated. Given the work we'd done together during the war, I was inclined to feel some loyalty toward him, and yet I couldn't deny I'd always been slightly wary of him. Even when I'd helped him escape to Holland after we'd discovered he was compromised. Even after everything between us that had followed. I wanted to believe I wouldn't have allowed him to get so close to me if I hadn't somehow sensed that at his heart, he was a good man, but the truth was I had been in a very dark place. I hadn't always been thinking clearly. As evident from my deep regret immediately following.

I shook my head, but that was allowing my head to go where I didn't want it. Not when I wasn't yet ready for the conversation to veer on that course.

"Perhaps his objective has something to do with this remote-control aeroplane Monsieur Chauvin mentioned," Sidney suggested, tipping his head close to mine so that we could not be overheard by the couple we passed walking in the other direction.

"I wondered the same thing," I admitted as we paused at a corner. "I'm also curious whether it's somehow connected to that aviator's map case I buried."

We fell silent as we crossed the street to the large square in front of the magnificent Palais des Princes-Evêques. There, among the archaeological ruins of the first St. Lambert Cathedral, German soldiers had marched and camped during the conflict. Though I had only passed through Liège once during the war, I found the changes to be slow and yet heartening. Here, Belgians were determined to move on with their lives, even in the very pockmarked shadow of the war.

But Sidney's thoughts had not followed mine, still lingering on Alec. "Well, I suppose we shall have to wait and see if he turns up again. Somehow I doubt we shall be difficult to find."

I had to agree. In a country already short of motorcars, Sidney's Pierce-Arrow would be highly conspicuous, especially in the more rural areas. Though grateful for the ease such transportation afforded us, I was a bit torn about it. Such a distinctive vehicle would make it easy for Emilie to locate us, should she wish to, once our search for her became known. But it would also make it simpler for someone to follow us. Someone I wasn't sure I wanted to lead to Emilie's door.

Almost as if summoned by my very thoughts, I felt a prickling along the back of my neck. I was well-trained enough not to glance over my shoulder. Instead, I slowed our steps, coming to a stop near the stone remnants of the cathedral. Smiling, I turned to press my hands to Sidney's chest, as if smoothing the collar of his coat. His hands lifted to clasp my waist and his eyes dipped to my mouth. The look in his eyes, the heat that sprang to life at this spontaneous overture of affection, made me sorry to disappoint him.

"Someone is watching us," I murmured as I searched the square over his shoulder.

The fire in his gaze banked as he peered beyond me, careful not to lift his head or shift abruptly. "Where?"

"I don't know. But I sense their interest." I brushed my fingers upward, fingering the neatly clipped hairs at the base of his neck. The ones I knew would curl upward if allowed to grow longer.

My thoughts first turned to Alec, curious whether he'd doubled back to follow us. If that was the case, he would have disappeared the moment I turned to face Sidney, well aware of just such a tactic, as we'd utilized it on two occasions during the war. I breathed slowly, trying to sense whether the person observing us was still doing so. However, the close proximity of my husband was proving to be a greater distraction than I'd anticipated, particularly when he stroked his fingers over my spine in lazy circles. Feigning affection with Alec had never caused me to break my concentration, but then again, I hadn't been in love with him.

Ignoring the fluttering in my stomach, I scanned the people beyond him through my lashes until a familiar figure caught my eye. He stood about twenty feet away near a street vendor, pretending to study the contents of a book.

I tilted my head to whisper in my husband's ear. "It's the gentleman from the séance. The one I told you I suspected was following me about London. Now that seems certain."

His hands tightened momentarily on my waist. Then he turned his head so he could nuzzle my ear. "I don't suppose this square would be the ideal place for a confrontation."

"No. A side street would be better." I wasn't altogether surprised by the breathless quality of my voice. Sidney's lips on my skin were making me feel a trifle lightheaded.

"Then let's see if he follows." His smug tone made it clear he had also noted his effect on me.

He pulled back, keeping his left arm wrapped securely around my waist and guided me toward the river. I played along, cuddling into his side as I gazed adoringly up at him. We turned off the larger boulevard into a quaint shop-lined side street, and then left into an even narrower deserted lane between two buildings. A few feet along stood an arched doorway with a small recess. Sidney urged me inside, and we pressed back against the wall, straining to hear the sound of footsteps.

My eyes widened in surprise as Sidney pulled a pistol from behind his back. Apparently, it had been tucked into the waistband of his trousers at the small of his back. For how long, I didn't know. But perhaps even more startling, it was a Luger, the Germans' sidearm, and not one of the Webley revolvers issued to British officers.

"You aren't going to shoot him, are you?"

He scowled. "No." But then added under his breath. "Not unless it's necessary."

There was the shuffle of feet, as if someone came to a sudden stop. Then footsteps advanced down the lane toward us, beating a rapid tattoo against the stones.

"Well, try this first," I said, stepping forward as the footsteps drew even with us. I swung out with my handbag, clipping him on his face just below the temple. Though deceptively lady-like, it had wickedly sharp corners—should they be needed—and enough heft to pack a wallop. During the war, I'd learned the value of a cleverly disguised weapon.

He howled in pain, and Sidney grabbed a fist full of his coat, propelling him into the alcove where he slammed him back against the heavy wooden door on my left. I flinched at the impact.

"Who are you?" he snarled into the man's red face. "And why are you following my wife?"

The man had the wind knocked out of him for he wheezed, struggling to form a reply. "I . . . I'm not . . ."

Sidney raised his pistol so that the man could see it. "Don't even try to lie."

His eyes widened in terror. "I . . . I mean her . . . no harm."

"Then why are you *following* her?" he bit out through gritted teeth.

"Sidney," I murmured, lifting a hand to intercede lest he go too far.

He relented a fraction, loosening his grip on the man's coat. "I'm not going to repeat myself again. Who are you?"

"Jonathan Fletcher," he whimpered.

I frowned. "The author?"

"Y-yes. I write crime novels."

Sidney glanced at me and I shook my head in confusion. "Why are you following my wife? She saw you in London and now you're here. Why?"

"And for that matter, how?" I interjected, unable to believe he'd trailed us all the way from London without our noticing.

Mr. Fletcher licked his lips. "Well, I hired someone to follow you when . . . when I realized you'd seen me in the park."

I arched my eyebrows. "And yet you followed us to Belgium anyway."

"Yes, well, my man telephoned to say he'd lost you in Ostend, but that he'd overheard you speaking about Liège on the boat. So I . . . decided I should join him." He huffed sheepishly. "That two of us were less likely to lose you again."

A thought occurred to me. "This man. Is he wearing a mask?"

Mr. Fletcher squirmed. "Maybe."

I scowled. The man from the boat. Well, that explained how he'd caught up to us in Liège, but it still didn't explain why they were here. A fact that also hadn't slipped Sidney's notice.

"Such a determined effort," he drawled sarcastically before leaning in to growl at the man. "But *why* are you following her?"

Mr. Fletcher winced. "I . . . I noticed the way she reacted to Madame Zozza's summoning her friend. It was the most interesting thing that happened that night. And . . . well, I needed an idea." He began to gesture more broadly with his hands. "The plot of my latest novel was going nowhere. That's why I decided to attend Madame Zozza's séance in the first place. I was hoping maybe I could utilize her as a character. Then I heard her home had caught fire the next morning. I only live a few blocks away. So I walked over to watch. And that's when I saw

Mrs. Kent." His eyes gleamed with excitement as he turned to me. "You were talking to her assistant and I thought, now, there's a story. So I decided to follow you."

Sidney's eyes met mine, echoing the exasperated disbelief that must have been reflected in mine.

"You followed me all about London and into Belgium, all because you were chasing a story idea for your novel?" I asked incredulously.

"I take it you're not an artist," Mr. Fletcher replied in affront. "Otherwise, you would understand how desperate one becomes when facing the blank page. And yours was the best idea I'd had in ages. Society girl kills medium in order to keep her secrets."

I stared at him in bewilderment, realizing he'd fashioned me into the villain of this story of his, whatever it was. In any case, his explanation for trailing after me was so outlandish, it could only be true. Sidney seemed to agree, for he released him and lowered his pistol to his side. Though I noticed he didn't put it away.

"My wife didn't kill anyone," Sidney retorted. "But write whatever story you please, so long as the woman does not resemble her in any way. And so long as you stay out of our way. If I should catch sight of you or your man in the mask again, I will not hesitate to use this." He gestured with the Luger.

Mr. Fletcher nodded frantically. "Of course. Of course."

Sidney stepped back to let him pass, but apparently Mr. Fletcher had decided to press his luck.

"Can I ask why you decided to travel down from London separately? For a moment, my man thought you were going to take the earlier boat as well. Nearly fooled him."

My eyes slid to Sidney in confusion. What earlier boat?

He glowered at the man. "No you may not. Now get out of here. Before I change my mind."

Mr. Fletcher moved quickly then, scampering back the way he'd come.

Once he'd gone, I crossed my arms over my chest and glared at him expectantly, waiting for an explanation.

One corner of Sidney's lips curled upward derisively. "Well, I doubt he's any danger to your Emilie."

"Sidney?"

His gaze dipped to my handbag, as he reached back under his coat to stow his gun. "That's some accessory. Had I known how effective it would be, I wouldn't have bothered to draw my gun."

"Don't think you're going to distract me. What other boat was he talking about?"

I could read in his eyes that he was considering lying, and I arched a single eyebrow, prepared to stand there all evening in the deepening shadows if he didn't start talking.

He brushed a hand back through his ruffled hair and shot his cuffs, settling his appearance back to one of careless elegance. "The boat to Calais."

I frowned. "But the note I left . . ."

"Said you were taking the one to Ostend. Yes, I know."

His jaw was tight as he glanced up and down the lane, and I realized there was something he wasn't telling me. I studied his profile as he linked my arm through his and guided me down the lane in the direction of our hotel. Where had I recently heard someone mention that French port?

I gasped, jerking Sidney to a stop. "You thought I was meeting Max!"

CHAPTER 18

I didn't." Sidney's brow furrowed. "Well, I suppose I wasn't sure," he reluctantly admitted.

"How could you even *think* I would do such a thing?" I wanted to swat him in the head with my lethal handbag. "I told you I wanted to try to make our marriage work, and I *am*. I would never just . . . just run off with another man." I narrowed my eyes. "At least, not without telling you that's *exactly* what I was doing."

My fury seemed to have succeeded in upsetting his cool insouciance, for he shifted his feet in agitation, his dark hair falling over his brow. "I didn't *want* to think you were. But I couldn't *help* but notice how comfortable you seemed with Max." His words sounded like an accusation.

"What's that supposed to mean?"

He shook his head, scraping his hair back from his face. "Nothing. Forget it. It's just . . . your ease with him only seems to highlight there's something lacking between the two of us. You can't tell me you haven't noticed."

I stilled, feeling oddly exposed having this conversation in the middle of a street in Liège, even a deserted one. I could hear voices somewhere nearby chattering softly. And yet, if I refused to discuss it, I was afraid neither of us would raise this specter again.

"Yes. I-I know," I replied softly.

"It's not like the way it was." He shoved his hands in his pockets, his voice tight with frustration. "Even during the war, I would come home on leave and be reassured that, in a world going to hell, at least everything between us was good. But now, it's like . . . it's like I can't reach you. It's like you don't want me to." His gaze seemed to implore mine, asking me to help him make sense of it all. He exhaled raggedly. "Or maybe I'm reaching toward the wrong thing. But whatever the case, the harder I try, the further away you seem to retreat."

For a moment I couldn't speak. My stomach was twisted in knots along with my tongue.

Everything he said was true. For I had felt it, too. We had always been opposed in that I tended to retreat to evaluate a situation when I felt threatened or uncertain, whereas he pushed forward, sometimes almost relentlessly—thinking he could conquer the situation with perseverance and resolve, or at least endure it. I had both craved and feared his determined pursuit of intimacy since our return from Umbersea Island, wanting to feel close to him again and yet knowing that would put my secrets at risk.

I knew what needed to happen. I knew I had to tell Sidney what had happened between Alec and me when I'd believed Sidney was dead. We would never be able to move forward until I did. But I was afraid that might also spell the end of us.

"Sidney, it can never be like it used to."

He looked up at me as if I'd just punched him in the gut, and it tore at my heart.

"Not exactly," I murmured to soften the blow. "You're different. I'm different. How can we expect our relationship to be the same when we aren't?"

He studied my features, considering my words. "You're right." His eyes were heavy with sadness. "I suppose . . . I'm having a hard time accepting that. The war took so much."

I moved a step closer, pressing my hand to his chest. "But it didn't take me. Yes, it changed me, but I'm still here. And so are you." I inhaled a ragged breath, remembering all the months I'd believed that wasn't so. "And I don't think I'm the only one who retreats when the subject gets difficult, or who worries the other won't like the truth."

Sidney's hands lifted to clasp my waist. His entire body seemed to heave a long sigh as his head fell forward, his forehead touching mine. "I suppose you're right."

I pulled my head back so that I could look into his eyes. "You suppose?"

His lips quirked, and he pulled my body flush with his. "I'm not retreating now."

I wanted to argue that physical intimacy had never been the problem, but the familiar heat blossoming inside me urged me to stay silent instead.

But before Sidney could make good on the promise flickering in his eyes, a pair of gentlemen rounded the corner. I buried my face in his chest as he lifted his head to greet the two men. I could hear the gentle humor in their voices, as well as Sidney's, who turned me in to his side to guide me out of the lane to the busier street beyond.

Neither of us spoke for several moments, and I might have been content to remain silent until we returned to the privacy of our hotel room. Until my hand brushed against the outline of his pistol beneath his coat.

"How long have you been carrying this?" I asked.

His eyes flicked down toward me before scanning the boulevard before us. "It seemed a good precaution since you didn't appear to know exactly what you were stepping into."

"Yes, but why a Luger?"

"Truth be told, Webleys are rubbish. I may be British, but I'm not so foolish as to equate loyalty to the Crown with carrying a British weapon now that the war is over. Especially when the Germans' Lugers are so much better."

I couldn't refute that logic.

"What of you?" he asked. "I thought you might have a small one tucked in your handbag you'd carried during the war."

I shook my head. "Too risky. The citizens in the occupied territories weren't allowed to possess firearms. And as often as one was searched, the chances of my keeping one concealed were minuscule. It would have been the quickest way to get myself detained or worse."

"So you've never fired a gun?"

"I didn't say that."

Sidney looked at me in question as we passed a restaurant with tables set out on the pavement. The hum of its patrons' conversations would have made our softly spoken words inaudible. So I waited until the voices had all but died away, leaving us alone in the dusky twilight that had settled over the city.

"Rob taught me. On his last leave before . . ." Before my brother's aeroplane was shot down over France. I didn't need to say the words, Sidney understood.

I swallowed the lump in my throat. "The trains running north were always so sporadic, so he spent his leave in London with me. He convinced me to drive up to Hampstead Heath so he could teach me to shoot." My lips curled reluctantly in a smile, one that was as painful as it was amused. "Of course, we treated it as a lark, but I knew it was meant for my own protection, seeing as I was alone in London with you away at the front."

I didn't know why I hadn't told my husband about this before, except that it was my last memory of my second brother. I suppose I'd been jealously guarding it.

"I asked for leave, you know."

I looked up at his shadowed features.

"When I heard he'd been killed," he clarified. "I knew you would take it hard. But it was denied."

There was no use asking why. If every soldier who ever asked for leave was granted it when a close friend or family member died, there would have been no one left to fight the war.

I inhaled past the tightness in my chest. "Yes, well, work kept me busy in London." C had offered me a leave of absence, but I had declined, preferring to push through the pain. Besides I was needed there. All our agents along one sector of the front had been reporting an extraordinary air of excitement, preparation, and heel-clicking among the Germans, and there were rumors the Kaiser would be paying a visit. Part of my job at that time was to help sift through that intelligence. If we could discover when and where exactly the Kaiser would be making his inspection of the troops, then a surprise run by our bombers might very well end the war.

Of course, we didn't succeed, and the war dragged on for over three more years. Even now, the Kaiser resided safely in exile in neutral Holland.

If only . . .

I internally shook myself. With all the near misses and foiled plots I'd been party to throughout the war, if I were to begin making "if only" statements, I might never stop.

We arrived in the tiny village of Macon along the Franco-Belgian border about an hour before midday. I had visited the town close to half a dozen times during the war, but never by direct route on the road from Chimay. The journey was always taken on foot through the rolling fields and woods, ever vigilant of German soldiers patrolling the area. It felt odd to drive straight into the village and halt in front of the St. Jean the Baptist Church. The leaves of the many-centuries-old linden tree in the square, its branches supported by braces, glistened bright green in the morning sun rather than the shadowy gray I was accustomed to.

Rose Moreau, code name Emilie, had lived in a house at the edge of the village, which backed up to the heavily forested land, which lined this stretch of the border. Although that part of France was also occupied by the Germans for most of the war, the boundary between the countries was surveilled almost as severely as the frontier with Holland. Not only was the region an important staging area behind their front lines, containing one of the crucial railway lines which ran parallel to the battlefront—utilized to shift troops and supplies from one area of the front to another—but it also boasted the headquarters of one of their armies at Château de Merode in Trélon. As such, the La Dame Blanche platoon operating in this area was of strategic importance to Britain and the Allies. Which was how I'd come to be in contact with Emilie so often during my time in Belgium.

Sidney and I decided our first visit in the village should be to the priest. In my experience, they often knew more about their parish and its residents than anyone, and their presence in wartime had proven no different. In fact, a fair number of La Dame Blanche's members, including three battalion commanders, were priests.

It did not take long for us to find him, for he stood next to the linden tree in his black cassock and a wide-brimmed hat, tending its branches. He stood watching us as we approached, no doubt having already surveyed our expensive motorcar and smart clothes and surmised we were not from this part of his country, if we were even Belgian at all. His expression was carefully genial as he greeted us in a Picardy accent.

"Good day, Monsieur and Madame. How may I assist you?"

"Good day, Father," Sidney responded, sliding his hands into his pockets as he cast a glance upward at the church's steeple. "It's good to see that not all the old buildings in this stretch of Europe were damaged by shell fire."

The priest, a man I estimated to be about forty, smiled reflexively. "Yes. Though we contended with our fair share of stray projectiles. Particularly at the end, as the Allies were advancing. The aim was not always true, no?"

That was an understatement, if ever I'd heard one. More often than not, the bombs and shells fired from both sides or dropped from the skies had missed their targets—and struck residences and places of business, killing civilians in the process. Nowhere had been truly safe.

"I can recall a near miss," I agreed, conceding his point. "Just west of town." I nodded in that general direction. "There's a crater in the woods."

His dark eyes studied me more carefully. "You spent time in Macon during the war?"

I nodded. "Briefly. Actually, that's why we're here." I drew breath to say more, but he surprised me by speaking first.

"You are Madame Moreau's friend."

The manner in which he spoke the word "friend" made it clear he meant something more.

I blinked, now scrutinizing him in much the

same way he had me moments before. "She mentioned me?"

"We spoke on occasion. I was her priest after all." He hesitated, as if considering how much more to reveal, and I got the distinct impression I was being weighed and measured, my worth calculated in a matter of seconds. "And . . . I acted as her letter box."

This astonished me, for I had never suspected there was another agent in the village. I'd always assumed Emilie carried the reports from Baives, France—several miles to the north—across the border, through Macon, and on to Chimay. I'd not realized this was where her relay ended.

"You were also part of La Dame Blanche?"

"Yes. And if I'm not much mistaken, you are Gabrielle Thys." He arched his eyebrows in expectation.

"I am. Or at least, that was my code name."

He clasped his hands in front of him. "She said you might be coming to see me."

Sidney and I shared a look of foreboding at this revelation. That Emilie should know me so well, that she should realize I would come looking for her. Or had she been the one to set me on the trail to do so?

"Then you know where she is?" I asked.

But he would not be rushed. "Come. Sit in the cool shade out of this hot sun and I will tell you what I know."

He gestured toward a pair of benches positioned between the wooden braces under the wide canopy of the linden tree. As the tree was in bloom with its buttery yellow, star-shaped flowers, I was instantly enveloped by its sweet perfume. The patented blend reminded me of honey mixed with the zest of lemon and attracted softly buzzing bees to gather its nectar.

I settled in the middle of one of the benches between the priest and Sidney, who reclined back to smoke one of his Turkish cigarettes. Its spicy sweet aroma was not an unpleasant combination with the linden tree and did something to discourage the bees from hovering over our heads.

"When did you last speak with Madame Moreau?" the priest inquired.

"A few months before the end of the war. Around mid-August."

"So you were not here at the end, when it became obvious the Germans were unraveling."

"No. I was needed elsewhere."

He dipped his head once in understanding. "Just so. Well, not long after that, Madame Moreau became concerned that someone was watching her. You can appreciate what a sensible, astute woman she is, I think."

I nodded.

"Then you will understand why she passed her courier duties on to another agent, anxious to keep the network from being compromised. In any case, by that point the Spanish influenza was running rampant through the village and countryside, and she was overwhelmed trying to do all she could to help those who were stricken. She even fell ill herself for a short time." He crossed one leg over the other. "As such, I saw little of her during that time. And even after the armistice and the Germans departed, she seemed to keep to herself."

His brow furrowed as he stared out into the village square. "Then a few months ago, she came to see me. She seemed agitated. She insisted we converse through the confessional, though more than once she broke off to check to be certain no one else had entered the church."

I frowned, that did not sound like Emilie at all. The woman I had known had always been incredibly cool in tense situations. I had watched her stare down German soldiers more than once, annoyed at them for questioning her special pass to move about freely on her midwife duties.

Even Sidney seemed to sense the gravity of this alteration in her behavior for he leaned forward, bracing his elbows on his knees, waiting for the priest to continue.

"What did she say?" I prodded.

"She told me she was going away for a time. That there was something she needed to look into, and that it wasn't safe for her to be here."

Alarm crept up along my spine upon hearing my suppositions were correct. Emilie had been in trouble. "Did she tell you why she wasn't safe?"

"She would not say." This seemed to trouble him greatly, for his eyes were clouded with worry. "But there was a fire at her home."

"What?"

He held up his hands to reassure me. "A small one. Easily put out. She wasn't injured. Though it might have been much worse had she not awakened," he admitted.

I shared a glance with Sidney, wondering if he'd noted the same thing I had. Emilie's house had caught fire, just as Madame Zozza's had. Had the one at Emilie's cottage also been set intentionally?

"She said that you might come looking for me," the priest continued. "And that if you did I was to tell you 'all her hens had come home to roost.'" His gaze searched mine, clearly ignorant of what this meant.

I frowned, feigning confusion. "That's it?"

He nodded slowly. "Yes. And that you could inquire after her at her sister's home in Quevy."

I did not fail to note the manner in which she'd worded this message. That I might ask for her in Quevy, not that she would necessarily be there. I also perceived that Quevy was one hundred kilometers or more from the village she told the chiefs of La Dame Blanche she was moving to.

I sat very still, contemplating these matters, and trying to determine the best way to ask what I wanted to know next, without drawing too fine a point on it. When Sidney exhaled a long stream of smoke and asked for me, almost as if he could read my mind, I could have kissed him for it.

"So she's not here in Macon?"

The priest shook his head. "I'm afraid not, Monsieur. She has not been here in many months."

"But she *is* planning to return?"

"Perhaps. I do know she hasn't sold her cottage. So perhaps she plans to return one day." He shrugged. "But I cannot tell you when."

I shifted to face him more fully. "Do *you* have any suspicions why she left? Why she thought she wasn't safe here? Other than the fire."

He did not answer me immediately, and I didn't think it was simply because he was sorting through his own impressions. I could tell there was something specific on his mind.

I pressed a hand to his arm. "I know you do not know me. That there is only my connection to Madame Moreau to recommend me. But it truly is most important I find her," I pleaded, hoping my earnestness would persuade him. "I do believe she's in danger, but I do not know from exactly what quarter, and without that I cannot protect her. Please, will you tell me what you know?"

He reached up to pat my hand. "I will. Because I believe Madame Moreau would want me to. And because she spoke highly of you."

Even so, it took him a moment to gather his words, his expression lowering as if a veil was drawn over him. "When one agrees to undertake such a role in an organization like La Dame Blanche, no matter how pure the motivations of patriotism and justice, one must also accept the necessity for some amount of deception. You must lie to your neighbors, your family, the enemy, and even yourself in order to preserve the secrets you have sworn to keep. And you hope, you pray . . ." he pressed his hands flat together as if in supplication ". . . that your actions will not harm the innocent. That the choices you make and the information you pass on will save more lives than it takes. That it will bring the suffering to an end and not make it worse. That you will not be forced to sacrifice your honor in the quest for what is right."

My chest tightened with each word he spoke until each breath was painful to take, for I understood what he was trying to convey intimately. I had wrestled with my conscience many times over the past few years. How much more so must have these agents who lived under harsh occupation, forced to watch their friends suffer, and even developed bonds with some of the individual Germans with whom they resided so closely?

I was not so narrow-minded as to not recognize that many of the enemy were good men caught up in the same cog of war that had entrapped us all. Men I would probably have befriended under other circumstances. It was foolish to think some of the Belgians and French had not also developed amicable relationships with some of their singular enemies even if they despised the German Army as a whole. To know that the intelligence they shared might cause their deaths, no matter how necessary in order to win the war, must have torn at some of them.

He heaved a heavy sigh. "But it is a long game, yes? And sometimes one cannot see the ramifications of one's actions until it is too late."

I nodded, feeling Sidney's gaze on my face, and afraid if I tried to speak, I might give away just how deeply the priest's words had affected me.

The priest returned my nod with one of his own, his uneasy gaze peering somewhere into the past. "As such, a woman came to see me about a month after the end of the war. She . . . she looked as if she hadn't eaten or slept in weeks— naught but skin and bones. But she marched forward and . . . and spit in my face."

I could hear in his voice that he was still rattled by this.

"She said that others might think me a hero, a patriot, but she knew the truth. That we were liars and charlatans. That we hadn't a care for the consequences to others." He glanced at me then. "She claimed her brother had been falsely accused and arrested because of some papers the Germans found burned in their hearth."

A sickening feeling came over me and I had to force myself to continue to meet his gaze.

"Papers she swore the midwife or her assistant must have burned there, not her brother."

I swallowed hard, fighting to maintain my composure. I frowned out into the sunlight, not daring to look at my husband, and refusing to allow myself to reach out to him in search of comfort. All the same, I could sense in his very stillness that he was thinking of the same thing I was, recalling a story I'd told only the day before. His leg shifted slightly, pressing against my own, a solid presence at my side.

"What happened to her brother? Was he merely detained or . . . ?" I didn't finish the question, not needing to.

"She didn't know," the priest replied. "She said she couldn't find him."

"And . . . her baby?"

"Taken by the influenza."

I forced another breath into my lungs. "What was her name?"

At first, the priest did not answer, but when I turned to look at him, I think it was evident I already knew it.

"Adele Moilien."

"Did she pay Madame Moreau a visit as well?"

"She didn't ask for her. Just cursed me and left. But I can only assume."

I nodded. "And a few months later, Madame Moreau departed Macon."

"Yes. Perhaps it had nothing to do with it."

"But perhaps it did."

CHAPTER 19

I assume you believe Adele Moilien was the mother Madame Moreau was attending to when you rifled through that aviator's map case," Sidney murmured as he turned off the road onto the overgrown lane that would lead us to Madame Moreau's cottage.

I blinked up at him, having fallen silent after directing him how to get there, my mind in the past.

He flicked a glance at me. "You said that when you learned there were Germans making random searches in the area, you dashed out to bury the map case while she disposed of the papers that were useless."

I inhaled a shaky breath. "Yes. The baby was safely delivered, and all was quiet when we left. But perhaps the Germans came later. Perhaps in our haste, not all of the papers burned to ashes." Though such carelessness was not like Emilie.

I was grateful when he didn't try to salve my conscience with trite words, for it would not be eased. It shouldn't be. We should have paid closer attention.

Instead he focused on the more pertinent ramifications. "Do you think Mademoiselle Moilien could be the person searching for Emilie?"

"She could be." My brow furrowed as the Pierce-Arrow rolled to a stop at the end of the lane. "But if she'd already found her before Emilie moved away from Macon, then why would she need to find her again? Wouldn't she have already said or done what she intended to?"

Sidney tilted his head, considering this. "Maybe she learned about her brother's fate and decided words weren't enough. That she needed revenge."

"And that fire was her first attempt to do so," I said following his line of reasoning. "But when that failed and Emilie fled, she had to pursue her."

Sidney must have heard the doubt in my voice. "Do you have a better theory?"

"No," I admitted. "Though I do wonder whether the matter Emilie said she had to look into involved tracking down this woman's brother. And if that was the case, then Mademoiselle Moilien couldn't have already known what exactly happened to him."

I pushed open the car door and stepped out into the dirt lane. Emilie's cottage nestled within a stand of ancient beech trees. Their knobby trunks and gnarled branches had always seemed peculiarly life-like in the dark of night, like ancient sentries. I was surprised to discover they appeared no different during the day.

I led Sidney up the walk to the white stone cottage. The overgrown path and rambling brambles gave it the decided air of a building unlived in, but I rapped at the door regardless. When no one answered, I tested the door handle to see that it was locked. Then I turned to follow the path around the side of the house, Sidney trailing after me.

"What are we looking for?" he asked

I glanced over my shoulder, arching my eyebrows. "Her roost."

"Ah," Sidney exhaled in understanding. "I wondered why she would leave such a message for the priest to relay to you. Does she have a henhouse then?"

I paused as I rounded the house to gaze up at the blackened and scorched roof of the northwest corner. Then I turned around to survey the back garden. To the right lay a patch of dormant soil, now overgrown with weeds. In warm weather, Emilie had planted whatever seeds she could get her hands on to grow food, all the while knowing the Germans would come along to confiscate seventy-five percent of it.

When Emilie had first joined La Dame Blanche, I knew she had utilized one corner of the plot as her hiding place. She'd buried the identification disk she'd been given, just as she'd been instructed. The disk she was not to disinter again until after the war. Any reports she could not immediately deliver were also stashed there. But after she'd returned home one morning to find the Germans tearing up her garden in order to requisition much of her produce, nearly unearthing the tin can filled with her secrets— she had decided it would be safer to move them to a different spot.

"Not a roost," I replied, striding across the lawn toward the split yarrow tree. Grasping one of the branches for leverage, I stepped up onto an exposed root. I grinned at him as I reached up toward the deep "V" formed by two of the appendages. "A nest." Pulling my hand from the tattered birds' nest, I showed him the battered tin can.

I hopped down from my perch and he moved closer to peer over my shoulder. My heart surged inside my chest as I removed the lid, curious to discover what she'd wanted me to find. However, my hopes were swiftly dashed, for there was nothing inside.

I stared blankly down inside the can, even tipping it upside down to upend it, but nothing tumbled out. "This doesn't make any sense." I tilted the can this way and that, searching for stray markings. I noted a series of tiny holes at the bottom, but nothing more. "Why would she have her priest give me such a message and then leave nothing inside?"

Sidney climbed up on the root, using his superior height to peer into the nest. He shook his head as he dropped back down. "Maybe she moved it."

I turned to look at the garden. "And put it in a different can? Possibly." I walked over to the vegetable plot to stare down at the dirt.

"I presume you're going to ask me to dig?"

I glanced up to find his mouth quirked upward at one corner. "Yes. If you don't mind."

"Let me find a shovel."

But even after turning over the soil in all four corners, we found nothing.

I planted my hands on my hips, shaking my head as I scowled at the earth. "I don't understand. Did she change her mind?"

Sidney finished unrolling and buttoning his shirt sleeves and bent to retrieve the coat he'd discarded. I was almost sorry to see him put it on, for his form showed to better advantage without it. "Perhaps she was worried someone was on to her and it would fall into the wrong hands," he remarked, shooting his cuffs.

I wanted to howl in frustration, but the sound of someone calling from the front of the cottage made me start.

"*Salut! Qui est là?*"

Sidney's eyes met my wide-eyed gaze and as one, we hastened to remove all evidence of our digging in Emilie's garden. He pushed the shovel under a bush while I slid the tin can into my pocket, hoping the bulge was not too noticeable. Just before the woman stepped into view, he slid his arm around my waist, joining me in my feigned examination of the scorched roof.

"There you are!" she declared triumphantly in lilting French. "I saw the motorcar and simply had to come and see. Are you to be our new neighbors?"

I recognized her now. This middle-aged woman with soft blond curls streaked with gray was the town gossip Emilie had pointed out to me from a distance and warned me not to be seen by. Not because she was malicious or colluding with the enemy, but because people with such loose tongues were always dangerous. Far too many times, agents had been compromised by the careless chatter of others. If word that a strange woman had visited Emilie reached the ears of the Secret Police, they would have descended upon her, demanding answers, and possibly revoking her special pass to travel about unrestricted on her rounds as a midwife.

However, now she might prove quite useful.

"Oh, we haven't purchased anything yet," Sidney replied, flashing the woman a charming smile. "But a friend of ours mentioned this place might be available."

"Oh, well, how delightful." She simpered under his regard. "I'm Madame Ledoq."

Sidney took her proffered hand, bowing over it a trifle too excessively. "Monsieur and Madame Kent."

I'd debated whether to reveal our real names or use an alias, but he made the decision for me. And it turned out to be the right one, for she gasped in recognition.

"Oh, but I knew you looked familiar." Her round eyes flitted between us. "And you look just as dashing in person as in the newspapers."

"You've seen our picture in the papers?" I asked, having been curious how widely our story had circulated.

"Oh, yes. Not the local ones, mind you. But Madame Laurent's daughter sometimes sends her the papers from Paris, and London, and sometimes even New York."

A tingle began at the base of my spine upon hearing the name, but I didn't wish to appear too eager. "Oh? Does she live in Paris?"

"London. Left during the war, like so many." She shook her head sadly. "And now, she has no wish to return. Part of me wonders if that's where Madame Moreau has gone as well." She gestured to the house, switching topics before I could stop her. "She simply packed a valise and left one day, without even a word goodbye." She peered up at my husband, a calculated gleam entering her eyes. "But perhaps you know her. She spied for the British during the war."

"Did she?" His voice was tight with suppressed amusement, and I nearly elbowed him in the ribs. Fortunately, Madame Ledoq seemed oblivious to it as she chattered on.

"Oh, yes. I don't have to tell you how shocked we all were to find out. Shocked and proud, of course. Somehow, she managed to fool us all, even *me,* and *I* am not so easily deceived. Let me tell you, not much occurs in this town without my knowing about it." She arched her chin, seeming infinitely proud of this.

I smiled. "I can imagine. Did you . . ."

"But the war made everything so topsy-turvy. You never could tell who was capable of what. Smugglers, informants, war profiteers, and young women fraternizing with the enemy." She "tsked" in disapproval. "Now there, Madame Moreau already knew more secrets than the rest of us and could be trusted to keep them." Her eyes had narrowed as if this displeased her. Perhaps she'd thought the midwife should share such information with her. "What company women were keeping, who the true fathers of their babies were. She ran a brisk trade during the war, I can tell you that."

I stiffened upon hearing her phrase it in such a callous and self-righteous manner. Whether their participation had ultimately been willing or not, many of those women would rather not have "fraternized" with the enemy. It had been a means to an end. It was easy for her to cast judgment when she condemned only herself to deprivation, but many of these young women were already mothers. To hear their young children cry from hunger and watch them shiver with cold, must have driven many of them to desperation, willing to go to any lengths to feed and protect them. I'm sure Emilie understood this better than even me.

"Yes, I'm sure every woman dreams of being conquered by the Bosche," Sidney drawled sarcastically, though his expression remained indifferent.

At first, this comment seemed to sail over her head as she nodded in agreement. But then she paused, glancing between us, perhaps sensing our disapproval, though she seemed to ascribe to it a different reason, and she hastily attempted to soften her comments. "Oh, but overall there was very little of that here in our village. Much less than elsewhere. Our girls were loyal. They knew their duty."

I waved this away with a gentle flick of my hand, tired of her opinions. "I'm sure. But this Madame Laurent? I believe I know a woman by that name. What did you say her daughter's name was again?"

"Pauline. But I doubt she runs in your circles. She's not so fashionable."

I wanted to exclaim in triumph, but instead I

answered Madame Ledoq serenely. "No. Different girl." I sighed, gazing up at the tiled roof as if smitten, despite the evident fire damage. "And you say you don't know where this Madame Moreau who owns the cottage has gone off to?"

Madame Ledoq hesitated before answering, her eyes growing more curious by the second. "No. The priest suggested she might have gone to visit family. We weren't allowed to travel far during the war or send letters, you see, so anyone further away than Chimay was effectively lost to us."

"Ah, well, we shall have to follow up with our friend then." I turned to Sidney. "Darling, your appointment?"

He flicked a glance at his wristwatch, following my cue. "Oh, yes! I'm afraid we must be on our way." He flashed her a dazzling smile. "Lovely to chat with you, Madame Ledoq. I do hope we shall have the chance to meet again."

Momentarily flustered, Madame Ledoq had little time to form a response before Sidney hustled me around the house and back into his motorcar. He lifted his hand in parting as she watched us reverse, a look of stunned bemusement on her face.

"That woman must have been a menace during the war," he declared ferociously. "If the Secret Police hereabouts were worth their salt, they must have loved to let her chuck her weight about. I imagine more than one citizen was betrayed by her mindless yammering."

"Yes, I was warned to steer clear of her." I turned sideways to face him. "But enough of her. What of Pauline Laurent? Did you recognize the name?"

"Madame Zozza's assistant."

I leaned toward him eagerly. "Dash it all, but I never suspected a thing. Did you?"

"That she had a connection to your Emilie?" He shook his head.

I scowled out through the windscreen. "And I *do* think she *still* must have a connection to her. It would be far too great a coincidence otherwise. The question is, what part does she play in all of this?"

Sidney's fingers tapped against the driving wheel in thought. "Madame Ledoq said she fled the country during the war, one of the thousands of refugees who flooded into England. But did she leave early in the war or later?"

"And did she witness anything before she left? Or perhaps she learned something from someone else later."

"Either way, I think we have to question whether anything she told us was true. After all, we only have her word for it that a strange man visited Madame Zozza, or that she saw him fleeing from the house the morning of the fire. For all we know, she could have been the one to convince the medium to pretend to summon Emilie, and then locked her in the house and set it ablaze to cover her tracks."

I rubbed my temple with my hand and grunted in frustration. "And now she's hundreds of miles away in London, beyond immediate questioning. Who knows? Maybe she's fled even further." I lifted my head. "Unless she followed us here." I swiveled to glance over my shoulder at the empty road behind us.

"Perhaps beyond our questioning, but what of your colleagues?" he proposed.

I doubted Major Davis would allow anyone at the Secret Service to knowingly lift a finger to help me. But if Captain Landau made the request, that would be a different story. And he did offer to assist in whatever way he could, either from his own inclination or C's surreptitious urging.

"You're right," I replied. "We'll have to find a telephone or, at the least, a telegraph office."

"Where am I going by the way? This sister's house in Quevy?"

"Not yet. First, I want to see if I can find that house where I buried the map case." My fingers tightened around the handbag I held in my lap. "Maybe Adele Moilien, the woman who confronted the priest and likely Emilie, will be there, too."

He slowed the motorcar and pulled toward the verge of the road. I could feel him searching my features, his gaze so intense it was almost tangible. He'd not offered me trite reassurances earlier when my distress had been evident, and I braced for them to be spoken now. But instead he turned to stare out at the waving grasses that lined the road before us.

"Not long after I was promoted to captain, there was a young lieutenant assigned to my company. A rather green fellow. Barely eighteen." He spoke softly, carefully, but I could hear the tension at the edges. "Suffered a fair amount of teasing from his fellow officers." His mouth flexed in a grin. "Especially after his mother sent him an undergarment of chain mail."

"You're jesting?"

He shook his head. "The poor woman thought it would protect him." He cleared his throat. "Young Atkins took the teasing well. He was a good sport. But the new officers always made me nervous. They made all the men nervous." A deep furrow ran between his brows. "They'd yet to be tried in battle, and you never knew how they were going to react the first time they faced a hail of German bullets."

His shoulders bunched and his hands tightened around the driving wheel before he dropped his arms into his lap. I felt an answering constriction in my gut, waiting on the hatchet to fall.

"As such, I preferred to keep them as isolated as possible," he explained. "Until they'd survived a few bombardments. Until they'd killed their first Jerry. Until I knew they weren't going to freeze, or leg it, or grandstand, and get my men killed because of their idiocy. So when my company was ordered over the top, I elected to leave Lieutenant Atkins behind in charge of the reserve platoon with a stalwart corporal to assist him." His expression turned grim. "Little did I know that away from the trench was the safest place to be, for a shell hit it dead on. Killed or injured three quarters of the platoon, including Lieutenant Atkins. And the worst part was, it was one of *our* shells."

My stomach quavered, wondering at the piece of luck that had seen that Sidney was not the officer in the trench.

He turned his head to look at me for the first time, his eyes stark with memories I was certain I couldn't begin to fathom, even knowing all that I did. "I tell you this because, the truth is war is hell on everyone who falls near its angry maw. The actions you take thinking to spare the innocent or inexperienced can just as easily cause their destruction, simply because the world is turned so bloody upside down. So don't take on the guilt of that woman or her brother's sufferings from where it truly belongs."

His voice was so vehement on my behalf that for a moment all I could do was stare at him. That he should so fervently want to ease my pain made a space in my chest that had grown cold begin to warm again, and I had to struggle to find my voice. In the end, I could only nod.

He searched my gaze a moment longer, as if to be certain I meant it, and then lifted his hands to grasp the driving wheel.

"But what about you?" I finally managed to say as he turned to look over his shoulder at the road behind us.

He scowled as he pulled forward, gunning the engine. "I'm a different story."

I frowned. "How can . . ."

"Now where to?"

"Sidney . . ."

"Where to?" he snapped.

I wanted to press the matter even though it was clear Sidney had no desire to discuss it further. On the roadside deep in the Belgian countryside, at the edge of the war-ravaged areas, hardly seemed to be the ideal place. But I could see how much pain it caused him, how much blame he carried around on his shoulders. And I was not going to forget.

CHAPTER 20

Rarely had my memory failed me. It was something I'd relied upon day to day, hour to hour during the war. As a Secret Service agent, it had been perhaps my greatest asset alongside sharp instincts and acute observation—enabling me to form connections between seemingly random bits of intelligence collected in other reports and develop a broader picture of the enemy's actions and intentions. It had enabled me to pour out the information I'd carefully memorized into my debriefing reports the moment I returned to Rotterdam, and expand on the data already included in La Dame Blanche's dispatches.

And yet I could not recall where the cottage was located where I'd buried that German aviator's map case.

I'd directed Sidney down numerous roads and back lanes between Chimay and the Franco-Belgian border, scouring the landscape for any clue as to where this home was situated, but I simply could not find it. The problem was that everything looked so different in the daylight. Had I set off from Chimay on foot under a full moon, I might be able to stumble upon it, but even that was doubtful. And I wasn't about to waste any more time on such a task.

I planted my hands on my hips, staring out over a dormant field run rampant with wild grasses and bounded by overgrown hedges. I stood at the edge of a wood, the boundary of which marked the border of Belgium and France. If I were uncertain of that, the remnants of barbed wire still strung between a few posts cleared up any confusion. It seemed so innocuous now, but I remembered how the sight of it looming up out of the dark made the heart pound with fright, knowing a German patrol could be but a few feet away.

Sidney toed the end of the line where it trailed into the grass. "Is this where you snuck across?"

Upon seeing the narrow trail leading away from the road toward the border, I'd decided we should follow it on foot to see where it led, but it hadn't led anywhere. I sighed, exasperated at the results of this last fool's errand. "Most likely not." I pointed before me. "These fields are too open. It would have been far too easy for a patrol to spot us crossing from a distance. Safer to either pass through an actual border post—and hope our passes, and identification cards, or a skillful bluff would see us through—or dart across in a heavily wooded area where the wire had been clipped."

He narrowed his eyes, squinting into the afternoon sun. "Madame Ledoq mentioned smugglers. Of what? Contraband?"

I grimaced. "Food. Potatoes typically. For every hardship the Belgians faced, the French in the occupied territories had it worse."

"No love lost between the French and the Germans," he remarked wryly.

"I don't think the smugglers made much profit. It was more like another form of resistance. In any case, they were invaluable help at times in transporting agents across frontiers. They knew all the paths through the wildest areas and were able to follow them even on moonless nights." I dropped my arms, shaking my head in frustration. "I keep thinking about all the things Emilie might have witnessed during her frequent treks to visit expectant mothers, all the secrets she potentially could have been keeping. It's impossible to know what exactly sent her into hiding."

Sidney lifted a hand to rub circles on my back. "Then let's start with what we *do* know."

I inhaled a deep breath, releasing some of the tension knotting my frame. "Yes, you're right." I knew better than to let my emotions run away from me. That way lay trouble. But calm, careful thinking would save you more often than not.

"All right, so we know that a few months after the end of the war, Emilie decided to move away from Macon for a time, not long after a fire at her home. She gave the priest a message to relay to me, but didn't tell him or any of her neighbors where she was going. And she gave the chiefs of La Dame Blanche a fake address. She may be at her sister's home in Quevy, as the message she gave to the priest seemed to imply." I grimaced. "But somehow I doubt it will be that simple. She obviously wanted to disappear, but from whom exactly? And why is she leaving *me,* of all people, breadcrumbs to follow her? How did she know I would come looking for her?" I bit my lip, contemplating the matter.

"We also know that someone who was privy to the knowledge that both you and Emilie worked for British Intelligence convinced Madame Zozza to pretend to summon Emilie and urge you to 'unearth her secrets,'" Sidney chimed in, shifting to lean back against the empty post on the opposite side of the path, its barbed wire already having been removed and taken away, probably by some farmer. "At the least, this person knows Emilie was the code name of Madame Moreau, and that you both operated covertly. The rest, perhaps, could have been inferred. For what person in such a situation doesn't have secrets to hide?"

"True," I agreed. "Although whoever it was, certainly thought it imperative enough to conceal their identity and intentions by killing Madame Zozza and setting fire to her house and all her notes. And now we know that her assistant, one Pauline Laurent, was a girl from the same village where Emilie lived, and must have played some part in the matter." I paused, a thought occurring to me. "In fact, Melanie Tuberow told me it was Mademoiselle Laurent who made the arrangements for Melanie to gift her session to Daphne and convince me to join her. At the time, it hadn't struck me as suspicious because such things are normally handled by an assistant."

"So whoever is behind all this has some connection to both Macon, Belgium, and London. That certainly fits Mademoiselle Laurent."

"Yes, but how did she come to be in possession of classified information?"

"Maybe it isn't Pauline Laurent. Maybe her mother or Madame Ledoq stumbled across Madame Moreau's code name. Maybe when they saw our picture in the newspaper, they mentioned seeing you about the village during the war." He tilted his head. "You pretended to be a relation or assistant of Madame Moreau's, didn't you? So others must have seen you together from time to time."

"Yes," I replied hesitantly, though I'd done my best to avoid it.

"Then if Madame Moreau's role with La Dame Blanche became known after the war, it wouldn't take a great leap of logic to realize you might have been an intelligence agent as well."

"That's possible," I conceded. "But if Mademoiselle Laurent has been in London all this time, why did Emilie feel threatened enough to move? And what possible motive could Mademoiselle Laurent have for harming her?" I straightened. "Unless she had a partner? A lover, perhaps." I frowned, feeling like I was grasping at straws.

"Maybe she's a German agent seeking revenge."

Daphne had mentioned Mona Kertle was included in MI5's Registry as a suspicious person. I wondered if Pauline Laurent was as well. But as for either of them being a German agent eager to avenge any wrongs, I shook my head. "No. Their networks fell apart at the end of the war. And with the state of chaos in Germany, I doubt they have time to worry about petty grievances, which is all I can imagine Emilie having anything to do with. She didn't kill anyone or double-cross them."

"That you know of." He arched his eyebrows significantly.

I allowed myself to consider the possibility. After all, war had forced so many of us to do things we would never have believed possible. But whatever the truth, I still didn't believe Mademoiselle Laurent could be a German agent.

"Unfortunately, I think a great deal of this comes down to motive, which isn't clear yet. And it might not be until we find Emilie. Which I think has to be our priority."

Sidney straightened away from the post. "Then on to Quevy?"

I gazed out over the border across the sun-drenched fields one last time and nodded. "On to Quevy."

Though we set out from Macon with what I'd thought would be ample time to reach Quevy, I soon discovered I hadn't taken into account the poor state of the roads in this part of northeastern France after the Germans' retreat. The most direct route to Emilie's sister's village took us north through one of the French peninsulas that jutted into Belgium, for the border between the two nations was by no means straight. Most of the roads we'd encountered in Belgium had been in relatively good repair, but here was more evidence of the greater animosity felt toward the French, as well as the fact that the further northwest we traveled the closer we came to the front.

However, Captain Landau had foreseen just such a difficulty. I'd been able to locate a telephone as we passed through Trélon and place a static-filled call to him in Brussels, asking him to send someone to speak to Pauline Laurent. I'd even been specific as to the agents I preferred to handle the matter. Whether London would honor that request was uncertain, but given that the directive came from Landau, I hoped we'd see results.

When he'd asked our plans, I'd told him I would have to telephone him, as I had no idea where we would be staying. But he'd known the area far better than I and suggested where we might consider stopping for the night. He instructed me to give them his name, and the best room would be ours. I'd thanked him, but privately dismissed the possibility of us halting our journey so soon. Not while the sun was still so high in the sky. But with each mile that dragged on, I began to understand his insistence.

I couldn't help but cast worried glances at Sidney from time to time as he navigated the pitted roads. His shoulders steadily inched toward his ears, and the cigarettes in his silver case dwindled. Near Trélon, where the German Army Headquarters had been located, we encountered an astonishing number of shell craters as well as the ravaged ruins of old buildings, their craggy turrets of crumbled masonry casting odd shadows across the landscape. Continuing north, we passed the charred remnants of once proud villages—evidence of the Germans' ruthless advance five years earlier when they'd set fire to some towns after claiming they'd been fired upon by civilians. In other places, we came upon slag heaps of spent shell casings and jumbled piles of railway track torn apart by the Germans as they retreated.

At Maubeuge, where the outer ring forts were pulverized into twisted wrecks of metal, we elected to halt our journey for the night just as Captain Landau predicted. The hotel he'd recommended was located near the middle of the city, and while somewhat austere given the depravities of the war, it was clean and comfortable, and the simple but satisfying food in their restaurant most welcome after a long day. Sidney seemed to agree, for the strain marring his brow during the difficult drive diminished as our meal took on the semblance of normalcy.

The food and wine had all but lulled me into a comatose state when the concierge unexpectedly appeared at our table. "Excuse me, Madame. This was just delivered for you."

I took the white envelope from his hand and thanked him. Thinking it was from Captain Landau, I only waited long enough for the man to depart before breaking the seal and extracting the paper inside. However, the contents all but erased the serenity of the moment before.

"What does it say?" Sidney asked.

I passed it over to him, knowing I couldn't very well hide the telegram from him.

LOCATED THE AVIATOR FROM CHIMAY—
(STOP)—KILLED IN ACTION JULY
1918—(STOP)—DEAD END
CAPTAIN ALEXANDER XAVIER

Sidney's mouth twisted in displeasure. "Why am I not surprised to hear from him?"

"He's merely trying to help," I replied, though I was no happier than he was that Alec had reinserted himself back into our lives, no matter the altruism of his motives.

"I suppose Captain Landau told him where to find us."

"Undoubtedly," I replied, tearing the telegram into neat squares.

He arched his eyebrows at my actions, and I stopped, setting the papers aside.

"Sorry. Just a habit from the war." It had been imperative to never keep incriminating evidence. I inhaled a steadying breath, trying to feign an ease with this new development despite the sharp glint in Sidney's eye. "So that aviator I stole the map case from is not our culprit."

Not that I'd actually believed him a good suspect, but it was good to rule out someone.

"Alec must still possess some extensive connections in Germany for him to have discovered that so quickly." His voice was tinged with suspicion.

Having worked with him during the war, I was less surprised. "Yes, well, Alec always was resourceful." I glanced toward the front of the restaurant, wanting to change the subject.

But Sidney seemed determined, now that he had me relatively alone, to pursue the matter of my and Alec's connection. "How then were you responsible for compromising him?"

I turned back to meet his gaze, realizing he was referring to the conversation we'd had in that café outside of Brussels. I'd not planned to tell him the entire tale of our most important assignment together, but it was difficult to explain my role in drawing the Germans' suspicion towards him without it. Still, part of me screamed at me not to speak, to avoid the discussion. But I ignored it, reaching out a hand that was surprisingly steady to straighten the cutlery beside my empty plate, and accepted the inevitable.

"Throughout the war, Alec had continued to make his way up the German chain of command, and in the summer of 1918 he was a hauptmann in charge of the coding division at the Kommandantur in Brussels. Early in the war, without the enemy being aware, the British had obtained a copy of the original diplomatic code book used by the Germans. It was a critical piece of intelligence. But apparently, the Germans had become suspicious because their coding office had been given a new book. One they had been ordered to begin using on a specified date, once copies had reached all other divisions. There was, then, a short window of opportunity for us to copy the new code before it was put in use, and without the Germans catching on."

Sidney sat back, lighting a cigarette he smoked

leisurely as he listened to me. His deep blue eyes seemed to take in every aspect of my demeanor, and though I strove to remain composed, I knew my agitation must have been evident.

"I was in Holland at the time, so when Alec's urgent missive arrived via courier, I was sent to Brussels to . . . pose as his mistress." I hadn't meant to stumble over the words, but I did nonetheless.

His only reaction was a slight furrowing of his brow.

"I took rooms at a hotel that Alec had arranged for me, just a simple Belgian girl from a small village near the border with Germany, an identity I'd used twice in the past. Every day at midday he would visit me, bringing a portion of the code book for me to copy onto tissue paper. He would return in the evening to assist me, though we still had to go out at night to dinner and parties with his fellow officers to maintain the ruse."

"Of course."

I couldn't tell if he was being sarcastic or not, so I ignored the comment and pressed on. "Then we would return to our room and I would continue to copy until the task was finished in the wee hours of the morning while Alec got some rest. At sunrise, he would return to the Kommandantur early and replace the pages he'd removed, so that the entire new book was accounted for during inspection, which most often occurred in the morning. That's why he could only remove a few pages at a time and not the entire manual, on the off chance his superiors asked to see it later in the day. In any case, we couldn't copy many more pages in a day than he removed anyway."

I paused as our waiter whisked away our plates, declining his offer of dessert. My stomach was already churning. I couldn't swallow a bite even if it was the most heavenly concoction on earth. My wine, however, was a different story. I took a long swallow as Sidney tipped the ash from his cigarette into a tray.

"And you repeated this day after day?" he surmised.

"Yes. I would rise each day around mid-morning and dress, wrapping the pages we'd copied around the bones of my corset and stroll to a café down the street from the hotel. It was a favorite among the German officers, which was, I'm sure, how it was able to get supplies when everywhere else had none. Though, at that late date, even the German generals were having to go without some things. However, this café also acted as a separate letter box for the British."

I could read in his eyes that he was impressed. "A viper at their breast."

"I would sip a cup of coffee and enjoy a pastry, and then slip into the water closet where I would remove the pages we'd copied, roll them into a tube and slip them into the hollowed-out handle of a broom stored there. A courier would then collect them and take them across the frontier into Holland." I smoothed my hand over the tablecloth, approaching the crux of my story. "I made certain to go at a different time each morning, hoping to avoid those officers who made a routine of patronizing the establishment. I kept to myself as best I could, while still appearing as if I was obviously a German's 'kept woman.'" I exhaled the breath I was holding. "But sometimes all the care in the world cannot save you from chance."

Sidney stubbed out his fag, resting his elbows on the table to lean closer to me.

I struggled to meet his gaze. "There were . . . certain German officers one knew to avoid. Men of black reputation who cared little about anyone's wishes but their own."

His jaw tightened.

"I suspect you know what I mean."

He nodded, reaching out a hand to take mine. And I let him, craving the warmth and reassurance of his touch, even though I knew very shortly he would snatch it away.

"I accidentally collided with one such officer, an oberst, when I was leaving the water closet at the café on the second to last day of this assignment. I recognized him immediately, though I pretended not to, and hurried on after a swift apology. Unfortunately, I'd dropped my glove, and he called me back to hand it to me. I spent a tense few moments conversing with him after that, half-afraid he was toying with me and knew exactly what I was up to. But his lewd perusal of my person and suggestive comments soon made it clear he was only interested in me for one thing. He asked me to lunch, and I declined as gently and blushingly as possible, protesting that I was already meeting Alec. But I could see in his eyes that the damage was already done. He'd taken an interest, and that could only spell trouble."

"Did you warn Alec?"

"I tried to. In fact, I was a bit frantic when he came to see me at midday with the last section of the code book. Especially when he told me the oberst had already come to visit him at the Kommandantur, asking about me. But Alec was unconcerned. In truth, he seemed to find the entire matter amusing. He said he was aware of the oberst's reputation and the fact that he was frightfully persistent, but that he would never pursue me across Belgium, where I would supposedly return to the next day. But I worried anyway."

"And you turned out to be correct?"

I nodded, staring down at where our hands were joined. "About a month later, we learned that Alec was under suspicion, and that an arrest seemed imminent. We could have left him to face the consequences, which would have almost certainly meant a swift court-martial ending in a firing squad. All of us who took on such work accepted the risk. Alec more so than others. But he was an important asset. One we knew possessed even more insights into the Germans than could be detailed in his reports."

I hesitated, allowing the soft murmurs of the other patrons and the clink of their silverware to wash over me. They only accentuated the unreal nature of holding this conversation in such a place.

"I would be lying if I didn't admit there was also a personal element to it. For Alec had become a friend. One I was never entirely certain of. But a friend nonetheless." I could hear how tightly strung my voice had become, but could do nothing about it, except lower it to a whisper so that the others in the room couldn't hear. "I couldn't sit back and do nothing while the Germans killed him. I'd believed I'd already lost you, and . . . well, there was also a degree of guilt. Though it couldn't be stated with any certainty, the fact that the oberst was at the center of the questions swirling around Alec seemed to point to the fact that my encounter with the man had something to do with it."

"So you went after him?"

I swallowed and shrugged. "An attempt needed to be made and I was in Holland. One of our best *passeurs* guided us part of the way, and helped ensure we made it across the electric wire, and over the border. But the rest of the extraction plan was on me."

"And you made it safely to the Rotterdam office?"

"Not the office," I protested. "I never visited the Rotterdam office. That would have been far too dangerous. Holland was a neutral country, and as such it was populated with not only our agents, but those of many of the warring countries, including Germany. As such it posed a particular challenge, and had to be treated as enemy territory. The Germans, of course, knew where British Intelligence's headquarters were located, as we knew theirs. So whenever I arrived in Holland, either from Britain or Belgium, I instead telephoned the office and used an assumed name, and they would tell me in code which of the many houses they owned in Rotterdam and The Hague to report to."

"So you made it safely to this house in Holland?" he asked, growing impatient. "Without incident?"

"Yes. Mostly."

But I could tell he knew that wasn't all there was to the story. I could read it in his watchful gaze, in the tautness of his mouth, and the sharp glint in his eyes. I could feel it in the restrained energy in the clasp of his hand in mine.

He sat back suddenly, pulling his hand from

mine. "Then I should think any guilt or gratitude in the bargain should now be on his end," he declared, pushing his chair back. "Have you finished?"

The last was added so abruptly, I didn't have a chance to respond anything but a stammered "yes."

The firmness of Sidney's grip on my arm as he escorted me back to my room left me with no doubt that our conversation wasn't finished. He'd simply been astute enough to recognize it should reconvene in a place more private. His steps were unrushed, his expression amicable, but I was not fooled. Either Sidney had already guessed what I hadn't yet confessed, or he suspected something similar. My days of evading the matter were over. I didn't even try to fight it.

While he shut the door to our suite of rooms, I switched on a single lamp and crossed toward the settee where I perched at the edge of the cushion, staring down at my hands. The fact that such a lovely sofa, as well as all the other furniture in the suite, had not been requisitioned told me that some German officer had used these rooms as his quarters. I suspected the entire hotel had been commandeered as barracks.

Sidney stood several feet away, his hands on his hips. He didn't speak, just watched me.

I knew it was cowardly not to meet his gaze, but still I struggled to lift my eyes. And when I finally did, it was like being pierced in the heart. Because for a brief moment, he had allowed his mask of impatience and anger to slip and I had seen the anguish underneath.

"Now, why don't you tell me what has you wracked with guilt?" he ordered in a carefully controlled voice. His eyes turned to chips of ice. "Or shall I guess?"

CHAPTER 21

Though my mouth was dry and my stomach quavered, I forced myself to speak. "On the night we returned to Rotterdam, I . . . I slept with Alec," I gasped, my voice trembling on the words. I inhaled a ragged breath, trying to fight back the tears burning at the corners of my eyes. "It was only the once, and I . . . I knew it was a mistake the moment it was over."

I spoke the last in a rush as Sidney whirled away from me, uttering a curse. He shook his head as if he couldn't even bear to look at me.

I slid toward the edge of the settee, pleading with my clasped hands. "I'm so sorry, Sidney. Had I known you were alive, I would never have even considered it."

"Are you sure about that?" he queried snidely, turning back to face me.

"Yes! How can you even think otherwise?" I protested, resentment trickling in to override some of my guilt.

"Because the two of you seemed quite cozy. And you already admitted you care for him."

I rose to my feet. "Not like I care for you. Never

336

that way. And had you not led me to believe you were *dead,* I would never have allowed him to get that close. I would never have *wanted* him to."

"So this is my fault?" he demanded incredulously.

"Yes. No." I clenched my fists in frustration. "Had I known you were alive, I would never have behaved the way I did. But my actions are my own. I take responsibility for that."

"So you're claiming you did what you did out of grief? That you drank, and flirted, and warmed another man's bed because you were missing me?"

"I didn't know how to deal with any of it, Sidney! The war, the work I did, Rob's death, the loss of all those men—so many friends. And then to lose you . . ." I choked on a sob and turned my head away, fighting back the emotion. "You can't tell me you handled everything any better?" I accused.

His eyes blazed with fury, the light of that single lamp making the hollows of his face dark pools of anger. "Why didn't you tell me any of this sooner?"

"Because I didn't know how. How do you tell your husband that you slept with another man? How do you raise that specter when the state of your marriage is already in peril?" I pleaded with him, trying to make him understand.

He stared back at me, his emotions so raw, so blistering that I wanted to shut my eyes. I made myself continue to meet his gaze, trying to communicate how much I regretted my actions, how desperately I wanted us to find a way past this. For a moment, I thought he might come to me. That he might take me in his arms. But then he did the exact opposite.

Lifting his hands as if in defeat, he backed toward the door. "I just . . . I can't . . ." He shook his head and whirled away. A moment later the door clicked shut behind him.

I stood staring at the dark wood, my mind blank, as if it could not comprehend what had just happened. My body caught on quicker. My knees gave out and I sank back onto the sofa as a sob worked its way up from my throat, bursting forth. I leaned forward and wept, pressing my hands over my chest as if by force and will alone, I could keep my heart from breaking. Yet again.

I had cried so many tears over Sidney. When I'd believed him dead in the sucking red mud of the Somme. When I'd discovered he was alive, but he'd placed his quest for vengeance over any devotion he felt for me. Not to mention all the times he'd returned to the front after a few days' leave. Each departure, each new offensive, each roll of honor printed in the newspapers brought a fresh wave of terror and grief. And now this.

Eventually, my sobs diminished, and I collapsed sideways on the settee, gazing forlornly at the door through which Sidney had departed. I wondered, almost idly, if he would ever return, or if he would just leave me here. I'd grown so used to his leaving, though it had been the war and not by his choice, that the event seemed somehow inevitable. As if he had always been meant to be an impermanent fixture in my life, flitting in and out, ravaging what was left of my heart.

How long I stared red-eyed at the door, wrestling with myself, I don't know. But at some point, my eyes grew heavy and I fell into a fitful sleep.

My eyes were gritty and my face swollen the following morning—as I hefted my valise and portmanteau, and emerged from the hotel into the dim light of dawn. A ceiling of gray clouds blocked the sun, casting a pall over the day. One that seemed fitting.

I'd woken sometime before sunrise to find that Sidney had still not returned. That revelation opened a pit in my stomach, and I'd rolled over to stare up at the ceiling, trying to come to terms with what I'd only feared the night before. That our short-lived reunion was truly over, and our war-torn marriage was at an end.

We wouldn't be the first or the last couple who wed during the feverish excitement of the war to discover afterwards it was a mistake. But that was no consolation now. No balm to my already battered heart.

I'd waited two more hours for him to appear, and when he did not, I'd forced myself to dress and pack my things. After all, Emilie was still in danger. She still needed to be found. My wreck of a marriage changed none of that.

I'd stopped to speak to the concierge, learning that while the train did not go to Quevy, there was a garage just around the corner that also operated a car service the hotel sometimes utilized for their guests. He offered to telephone them, but I declined, not wanting to remain in the hotel a moment longer than necessary now that I'd made up my mind what must be done. Eventually, Sidney would have to return for his things, and as he seemed to be giving me time to clear out before that, I resolved to do so.

But standing on the pavement now, I felt a profound sense of loss, of aloneness. In the five weeks since Sidney's return, without realizing it, somehow, I'd grown attached to the comfort of believing I was no longer alone. Throughout the war and especially after his reported death, I'd felt isolated, singular. And the consequences of that loneliness had at times been cold and cutting.

But then Sidney had come back, and despite the difficulties, despite the uncertainty, he was alive and so was I, and at least there were two of us.

Now that proved to be a lie. And the yawning reality of it held me immobile.

How long I stood that way, I can't say, but the shuffle of footsteps behind me alerted me to the presence of another. I lifted a hand to adjust my hat, forcing movement back into my limbs before I glanced over my shoulder. Only to be staggered by the sight of Sidney standing against the wall, watching me.

His face was haggard and pale, and his hair kinked and curled, as I knew he hated it, falling over his forehead. But even looking as awful as he did, he was still the most beautiful human being I'd ever seen. That knowledge cut like a knife through my breast.

He ground out the cigarette he'd been smoking and approached me, his gaze dipping to my luggage. "Leaving me, are you?"

For a moment, I couldn't speak, only stare into his deep blue eyes rimmed with dark circles, almost as if he'd been punched. Though the rest of his face was subdued, his eyes gleamed at me with a dozen questions. All I cared about was that there was no trace of disgust or fury.

"I thought I'd change it up for once," I finally replied.

The joke fell flat, and the moment it had passed my lips, I wished I could take it back. It was too soon. But Sidney only tipped his head, acknowledging the truth of that statement.

"Where did you sleep?" I asked softly, for he looked as if he were about to keel over.

"I didn't. I just walked," he added, anticipating my next question. "Thinking." He shrugged. "It's not the first time I've done so."

It wasn't an invitation to ask questions, but I did so anyway. "The war? The traitors?"

"Some." His gaze dipped to his foot, where he pushed aside a stray stone. "But a lot of times it was you." His eyes searched mine before he murmured. "It was hard not to think about you at night."

My chest tightened with the same longing I heard in his voice, and I wanted to reach out to him, to move closer, but I couldn't. Not when I didn't know what his plans were. Did this mean he wasn't leaving me, or was he simply trying to say goodbye?

He inhaled a deep, hitching breath and glanced at the hotel. "Will you let me fetch my things and then we'll set off for Quevy?"

It wasn't a declaration of forgiveness or a clear statement of intent, but I figured it was the best that could be expected at the moment. Too quick a reconciliation would have seemed false. Better to take it by increments.

I nodded, swallowing the lump in my throat. "So long as you let me drive for a spell."

He arched his eyebrows at this demand, but before he could insist he was fine, I cut him off.

"You may be alert enough to drive, but I need you to have your full faculties in order to help me unravel this riddle."

When he still looked as if he wanted to argue, I arched my chin.

"Did you or did you not teach me how to drive before the war? And I've been doing so for nearly five years in your prized Pierce-Arrow, with nary a scratch." In a gentler voice, I added, "I can handle her, Sidney."

He exhaled, finally relenting. "I suppose I could take a short doss."

I didn't reply, determined he'd sleep the whole way to Quevy, no matter how long it took to traverse the twelve kilometers on these roads.

Though we didn't know the exact direction to Emilie's sister's house, in a tiny village like Quevy, everyone knew each other, and we were swiftly directed to her cottage. At first, upon seeing the petite woman with frazzled hair and quick, darting eyes, I thought we might have come to the wrong place. She was as different from calm, contained Emilie as could be. But she ushered us inside when I mentioned Rose Moreau, as if worried the trees bordering her home might be listening.

She gestured us toward chairs at a battered, round table. "Yes, Rose Moreau is my sister," she confirmed after closing and locking the door.

Sidney and I exchanged a look as she fluttered about, twitching curtains before joining us at the table.

"Is she here?" I asked.

Her eyes immediately narrowed in suspicion. "Who wants to know?"

"My name is Verity Kent. Though your sister would most likely have known me as Gabrielle Thys." When this elicited no response from her, I tried something else. "Her priest in Macon told us she left a message for me saying I could find her here."

She leaned forward in challenge, unsettling me. "Is that actually what he said?"

"Well, no. He said I could inquire after her here."

Her eyebrows arched, as if anticipating more.

"And that the hens had come home to roost." I wasn't sure how this was pertinent to her, but it seemed to galvanize her into action.

She jumped up from her chair and crossed the room toward a cupboard. "Did you bring the can, then?"

I blinked in surprise. "Yes, actually. Though it's out in the motorcar."

She waved her hand at us as she bent forward on her hands and knees to rummage through the items stored in the lower compartment. "Well, go fetch it then."

"I'll go," Sidney offered, rising to do so.

I watched the little woman in bemusement. It was only by a stroke of luck that I'd taken the can with me. I'd intended to leave it where I'd found it, but then Madame Ledoq had interrupted us and I'd never removed it from my pocket until we returned to the motorcar.

Exclaiming in triumph, Madame Moreau's sister emerged from the depths of the cabinet, brandishing a thick book as if it was the Holy Grail. She dropped it on the table before me with a *thunk* and then planted her hands on her hips. It was a Bible, and an old one at that, but I had no idea what she expected me to do with it.

Sidney returned then, looking between us as he passed me the tin can.

"Are there no further instructions?" I asked.

"If you are who you say you are, then you'll know the game as surely as you know your name," she declared before walking away.

Scowling in confusion, I studied the can and the Bible. Clearly, I was missing something. Something important.

"I take it you don't know what to do?" Sidney inquired.

"Just . . . give me a moment."

Removing the can's lid, I looked inside again to still find it empty. Should there have been some message inside? Had someone else taken it? Or was the can to be used in a different way?

I turned it this way and that, searching for

random markings. Closer examination showed there were five dented holes in the bottom, but they didn't follow any discernable pattern I could see. I reached out to flip open the Bible. Perhaps there would be a note or random marking for me to follow.

But then why did I need the can?

Huffing in exasperation, I set the can down on the open page of the Bible to glower at it. If this was some coded message, Emilie was certainly going to extremes to keep her location a secret.

Which in and of itself was peculiar. She was such a straightforward, no-nonsense person. All of this subterfuge was making me uneasy. Either she was extremely wary of someone finding her and uncovering whatever she knew, or she wasn't the one sending me on this scavenger hunt. But who else knew about the can and the other things?

"Verity."

Hearing the wariness in his voice, I glanced up at Sidney.

He stood next to the cupboard, holding one of the books from its upper shelves. "I think you should see this." He held the book in front of me so that I could read the cover.

"That's one of Jonathan Fletcher's novels." The middle-aged man from the séance who we had confronted in Liège for following me. "But why . . ."

He flipped the book over so that I could see the back, pointing to the photograph of the author. The distinguished older gentleman in the image was decidedly not the man who had claimed to be him.

"He lied," I murmured rather needlessly.

Sidney nodded. "Yes, and we didn't catch it."

I scowled, feeling the same anger I heard in his voice over our being duped. "Well, dash it all. And he's probably still following us."

"If he is, he's doing a much better job at it. I haven't seen him lurking about, and I've been paying attention."

"So have I," I admitted. Had his bumbling nature been an act? To what end?

I glanced down at the book again. "I suppose the photograph could be fake," I suggested hopefully. The man captured there looked like the sort of person one wanted a gifted author to appear like. Maybe Mr. Fletcher didn't want his real face plastered on the back of his books.

Sidney didn't say anything, merely arched his eyebrows letting me know he realized I didn't believe that any more than he did.

I frowned at the open page of the Bible as he replaced Mr. Fletcher's book on the shelf.

The corners of his mouth quirked upward in sympathy at my evident frustration with Emilie's code. "Perhaps the sister can be persuaded to tell us where Madame Moreau is."

I could hear the sounds of her moving about in the next room. "If she even knows."

"It's worth a shot."

But his steps were arrested before he'd even taken one. He loomed closer to stare down at the can. "Did you know you can see letters through the holes at the bottom?"

I leapt to my feet to lean over the can. He was right. You could see individual letters through the punctures.

My heart surged in excitement. "It's a cipher." I paused. "But what page?"

I thought back over everything we'd learned, over all the memories I'd relived this week about my time spent with Emilie. And then my thoughts returned to what her sister had just told me.

"You'll know the game as surely as you know your name," I repeated.

Emilie had known me as Gabrielle during the war. Could she be referring to the angel Gabriel? But which verse?

I began to flip the pages to the New Testament, but then the Book of Psalms caught my eye and I paused. There must be a half dozen or more verses that included Gabriel by name, but I could think of only one that mentioned verity. My mother had quoted it often enough to me, for that was how she'd chosen my name. It was verity the virtue and not Verity the name, but I didn't think the distinction mattered.

Turning back several pages, I located Psalm 111 and rested the can on the page just below the line with the word "verity" at the center. I had to rotate the can a bit, but sure enough the holes lined up to pick out the letters *h, a, v, a, y.*

"What's 'havay'?" Sidney asked, reading over my shoulder.

"Havay is a village a short distance from here." But this answer only raised more questions. Namely about the village itself. For I was familiar with Havay, and I knew there was very little chance Emilie was staying there. Yet another breadcrumb on her trail?

I looked up to find her sister watching me from the doorway. Her only parting words were, "Step with care."

CHAPTER 22

A ll right, out with it," Sidney declared as we returned to the road. "What's made you so windy about this village?"

I gazed out over the golden fields now fallen silent when not so long ago they shook with the thunder of artillery guns. I knew I couldn't keep this from him. He would see the truth for himself soon enough. And perhaps it was better if he was prepared.

"In early 1918, the Germans evacuated Havay and then used it as a training ground for their heavy bombers. They wanted to test their latest large-caliber bombs in real situations before using them in operations."

Sidney glanced over at me. "You mean . . ." He couldn't seem to finish the words.

"They leveled it."

It would be little better than the war zone, minus the squalid trenches and rotting corpses.

I watched as the reality of what we were about to drive into settled onto Sidney's shoulders. His hands tensed around the driving wheel.

Why Emilie was sending us to such a place, I

didn't know. Unless it had something to do with the wireless-controlled aeroplane she had been searching for evidence of. Had the Germans' capability with such a weapon progressed to the point that they were testing it in the field? Monsieur Chauvin's comments had led me to believe the matter was still in the earliest stages of development, but perhaps I'd misunderstood. After all, one significant cause of the collapse of the German Army had been the revolution that occurred in Germany, overthrowing the Kaiser and his imperial regime. Given another few months, would things have changed considerably?

Whatever the truth, the proof of the Germans' destructive capabilities soon came into view. We crested a small rise, and there unfolded before us a scene of utter destruction. I'd heard another agent describe Havay as a modern-day Pompeii, and the comparison was an apt one. Not a single building still stood. The town hall, the church, every house and farm had been reduced to rubble. And the land, which had undoubtedly been fields of rich soil, was pitted with craters and the splintered ruins of trees, much like I had witnessed along the front.

Sidney slowed the motorcar and came to a stop in the middle of the road. Though he didn't speak of it, I could sense the turmoil within him. The air was thick with it. I knew his memories of the war were not far from his thoughts. He'd twitched with them in his sleep as I drove us to Quevy.

"Why did she tell us to step with care?" he asked. "Are there unexploded shells?"

"It's possible. It doesn't look like anyone has done anything to begin clearing this debris to rebuild the town. If they even mean to." I squeezed my hands together in my lap. "They trained some of their miners here as well, so there may also be undetonated mines."

Sidney turned to stare at me incredulously. "Does this Emilie *mean* to bump you off?"

I smiled weakly. "I don't know what her intentions are in bringing us here. There must be something she wants me to see."

He snorted in dissent but began to inch forward again.

"But even so," I added. "Let's leave the motorcar at the edge of the destroyed area."

A profound sadness overcame me as I gingerly picked my way through the dust of what had undoubtedly been a flourishing village before the war. This place where people had lived and loved and dreamed had been turned into mere fodder for the enemy's weapons. A quick glance at Sidney's face showed that he was digesting the same thoughts, though he seemed more inclined to anger than dismay.

We made our way through and around the heaps

of rubble and skirted by the craters, walking several feet apart so as to distribute our weight across a greater area. Except in a few places where the going was rough, and he assisted me over the loose rocks and debris. The air was too quiet. Not even a birdcall to break the silence. Tufts of plants had begun to reclaim the soil in spots, growing wildly amidst the ruins with a few of the ever-present poppies that seemed to spring up in seemingly the most improbable places— just as those flowers had in the battlefields of Flanders. Even so, these blossoms were late bloomers; but our spring and early summer had been cool.

It was a trail of these brilliant red poppies that led my gaze toward the wreckage of an aeroplane half-consumed by the ruin of a building. The aircraft must have been one of the last to fly over the area, for otherwise it would have been reduced to almost unrecognizable rubble like all the rest.

I pointed to it, and Sidney and I made our way through the debris field closer to it. I'd only stood near an aeroplane once before, but as then, I was astonished by how flimsy and insubstantial the flying machine seemed. Particularly knowing it carried men up into the heavens, holding them aloft with nothing to catch them should it fail.

I couldn't help but think of the aviator from whom I'd stolen the map case. In the haze of his drunken bragging, he'd admitted that if not for alcohol, he would never have had the courage to leave the ground. And he was one of Germany's crack pilots, with over twenty-five successful flights to his name. It was no wonder they'd kept the aerodromes stocked with kümmel.

"I'm no expert. But doesn't it look smaller than the aeroplanes we normally saw?" I offered hesitantly. "Even the Germans' little Albatrosses?"

Sidney nodded. "But who knows what aircraft they had in development by the end of the war?" He ventured closer, surmounting a pile of masonry as he leaned this way and that to examine the aeroplane.

"Careful," I gasped as his foot slipped, shifting the rubble beneath him. He paused, extending his arms to balance himself before continuing on.

I moved a few steps to the right on the more level ground to see the aircraft from a better angle. The single wing had buckled over the cockpit and the front had all but been crushed by stones, but the tail, marked with the Germans' black cross, was relatively unscathed.

"Didn't the lighter fighters, like the Albatross, usually escort the heavy bombers on their raids?" I asked, curious whether that was how this aeroplane had come to be here. But why would the swift, darting fighters be used on a practice run if the main goal was for the bombers to

354

improve accuracy? I supposed they could have proved a distraction for new bomber pilots, so they'd sought to acclimate them to flying through the heart of those dizzying dogfights. Though something had definitely gone wrong here.

When Sidney didn't reply, I glanced toward where he arched up on tiptoe to peer into the cockpit. The look on his face was pinched and drawn, and I cringed at the possibility some evidence of the pilot's battered body still remained.

"What was inside here, I can't say with any certainty," he said, glancing up at me over the wreckage. "But I don't think this was piloted by a human."

My eyes widened. "Why do you say that?"

"There's no space for a man. Unless he's the size of a child. And all the controls have been ripped out."

"They wouldn't have done that unless they wanted to salvage what was there because it was particularly exceptional, or . . ."

"They wanted to keep it from falling into the wrong hands," Sidney finished for me.

Neither of us had to say the words, for we were both thinking the same thing. It appeared Emilie's report of tales of a remote-controlled aircraft may have been based on fact after all, and not merely the usual German optimistic exaggeration.

I studied the aeroplane with new eyes, not sure I wanted to believe such a thing was possible.

"Of course," Sidney spoke up again, interrupting my horrified musings. "The controls might not have been removed by the Germans."

He was right. There was no way to know who exactly had confiscated them. Just as there was no way to know precisely what had been there for them to take.

But Emilie had wanted us to see this. I felt certain of it now. Why else send us here?

Now, what were we supposed to do with this information?

As if in answer to my silent question, something fluttered in the corner of my eye. I turned to see a piece of faded, yellow fabric billowing in the breeze. I was drawn toward it and noted that one end of the cloth appeared to be trapped beneath a rock next to the squat remnants of a wall. Somehow, I doubted it had survived this way for nearly a year since the village's destruction.

I was rewarded for my curiosity, for at the base of the wall I could see words written in English painted in stark white against the gray stone.

If you dare not grasp this, you should not seek me.

Another code.

I sighed and reached out to touch the stone with my gloved fingers, ruminating on her riddle. Something about the phrasing niggled at the back of my brain, but I couldn't recall why.

Behind me the crunch of Sidney's footsteps came to a stop. "Another message from Emilie?"

I rose to my feet. "Yes. Though I'm not quite certain how to decipher it."

Sidney leaned down to read the words before standing again. "Sounds like something from a poem."

"Yes, I had a similar thought." I chewed on my lip.

"Maybe Byron? Or Tennyson? Or Shakespeare?"

I glanced at him in amusement. "Or Chaucer or Wordsworth?" Poetry had evidently not been my husband's favorite subject if he was merely going to rattle off some of the most famous names.

He shrugged, accepting my teasing without complaint.

I felt a drop of water on my forehead and then another, and glanced up toward the sky. The rain that had been threatening all morning began to fall somewhat sporadically, almost as if it couldn't make up its mind.

But just in case it decided to begin in earnest, we began to make our way back toward the motorcar. It was as we passed a pair of red poppies sprouting on a grassy verge that the answer came to me.

"It's Brontë," I gasped.

"Emily?"

"No, Anne. 'But he that dares not grasp the thorn should never crave the rose.'"

"I see. She's the rose, since that's her real given name." Sidney opened the motorcar door for me. "But how does that tell us where to go?"

I frowned, arrested in thought. "'If you dare not grasp this,'" I murmured, turning my head to gaze out past Sidney's arm toward the trees growing in the distance, spared from Havay's destruction. "'This.' The thorn."

"I assume you can ponder the matter just as well *inside* the motorcar."

I glanced up to see humor glinting in his eyes as the rain fell softly around us. The sight of him smiling at me did something funny to my insides, making it difficult to breathe. And all of a sudden, I was arrested for an entirely different reason—struck mute by the fact that I'd feared I would never again see such a gentle expression on his face when he looked at me.

As if grasping the magnitude of this moment, his smile faded, but the tenderness remained. His hand lifted to cup my face, and I was certain he would have kissed me. Had the sky not decided right then to open up and pour.

He pulled back, ushering me inside the vehicle before he darted around to the other side through the cold deluge.

"Dash it all," he cursed as he fell into his seat.

Shrugging his shoulders, he tried to shake off the dampness.

I passed him a handkerchief so that he could mop his face.

"Well, I'm certainly awake now," he quipped.

Whether it was the gamut of emotions I'd run in the past twenty-four hours or our foiled kiss. Whatever the reason, he suddenly seemed impossibly handsome to me, even with his skin glistening and rain dripping from the brim of his hat. I was forced to clear my throat before I could speak, lest I make a cake of myself. "All the better to help me puzzle this riddle."

"The thorn, hmm? There isn't a village by that name, is there?"

"Not that I know of. Although . . ." I paused, as an idea took hold in my brain, becoming more plausible the longer I contemplated it. I sat forward in enthusiasm. "Of course. I'm not sure how they met, but surely it's possible."

"How who met?"

I swiveled to face him. "So 'the thorn' in French translates to 'l'epine.' And I just happen to be familiar with a Madame de l'Epine." I arched my eyebrows at the significance. "She hid me in her home in Tourcoing, near Lille, one night."

But rather than excitement, his face blanched. "That close to the rear of the German front?"

"Well, yes," I fumbled to respond. "Though

assignments that required me to be so close to the fighting were rare."

"Because they were dashed risky."

I didn't deny it. Security in those areas had been rigorous. If I had been stopped and they'd bothered to check their rolls of citizens, as an outsider I would have instantly been arrested or shot. But I wasn't about to explain myself now, nor the necessity of my being there.

"All that is not of the moment," I replied calmly. "But the fact that Emilie is possibly in Tourcoing is."

"So that is where you wish to go?" Sidney replied grimly.

I nodded, knowing full well what that meant for him.

He inhaled a deep breath as if to ready himself. "On to Tourcoing then."

Fortunately, as we traveled out of Havay, the rain ceased. Though the heavy gray clouds remained in place, threatening to drench us again at any moment. Some distance outside of Mons on the road to Tournai, in the hotly contested country fought over during the Allies' initial disastrous retreat in August 1914, we stopped at a café in a small village for coffee and sandwiches. Sidney was pleased to find the town had a supply of petrol, so he filled the motorcar's tank and performed some other maintenance with the help of a man with a booming laugh who had been a mechanic in the Belgian Army. All while a swarm of local boys clustered around him, buzzing excitedly like bees. They asked a hundred rapid-fire questions in their peculiar slang, all of which Sidney answered patiently, happy to find someone as interested in motorcars and engines as himself.

I smiled at the sight, amused by all of their boyish enthusiasm, and strolled down the street to the Hôtel de Ville. They professed they were delighted to let me use their telephone, and I rang up Captain Landau's office in Brussels. As was the case earlier that day when I'd called from the hotel in Maubeuge while waiting for Sidney to shave and gather his luggage, his secretary claimed Landau was not in. So I left another message stating I would telephone again when we reached our destination. She had no news for me, and while frustrated, I wasn't overly concerned. It might take some time for the agents in London to track down Pauline Laurent, and I was well aware that Captain Landau was busy with other matters. I trusted he would find a way to get in touch with me if the situation turned urgent.

Sidney had told me he would swing around with the Pierce-Arrow to pick me up at the town square, so I crossed the road toward the green space. Or what had once been green. But the grass was all but stunted, and I could only surmise the Germans had commandeered this square for their use like so many other places. Many of the trees were shorn in half, splintered by shells, but a few remained to offer their welcoming shade on hot days. I strolled down the pathway cutting diagonally across its center toward a statue in the middle, happy to stretch my legs after so many days spent in the motorcar. However, my contented idyll was short-lived.

As I neared the limestone figure, a prickling sensation began along the back of my neck. One I'd long ago learned to heed. I glanced about me slowly, as if surveying the park. There were a few other figures milling about, but none of them seemed to be paying me the slightest attention. I lifted my eyes to the buildings ringing the square that still stood, but there again I was foiled for it was impossible to see through the windows from such a distance. Nevertheless, I felt certain someone was watching me.

I continued through the square, ever mindful of those around me. When I saw the Pierce-Arrow approaching, I abandoned all pretense of ease and turned abruptly to scan the park behind me, hoping to catch them off guard. On the left, a tall man with his hat pulled low hurried away, passing behind two trees. I narrowed my eyes, trying to tell if any part of his walk or appearance seemed familiar to me.

Sidney leaned across to open the motorcar door, and I slid into the passenger seat.

"Drive around toward that direction," I instructed him, wondering whether we could intercept the man before he disappeared.

Sidney did as instructed, accelerating sharply around the square, but there was no such man in sight. Only a woman pushing a pram who leveled a fierce scowl at us. Sidney stopped short, allowing her to pass while I searched the buildings.

"Did you see someone?" he guessed.

"I don't know," I prevaricated, not wanting to speak the name of the person I thought it might have been. "Maybe. But I could have sworn someone was just watching me. And the man I saw move this way was too tall to be that fellow from Brussels who claimed to be Jonathan Fletcher."

I turned to find Sidney watching me, a shrewd look in his eyes.

"You don't have to avoid saying his name, you know. I promise I won't order you out of the car and drive away."

I inhaled past the tightness in my chest. "Well, you can hardly blame me. For a man who usually charges directly at difficulties, you've been doing a remarkable amount of walking away."

Something shifted behind his eyes, something bleak and heart-wrenching. He stared straight ahead through the windscreen, inching the motor-car forward again. "Yes, well, I'm not always certain I have complete control over myself any-more. It seems better not to risk it."

I could tell how much it had cost him to admit such a thing, and it only made the confession all the more distressing. For what could I say to that?

I knew the war had changed many men, and often not for the better. Those who would have never lost their temper or lifted a hand in violence, suddenly found it difficult to contain themselves even over the most trifling matters, let alone the larger ones. For them the war was still in the back of their heads, and the instincts and habits they'd fine-tuned over the years of conflict, in order to stay alive, could not be turned off in an instant. Even those who did not suffer from shell shock had nerves twisted and frayed, sometimes almost to the breaking point.

So many of them struggled to let go of the war. I'd wondered if Sidney was one of them, and now I knew.

Swallowing hard, I choked down the lump that had formed in my throat and reached over to gently touch his leg. I didn't dare look at him. I knew he didn't want that. And I feared if I did so, I might not be able to contain my brimming emotions.

For several moments, he didn't move except

for the actions required to drive his motorcar. But then his hand dropped to cover mine, squeezing it tightly before he relaxed his grip.

We fell silent as the village fell away and we ventured deeper into the open fields of the torn countryside. Much of it was still barren and fallow, trampled and mismanaged during the years of German invasion and occupation, or marred by shell holes. But here and there were encouraging signs of regrowth—the green leaves of sprouting potatoes and waving stalks of barley.

I had traveled through this area a few times, cutting across the country from Holland and Brussels toward the French border, often with the aid of a *passeur* or other guide, largely avoiding towns. The sight of this landscape now tugged at something inside me. I felt a peculiar sense of almost melancholy. Not for the war and all the danger involved, but perhaps for the purpose I'd felt.

"This would probably be a good time to tell you that I spoke with my friend at Scotland Yard," Sidney said.

I glanced up in surprise. "When?"

"I telephoned him this morning. I wanted to hear whether Pauline Laurent had revealed anything more when they questioned her. She did not."

"But . . . ?" I could hear the word fairly ringing in his silence.

His eyes darted toward me rife with cynicism. "But she's no longer at the address she gave them. He went to ask her a few more questions and the proprietress told him she'd departed some days before and most of her things were gone from her room."

I sat back, somehow not surprised. "Well, that's suspicious."

"To say the least."

"So why did she leave so quickly?" I contemplated. "And where did she go?"

As if in answer to that question, the crawling sensation along the back of my neck began again. I swiveled to look over my shoulder.

"There's another motorcar some distance behind us," Sidney said, correctly construing my concern.

"Has it been following us for long?"

"I didn't see it before our stop, but it might have been there." He flicked a glance into his wing mirror. "If either the sun would appear or the sky would get dark enough to force us to turn on our headlamps, it would help. As it is, the vehicle almost blends in to the horizon."

I scanned the road ahead of us, gnawing my lip in thought. Ahead of us, I saw a crossroad leading off toward the east. I pointed. "Turn here."

Sidney immediately complied, though he had to brake hard to do so. He slowly motored forward on the dirt lane while I turned in my seat, waiting for the other vehicle to appear. About a minute and a half later, a gray motorcar came driving down the road. But it didn't even brake, simply continued to move forward and carry on to the north, disappearing from sight.

I sank back into the leather, wondering what that meant, if anything. Perhaps, I was imagining things.

"Shall I turn around?"

I gestured incredulously to the muddy mires lining either side of the narrow road. "Where?"

"I'm sure I could manage it."

I arched a single eyebrow at him, not keen on the idea of watching him attempt such a feat. "Just keep going. We should be coming up on another road cutting back toward the north."

This proved to be a mistake.

CHAPTER 23

We did, indeed, find the crossroad cutting north. And it was wider than that single dirt lane. But about two miles from the turn, Sidney's motorcar suddenly began to hiss and splutter, and steam seeped from underneath the bonnet.

A ferocious scowl transformed his face as he pulled the Pierce-Arrow to a stop. "What's this? I just checked her over." He threw the vehicle into park. "Unless she jostled something loose on these rubbish roads."

I wisely remained silent as he climbed out, removed his coat, and rolled up his sleeves so he could look under her bonnet. He cursed, leaping backward as more steam billowed forth. Once it had cleared, he moved forward again to examine the engine.

"What is it?" I asked as he stomped toward the far side running board, muttering to himself.

I heard the clink and clatter of tools shifting about in the small storage box strapped there, and then a softly muttered oath. In the wing mirror, I watched as he threw down the rag he'd been wiping his hands with and then turned to pace away, his hands on his hips. After a moment, he retrieved the rag from the ground and returned to the bonnet.

But it wasn't long before he slammed it shut again and turned to me. "The radiator has sprung a leak." He stared up and down the empty road. In all the time we'd been parked there, not a single vehicle had driven by. "If I had my pliers, I could patch it long enough to get us back to civilization, but they appear to be missing, even though I saw them not three quarters of an hour ago."

"Oh, dear," I replied evenly, wondering if one of those animated boys might have had something to do with it, even if by accident.

He began unrolling his sleeves in sharp movements. "I suppose we'd better start walking."

I offered him a smile of commiseration and gathered up what I thought shouldn't be left behind and tossed it into the shoulder satchel where I'd stored some food and a bottle of cider. I couldn't help shooting an anxious glance up at the sky heavy with clouds. It was difficult to tell whether the light had grown dimmer because rain was imminent or daylight was merely beginning to wane. Sidney seemed to share my concern for he retrieved a blanket from the rear seat and draped it over his arm before taking the satchel from me to loop it over his shoulders.

We set off down the road toward the north.

There was little evidence of human habitation, and the homes and barns that did exist were badly damaged, or little more than charred remains. Yet more sins to lay at the advancing German Army's feet. Still the walk was easy, and I quickly found my stride again, even after almost a year's absence from this terrain.

Sidney marched along just as effortlessly, though I could tell he had adjusted his gait to match my shorter one. I worried the shoulder satchel might pull uncomfortably at the healed bullet wound in his chest, but he didn't appear to be troubled by it. Nevertheless, I was about to ask him about it when he spoke.

"I suppose you're accustomed to this?"

I looked at him in question.

He gestured broadly with his hand. "Walking cross-country like this. Though I suppose much of it was done at night." He sounded genuinely interested, but still I demurred.

"I never really got *used* to it. Not when I knew I could stumble across German soldiers at any moment." I glanced about me at the flat terrain. "After all, when they called out to you to stop, you had better do so."

"Weren't you afraid?"

I glanced up into his wide, troubled eyes.

"We heard the stories at the front, read the newspapers. I know they were censored and exaggerated, but, nevertheless, the Americans

370

didn't dub the Germans' actions 'The Rape of Belgium' for no reason."

I knew what he was really asking, and I sought to reassure him. "Of course, I was afraid. How could I not be? And yes, I was . . . pestered to a certain degree. As all the women were. And I didn't like it." I crossed my arms over my chest, feeling sullied even now. "I cried the first time it happened. But then I knew it could have been so much worse. And . . . and one simply had to carry on. The German command certainly wasn't going to stop their men from doing such things."

I inhaled a steadying breath, lowering my arms. "The best thing I could do, the only thing, was to complete the tasks assigned to me, and help to defeat them, and drive them out of Belgium. And in time, the acuteness of the terror faded. Didn't it for you?"

He frowned down at his feet. "Yes, I suppose so." Then he surprised me by adding. "Or perhaps it was more a matter that one stopped caring altogether."

His gaze lifted to my shocked one and his lips twisted in irritation. "Not that I was suicidal. Merely that it was easier to just follow orders and stop concerning yourself with everything else."

I could hear in his voice that he wished this was genuinely true, but I knew better. "Now why do I suspect that's a lie?"

His head turned abruptly taking in my gently chastising expression.

"Sidney, I've seen the way you treat your former soldiers. I watch how it tears you up to see their lost limbs and low spirits. I mean, for heaven's sakes, you faked your own death so that you could search for evidence to expose a traitor among your ranks! And you told off those two busybody ladies in that café for being insensitive." He opened his mouth to argue, but I cut him off. "*Not* that they didn't deserve it. But don't try to tell me you stopped caring."

When he didn't respond, I decided to push a little further.

"Somehow, I suspect you know the exact number of men you killed with your own hands," I murmured.

His face seemed to close in on itself, struggling to contain the dark emotions I sensed roiling underneath. But he didn't deny it, and I suspected that was as near a confirmation as I was going to receive. His shoulders seemed to bow, shouldering all the weight of that pain, that guilt, and I wished there was something I could do for him. Some way I could ease that suffering. But that was not my absolution to give.

"It was hell, Sidney," I said, knowing full well it was not enough. "All you could do was survive it and help as many of your men as possible survive it."

He didn't speak for a long time after that. We marched along with nothing but the rustle of the wind through the grass at the side of the road, and the honking cry of a flight of geese overhead to break the stillness, as the light continued to fade. But there was still one more thing bothering me, one more concern. Given all the other revelations of the previous evening and today, I finally felt brave enough to voice it.

"Do you really mind it so much, then?" I kicked a stray rock toward the verge of the road, feeling his gaze lift to look at me. "The fact that I worked for the Secret Service? Does it bother you?"

"Is that what you think?" His voice was more serene than I expected.

"I don't know what to think. But I see the way you look at me. I see the doubt, the uncertainty . . . and I can only wonder."

He blew out a heavy breath. "I suppose I have been doing that. But it's not that I doubted *you*. Or rather . . . it's that I doubted everyone." His mouth flattened into a humorless smile, recognizing he wasn't making sense. "I suppose I'm wary of being duped again."

I stiffened, but tried to follow his rationale. "Because of the war?"

He nodded. "All the bloody lies they told us to rationalize the loss of so many lives. All the bloody lies some of my closest friends and fellow officers told to hide the fact that they were committing treason." He halted and turned to me. "Once you began to reveal just what part you had played in the Secret Service, I started to wonder if I was being deceived again."

"And then last night I confirmed it," I whispered.

But he shook his head, reaching for my arm. "No, Verity. What happened between you and Xavier? That was different. I can see that now." He grimaced. "And I only have myself to blame for allowing you to believe I was dead." He leaned over me so that our foreheads nearly touched. "It doesn't mean I like it. But . . . I accept it."

I inhaled a ragged breath. "Thank you."

"Don't thank me," he insisted. "And don't for a minute think I'm not proud of the work you did during the war." His lips quirked upward at one corner. "It just took me a little while to come to terms with it, that's all. I'm afraid no man likes to hear his wife has placed herself in such danger, even for a good cause."

I smiled up at him, blinking back tears as emotion welled in my chest.

It was then that a rumble of thunder rolled in the distance. We turned as one to stare up at the sky, and I touched my cheek, swiping away a raindrop.

"We'd better find shelter."

Unfortunately, the only thing still standing within sight was an old barn about a quarter of a mile down the road. We hurried toward it, breaking into a run as the rain that had dogged us all day let loose. The blanket Sidney had brought and held over us did little to keep us dry. So by the time he pulled aside the door and we slipped inside, we were both sodden.

I struggled to catch my breath as I removed my hat from my head and shook it out. Turning to survey our surroundings, I discovered the barn was really more of a stable. One that was empty of any animals except perhaps some mice. The roof was damaged over the far end, allowing rain to pour through in a thunderous cascade, but at the front the shed remained dry.

Sidney's footsteps crunched on the dirt floor as he walked from stall to stall, pausing just outside the second on the left. "There's straw here, and it appears to be relatively fresh."

I followed him, watching from the entrance as he shuffled his feet through it, stirring up the earthy scent. "Perhaps one of the farmers nearby still uses the barn for his livestock."

Though where they were now was anyone's guess. Likely slaughtered for food.

"I'm not going to question how it came to be here," he said. "I'm just going to be grateful for it since it looks like we're going to be spending the night here." He spread the blanket over the wall of the stall to dry and dropped the satchel on the floor next to it. "I'll check the tack room for any supplies. Perhaps there's a set of tools I can use to fix the motorcar."

I removed my coat and hung it on the stall next to the blanket. I would dearly have loved to change into something dry, but we'd left our valises back in the Pierce-Arrow. Wrapping my arms around myself, I rubbed them trying to generate some heat against the chill. The thumps and clinks coming from up and down the aisle indicated where Sidney was, but instead of following him, I moved back toward the main door.

As darkness fell, the rain drummed against the earth, falling in a curtain that obscured much of the world beyond. An ache began in my breast, like the one I'd felt the last time I'd stood alone this way, watching just such a rain. Though then it had been through a window in Rotterdam, not a barn door somewhere in Belgium, and the man with me was not my husband. The pain was so acute I closed my eyes, wondering if the weather had conjured the memory or our words on the road.

Sidney joined me, pausing just behind my shoulder. The warmth radiating from him penetrated through the thin fabric of my summer blouse and skirt. I thought he might speak, that he might tell me what he'd discovered in the tack room. If he had, it might have broken the spell. But he merely stood behind me, silently watching the rain.

"When you died, I had to stop myself from feeling or else go mad," I began hesitantly, trembling slightly at the confession. "I . . . I'd already started to numb my mind with gin, but I couldn't stop myself from physically wanting you. And I thought . . . maybe . . . if I wanted someone else, maybe it would make it stop." I exhaled a ragged breath. "It wasn't until after that I realized what a bloody fool I'd been. That I would never stop wanting you." My voice broke on the last as I finally turned to face him. "Not until the day I died."

His face was filled with such poignant yearning, such desire, that I couldn't withhold anything from him as his mouth claimed mine. I couldn't breathe for wanting him so badly. And apparently, he felt the same, for his kisses and caresses were like a fever.

I didn't even think of resisting when he pulled me into the stall and laid me down on the blanket he spread over the soft hay. Because for the first time since his return from the grave, there was nothing between us but the sweat of our own skin.

Later, we lay wrapped in the warmth of each other, the woolen blanket rasping against my still flushed skin. We stared up at the dark ceiling, beyond the glow of the lantern Sidney had found, as the rain continued to fall outside. His fingers toyed with my hair, and I inhaled the scent of his skin and the crushed straw, and savored the contentment seeping into my limbs.

Perhaps I should have halted his advances, but it seemed fitting somehow that we should find each other again in such a humble place. For all that we were wealthy Londoners, we had both lost whatever pretensions we'd clung to during the long years of war. We'd both witnessed the worst and best of man. We'd both roughed it, sleeping in such lowly hovels as trench dugouts and barns. Perhaps it was in these unassuming spaces that we were truly ourselves.

In any case, I was not going to regret it now. Not when I felt fully connected to Sidney for the first time since his disappearance, since before the war. Perhaps even earlier than that. For there was a depth to our relationship now that the naïve eighteen-year-old girl I'd been could not have achieved. For the first time in a long time, I felt a sense of permanence being with him. I realized in the back of my mind I'd formed contingency plans, planning my course of action should the damage to our marriage prove irreparable. But in the space of the last hour, I'd let those go.

As if he'd been contemplating the same thing,

he turned his head to press a kiss to my temple. "I hope you don't mind I didn't take precautions."

By unspoken agreement, we'd taken steps to prevent my becoming pregnant until we'd worked out our differences. While I might not have rushed to this step so quickly had the necessary items not been back in the motorcar, I was also not upset.

"No, I don't mind."

"It may not even matter," he remarked off-handedly. "It never happened before."

I stiffened, not having planned on sharing this here.

He pulled his head away from mine to see into my eyes. "Has it?"

My gaze dropped to his chest, where my fingers combed through the dark whorls of his hair. "Once. Briefly. It was over before I could tell you. And then . . . well . . ." I risked a glance up at him. "You were different the next time you had leave from the front, and I decided not to tell you. Not then, at least." I shrugged. "And then you died."

He stared down at me a moment longer, before pulling me close again. "Oh, darling," he murmured into my hair. "I'm sorry."

I clung tightly to him, absorbing his strength. "Me, too."

We lay like that for some time, but I couldn't brush aside the urgency of our situation for long.

Especially now that we were stranded without his motorcar.

"Did you find any tools in the tack room?" I asked.

His cheek was pressed against my forehead, and I felt him smile. "Back to business, is it? I feel like I should take offense," he jested, and then more seriously. "No, I didn't. Nothing useful to our predicament at any rate."

"You said you checked the motorcar over at our last stop, and that your tools were all accounted for then?"

"Yes."

"Did you step away from your motorcar at any point?"

He rolled so that he faced me. "Are you trying to suggest it might have been sabotage?"

"It just seems highly suspicious that such a thing should happen when you just checked the engine, and the particular tool you should need to fix the problem should be missing."

"I'm not trying to refute you. I had the same thought."

"Then you did step away for a moment?"

He nodded. "And either that mechanic or one of those boys could have tampered with the radiator."

"But why?"

"I can't answer that." He arched his eyebrows. "Unless someone convinced them to do so."

"Someone who doesn't want us to reach Emilie," I finished for him. "Or at least wants to delay us." I frowned. "But for what purpose?"

"That is the question, isn't it?"

How long I'd been sleeping, I didn't know, but something woke me with a start. I lay still, searching the shadows overhead as I listened for the sound that had roused me. A few moments later, I heard it again. It was a sort of thud, followed by a splashing sound.

I rolled my head to look at Sidney, relieved to see he was already awake. He lifted his hand to keep me from speaking, before slowly sitting up. The night being too cool, and our position exposed, we had re-dressed before falling asleep. Now I was glad of it.

We both strained to identify the sound. At some point, the rain had stopped, and a hush had fallen over the barn.

There it was again—a sort of sloshing sound. I began to wonder whether there was a downspout somewhere, but the noise appeared to move along the outer wall, not remaining fixed.

That was when a subtle smell assailed my nostrils. I wrinkled my nose in distaste before sitting upright in horror, for I recognized it. Kerosene.

CHAPTER 24

S idney grabbed my hand. "Come on."

He passed me our shoulder satchel and then peered around the edge of the stall. Tugging me forward, we inched along the wall toward the door. A few steps outside the entrance stood a man. In the darkness it was difficult to tell who he was, but he seemed familiar. Something in his fidgeting stance reminded me of someone.

Sidney palmed his pistol, frowning fiercely. I could tell he was tempted to rush him, but though we knew at least one other man was out there dousing the barn, we had no way of knowing how many others we couldn't see. Whatever the odds, we weren't going to escape that way without being seen and plausibly shot at. So I trusted he knew what he was doing when he pulled me deeper into the barn. Sure enough, in a stall closer to the far end, one of the boards was missing from the bottom of the outer wall, and the others were rotting away.

He began kicking at those boards with his heel, widening the gap through which I could see the outside. The smell of smoke assaulted my nose, and I glanced behind me, searching for flames. When the space seemed wide enough, he knelt and cautiously peered out. Pulling his head back inside, he urged me to scramble through.

The scent of kerosene was strong, and I realized I was crawling through a puddle of it. Stumbling forward, I kneeled in the sodden grass several feet away, scouring the length of the barn as Sidney struggled to squeeze his larger frame through. Once he was free, we wasted no time in making a hasty retreat deeper into the field. The clouds above obscured the moon, and I prayed whoever was behind us setting fire to the barn did not see us running away.

Several hundred feet from the structure, Sidney pulled to a stop and we swung around to see what was happening. Flames licked up the front of the stables over the space where we'd slept, slowly spreading over the wood. At the corner near the main door, we could see at least two silhouettes watching it burn. Two men who obviously expected us to be inside, burning along with it, for there was no urgency in their movements.

I tugged against Sidney's hand, pulling him away. There was no use in attempting to confront them now. They would see us coming long before we could do anything to stop them, unless he planned to crawl on his belly through this muddy field. It seemed best for now to let them believe we were dead. And that meant we needed to flee further before that entire barn went up in flames, illuminating the night for some distance.

We stumbled forward as quickly as we dared so as not to risk either of us being hampered by a twisted ankle or worse. Every once in a while, one of us would glance behind us to be certain we weren't followed. However, when the darkness closed in around us again like a comforting blanket, and it became obvious we had escaped without being seen, we slowed our steps to a walk.

At the edge of a tiny stream, I asked to stop in order to catch my breath. Sidney turned with hands on hips to watch the inferno in the distance, but I kept my gaze resolutely away from it, allowing my eyes to fully adjust to the blackness of night. Wiggling my fingers inside my gloves, I studied the rise and fall of the land and the landmarks I could see.

The stream formed a large arc in the middle of the field before continuing westward. Rather helpfully, the moon peeked through in snatches as the clouds scuttled by overhead. It was during one of these short intervals that I noticed the copse of trees about three quarters of a kilometer distant from us, toward which the stream flowed.

"This is perhaps going to sound unbelievable, but . . ." I glanced at Sidney. "I think I recognize where we are."

He stepped closer as I lifted my arm to point toward the trees.

"If I'm right, then there's a house on the other side of that wood. I rested there one day with a downed British pilot we were endeavoring to guide to Holland. It may not be stocked like it was during the war. In fact, it probably isn't. But there's a chance there may be fresh clothing and tools to fix your motorcar." I paused, grimacing at the thought. "If those men didn't fire that as well."

"Don't even say it," Sidney snapped.

I lifted a hand to his arm in commiseration. I knew how attached he was to his Pierce-Arrow.

He sighed in resignation. "Lead on, then. What do we have to lose?"

I turned to follow the course of the stream and Sidney fell into step beside me, taking the satchel from me.

"Who do you think those men were?" I asked, wondering who had attempted to kill us. The thought made my stomach quaver now that we were further from the danger. "You got a better look than I did. Did you recognize the man by the door?"

From his answering silence, I could tell he did. "It was the man we confronted in Liège. The one who claimed to be that author."

"Jonathan Fletcher?"

"I should have pummeled his lights out then," he growled.

"But why? Who is he really?"

He shook his head. "I don't know."

"And who was with him?"

"I don't know that either," he snapped angrily. "Maybe that fellow in the mask you saw on the boat. Or perhaps it was Xavier come to finish us off."

"You don't have to snarl at me," I retorted, lengthening my stride to charge ahead of him.

Unfortunately, with his longer legs he had no problem catching me up.

"I didn't ask for any of this to happen. But it is proof that there's something wrong. Something very wrong. Why else would someone wish to kill us?"

He grunted his agreement. "Well, whatever the reason, I suppose we should be glad their preferred method of murder is setting fires. After all, there are a lot more effective ways to kill someone."

I nearly stumbled. "You're right. The fires all do seem to connect to one another. First the attempt on Emilie, then Madame Zozza's death, and now this. Killers do tend to stick to the same modus operandi. It's what they know."

Sidney turned to look at me, and I could practically hear the thoughts in his head spinning, wondering where I'd learned such a thing, but now was not the time to elaborate.

As we entered the copse of trees, our steps slowed as we cautiously picked our way through them. I drew to a stop when the house with three gables came into view through the branches. All was dark and quiet, but that was to be expected in the middle of the night. We approached silently, alert for the slightest indication that anything seemed off.

The entrance to the house was through a little door in the left gable, and as I drew near I noticed the windows were still boarded up. If someone had intended to return here, they'd either been unable or elected not to. I moved to open the door, but Sidney stopped me with a hand on my arm, insisting on going first. Holding his pistol at the ready, he stepped through the threshold. I glanced behind us, scanning the trees before following him inside.

The door opened into a spacious room which seemed to echo with loneliness at its abandonment, just as it had during the war.

"Stay away from that corner," I directed Sidney as I moved toward the large stone fireplace, its carved ornamentals shrouded in dust. "Some of the floorboards and wooden wall panels are crumbling with rot."

I reached for the door of the cupboard to the right of the hearth, its rusty hinges complaining from disuse. Inside it appeared like the normal wooden interior of a closet, but I knew better. Bending over, I pushed against the back wall near the bottom. It swung inward as the top swiveled outward, with the pivot at the center of the wall.

I glanced back to find Sidney leaned over watching me. "Close the cupboard door and follow me."

He did as he was told, crawling after me into a dark, eight-by-eight square room. Underfoot crunched hay strewn across the floor. Once he was through, I let the wall drop back into place and reached up and then down to shoot bolts into sockets in the ceiling and floor, preventing anyone outside from opening the hidden door.

"Very clever," Sidney proclaimed, examining the mechanisms.

"Yes, it came in quite handy at times for our agents. The local German patrols and gendarmes liked to stop in this house to warm up, never knowing there was a secret room just beyond the cupboard, hiding the enemy."

He turned to look around at the hay-strewn space, its only contents a few boxes, an old carriage lamp I was lighting, and a partially burned candle. "But what if they discovered you were here? Wouldn't you be trapped?"

I shook my head, striding toward one of the far corners and bending over to search for the rope buried by straw. "This is a trap door leading into the cellars. And then from there one could escape through a grating in the outer wall."

"This space was well-planned."

I couldn't help but chuckle at the impressed

tone of his voice. "Well, I don't know who precisely to credit with the design. Perhaps it was here before the war. Either way, we put it to good use."

I knelt to rummage through the boxes, eager to be free of my kerosene-soaked skirt. Fortunately, there were a few ragged items of clothing—an old gray skirt for me and a pair of brown trousers. They were hardly ideal, but given the alternative, I was happy to have them.

Sidney seemed of the same mindset, swiftly exchanging his pungent, wet bottoms for the ragged pair. Though he did sigh rather heavily to see they were at least three inches too short for his frame.

The first box also contained a blanket, and he located a small collection of tools in the other, including a pair of pliers. So with that matter sorted, we bedded down together on a mound of hay for whatever remained of the night.

I'd only just settled comfortably when I heard his breathless snorts of suppressed laughter. Sidney struggled for a few more moments, before I glanced over at him where he lay on his back.

"What is so funny?"

He cleared his throat. "Nothing. It's just . . . I used to lie awake during the war sometimes aching for you. But I didn't expect when I returned that I would find myself lying awake beside you aching in every *other* muscle." He guffawed.

I rolled over to swat him. "Sidney."

He wrapped his arms around me, pulling me close even as he still trembled with laughter. I stared up at him in disapproval, though it was almost certainly foiled by the smile that tugged at the corners of my lips.

In the windowless room it was difficult to tell how much time had passed. It was surprisingly warm and cozy. I recalled thinking the same thing the last time I'd stayed there. Though, at the time, I'd believed it was exhaustion that made it so. Perhaps it still was.

Whatever the case, some hours after our arrival I was woken by the sound of the cupboard door opening. I sat upright almost at the same time Sidney did. He began to scrabble for his pistol, but I placed a hand on his arm and shook my head. With the bolts in place, no one could open the secret door. *If* they even knew it was there.

That was the question. For it could well be a passing traveler, searching for a warm place to rest. Or just someone exploring the vacant house.

But if they knew about the secret door and this secret room, well, then that signaled something quite different. Either someone privy to the knowledge had shared it with an outsider, or someone working with the intelligence networks in Belgium during the war was outside that door.

I had a difficult time believing the timing of such a visit did not indicate the latter.

Something scraped against the wall, as if feeling along it. My heart lodged in my throat as I glanced at the trap door, wondering if we would have to attempt to flee. If the men from the barn had realized we'd escaped, perhaps they'd guessed where we'd gone and planned to set the house ablaze as well.

So when someone suddenly rapped on the wall as if paying a call at the door to our flat, it was understandable that I should jump.

"Verity, Sidney, I know you're in there."

My eyes met my husband's. Both of us recognized the voice.

"Let me in. I have information you need."

Sidney arched a single eyebrow in skepticism.

When neither of us answered, he spoke again in a wry voice through the wall. "You can't think I mean you any harm."

I frowned, whispering to Sidney. "What should we do? We can't just sit here."

It was his turn to glance toward the trap door, but I shook my head in impatience. "If he knows about the secret door, then he likely knows about the second exit."

He sighed, but reached over to light the carriage lamp, and I blinked at the muted glow.

"Verity?"

I looked to Sidney, and he nodded.

"Just a minute, Alec," I snapped back, not wanting him to think for a moment his presence was welcomed.

"You open the door," Sidney murmured in my ear after positioning the lamp where he wanted it. He drew his pistol, standing in the shadows as he leveled it at the spot where Alec would emerge "But stay to the side as he crawls through."

I wanted to trust he wouldn't shoot him unless it was absolutely necessary, but given our trio's complicated history, I would be lying if I didn't say I harbored doubts. Sidney noticed my hesitation and cast his black scowl my way. Lifting up a prayer that there wouldn't soon be blood on my hands, I reached down to release the first bolt and then stood on tiptoe to trigger the second.

Just as I stepped to the side, the wall swung inward and Alec's dark head poked through. He shimmied through the opening, only to rise to his feet to find Sidney's Luger pointed in his face.

His mouth twisted into a sardonic grin. "So that's how it is, is it? Though, I suppose I can't blame you given the night it appears you've been having."

"Search him," Sidney told me.

I thought about arguing, for the last thing I wanted to do was run my hands over the body of the man I'd told my husband less than thirty-six hours before that I'd slept with when I'd believed he was dead—all while my husband looked on. But he was right. We didn't know if we could trust Alec. It would be foolhardy in the extreme not to confiscate any weapons he might be carrying. Not that I didn't think he could be equally as deadly with his fists if the situation called for it. But the less options for him to do harm, the better.

It didn't help that Alec seemed to find the entire exercise a colossal joke. "Is this retribution for that time I had to search you?" he quipped as I slid my hands over his arms and then along his torso, harking back to our first meeting at the Kommandantur in Brussels.

"It's not retribution if you're still enjoying it and I'm not," I retorted, amazed at his cheek in flirting with me in front of my husband. Then again, he didn't know that Sidney now knew about us.

"Ah, right," he murmured, though the gleam in his eyes clearly communicated he thought I was lying.

I rolled my eyes as I knelt to search down his legs, doing so more roughly than was necessary. Lifting up his right trouser hem, I extracted a dagger from a holder attached to his ankle and sank back on my heels to hold it up for both men to see. I arched my eyebrows pointedly at Alec.

"Did you honestly think I would be completely unarmed? I had no idea what I would be walking into after seeing that blazing inferno of a barn in the distance from the main road. And then when I spotted what a wreck they made of Sidney's Pierce-Arrow."

I withheld a gasp, though I couldn't stop from turning my head to look at Sidney. The dim light of the carriage lamp cast stark shadows over his features, making his hard jawline even more pronounced, as well as the anger glittering in his eyes.

"Is he clear?" he bit out.

"Yes, just the knife," I replied, rising to my feet.

Sidney lowered his pistol, transferring it to his left hand as he approached.

"Well, now that that unpleasantness is over with . . ." Alec began, only to be cut off by Sidney's swift punch to his face.

CHAPTER 25

Alec was knocked back into the wall, which wobbled from the impact, the bolts not having been thrown back in place. I stared wide-eyed at the two men, braced for them to come to blows. But instead of continuing to pummel him, as he'd clearly caught the other man off-guard, Sidney backed away, shaking his hand twice before lowering it to his side.

Alec regained his balance and pressed a hand to his lip, which was stained with blood. "Don't blame the messenger, old chum," he drawled, perfectly sanguine about the entire altercation. He rolled his jaw. "I didn't know you were unaware they'd torched your car." But in the silence that fell, his eyes darted first to mine and then Sidney's, dawning with understanding. "Ah. I guess you told him."

I nodded.

"Sorry, old chap," he replied affably, as if he were apologizing for beating him at cards and not adultery with his wife. "She never would have looked my way if we hadn't believed you were dead." He shrugged, checking his lip for blood again before reaching into his pocket for a handkerchief. "Even then, she was still in love with you."

My cheeks heated at the realization my feelings had been so evident. Having this discussion was slightly akin to a nightmare, and I was eager to be done with it.

Fortunately, so was Sidney. "Why are you here?" he demanded. "And what is this information you have that is so important you tracked us down to tell us?" He didn't bother to hide his mistrust.

I thought Alec might take offense at that, but he brushed it off like all the other slights. I supposed spending four years posing as a German officer had taught him how to ignore insults quite effectively.

"After I separated from you in Liège, I couldn't stop thinking about the matter, so I decided to do a little investigating of my own." His expression turned serious. "And what I discovered convinced me you might be in danger."

"How did you know where to find us?" Sidney charged, still dangling his pistol at his side.

"You kept tabs on us through Captain Landau's office?" I guessed, having already deduced that was how he'd known where to send his last message.

He nodded. "I was already on my way to find you when I checked in with the office in Brussels and discovered you were headed to Tourcoing. I saw the flames from the road, and decided it was too much of a coincidence not to investigate. And then when I saw the state of that beautiful Pierce-Arrow . . ."

Sidney winced.

"Well, I knew something must have happened to you. But if you escaped, you would likely make your way here."

I crossed my arms over my chest, scrutinizing his features. "I didn't know you were aware of this house."

His lips creased into a tight grin around the handkerchief still pressed there. "I'm aware of a great many things." He tilted his head. "Like the fact that Monsieur Dewé and Monsieur Chauvin do not trust me. I suppose because of the role I played during the war. And that is why Monsieur Chauvin pretended he wished to show you his orchids so that he could tell you what Madame Moreau discovered about the Germans' wireless-controlled aeroplane."

I dropped my arms to my sides in surprise. "You knew about that?"

He nodded. "But what Chauvin and even Captain Landau don't know is that the British Royal Flying Corps had already successfully developed such an aircraft and tested prototypes earlier in the war."

"What?"

"But why did we never hear of such a thing? Why wasn't it put to use?" Sidney demanded.

"Because the craft was never perfected." He removed the handkerchief from his mouth, stuffing it back into his pocket. "And because the top brass lost interest."

Sidney huffed as if that explained a lot. "Then why was British Intelligence so anxious for Madame Moreau to uncover more information about the Germans' invention?"

I already knew the answer to that. "They needed to know how far along the enemy was in developing it. Whether it was a cause for concern or little more than a concept."

Alec held up his hand. "Don't get me wrong. The concept is still valuable, no matter where it comes from. Especially if the inventor was able to work out the difficulties the British scientists and engineers were struggling with. Someone could sell that information for a pretty penny."

My gaze lingered on Alec's face, somewhat surprised to discover he was more knowledgeable of intelligence matters than I'd realized. That or he had a lot of highly placed friends. Though they were both captains, he certainly outranked Landau in some unilateral way.

"Is that what you believe happened?" I asked him. "That someone is after that information, and they think Emilie has it?"

"I'm only saying I'm guessing that's one of

your suspicions given your visit to Havay, and that it's possible. Though not necessarily for the reason you think."

I glanced at Sidney, wondering what he thought of this disclosure. He still glowered at Alec, but he appeared to be mulling over the matter.

However, Alec's revelations were not complete. "I also thought you would find it interesting that Landau was in London the morning Madame Zozza, one Mona Kertle, was killed."

A sinking feeling began in my stomach. "That's something he failed to mention. Though not incriminating on its own. After all, weren't you there as well?"

His eyes sparked with amusement. "*I* was not."

My and Sidney's gazes met in confusion.

"I take it that's one of the reasons for your charming welcome," Alec drawled flippantly. "The fire happened the morning of the eighth, did it not? Well, I was in Paris until the evening of the ninth when I traveled back to London, where I chatted with your friend, the Earl of Ryde, in the War Office the afternoon of the tenth."

I supposed that meant he couldn't have been the one to kill Madame Zozza. At least, not directly. After all, we knew that somehow the man masquerading as the author Jonathan Fletcher and a compatriot of his were involved, whether as the main culprits or henchmen.

But Alec had never struck me as the type to

399

involve others in what must be done unless it was necessary. More people meant more loose lips, loose ends, and potentials to be caught. For instance, when we'd copied that codebook, he'd only asked for one person to assist him, though a dozen could have copied the book in one night. The thought of that bumbling Mr. "Fletcher" being employed by suave, careful Alec was laughable.

When the silence stretched too long, some of the humor faded from Alec's eyes to be replaced by something hard. "There were numerous witnesses, should you need to speak with them."

I shook my head, brushing aside the matter for the moment. "What else did you discover about Captain Landau?" I asked, knowing him well enough to tell there was more. Otherwise he would never have raised the guise of Landau having been in London the day Madame Zozza died.

He dipped his head, as if in approval. "I always did like that about you, Verity. You never let me dither around the point."

I arched a single eyebrow, indicating that's exactly what he was doing now.

His eyes flicked to the pistol in Sidney's hand, his voice strained at the edges. "Are you going to put that away now?"

He narrowed his eyes in challenge. "Does it make you nervous?"

"My good nature lasts longer than most, but there gets to be a point when having another chap feel the need to have his weapon drawn becomes an insult."

Sidney looked to me, asking my opinion, and I nodded. I didn't think Alec meant to harm us. At least not here, not now.

He studied the man across from him a moment longer and then slid the pistol into the pocket of his coat.

Alec seemed to relax by a degree. "Landau never reported the threats to the members of La Dame Blanche. He also scarcely mentioned the potential for reprisal by German loyalists in his dispatches."

"And yet he seemed to make a particular point to mention that to me," I murmured, thinking back over our conversation in his office in Brussels.

"I noticed that as well."

I dipped my head to stare at the hay-strewn floor. Could Landau be behind all this? Madame Zozza's death, the attempts on Emilie's life and mine, Emilie's subsequent decision to go into hiding? It seemed impossible. The man I had known and worked with upon occasion in Rotterdam during the war had not seemed capable of such deception, of such cold-bloodedness. But then again, it was often those who seemed least capable who proved to have the greatest aptitude at it. That had certainly proved true during our last investigation.

"So, he needs me to find Emilie so that he can obtain whatever information she has on the Germans' wireless-controlled aeroplane?" I speculated aloud. "But then why did he try to kill us last night when he was content to merely follow us before? We haven't found Emilie yet, so why the sudden escalation to violence?"

I felt sick at the idea that my former commanding officer, a man I'd considered a friend, had been the second man outside the barn. Or that he'd ordered such an action. But I also couldn't help but note that he had not been in his office in Brussels either of the last two times I telephoned him. He easily could have caught up with us in Maubeuge, where he predicted we would need to spend the night.

Alec shrugged. "Perhaps he was worried you were too close to the truth. People under the strain of detection often make mistakes."

"Or maybe he was anxious we'd discovered something he hadn't planned on. Something at Havay." The grave look in Sidney's eyes made it clear he was thinking of something in particular.

"That crashed aeroplane?" I asked.

"Yes, but more specifically that something was missing from it."

"The wireless equipment?"

"Maybe."

But the hesitancy with which he spoke and the look he shared with Alec told me there was something I hadn't deduced yet.

"What else was missing?"

His gaze met mine squarely. "The bombs."

I shook my head in confusion. "I assumed the aircraft must have already dropped them, otherwise wouldn't it have exploded when it crash-landed?"

"Not necessarily. There have been plenty of aeroplanes that managed to make distressed landings without detonating their incendiaries."

"But how can we know?"

"We can't. Not for sure."

The room seemed to echo with that knowledge as a new and more horrifying possibility opened before us. If there were bombs missing from that plane, then where were they? And if someone was willing to kill to keep that knowledge secret, then what were they intended for?

Naturally my thoughts went to the bombing at the Blankenberge Police Station, which I assumed had been done with a small incendiary considering the low number of casualties. The explosion caused by a shell the size the aeroplane would have carried would create a crater.

"I was led to believe there were still unexploded shells all over at the front," I said, still trying to come to terms with it all.

"There are," Alec confirmed. "But many

of them are buried, and likely to go off at the slightest touch. And the ones that are known of are monitored, as are any still left in the towns and villages stretching across the area. However, Havay is not."

For someone looking to cause trouble, the situation couldn't be more ideal. But how did that connect to Landau? Or didn't it?

"We need to get to Tourcoing and find Emilie," I stated decisively, a sense of urgency surging through me.

"I have a motorcar out front," Alec offered, reminding us that Sidney's beloved Pierce-Arrow would not be taking us anywhere. "I would be happy to give you a lift." His eyes dipped to the skin exposed above Sidney's socks. "I can also lend you a pair of trousers, mate."

Sidney started to scowl, but then relented almost wearily as he tugged at the seat of his trousers in a rather ungentlemanly manner. "Yes, I would be most grateful."

On the chance that any of our belongings had survived the fire, we drove past the still smoldering wreckage of the Pierce-Arrow, but all had been consumed. So we pressed onward toward the north, pausing at a café in Tournai to eat, and find me and Sidney a change of fresh clothes. After scrubbing my hands and face, and donning a blouse with cobalt blue polka dots and a black serge skirt, I felt revived, and went in search of a telephone.

We had decided to risk calling Landau in Brussels, and that I should be the one to do it. For one, I wanted to discover if he was in the office rather than gallivanting across the Belgian countryside setting things ablaze. I was conscious of the possibility I would be tipping him off to the fact that Sidney and I were still alive, but I thought it more imperative we discern his reaction to hearing my voice over the telephone. There was a strong chance he might give himself away.

When the call connected, I expected his secretary to fob me off again with some paltry excuse. So when she asked me to hold, for a moment I vacillated between remaining on the line and hanging up. Landau's voice came through the headset before I could decide.

"Verity, I'm afraid I don't have anything for you yet on Miss Laurent." He sounded bored, almost distracted. Papers shuffled in the background.

"Oh," was all I managed at first.

"Apparently, they haven't yet spoken with her. I'll press them on it. Did you make it to Tourcoing? Is there an address I may ring for you at?"

I recognized that Landau could be a more gifted actor than I realized, but I didn't think so. Not when so little time had elapsed between the secretary informing him of who was on the line and his answering. He was obviously in a hurry to end the call, his mind elsewhere. There wasn't a trace of anxiety in his tone.

So I made the split-second decision to trust him.

"We've run into a bit of trouble here," I said softly into the mouthpiece, turning my head so that the chemist who'd allowed me to use his telephone could not read my lips.

"What's that?"

"Someone tried to kill us."

This finally served to cut through the haze of his preoccupation. "Wait. What?!"

"I can't go into the details now. The pertinent thing is that Sidney and I are both fine. But I need some information from you. And I need it now."

Whatever he'd been fidgeting with before, he set aside, and I could sense his focus was fully directed at me. "Go on."

"What do you remember about the wireless-controlled aeroplane Emilie reported that the Germans were developing?"

"Not much." He seemed to exhale in frustration. "We asked her to uncover more information about it, but her next report said her informant had died."

"Did she give his name?" I asked as the line crackled.

"She called him Zauberer, but I'm not sure that was his name. In fact, I'm fairly certain it wasn't."

Given the fact that "zauberer" was the German word for "wizard," I suspected he was right.

"And she mentioned something about Buzancy."

Something about those two words tugged at my memory, but I couldn't recall why. "Wasn't there a German aerodrome in the Buzancy commune in the Ardennes of France?"

"Yes. One that was difficult to penetrate given its location."

"Right. I remember now. Once the Charleville platoon was established didn't they send out a flying squadron trying to establish a new branch in that direction?"

"Yes. Though ultimately, most of the information that came out of that area came through the train-watching posts along the rails in neighboring Vouziers, whose reports ran through the Chimay company."

It struck me then like a bolt to my brain why the words "Zauberer" and "Buzancy" seemed so familiar. They had been scrawled in the margin of one of the charts we'd pulled from that German aviator's map case. The aviator I'd met coming from the Moiliens' cottage north of Chimay. The same cottage where later we'd buried the map case and burned the papers we didn't send on to Holland. The same Mademoiselle Moilien who traveled to Macon after the war to confront the priest and likely Emilie.

I wondered if Emilie had gone searching for the reason those two words were scrawled in the margin or if she'd stumbled upon it later and remembered. Either way, all of it seemed too much of a coincidence for there not to be some greater connection. Particularly when one had been privy to the German ace's drunken rambling as I had.

As typical of men pleasantly oiled with alcohol, he bragged in a meandering manner about a number of things, including his skills as an aviator, the greatness of Germany, and how the war would be soon over, and the enemy would never know what hit them. At the time, I'd paid little attention to such boasting as most of the Jerrys were prone to do so from time to time, ever hopeful that each new push would crush the Allies. Just as I'd paid little attention to his mention of Havay, as I was already aware of the village's use as a testing ground for the Germans' bombers, and it was only natural an aviator would be familiar with it, too. I'd simply noted those things in my debriefing report when I returned to Holland and filed them away in the recesses of my brain.

But now I had to wonder if the pilot had known something about the wireless-controlled aeroplane, if somehow he'd been involved. Alec said he was dead, and I trusted his inquiry into the matter had been thorough. But there was one man connected to that situation we didn't know the fate of.

"It would have been good to get a bit more information on their invention," Landau was saying, oblivious to my thoughts. "But then the war ended. I suppose we may never know."

"This may seem unrelated," I said, cutting into this soliloquy. "But are you by chance cognizant of a man by the name of Moilien?"

At first this question was met with silence and I worried we'd lost our connection. But then over the crackle of the telephone line I heard his astonishment.

"If you're referring to an Étienne Moilien, then yes, I am. And given your question, I'm guessing you won't be shocked to hear there may be a connection to Emilie."

CHAPTER 26

"Had I known it would have any bearing on your search, I, of course, would have told you before," Landau hastened to assure me. "But, how could I?"

I felt a tingling along my scalp that we might finally be close to some answers. "Go on. How do you know Monsieur Moilien?"

"He came across the frontier into Holland. This was sometime in early 1918, oh, about the time of the Germans' big push. Made a lot of noise, demanding to speak to British or French Intelligence. Well, the French didn't want anything to do with him, not when he was drawing so much attention to himself." He sighed. "But I agreed to speak with him."

"What did he say?"

"He handed me a bunch of jumbled notes filled with random information, most of it not very useful, though some of it was definitely not common knowledge."

"Did he tell you how he obtained the information?" I smiled reflexively at the chemist, who must have sensed my growing excitement for he looked up at me from where he was making pills behind his counter.

"He said he was friends with a number of German officers. That his sister was the particular friend of a few. I asked him if his sister had fled Belgium with him, and he said she'd remained at their home outside Chimay. That he told her to continue to collect information while he delivered what they'd already discovered to us. He informed us they would work as spies for us."

"He meant to go back?" I gasped, stunned by the man's brazen ineptitude. Not only were the German Secret Police undoubtedly already aware of his presence in Holland and his visit to British Intelligence after the fuss he'd raised, but he would have missed a number of roll calls, so the Kommandant in Chimay was also aware of his absence.

"I had the same reaction and told him he would be arrested or shot if he returned to Belgium. But he insisted he knew what he was doing." In my mind, I could see Landau rubbing his forehead as I'd watched him do numerous times when confronted with other people's incompetence. "We, of course, declined his offer. The man could have been sent by the Germans, though his general incapability made that seem unlikely. But I'm sure you recall how it was. The enemy was always trying to fool us, sending us men masquerading as deserters or refugees who tried to sell us faulty information. And they'd grown craftier as the war dragged on." His voice had tightened with remembered frustration, and he sighed. "But whatever the case, I certainly wasn't going to trust him with even the minutest details of our intelligence networks, and I wasn't going to expose any of our other agents to him, either."

"How did Moilien react?"

"Oh, he was furious. He couldn't believe we weren't showering him with gratitude over his offer. He insisted we pay him for the information he gave us, and we did. Though it wasn't enough for his liking." His voice lowered. "Quite honestly, Verity, the man concerned me. He was erratic and a bit overzealous."

"Never a good combination in an agent."

"Precisely. If he wasn't already a German stool pigeon, I wondered whether he would go to them to offer his services just to spite us. So, I had one of our men follow him. But only as far as the wire, where he safely made his way across and back into Belgium."

"And that's the last you heard of him?" I asked, staring through the shop's window toward the café across the street where Sidney and Alec could be seen seated at a table. Every once in a while, one of them, usually Sidney, would dart a glance in the direction of the chemist.

He gave a short humorless laugh. "Oh, no. He came to see me again. In Brussels."

I clutched the mouthpiece tighter. "You saw him after the war?"

"Yes. He charged into my office and demanded we give him compensation for the time he spent in a German prison. Claimed he was captured while he was gathering information for us, so we owed him. I reminded him we had not authorized him to do so, that I had even tried to discourage him from returning to Belgium, that he was certain to be apprehended. But he would not listen. He called me a liar. And worse, he accused us of having him framed. That we tipped off the Germans, and that's why he was caught, not because of his own stupidity."

Was he caught because of the aviator's papers Emilie and I had burned in his hearth, or had his sister lied or misunderstood? Had they already intended to come for him because they were aware of his trip across the wire into Holland?

I heard his chair squeak as he sank into it. "I felt sorry for the fellow. I genuinely did. I don't know what they did to him, but it wasn't pleasant. He was cadaverously thin, one hand was misshapen, and he sported a nasty looking scar across the entire left side of his face. But he was never in our employ, and there was nothing I could do."

I stiffened at his description of the man's scarred face. For men often concealed such injuries behind a mask, and I had seen just such a man. Very recently.

Moilien was the man on the boat. I felt certain of it. The way he'd moved, how he'd hurried around the corner of the cabin.

In his mask he might have been following me long before that without my ever realizing it. With all the journalists and photographers hounding Sidney and me, attempting to snap our pictures and report on our *on-dits*, I hadn't exactly been paying particular attention until Madame Zozza's sham summoning forced them back into focus.

"Why are you asking about him?" Landau asked, confusion tightening his voice. "Do you think he's involved somehow?"

"I haven't time to explain. Not until I know more. But yes. Yes, I do. Will you still be in Brussels this evening?"

"I will. I usually let the telephone ring in the evening after everyone has gone, but if you intend to call, I'll answer it."

"Please do."

"But Verity, what is going on?" he demanded in concern, clearly hearing the alarm in my tone.

"I will tell you more tonight," I assured him, anxious to be on our way again. "Just know that my husband and Captain Xavier are with me." I rung off, thanking the kindly old chemist, and turned to hurry back across the street.

"I take it Landau was in Brussels," Sidney declared with wry amusement as I dropped into my chair. "Or were you waiting on that chemist to grind and crush the willow bark for some headache powder."

Eager to tell them what I'd learned, I ignored his pitiable jest. "Yes, Landau was in. And he actually had more pertinent information than I expected." I swiftly informed them what Landau had told me, minus a few details. "So it appears Monsieur Moilien may be the mysterious figure behind much of this. He's almost certainly familiar with Havay through his sister's gregarious aviator friend, and he had dealings with Emilie and me, no matter how brief." I took a sip of my now cold coffee and grimaced, setting it aside.

"I guess you've decided to trust Landau then," Alec said, stubbing out his cigarette.

"He's not our man. His manner was too natural, his reactions too genuine for him to be the culprit. Not to mention the fact that he was in Brussels. And . . . I saw Moilien on the ferry crossing from Britain."

Sidney's eyebrows arched. "That masked gentleman you thought you recognized?"

I nodded. "Why he's doing this, I don't know? Money? Revenge?" I shrugged and shook my head. "Whatever it is, Emilie may know. And she will hopefully know what he intends to do with those bombs."

"What of Pauline Laurent? If she's gone into

hiding, doesn't that seem suspicious?" Sidney pointed out.

"It does. But at this point, I have no idea how she fits into this plan. Perhaps she knew the Moiliens and agreed to help them without realizing what she was getting herself into. She and Adele Moilien would be about the same age."

"And who is this partner of Moilien's? The man pretending to be Jonathan Fletcher?" Sidney sat forward as if he was going to answer his own question. "You know, I think I may know a way to answer that."

Alec and I watched as he strolled across the street, entering the same chemist's shop I'd just vacated.

"What does he intend to do?"

I turned to look at Alec where he lounged, leaning to one side of his chair, his eyes narrowed against the glare of the sun. "We aren't the only ones with connections," I answered obliquely, having already deduced Sidney's objective.

Alec's eyes glinted with good humor as if to say, "Touché."

I reached for my handbag. "If you want to bring the motorcar around, I promise to not let him share his scoop until you return."

He chuckled, rising lazily to his feet. "As you wish, m'lady."

Either Sidney had been unsuccessful, or his

telephone conversation had not lasted long, for he soon hurried back across the street, reaching my side just as Alec's borrowed Porter pulled up to the pavement.

"Any luck?" Alec asked as he accelerated down the road toward the north.

Sidney swiveled so that I could hear him from my position in the rear seat. "I telephoned Rawdon, a war chum at Scotland Yard, and he recognized the fellow by description immediately. His real name is Peter Smythe. Apparently, this isn't the first time the chap has told people he's Jonathan Fletcher. He's done so a number of times to get out of sticky situations."

"*Illegal* situations?" I pressed.

"Some of them. Others are merely on the suspicious side. Like his following you. And Rawdon gathered he's a frustrated writer of some kind. But Smythe also has an arrest record that indicates he has no qualms about engaging in more . . . unsavory dealings."

"So he's a hired man, a torpedo, so to speak?"

"Sounds like it. Though if he knows about Moilien's plans with the bombs, he must also have his own beef with the war or Britain. Maybe he's a German sympathizer."

"One would think so, but some men simply have few scruples, and even less of a conscience," Alec countered almost wearily.

"There are not just men like that," I corrected

him, turning to stare out at the sun-dappled countryside.

If not for the sobering nature of our discussion and the seriousness of our quest, it would have seemed the perfect summer day. When I closed my eyes, just for a second, I could almost believe we were driving into the Sussex countryside for a picnic. But then Alec wouldn't be with us, and Sidney's Pierce-Arrow would still be all apiece.

I sighed one last breath of regret and then refocused on the problem at hand. Namely, finding Emilie.

The city of Tourcoing was situated along the Franco-Belgian border to the northeast of Lille, beyond Roubaix. Consequently, it had not suffered as greatly from the repeated bombings and shellings as the other two cities had. However, the occupation of the Germans had been just as harsh, and Tourcoing's main form of industry crippled. The entire area had been a renowned wool manufacturing center with thousands of looms and specialized equipment, all of which had been seized and carted away into Germany or smashed and burned.

I directed Alec to drive toward The Grand Place where the Church of St. Christopher still towered overhead, having somewhat miraculously survived the war with little damage except to its famous bells, which the Germans confiscated to melt down for bullets. It was a market day, so the square bustled with activity, perhaps more so given the reduced circumstances that continued in this area. I stood along the northern end in front of three small shops next to the Hotel Cygne, struggling to recall which shop I had called in to during my last visit to the city in order to make contact with Madame de l'Epine. The proprietors had definitely changed.

I swiveled to stare over the stalls of vendors across the square. Or else I'd gotten myself turned around. My gaze snagged on the church's tall steeple. No, this was the right place. I was sure of it.

Then I felt something brush up against my side and I instantly reached to secure my handbag. A lean-cheeked boy of about eight grinned impishly at me several steps away.

"S'il vous plaît, Madame Gabrielle. Par ici."

He turned to scamper onward before I could do much more than blink. I hurried to follow, trusting Sidney and Alec would either catch us up or I would find them again later. In any case, I could spare them little attention as the boy darted into a group of lads approximately his own age before they all scattered in different directions. I kept my gaze glued to the faded blue of his cap, watching it bob along through the crowd in front of me.

I wasn't entirely surprised Emilie had borrowed

this method from Madame de l'Epine to lead me to her. And I *did* believe it was her given the fact that the boy had used my code name. During the short few days I had stayed in Tourcoing on a time-sensitive assignment during the war, Madame de l'Epine had utilized just such a method to circumvent the heightened security the city was blanketed under given its location so close to both the front and the border with Belgium. The Germans' heavy guns had been so close to the city, I could remember the ground fairly quaking from the noise of their nightly bombardment of the Allies' lines.

The lad was devilishly quick, and I struggled to keep up with him as we meandered through the streets of the city. We passed the impressive edifice of the Hôtel de Ville with its French Renaissance architecture and dome, but after that I soon lost my bearings. Several times I feared I'd lost him around a corner or in the crowd of a busy street, only to see his mischievous grin flash over his shoulder, clearly enjoying this game.

At what point we doubled back to approach the cathedral adjacent to The Grand Place, I don't know, but the Gothic-style building of brick and stone loomed large at the end of the narrow alley the little imp darted into. Several feet into the shadowed passage, I stumbled to a stop, realizing he was no longer in front of me. I knew he'd scampered in here, but still I glanced behind me, wondering if I'd been fooled.

Sidney and Alec stood behind me, both having deduced the reason for my actions, for neither demanded explanations.

"Where did he go?" Sidney asked, expressing the same bafflement I felt.

"I don't know," I replied, advancing deeper into the alley. "He must be here somewhere."

As if in answer to my statement, a door to the left opened and a woman peered through. "Madame," she whispered, gesturing to me to come inside.

Her eyes widened at the sight of two men behind me, but I assured her they were with me. She nodded hesitantly but did not object.

She led us up a steep flight of stairs and then down a narrow hall to another. At the top of these, she paused before a door, rapping once sharply.

"*Entrez*," a voice called from inside and I hastened forward without any urging, for I already recognized that alto voice.

There, before the single window which looked out over the alley, stood Emilie. Or rather Rose Moreau, her real name, as I probably should begin calling her.

She glanced away from the window as I advanced into the room, her face creasing into a weary smile. "Ah, at last you have found me."

CHAPTER 27

I moved forward into the light of the window, grasping her forearms as I leaned forward to buss her on both cheeks. She appeared much as I remembered her, though there was now more gray in her hair than brown, and the lines bracketing her mouth and eyes appeared deeper.

"Well, you certainly didn't make it easy," I replied in French.

She sighed. "Yes, well, I'd hoped to avoid such a thing. But Pauline always was one for theatrics, and my plan wasn't flashy enough for her."

"Wait. Pauline Laurent?" I felt like I'd been struck in the head and my mind was struggling to regain traction. "*You're* the one who asked Madame Zozza to pretend to summon you?"

"No. That was entirely Pauline's doing." She sniffed in affront. "As if I would ever do something so ridiculous. That girl was simply supposed to pull you aside and tell you that you might be in danger, and that I needed your help."

"Oh, only that?" Sidney drawled.

Rose and I both turned to look at him where he

stood in the middle of the room, Alec hovering at his elbow.

"I dare say this is your husband," she deduced.

He moved forward, accepting her proffered hand while I performed the introductions. They greeted one another cordially enough, though I could tell they were both taking each other's measure. Then Rose's mouth curled into a genuine smile, clearly realizing the same thing. "Good man," she murmured, patting his hand where it still clasped her other one.

A flash of amusement crossed Sidney's face before we all turned to Alec.

"And this is Captain Alec Xavier, one of my colleagues from the Secret Service," I explained. "He worked covertly in Belgium during the war."

She narrowed her eyes, scrutinizing him even more closely. Alec, for his part, was wise enough not to display his usual insouciance, sensing correctly that it would not endear him to her.

"As one of the Bosche, no?"

How she'd deduced he'd infiltrated the German Army, I don't know. Perhaps after observing his comportment, she'd discarded all the other usual possibilities as unlikely. Whatever the case, I could tell that for Alec her estimation had just gone up.

"Can he be trusted?" she asked me without removing her eyes from his.

I knew that for her, nothing short of a confident

answer would do, so I gave it to her despite my remaining reservations. "Yes."

Then she surprised me by addressing Sidney. "And what of you, Mr. Kent? Do you think he can be trusted?"

I turned to my husband, curious what he would say, and certain that whatever it was, Rose would heed it. Sidney did not respond at first, instead turning to study Alec with an air of almost detachment. But when his gaze shifted to meet mine, I could see that he was far from detached. The knowledge of my and Alec's past relationship flashed in his eyes.

But in spite of that, or perhaps because of it, I felt myself relax. Sidney had served as an officer on the Western Front. He had assessed the fitness of thousands of men, sized them up in the heat of battle when death was but a fingertip away. I realized I trusted him to make this call. That unlike during the war, it didn't all come down to my judgment alone. I could rely on him.

Whether Sidney understood I'd come to this epiphany or not, the lines at the corners of his eyes and mouth softened. He nodded to Rose. "Yes, I trust him."

Alec's face registered briefly with shock, something I wasn't sure I'd ever witnessed. It was immensely satisfying. Particularly knowing that my husband had caused it.

"Then let us sit down and I will explain what

424

this is all about," Rose declared, gesturing to the table and simple ladder-back chairs, which were the only furniture in the floral wallpapered room other than a narrow bed and battered chest.

"What of Madame de l'Epine?" I asked as we sat. "Will she be joining us?"

Rose shook her head. "I'm afraid not. The good woman died just a week before Tourcoing was liberated."

"Oh, how sad," I replied, having known the older woman was battling a grave illness. And yet, still she had done all she could for the Allies and her fellow countrymen.

"But I trusted you would decipher my riddle and know to find me here. And so you have." She exhaled, clapping her hands. "But on to my tale. Some months after the war was over, I received a visitor." She glanced at me. "You will recall Adele Moilien, I believe. I delivered her baby the night you stole the map case from that German aviator."

I nodded.

"Well, the first time she came to see me, she was furious. Though, truly she was more dis-traught. She'd lost so much, including her baby to the influenza. Much of the village all but shunned her for daring to take the Bosche as lovers, not understanding she hardly had a choice in the matter. Certainly not the first time." She shook her head angrily. "She informed me that her brother, Étienne, had been arrested the day after her baby was born and sent to prison in Germany. And then she accused me of framing him, of leaving behind incriminating evidence in their home and informing on him to the Bosche. I knew better, of course. I would never have been so stupid as to leave anything more than ashes for the Secret Police to find."

I'd thought as much, but I'd left the task in her hands as I hastily buried the map case, so I hadn't been able to recall with certainty whether that was true. But if Emilie said it was so, I believed her.

She spread her hands wide. "I offered the girl what comfort I could, and when she told me she didn't know what had become of her brother, I told her I would help her find out. After that, she came to see me many times, and a sort of friendship developed between us. I think she had no one else." She grimaced, but then held up her finger. "But I could tell there was something she was not telling me. When I told her I'd discovered her brother had survived the end of the war and returned to Belgium, her reaction was not at all what one would expect. So I surmised this must be what she'd been hiding. That she must have already known."

Her eyes hardened. "But then, someone set fire to my house. Fortunately, it was sloppily done and I was not asleep. I smelled the smoke and with the help of a few neighbors, was able to douse the flames before they could do more than minor damage. But I knew then that she had not told me all.

"I was debating what I should do when Adele came to see me the next day. She was frantic and weeping inconsolably. She told me she'd known her brother was alive, that he'd been quizzing her for information about me. That she was certain it was he who tried to burn my house down. It was evident the girl was terrified of him. He claimed he'd worked for British Intelligence during the war, but that they had double-crossed him. That it was they who informed on him and planted evidence so that he would be arrested by the Bosche." She pressed a hand to her chest in outrage. "And *I* had been the one to do it." Her dark gaze flicked to me. "Or Verity."

I couldn't withhold a flinch. "Because of the map case?"

"Adele had found it some months earlier and not known what to make of it, but apparently Étienne saw it as confirmation. She said he would not stop until I was dead. And that she feared he was planning something much worse, though she could not tell me what."

She stood, crossing to the door to speak with someone outside in a soft voice before returning. "I decided then that the best course was for me to go into hiding until I understood better what

Monsieur Moilien planned. Though I do not like to admit it, I will tell you the man gave me quite a turn. Here, I thought my instincts were as keen as ever, and yet not for a second during the war had I suspected him of being any sort of agent. I was aware of his history. Earlier in the war, he'd been rounded up and taken to another part of Belgium where he was forced to work in the fields, leaving his sister unprotected."

"Which was, I imagine, how she'd ended up entertaining German officers in the first place?" Alec's mouth twisted cynically. "Who better to prey on but the defenseless?"

A furrow formed between Rose's eyes. "Because of this, I always suspected he'd harbored a particular hatred toward the Bosche, even though he sullenly knuckled under, but I'd never believed he actively resisted. And now this man is telling his sister he was an agent? Who was I to say for certain? I had only been connected to British Intelligence through La Dame Blanche. And I'd never met any agents outside of it save you." She gestured to me. "So I elected to keep the matter to myself at first."

I nodded, understanding her logic for doing so in the beginning, and hoping she would clarify why she'd continued to do so.

"It was relatively easy to confirm he'd never been a member of La Dame Blanche, but there were always lone agents and small bands of citizens working separate from us. And I didn't know in what capacity he had performed his role."

"What of Adele?" I asked. "Perhaps she could have gotten more details from him."

"*Mais oui*, Gabby, I am coming to that," she reproved me gently, using my code name. She pressed her hands flat on the table, staring down at them as her brow grew heavy. "All this time I continued to correspond with the girl, in code, mind you, through an anonymous letter box asking for any information she could share. But mostly encouraging, nay, *begging* her to consider leaving Belgium. Her brother's behavior toward her had grown increasingly worrisome and I feared the worst. I even told her I had a friend in London who could help her find a place."

"Pauline," I guessed.

She glanced up at me and the look in her eyes made the back of my neck prickle with dread. "I thought I'd finally convinced her to leave when I learned that she'd died. Burned to death in her cottage."

I turned aside, swallowing hard to contain my shock and outrage. That explained why we hadn't been able to find the Moilien's cabin. "So Madame Zozza wasn't his first success at murder."

"It was his sister," she stated succinctly.

There was a rap at the door then, a blessed

reprieve as the woman who had guided us inside entered, carrying a tray filled with coffee and little pastries. Rose began to pour for each of us, releasing the aroma of the roasted beans.

"What? No roasted oat chaff or pea shells, simply for old time's sake?" I jested in an attempt to lighten the weight of her most recent disclosure. Such items had been the poor substitutes the people in the occupied territories had to put up with during the war.

Rose scoffed. "You can take a stroll down memory lane if you like, but I'll keep my java." She dipped her head toward the plate. "And don't be telling me you wish the jam in those tarts is sugared potato pulp either."

"And here I'd thought we had it bad eating bully from tin cans," Sidney remarked, referencing the tinned corned beef that was often part of the men's rations while in the trenches. "I don't think I'll be complaining ever again."

We all looked to Alec as he lowered his coffee after taking a drink. "What? Don't look at me. I was one of those bastard Bosche officers back at headquarters for much of the war. We certainly weren't going to deprive ourselves of a good meal even if our men in the trenches and the good German people back home had none." He stared down at his cup morosely. "Honestly, it could put you off food forever."

On that somber note, Rose resumed her tale.

"After hearing about Adele's death, I ordered the friend who was checking our anonymous letter box for me to stop going. I was afraid her brother might have extracted the information of its location from her. But then a few weeks later, I received a message through a different anonymous letter box I'd set up in another village." She tapped the table with her finger. "Except this address I'd only given to La Dame Blanche. And, yet, who should utilize it but Étienne Moilien."

My eyes widened in surprise. "How did he get the address?"

"I don't know. But that's one of the reasons why I feared involving La Dame Blanche and British Intelligence. Because either he was an agent, or he had a contact who was."

"What did his letter say?" Sidney asked as he began to remove his cigarette case.

But she halted him with a lifted hand. "No smoking, please. Not in here. It inflames my asthma."

"Of course." He dropped the case back into his pocket.

"He blamed me for the fact that Adele had to die. And told me she wouldn't be the last. That if the British were so eager to sacrifice others to their cause, he would help them along." Her gaze shifted to meet mine. "And that I and my assistant were next."

Sidney's brow furrowed. "How did he know who Verity was?"

"He didn't. Not at first. And I prayed she was safely in London, her identity protected." She folded her hands together. "But then you made your return from the dead in such spectacular fashion."

Sidney's eyes closed and his head sank back as he grasped what I already had. "The blasted newspapers."

Rose nodded. "Yes. Your photographs were posted in many of the papers in Belgium and France. And I knew it was too much to hope Moilien hadn't seen it, or that he wouldn't recognize you. So I asked for Pauline's help. I was hesitant to contact you directly," she told me. "Lest I was being followed, or surveilled in some way, and lead him straight to you or vice versa. And I was equally afraid he was aware of Pauline given the fact that I'd urged Adele to flee to London and contact her. She was not supposed to come straight to you, but conceive of a way to happen upon you in a shop or coffeehouse. Somewhere that appeared natural."

She reached up a hand to rub her temples. "But as I said, that wasn't exciting or daring enough for Pauline. She insisted on luring you to that preposterous medium she worked for. I told her you would never come, that the woman I knew would never be taken in by such charlatanry, but she insisted she would find a way to get you there. Even then, she agreed to merely pull you aside and relay my message." She shook her head. "But that is not what she did. And this is where all control slipped from my fingers."

"She told Madame Zozza about me," I surmised, having already been told by Pauline that she often fed her employer information about her clients that would prove useful. "She thought channeling you would prove more . . . impactful." That was as diplomatically as I could phrase it.

"And it likely got the foolish woman killed." She pressed a hand to her chest where underneath her dress, I knew hung a gold crucifix. "Whatever exactly happened, Pauline contacted me in a panic. She said everything had gone wrong. That the medium had deviated from the plan."

I sat taller at those words, for Pauline had also uttered them to me, but I hadn't known what they meant.

"That she'd delivered the type of oblique message she often gave clients to milk them for more money, but you had been furious and hadn't fallen for any bit of it. And then she told me her employer was dead. That she'd seen a strange man leaving the house just after it was set on fire."

"Moilien," Alec declared.

She nodded once in confirmation. "From everything I knew about Moilien's previous crimes, I was certain it must be him. Adele must have told him what I said about Pauline and he followed her trail from Macon, for Pauline said she was almost certain he was the same man who had paid a visit to her employer a few weeks prior. Why he decided to kill this medium, I do not know. Maybe he convinced her to alter the plans, maybe she tried to blackmail him. Whatever the case, he killed her. And I told Pauline she was dashed lucky to be alive."

"By the skin of her teeth," Sidney confirmed, for we had seen how quickly that house had gone up in flames.

"I told her if she valued her life at all, she would go into hiding. That I would contact her again when it was safe."

"But I don't understand," I interjected, gesturing between me and Sidney. "We talked to her on the street while they were struggling to extinguish the fire. She could have told us then what was going on. She could have relayed your message. Why didn't she?"

Rose had fiddled with the handle of her coffee cup while I asked my questions, and now as if realizing it, she pushed it resolutely away. "I asked her the same thing, and I do not have a satisfactory answer for you. In all honesty, I think the girl was in shock and riddled with guilt. She knew her tomfoolery had contributed to her employer's death, and I think she was too scared to trust you with the blatant truth, especially since you had reacted so hostilely at the séance. And yet, at the same time, she didn't want you to be unaware there was a dangerous man involved. She said she told you that much, but she wanted to speak with me first before saying more. But by then, I knew it was too late. That Pauline needed to disappear before Moilien caught up with her."

I brushed my lank hair back from my forehead, trying to make sense of it all, for it seemed hopelessly muddled. "And so the codes you left me? They were all what? Your contingency strategy?"

"I appreciate how convoluted all this seems," Rose replied, obviously sharing in my frustration. "It wasn't supposed to be this way. But I didn't know who to trust, and this was too important to risk it. I was fearful for your life, Gabby." She reached her hand out to rest it over mine where it laid on the table, her eyes dipped before rising to meet mine again. "And I knew, of all people, I could trust you."

Rose was one of the least demonstrative people I knew, so for her to speak this way, and to touch me while doing so, meant she was being extremely earnest.

"I had to make those clues difficult, or else anyone could have followed them. And when I laid out the breadcrumbs, I thought the only chance you would be using them was if Pauline failed or something had happened to me." She released my hand, sinking back in her chair as she sighed heavily. "And now I fear it may have all been too late."

I sat taller, glancing at Sidney and Alec. "You're speaking of the aeroplane in Havay?"

She nodded. "I stumbled upon it just after the war. Though it all started months earlier. From the papers in that German aviator's map case, actually."

"Zauberer—Buzancy," I replied, repeating the name and location scrawled on those papers.

Her gaze sharpened. "You do know then?"

"Captain Landau helped me fill in some of the blanks," I confirmed. "Though he didn't know about the aeroplane in Havay."

"Well, after I discovered what Moilien was capable of, I remembered that aviator had been rumored to be one of Adele's particular friends. She admitted the young ace had been prone to brag, and though she had little interest in aeroplanes and such, her brother did. Given that, I figured he must be aware of Havay."

"So you went back to Havay," Sidney concluded, his hands pressed flat to the table. "And the bombs were gone."

I expected Rose to be surprised by this swift bit of deduction, but perhaps the implications were too grim for such considerations. Instead, she replied with a simple, but foreboding, "Yes."

None of us spoke for a moment, perhaps all trying to come to grips with the reality that our worst suppositions were true.

Alec was the first to find his voice. "How can you be certain it was he who took them? Perhaps the army retrieved them as they are doing all the others."

"That's what I'd hoped had happened," Rose admitted. "But I asked those who lived closest to Havay. No one had come to clear the site. The only visitors in vehicles that ever drove that way were the occasional morbid tourists. And their motorcars weren't military lorries."

Sidney blew a breath out through his lips, pushing back a distance from the table, his voice growing more strident and bewildered with each word. "So, Étienne Moilien intends to use these bombs somehow to get back at the British government because he believes they framed him, and turned him over to the Germans, and then refused to pay him restitution. Why not the Germans? They're the ones who imprisoned and tortured him after invading his home and harming his sister."

No one seemed to have a ready answer for this, for it did seem more logical to blame the Germans for his suffering. But I endeavored to make sense out of it anyway.

"Perhaps it's a matter of disillusionment. He obviously saw the British as agents of good, and he tried to ally himself with us, to do his own bit of good. Instead we rejected him, we foiled what he saw as his chance to rebel against an intolerable situation. And then he was captured by the very people he was trying to inflict harm upon and they turned that harm back on him tenfold. Maybe when he visited Landau after the war, it was his last chance to give some sort of meaning, of honorability, to everything he and his sister endured."

"But he was rejected yet again," Sidney finished for me. "Yes, I can see that. But why not both the Germans and British? Why is he directing his anger at only the British?"

"Because, in his mind, we've suffered the least," Alec stated. "At least, if one confines their scope to the Western Front. The Belgians and French were invaded. Portions of their countries were ripped apart by trenches and destroyed by shells. The Germans, while the perpetrators of his torment, are starving to death by the tens of thousands. The country has been picked clean by war." His expression was grave. "Moilien was imprisoned in Germany. As he made his way home, he would have seen it. They are already suffering for the part they played in the conflict. But the British and the Americans are a different story."

He frowned. "The Americans are too far away for him to contemplate, but the British are not.

And while we have endured our own share of suffering in the loss of life, we aren't starving, and save for the Zeppelin bombers, our country largely avoided any direct devastation. Think about it. All he sees are the British officials, and the well-nourished, well-dressed tourists flocking over the channel—to gawk at the destruction, shed a few tears, and then return to their land of plenty. Tourists like those women at the café outside of Brussels."

Sidney scowled at the reminder and turned to Rose. "Is that why we're here? Because of the tourists?"

"One of the last things Adele told me was that her brother had been spending a great deal of time somewhere near Lille, France, so that's why I'm here. Why you're here," she added glancing around at us.

"Have you been able to locate him? To uncover what he plans?" I asked anxiously.

She lifted her hands in frustration. "I do not know. One of my men located him in Lille some weeks ago, but then lost him again. Before the war, it would have been easy to locate a man with such facial scarring, but now there are so many with such injuries. And just as many who wear masks to hide them. It is all too easy to pass by unnoticed. Just another faceless, nameless suffering soldier.

"I suspect he means to harm the tourists in

some way," Rose added. "But where? And when? They are crawling all over this area of France and along this sector of the front. New ones arrive every day. Especially in these warm summer months."

"So we have nothing else to go on?"

She shook her head. "I am sorry, *ma rouge-gorge*. In this, I have failed."

CHAPTER 28

M aybe not," Alec interjected into our uneasy silence. "For I also have some information to share."

I could read from his expression that he'd only just decided to part with it, and that he was still hesitant to do so. I felt my temper spark, though I tamped it down, for it seemed almost inevitable that he should be keeping something from us. He always had held everything but the bare essentials close to his vest.

"About six weeks ago, the War Office received a threat from 'an anonymous Belgian.' That's what he called himself. The letter was filled with a lot of angry rambling, and it was unclear whether it should be taken seriously. So, I was tasked to find out who the sender was and assess the significance of his intentions." He glanced between Sidney and me, at least having the grace to appear a little remorseful that he'd been deceiving us. "Because in the midst of his incoherent tirade, he'd sworn that 'the silence of the battlefield would be broken by one last cry of vengeance, that the peaceful would be shaken from their repose, and that the travelers' displays of false grief would be transformed into cries of anguish.'"

"And you just *now* decided to tell us this?" Sidney snapped. His eyes blazed with fury.

"The information was classified," Alec replied. "You served in the army. You know how it works. I shouldn't even be sharing it with you now."

Sidney turned away, muttering a curse.

"Now that you're being so forthcoming," I drawled sarcastically, equally as frustrated even if I accepted the reasons for his withholding what he knew, "can you tell us if you discovered that sender was Moilien?"

"Until you arrived, I'd had little luck in the matter," Alec admitted. "Truthfully, it had not been made a priority. I was to pursue it in the midst of my other duties. But then Lord Ryde stopped to ask me those questions on your behalf." He nodded to me. "And I began to wonder if whatever you were pursuing might be related. You always did have a nose for sniffing out trouble."

I arched a single eyebrow, not certain I liked having it phrased precisely like that.

His lips quirked, obviously enjoying having irritated me. "So I hung back in Brussels longer than was strictly necessary, hoping to bump into you."

I glanced at Sidney, whose anger seemed to

have devolved into resignation. His eyes gleamed at me as if to say, "didn't I tell you so?"

Ignoring him, I resumed questioning Alec. "When did you realize we were pursuing the same man?"

"Not until later. I wondered at first if that aviator whose map case you'd stolen could be our man, but when I discovered he was dead, I started to look into those around him. Especially when the town of Havay appeared in his records."

I'm not sure why I was surprised he'd gotten access to German Army records so quickly, but I was. "And you already knew about the wireless-controlled aeroplane there."

He nodded.

"But what about that bit about Landau?" I charged, recalling how he'd seemed to point us in his direction.

"All true. I was suspicious of him. But I'm glad you were able to clear up the fact that he's not involved."

"So this is real," Sidney stated in summary. "Moilien means to use those bombs to harm British tourists somewhere near the front." His face was pale. "But we don't know precisely where or when."

"Now you understand what my predicament has been," Rose told him. "All I can think is that he means to target one of these tours." She shrugged. "But which one?"

"I heard there are casualties almost daily from unexploded shells," I said.

Rose nodded.

"Perhaps that's how he hopes to get away with it. Maybe he already has," I suggested, knowing even as I said so that couldn't be right.

"No, he will want the credit," Alec stated definitively.

How else would the British know? How else would they learn to regret not accepting him?

I exhaled in resignation, spreading my hands flat on the table. "Well, let's think about this logically. Most of the tours in this area begin in Lille, do they not?"

Sidney suddenly jolted forward in his chair. "A cemetery." His eyes were wide as he looked at all of us in turn. "He means to hit a cemetery while a group of tourists is there."

"But how . . ." Alec began, but he cut him off.

" 'The peaceful will be shaken from their repose.' Is that not what the letter said?" He stabbed the table with his finger. "It's a cemetery. It has to be."

I reached over to grab his hand. "I think you're right." A sick swirling began in my stomach as a new horror began to dawn inside me. "And I think I might know which one." I pressed a hand to my forehead as the full implication of it slammed into me, and I had to struggle to force my thoughts back into order.

"At the séance, Lord Ryde's aunt, Lady Swaffham kept asking about a cemetery at Boeschèpe outside Poperinghe. I take it her son is buried there." I swallowed, meeting Sidney's eyes. "Moilien's henchman was at the séance. He heard her mention she planned to visit it. What if he told Moilien?"

Sidney quickly grasped what I was trying to say. "And what better way to draw attention to your grievance than by killing not only British tourists, but also an earl and a lady."

"That sounds like exactly the type of thing he would go in for," Alec declared, though neither of us paid him much heed.

The thought of Max being in such danger, and completely oblivious to it, made my chest seize up in panic. He was my friend. Someone who had been there for me when I needed someone most. And yet our relationship was somewhat delicate because of the troubles that had been in my and Sidney's marriage. I squeezed Sidney's hand, imploring him with my eyes to understand.

He nodded, squeezing back. "Do you recall Ryde and his aunt's itinerary? When were they going to be on the tour?"

I pushed the fright away, knowing it would do no good to give it any sway. "Let's see." I thought back to what Max had told us. "They departed the same day we did, the eleventh. Three days in Calais and then a day to reach

Lille. So the tour would have begun . . ." My eyes widened. "Today!" I pushed to my feet, glancing around me. "We need a guidebook. All the tour companies essentially follow the same route."

"I do not have one," Rose replied.

I shook my head. "Of course not." Then I sprang toward the door, retracing our steps to the stairs.

"I do not know if the bookshops will have one either," she called after me as I clattered down the stairs.

"I don't need a bookshop. Just a tourist."

I burst out through the alley door, no longer caring about stealth. I turned my feet toward the spire of the Church of St. Christopher, anxious to discover whether we were already too late. The sound of footsteps hastening after me alerted me to Sidney's presence before he reached my side. He didn't check my stride, but he did reach over to clasp my hand. "I hope we're wrong. I hope he isn't going after Ryde."

I glanced up at him, surprised and yet heartened by his sincere words. I pulled him to a stop, arching up on my toes to press a kiss to his mouth. "I hope so, too," I whispered.

Then I turned to hurry us onward.

Fortunately, there was a large cluster of people milling about before the cathedral. Several of them clutched books before them, and I directed Sidney to speak to the man in a pin-striped suit while I approached a pair of younger women.

"Pardon me, are you by chance from England?" I asked, as my gaze dipped to scan the pages of the book the woman in the broad-brim hat was holding.

"Why, yes. Yes, we are."

"Is that the Michelin Guide to Ypres?" I asked.

"Well, no." She closed the book so that I could see the cover. "But I do have it."

"You do? Might I look at it for just a moment?"

She exchanged a glance with her friend. "Of course."

The friend's eyes scrutinized my matted hair and lack of a hat, for I'd raced out without donning it. I could only imagine what they thought of my ramshackle appearance, but truthfully, I didn't care so long as I could see their book.

The woman removed it from her shoulder satchel and I thumbed it open to the index page, searching for Boeschèpe. Finding the page with a picture of the cemetery, I flipped backward, discovering it was included in the second day of the itinerary. Max and his aunt would not be visiting it until tomorrow.

I nearly wept in relief. "Thank you," I replied, passing it back to them.

Ignoring their looks of intense curiosity, I swiveled about to find Sidney. It took me a moment to locate his dark head among the crowd, but I soon spotted him near the cathedral entrance. I hurried over to him, my steps lighter than they had been moments before.

"Tomorrow," I gasped. "They won't reach Boeschèpe until tomorrow."

"Then we'd best reach it first."

My eyes dipped to the book in his hands. "Did you buy that man's guidebook? Why?"

"I noticed it has maps and describes the most passable roads. If we're to navigate our way through that mire without getting stuck, we're going to need it."

I studied his wan face and the dark circles around his eyes, realizing that of all of us, he would know best what we were headed into. "I'm sorry," I murmured, hating that it had come to this. That I had to ask him to step into that hell again. I knew it wouldn't be easy. That the memories would undoubtedly be thick around him.

He didn't pretend to misunderstand. His gaze strayed toward the brick of the church, following it up the edifice toward the roof line. A thin strip of dark stubble he must have missed during this morning's makeshift ablutions bristled on the underside of his jaw. "It will not be pleasant."

I reached for his hand, and his eyes lowered to meet mine, stark with shadows.

"Let's go tell the others what we've discovered," he said.

We returned to the room to find Rose waiting for us.

"Where's Captain Xavier?" I asked. I didn't think he'd followed us from the building.

"He asked to use the telephone," she replied.

Perhaps he was informing the War Office. Maybe there were men they could send to assist us. Or perhaps the Belgian government could be counted on to lend their aid since the cemetery rested on their soil.

Whatever the case, we filled Rose in and then set down to study the guidebook and make our plans. Alec returned some minutes later.

"Lord Ryde was, indeed, staying at a hotel in Lille," he informed us. "But he left this morning. They expect him back tomorrow night after the tour is complete. He'll be staying somewhere along the route tonight. Likely in Poperinghe."

"How did you discover that?" I inquired as he joined us at the table.

"By telephoning the most notable hotels still standing in Lille. There are not many, so he wasn't difficult to find."

"That certainly fits this timeline." I nodded at the guidebook laid open before Sidney.

Alec's brow furrowed. "Unfortunately, the War Office is not proving so amenable. They found our evidence less than compelling, and without definitive proof that Moilien either has

449

those bombs in his possession or intends to use them at Boeschèpe, they don't wish to create an incident."

"Don't they understand the ramifications if we *are* correct?" I demanded.

"The most they'll do is inform the gendarmes in Poperinghe to be on the lookout for a man bearing Moilien's description."

"And if he's wearing his mask?"

Alec shrugged, his expression thunderous.

I closed my eyes, took a deep breath and exhaled, forcing calm through my body. It wasn't his fault the War Office was being so intractable. "I'll telephone Landau. Perhaps he has some resources or connections that can help us." After all, C had told him to help me in whatever way he could.

"Whatever our plan is, whatever our resources, we need to be on the road to Poperinghe within the hour." Sidney glanced out the window. "We still have plenty of daylight, but it will take hours to reach on these blasted roads." He smacked the map on the page of the book open to him. "Though we're going to bypass some of this, and take the road up to Menin, and through Gheluwe before detouring—as they've recommended since part of the main road to Ypres remains unpassable." He glanced at Alec. "Unless you know a better way."

Alec's eyes narrowed as if suspecting Sidney

of making a dig at him because he hadn't spent his war in the trenches. "I know next to nothing about it."

But Sidney did not take the bait. "Then this is our plan of approach. What we do when we get there remains to be seen. I suppose we attempt to locate Moilien and his bombs before he can place them."

I nodded and turned to Rose. "Do you intend to come with us?"

She glared at me as if in scolding. "I don't intend to stay behind."

"Then let's gather what supplies we need and prepare to leave," Sidney instructed as he closed the guidebook and rose to his feet.

"I'll bring the motorcar around," Alec growled, as if happy to be free of us, at least for a few minutes.

Rose began issuing instructions to the woman who had initially let us into the alley door while I waited for her to lead me to the telephone. She had just turned to address me when suddenly a shot rang out. It had come from the direction of the alley.

I dashed down the steps with Sidney close on my heels, only to stumble to a stop to find Alec lying in the open doorway.

"Son of a . . ." he cursed, grimacing in pain.

I dropped to my knees and crawled toward him. "Where are you hit?" I asked, even as he

451

lifted his hand away from his arm to reveal blood before clasping it back again.

Another bullet struck the wooden doorframe, sending splinters flying.

"Pull him back out of the doorway," Sidney ordered, as he kneeled and grasped Alec's legs.

Alec grunted in pain as we unceremoniously hauled him back inside. "I'm not helpless," he groused as he struggled to sit up.

Sidney pushed him down again, making him utter another foul curse. "Wait until you're clear of his line of fire."

Once Alec was safely inside, I expected Sidney to let the door close, but instead he reached for a piece of wood tossed in the corner they must have used as a prop. He jammed the piece between the door and frame, leaving a small gap.

"What are you doing?" I demanded as Rose and an older lad who had come down the stairs after us helped Alec to his feet.

Sidney withdrew his pistol. "I'm not going to give whoever this is the chance to come after us again." He peered cautiously through the gap, before withdrawing his head again. "I suspect I'm a better shot than he is if the chap was aiming for Alec's head or heart." He nodded at the man with blood pouring from his shoulder.

"Looks like he got close enough to me," I snapped and then cringed as a shot struck the stone of the building outside.

But Sidney was not even fazed, and I realized I was seeing him as he had been in the trenches. Focused, determined. As much as I wanted to yank him away from that gap in the door, I knew he was correct. Better to face this man now than have him shoot us in the back later.

"We need a diversion," he declared.

I hurried to follow the others up the stairs to wherever they were leading Alec. "Rose, where are those boys you hired to run interference?"

She glanced down at me in surprise. "Some of them are in the kitchen. Or they were." She nodded down the passage to the left as we came to the top of the steps.

I strode swiftly down it, listening for the sound of voices. Through the door at the end, I found four boys greedily stuffing their faces as an older woman clucked around them, dishing out more food.

"We need your help," I declared without pre-amble.

They all turned as one to stare up at me, their cheeks bulging with food as they chewed, but none of them seemed the least interested in moving from their chairs. Having grown up with three brothers and an innumerable number of their friends, I knew how to get their attention.

"It's dangerous. I'm quite certain I shouldn't be asking you."

The tallest one swallowed quickly, his dark

eyes avid with interest. "We'll help, madame."

The others nodded eagerly and I bit back a smile of triumph. "Excellent. Here's what we're going to do."

CHAPTER 29

Where on earth the boys had scrounged up the whizzbangs they set to lighting with such relish, I didn't know, but after hearing my initial plan, they were having none of it. They insisted instead on using these contraband explosives. Time being of the essence, I was hardly in the position to argue. At least the poppers would be used in a constructive way.

I stood at the corner of the building, watching as they lit their fuses and then lobbed them into the entrance to the alley. A few seconds later, a series of loud pops and bangs echoed out of the narrow passage, startling passersby in the street as the boys cheered and slapped each other on the back. When one of them would have darted around me to see the damage, I yanked him back by the shoulder.

I only hoped Sidney had realized what we were doing and taken advantage of any wavering in the shooter's attention. Moments later, I had my answer.

"I should have shot you in Liège," I heard Sidney snarl.

I risked peering around the corner to see him leveling his pistol at a man on the ground howling in pain.

He flicked his gaze up at me briefly as I stepped into view. "Grab his gun."

I hurried forward, the boys at my heels, and knelt to pick up the Webley.

"Nice job, boys," Sidney told them, speaking in French as I had. His gaze remained leveled at the man who I could now see was Peter Smythe. "I'm guessing I have you to thank for that stroke of brilliance."

"*Oui, monsieur*," they declared, and then proceeded to ask a dozen questions in their curious street patois.

Sidney ignored them all. "You shall be handsomely rewarded. But first I need you to fetch a gendarme. Can you do that?"

"You're not going to kill him?" one particularly blood-thirsty lad asked.

"No. Not today," he replied. The anger he was keeping banked flared in his eyes. "Though that doesn't mean I won't shoot you in your leg if you don't talk," he snapped at the fellow.

The boys would have stood there avidly staring if I hadn't shooed them toward the street to do as Sidney had asked.

"Where is Moilien? Where are the bombs?" he demanded of Smythe.

He whimpered and cursed, clutching his bloodied hand before him.

Sidney kicked him in the leg. "Where is Moilien? Where are the bombs?"

I silently begged Smythe to answer. We needed that information, desperately, but I didn't want to watch my husband have to shoot him again. I didn't want Sidney to be forced to do it. But he simply kept muttering, "my hand, my hand, my hand." I wondered if he was in shock.

Then Sidney lowered the aim of his pistol. "Your leg then," he threatened.

This galvanized Smythe to speak. "Wait! Wait! I'll tell you. Wait!"

Sidney dropped his gun to his side, giving him a reprieve. "Then talk!"

"He's in Pops," he bit out through clenched teeth, using the soldiers' popular nickname for Poperinghe, and confirming what we already knew.

"And the bombs?" Sidney pressed.

When Smythe hesitated, he lifted his gun again.

"He's burying them in the road somewhere," he snarled.

Sidney lifted his gaze to meet mine. I think we were both astonished to discover what we'd feared was true. Moilien did have the bombs. And he intended to use them.

"Where?" he pressed.

"I don't know where. Somewhere near Ypres. I think."

"You think?" Sidney's glare turned deadly again.

"He didn't share his plans with me," he snapped before whimpering again. "I need a doctor."

"Not yet. How did you know we'd be here?"

"I didn't. *You* were supposed to be dead." He glowered at us as if we were somehow to be blamed. "But you told that mechanic you were headed toward Tourcoing, so we figured Madame Moreau must be nearby. And then lo and behold, you two come striding into the church square. I thought at first you were ghosts, but you're flesh and blood all right."

The gendarme arrived then, cutting off our interrogation. We told them Smythe was a wanted fugitive from Britain and how he had shot our friend when he recognized him, leaving him in their charge.

I hurried inside to find Alec sitting upright as Rose bandaged his upper arm.

"The man refuses to lie down," Rose groused.

"It's merely a flesh wound," he snapped back.

"One that took a sizable furrow out of your flesh. You'll have a nasty scar. And if you're not careful, it will become infected."

"So give me another one of those shots. And give me a shot of morphine while you're at it. We

need to get to Poperinghe." He glanced up at me. "Did Sidney disarm him?"

Before I could answer, Rose yanked the bandage tight. "You were just shot. You're not going anywhere."

"As I said before, it's no cause for concern," he retorted through gritted teeth. His face was pale with pain. "Just give me the morphine."

Sidney returned to stand behind me, sizing up the situation quickly. "We can't make accommodations for you," he told Alec. "The roads between here and Pops are going to be pockmarked and uneven. It will not be a comfortable ride."

"I'll be fine."

"And how exactly are you going to help?" Rose huffed. "You can't even lift this arm."

"I'll be fine," he reiterated, glaring up at her.

Rose looked to me for assistance, but I shrugged. Alec was as stubborn as they came, and he certainly wasn't going to listen to me. Let him suffer if that's what he wished to do.

"Give him the morphine," Sidney told her grimly. "I'll get the motorcar." His arm touched mine. "You call Landau."

To say the drive to Poperinghe was hellish would be an understatement. It wasn't far outside of Tourcoing that the trappings of modern civilization seemed to completely drop away, replaced by the devastation of war. First, it was only the shelled wreckage of buildings crumbling between the homes that were pockmarked but had still been spared. But those buildings still standing became fewer and fewer—until all that was left were piles of rubble lining the dirt roads, and the cement bunkers and machine gun nests of the enemy.

Nothing of any height stood from horizon to horizon in the failing light. All the trees had been shorn and splintered to pieces, so all that was left were the severed trunks pointing straight up at the sky, though none reached far. The fading daylight made the churned and scarred landscape appear all the more desolate and mournful. It sent chills up my spine to think of the untold number of lives destroyed on this soil. In some sense, it seemed as if they were still there, hovering at the corner of my eye. That if I turned my head fast enough, I might see them.

However, the fall of darkness, while increasing the hazards—particularly in the sections which required us to drive over temporary bridges and boards rigged over streams and shell holes—brought its own reprieve. The stomach-churning smells released by the heat of the day lessened in the chill of evening as a blessed breeze of fresh air blew in from the west.

Rose and Alec sat in the rear seat, where he struggled in vain to hide his discomfort. But it was Sidney I felt most worried for. With each mile we drove into the devastated lands, the darker the shadows seemed to gather around him. His hands gripped the steering wheel as his eyes glared fiercely ahead, and I wasn't quite sure whether he was seeing the present or staring into the past.

Sometime an hour after sunset we reached Ypres. Or rather, what was left of it. This was somewhat familiar country to me now, for I had been here once during the war. I had witnessed the utter destruction. I didn't need to see it again. In any case, it required all my concentration to flip between the pages of the guide-book, reading by the light of my torch, to direct Sidney on the swiftest route through the ruined city.

Once we were on the much-traveled road between Ypres and Poperinghe, where troops and supplies were constantly moving up and down to the front and back, Sidney seemed to settle within himself. Perhaps he realized we were through the worst and headed to the rear, so to speak. Perhaps he was reliving the sensation that he had survived yet another rotation in the trenches. Or perhaps he was merely tired. Whatever the case, he relaxed into his seat.

"Are you all right?" I asked softly. "Can I get you anything?"

He risked a glance at me before refocusing

on the road. "No. I just . . . I can't stop thinking how deranged it feels to be racing across this benighted country to stop a madman."

"War makes the irrational rational," I replied simply and then sighed. "I know this isn't war anymore, but . . ."

"But it sure bloody feels like it." His gaze met mine again briefly, and the warmth of our solidarity wrapped itself around me like a cozy blanket. We might be hurtling toward an unknown danger, but at least we would be facing it together.

A short distance past the partially demolished village of Vlamertinghe, everything changed. It was almost startling in its abruptness. Here the heavy shelling and artillery barrage had stopped, and so large shade trees lined the road. Beyond them lay the wavering, glistening tips of hops in the moonlight.

We reached Poperinghe just before midnight, finding most of the town slumbering. The city had operated as a billet town and a divisional headquarters for the British for much of the war. Consequently, it had flourished, protected from the Germans' artillery by the notorious Ypres salient bulging outward toward the east, even while the countryside surrounding it on three sides had not. What a precarious situation it must have been to live here though, never knowing if the Allies' lines would hold. Had that salient been lost, Poperinghe would have been reduced to rubble just like Ypres.

Sidney parked Alec's Porter near The Great Market and we split into pairs. Rose and Alec would go to the Gendarmerie, or rather Rijkswacht, as it was called now that we were in Dutch-speaking Flanders, to enlist their aid. With any luck, Landau had gotten through to them already and they were anticipating our arrival. If not, then perhaps the sight of Alec's gunshot wound, if not his foreboding, pain-pinched face, would propel them into action quicker.

Sidney and I planned to visit the hotels to locate Max and his aunt, and warn any other tourists, and the officers working for those tour companies, about the road to Boeschèpe and the cemetery there. Fortunately, there were not many hotels of the quality Lady Swaffham would expect. At the second one we tried, we were forced to wait to speak with the clerk, so I wandered deeper into the lobby, peering into the drawing room. Finding it empty, I turned back to rejoin Sidney, when a familiar figure suddenly strode down the hall toward me.

"Verity? What are you doing here?" Max asked in shock. His face was more haggard than I'd ever remembered it being, and the lines bracketing his mouth seemed deeper than ever. I could guess what had caused it, and I cursed his aunt for dragging him through this. If our trip through the devastated country this evening had been bad, I could only imagine what a full-day's detailed tour would be like.

"Thank heavens," I gasped in relief, reaching out to touch the sleeve of his coat. Part of me had continued to worry we might not reach him in time.

His eyes continued to scan mine in bewilderment.

"Is there a place we can sit down?" I glanced behind me at Sidney, who had seen Max and was now joining us. "We have something urgent we need to tell you."

Given the animosity of their last interaction, I expected a bit of awkwardness between the two men, but they seemed to gloss over it easily enough as they shook hands. Although, if possible, Max looked even more perplexed.

"Kent, you're here, too. What is going on?"

Sidney's expression softened to one of empathy, perhaps noting the same changes I had in Max. "Come on, Ryde." He pressed a hand to his shoulder, guiding him toward a settee beside the entrance to the drawing room. "Have we got a story to tell."

By necessity it was brief, but no less affecting at that.

"So, this Moilien intends to bury bombs in the road so that our tour company will drive over them, all because he wants revenge on the British," Max summarized, shaking his head at the lunacy of such an idea. "How can he be sure it will be our motorcars that trigger them?"

"I don't think he can," I admitted.

"But . . . but that's insane."

"We know. But the insanity of it all only makes Moilien more dangerous. He's erratic and unpredictable. The logic one would normally use doesn't seem to apply."

Max looked as if he wanted to argue further, but he scrubbed his hands over his face and nodded in resignation. "If you say it's true, then I believe it." He glanced at Sidney. "What do you want me to do?"

Sidney stubbed out the cigarette he'd been smoking. "Speak to all the tour company operators. Stop them from taking the road to Boeschèpe and the cemetery."

"But how can you be certain it will be the road to Boeschèpe?"

"Because that middle-aged man who was so eager to sit next to Madame Zozza at the séance was working for Moilien. He heard your aunt talk about the cemetery," I explained.

"Yes, but that's not the only site she mentioned."

I sat forward. "What do you mean?"

He frowned. "Perhaps you weren't attending, but she also talked about Kemmel Hill. That's where her son fell. He was later transferred to one of the casualty clearing stations at Remy Farm near Boeschèpe, where he died."

I glanced at Sidney in alarm. What if we were wrong? What if it was at Kemmel Hill where he meant to enact his revenge?

"It must be the road to the cemetery at Boeschèpe. His letter to the War Office specifically said 'the peaceful would be shaken from their repose,'" Sidney argued.

"Yes, but there's also a cemetery next to where Kemmel Château once stood," Max said.

Sidney rocked back in his seat, taken aback by this new information.

"There's an older gentleman on our tour," Max explained. "Considers himself an amateur historian, and I've been listening to him drone on all day about these things."

I only listened with half an ear, studying my husband's face. "Moilien's letter also said 'the silence of the battlefield would be broken by one last cry for vengeance.' And I'm not sure I would call a farm filled with casualty clearing stations a battlefield."

His head turned so that he could meet my gaze and he nodded. "I guess we'll have to go to both. For he must be planning to bury the bombs tonight if he intends for them to explode in the morning. There will be less chance of interruption."

"You said he intends to bury the bombs," Max interrupted. "But what type are they?"

"Some type of aerial shell."

He frowned. "Then they must be fitted with impact detonators. Which means he's going to need the motorcars to do more than drive over them. That won't be enough to set them off. He's going to need to cause the wheels to drop down on them with as much force as possible. And that still might not trigger them." He tilted his head. "Of course, that's assuming he knows what he's doing."

Sidney reached out to grasp Max's arm, halting his words. "Do you know a place where the road drops?"

"I think so. And it's out by Kemmel Hill."

"Then we definitely need to check it out," Sidney replied, rising to his feet. "We can send Captain Xavier, Madame Moreau, and whatever Rijkswacht officers they are willing to spare out toward the road to Boeschèpe. If we find Moilien, we can always double back for reinforcements," he told me.

Max held up his hands. "Now, hold on. You two aren't going alone. I'm coming, too."

"Then who's going to warn the tour companies," Sidney pointed out.

"I'm sure my amateur historian friend would be thrilled to. Besides, no one is going anywhere until the morning." He slid his hands into his pockets, arching his eyebrows. "In any case, you don't know the site. You'll find it quicker and be able to rejoin the others if we're wrong. And if we're right . . . well, you might need all the help you can get."

Sidney scrutinized him, and I rolled my eyes at the sheer obstinacy of men. And they called *me* stubborn.

"Do you have a pistol?" he relented.

Max nodded. "Just allow me a few moments to collect it and contact that fellow."

CHAPTER 30

In a quarter hour, we were back in the Porter, driving southeast of Poperinghe back into the war-torn countryside. Landau's telephone call had proved effective, for the Rijkswacht were being more than cooperative, eager to spare any lives they could after so much devastation. They did not have a large force, but what officers they could, they put at our disposal. Several accompanied Rose and an injured Alec out to the Boeschèpe cemetery, while others would be positioned to block any vehicles from traveling that way. Another pair of officers would be sent after us toward Kemmel Hill as soon as they could be roused from their sleep.

This part of Flanders was covered in undulating hills with a larger ridge stretching from east to west, across the French border. In the darkness, we could not see the knolls, but the guidebook assured us they were there. The state of the roads steadily declined as we entered the old battlefields and winding lines of trenches.

"Has the tour more or less followed the same route as the Michelin Guide?" Sidney asked.

"Mostly," Max replied.

"Then we should make the turning at La Clytte and approach Kemmel from Locre," I directed Sidney as I examined the map in the light of my torch.

"No, I think we should go the other way," Max argued. "Come up on him from behind."

I glanced at Sidney, bowing to their greater knowledge of such tactics.

His brow furrowed in concentration, his eyes glued to the dusty road and rubble illuminated in the headlamps. "Explain to me the lay of the land."

"If we continued straight, we'll reach Kemmel village. Or what remains of it. Which according to this, is basically nothing but ruins. Beyond it lies the remnants of the château and its cemetery. To reach the hill, we have to turn right at the village. The book warns that the road skirting the foot of the hill is completely churned up and only passable because of a series of bridges, which have been thrown up over the shell holes." Having crossed over these rickety contraptions on our drive earlier that evening, I did not look forward to doing so again. "The road to the top of the hill is inaccessible."

Having absorbed all this, Sidney flexed his fingers around the driving wheel. "Then I suspect you believe he intends to utilize those existing shell holes in some way," he said to Max.

"That was my first thought. If he could find a shallow enough one and dislodge the bridge or camouflage the depth, then when the motorcar dropped into the hole, it *might* generate enough force to trigger the bomb." He sounded unconvinced. "It would be more likely if he tampered with the mechanism in some way."

"Well, it's too late now to wonder whether the man is familiar enough with ordnance to make certain they detonate," Sidney replied. "I think we have to assume he does and pray we're not too late to stop him from succeeding."

We all fell silent as we steadily drove onward into the night. A creeping mist began to rise up from the soil and debris in patches, coating the ground in gossamer blankets. There was no sound beyond the purr of the motorcar engine.

At Kemmel village, I directed Sidney through the narrow turnings between the ruins of wood and stone onto the road which hugged the base of the hill. There he rolled to a stop, switching the headlamps off.

Blackness enveloped us, thick and cloying with the scents of exhaust, Flanders mud, and decay. Hours seemed to pass, even though I knew Sidney was merely waiting for our eyes to adjust to the darkness. It was impossible not to be conscious of my heart beating a steady tattoo inside my chest, as well as the breathing of the two men on either side of me. I knew I had made my choice, that my heart was already given to Sidney, and yet the warmth of Max's leg pressed against mine was not unwelcome.

Sidney was the first to move, shifting the motorcar into drive. "If we have any luck," he murmured, "we'll see the light of his lamps long before he hears us."

We slowly rolled forward, the tires crunching in the dirt. At first there was nothing but the same devastation we'd viewed through the headlamps, just with a narrower, shrouded view. The shape of Kemmel Hill was visible as a darker line against the starry sky. We passed the ruins of a few machine gun nests, and then the road rounded a turn.

I reached over to grip Sidney's arm just as he came to a stop.

"I see it," he whispered.

In the distance shined a hazy light obscured by mist.

"Got you, you son of a . . . ," he swore, inching forward again.

"Should we be moving any closer?" Max murmured. "Sound travels further in the night."

"Yes, but not that far. And not in this mist. Just a little closer . . . There." He braked at the edge of a shell hole and its temporary bridge, and turned off the engine.

"Now, what's the plan?" Max asked.

"Well, I see at least two shadows moving in

and out of that light, but there may be more." He glanced to the side out over the morass lining the road. "I wonder how passable the terrain is around that hole. The safest bet would be to somehow sneak up, surround, and incapacitate them."

"I agree. I'd rather avoid actually firing our pistols. Who knows if they have guns?"

"I would assume they do," I said, my mind turning over an idea.

"What are you thinking?" Sidney turned to ask, evidently having heard the contemplation in my tone.

"Maybe we should use Moilien's paranoia to our advantage."

"Go on."

"Well, he thinks we're dead. That's what Smythe said. And this landscape . . . with the mist . . . and . . . well, we all know it still contains corpses yet to be unearthed." I glanced between the men. I couldn't see their faces clearly in the darkness, but Sidney's voice was grave.

"I think I know what you're suggesting. Tell me how we do it."

I shivered as the breeze brushed through my loose curls and across my neck. The night air was certainly cool, but that was not what had made the tiny hairs along my arms and down my back stand on end, my senses finely tuned to my surroundings.

Before me, several yards further down the road, stood Moilien in a shallow shell hole with another man I'd never seen before, working in concert with him. I could hear their muffled voices, the strikes of their shovels, and the shuffle of dirt. At least one of the bombs had already been lowered into the crater, for we had watched them carry it over from their vehicle.

Sidney and Max had both scrambled out in opposite directions over the quagmire of the surrounding fields and the slope of Kemmel Hill. Their paths had to be wide enough so that Moilien did not spot them as they circled around, but not so deep that they became stuck in the mire. I could only be grateful the top layer of soil was fairly dry, otherwise their slog through the sucking mud would have been even more difficult.

For my part, I simply had to wait on the road for their signals. This seemed the easier task, but I found that as the minutes stretched by, so did my nerves. I had thought the abandoned battle-field quiet, but I discovered I was wrong. The scrabbling of rats through the dirt, the clicking of insects, the whistling of the wind through some hole in the twisted metal wreckage—all was amplified.

And then there was the knowledge of what lay

out there under the upheaval of that earth. Left out here on my own, it would be all too easy to fool myself into believing the spirits of those who died were still wandering these unhallowed fields.

Which gave me heart that this plan just might work. For surely, I wasn't the only one unnerved to be standing on this unholy ground in the black of night.

I expected to see Max's lighter flicker first, for he had the easier of the two hikes, but it was Sidney's lighter that flared a short distance up the expanse of Kemmel Hill. Then a moment later, I saw Max's. Both were barely a glimmer, like a firefly passing through a forest, but I knew it was them. Inhaling a deep breath, I moved forward, praying this would work.

Steadily, I drew ever closer, shocked Moilien and his partner hadn't yet noticed me. When still they didn't look up, even though my steps were taking me nearer than I felt comfortable, I elected to moan. At first I felt ridiculous, but the longer I did so, the more fitting it seemed as I poured myself into playing my role, mourning my supposed, untimely death. Both men slowly lifted their gazes as I came to a stop about twenty yards away, purposely halting at the edge of a shell hole, as if to hover over it in my rippling skirt.

At first, neither of them moved, but then

Moilien shook his head. In the moonlight, I could see he'd removed his mask. "No. It can't be. You're dead."

The second man dropped his shovel and stumbled backward. He tripped over his own feet, falling to the ground. That's when Max scrambled up onto the road to stand over the crater, pointing his pistol down at the man. Sidney emerged more sluggishly from the muddled dirt of the hillside, his gun aimed at Moilien.

But this proved too much for the man, for he let out an infuriated, terrified cry. He clambered out of the shallow hole and darted into the field from which Max had emerged. His steps were too quick for him to be paying any heed to where he was stepping. Then Sidney lowered his weapon and took off after him.

"No!" I shouted even as he vaulted over a pile of debris. "Sidney!" I moved to the edge of the road, searching for his silhouette against the horizon, but his form had been swallowed up by the darkness. "Forget him. It's too dangerous."

Initially, I could hear the sounds of their fumbling footsteps, but even that was soon lost to the night. Clenching my fists, I paced a circle in the road. "Blast him! Blast him!"

"It will be all right," Max assured me as he ordered the other man up out of the hole. "Sidney knows what he's doing . . ."

Before he could even finish that statement,

there was a tremendous boom. It shook the earth and knocked me to the ground. At first, I worried one of the bombs Moilien had been burying had exploded, for who knew how he'd tampered with them. But then I realized I was not hit, and the terrifying flash of light had come from the middle of the field, not the roadway.

I pushed myself upright, staring out over the black field, my eyes momentarily blinded in the darkness that descended after the searing light. The patter of dirt raining down filled my ringing ears.

"Sidney," I gasped, blinking into the distance, trying to clear my eyes. I couldn't see him. I couldn't hear him. Where was he? "Sidney!" I screamed.

Oh, why had he followed that madman? Why? He could have let him go.

How close had he been to that blast? Could he have survived? Was he lying out in that field injured?

I couldn't see!

"The lights, the lights," I turned to yell at Max, who was kneeling in the dirt. "Point them at the field."

He was stumbling to his feet to do so when the sound of something approaching arrested us both. Through the darkness, a figure emerged. My every nerve strained toward it, desperate for it to be my husband.

When his features began to take shape, I clasped my hands over my mouth, unable to withhold the sob that had been building in my chest. He staggered over a depression in the earth and clambered up onto the road, sizing up the situation in one glance before dropping to his knees before me.

"You . . . you wretch!" I cried, swatting at him even as he pulled me to his chest. I collapsed against his shoulder, gripping the sides of his coat in my hands as I wept.

"I'm all right, Verity," Sidney crooned rather stiltedly. In truth, he sounded a bit stunned.

I pulled back, swiping at the tears on my face, and lowered my hand to find it covered with grit. It was then I realized that he was coated in a fine powder of dirt.

I lurched away from him, scanning his face and torso. "Are you injured? Were you hit?"

He shook his head. "No. I . . . I stopped to turn back about a minute before . . ." He swallowed. "Before the explosion." His body trembled as he inhaled a deep breath. "He must have stepped on a buried shell or mine."

"Why did you go after him?" I demanded, my anger returning now that I knew he was safe.

"I couldn't let him get away. The man meant to kill you." His eyes gleamed with fervor. "I wasn't going to give him the chance to try again." He lifted a hand, smoothing my hair back from my jaw. "But then I realized it was suicide. That there were too many unseen hazards. Trenches, and shell holes, and coils of barbed wire, and . . . and unexploded shells." He paused, searching my face. "That I had no desire to actually leave you a widow. Not when there are so many men already waiting in the wings."

I shook my head. "Oh, Sidney. You know they . . ."

He never let me finish my sentence, capturing my mouth with his own. I wrapped my arms around him, never intending to let go.

Then a voice to my left cleared its throat, and I pulled back, though not too quickly, for Sidney would not allow it. I flushed, looking over to where Max still stood with his gun pointed at Moilien's collaborator.

He smiled good-naturedly. "Pardon the interruption, but what would you like to do with this fellow."

Sidney opened his mouth to answer, but the sound of voices calling to us in the direction of our parked motorcar made him reconsider. It was the Rijkswacht officers who were supposed to join us. They must have heard the explosion.

He shrugged his head in their direction. "Why don't we ask them."

CHAPTER 31

N ice work."
I blinked my eyes, realizing I'd been staring sightlessly at the urn of flowers on the table across from the sofa where I sat. Captain Landau stood over me, his mouth curled in a knowing grin.

"What are you doing here?" I replied in startlement, setting my cup of now tepid tea next to my other half-empty cup on the table beside the sofa.

Once Étienne Moilien's associate—a man from Lille he'd hired solely for this purpose—had been taken into custody and the bombs had been roped off and marked for immediate removal, we had returned to Max's hotel in Poperinghe. Alec and Rose had already been there waiting for us, after finding no trace of Moilien or tampering with the road to Boeschèpe. Though Alec had stubbornly awaited our arrival, Rose had soon bustled him off to rest. He had aggravated his injury, and Rose was intent on bullying him into taking care of it.

Meanwhile, Sidney, Max, and I had remained

in the drawing room to answer questions. It was already mid-morning, and the night without rest, and far too much strain, had taken its toll. My eyes were gritty and I struggled to stay awake. Though what I wanted most was to bathe away the dirt and muck that seemed to permeate my every pore. It had been two days since I'd had a proper bath. Two days of travel, and sleeping in a barn, and crawling through kerosene, and wading through the morass of the devastated lands. I was filthy and grimy, and probably smelled even worse.

Landau sat down next to me. "Well, I wasn't going to leave you to face this bureaucratic mess alone." He glanced across the room toward Sidney, who was shaking hands with two Rijkswacht officers. "Though it appears you've navigated through it well enough on your own and resolved this tangle with admirable speed."

"This *tangle?*" I arched my eyebrows, ever bemused at the government's ability to understate any incident.

"The Belgian government, as well as our own, will be reporting the matter as just another terrible accident. A tourist wandering into an area where he shouldn't be."

I'd figured as much. No one wanted the public to know that leftover German bombs had so easily fallen into the hands of a lunatic.

"Noted."

"But even though you're no longer an agent, and this incident never happened, I'm afraid I'm still going to need a debriefing report." He at least had the grace to appear contrite while making such a high-handed request. "Take your time. The end of the week is soon enough to send it to me."

As it was already Wednesday, I could only sigh and roll my eyes at this magnanimous gesture. "I do have one question we haven't been able to answer that perhaps you can clear up." My tone of voice made it clear he'd better not withhold anything. "How did Moilien obtain the address Madame Moreau gave La Dame Blanche?"

Landau grimaced. "We're still trying to confirm, but we think he cultivated a friendship with one of the agents of La Dame Blanche in Liège, one who assisted Dewé and Chauvin as we've worked to liquidate the network."

"One of the couriers?"

"Possibly. Whoever it is, we suspect Moilien somehow convinced them to share Madame Moreau's address."

"Never knowing it would place her in danger."

"Undoubtedly."

I shook my head. "That's why she didn't share what she knew with La Dame Blanche, and consequently British Intelligence. She didn't know who could be trusted."

"Well, fortunately, she found a way to lure you into it."

"Lure" certainly felt like the operative word, but I didn't regret it. I couldn't. Not when we'd foiled a murderous madman, and in the process saved countless lives, including my own and Rose's. And just possibly salvaged my marriage.

Landau clasped his hands in his lap. "C sends his regards, and his deepest thanks."

So the chief *had* been kept apprised. Somehow I wasn't surprised.

"Unofficially, of course," I said.

"Of course." Landau smiled. "It's been good to see you, Verity."

"Likewise. Look us up next time you're in London."

He pushed to his feet. "I will."

And with that, he was gone, and my association with the Secret Service was severed yet again. Though, somehow, I wondered if it truly was. If it truly ever had been.

Max joined me a moment later, passing me yet another cup of tea.

"You and Sidney need to quit Mother Henning me. You must think I'm dying of thirst." I gestured to the table full of cups. "If you must bring me something, you could at least have the decency to make it gin."

His lips quirked. "Yes, well, it is only ten in

the morning. I was worried I might shock the natives."

I gestured toward my disgraceful appearance. "After seeing me, I think they would understand."

His eyes flicked over me. "You look lovely, as always."

"Stop it," I retorted in aggravation. "I'm more ragamuffin than woman. Or do you need your eyes examined? Perhaps that flash damaged your corneas."

He chuckled. "All right, I concede. You do rather resemble a dusty mop."

I arched my chin. "Thank you."

Silence fell as we stared at one another, and while it wasn't precisely uncomfortable, it wasn't easy either. His smile slipped a degree, though the warmth never faded from his eyes.

"You and Sidney seem to have resolved your differences."

"Yes, more or less."

"I'm glad."

It might have been merely a courteous statement, but I didn't think so. I believed he meant it.

"I'm sorry you got dragged into this mess," I replied, not knowing how to address the other.

"I'm not," he answered modestly, catching me off-guard. Then he leaned forward to press a gentle kiss to my cheek. "See you around, Verity."

I watched him go, wishing there was a way I

could give him the happiness he deserved. But it was not mine to grant.

My gaze shifted to the right to find Sidney studying me, a curious light in his eyes. I smiled wearily, and he crossed the room to join me.

"You look about as tired as I do," he remarked, sinking into the cushions with a sigh.

"Given the lack of sleep you've gotten in the last three days since we left Liège, I think that's doubtful." I pressed my fingers into the front of his coat. "I suspect you're dirtier, too, and I feel as if I've been dragged through a sandpit." Dropping all pretense at good humor, I settled into the sofa beside him. "Please, tell me they have a room for us."

He smiled, draping his arm around my shoulders. "They're preparing it for us now. And I asked them to go ahead and draw us a steaming bath. I'll even let you go first."

I sank my head down on his shoulder. "I knew there was a reason I married you."

"Yes, well, remember that the next time you drag me on one of your exploits."

I began to nod, until his words fully penetrated through the haze of my fatigue. "The next time?" I lifted my head to look at him.

He yawned. "Yes. Somehow, dear wife, I suspect this is only the beginning."

I couldn't tell whether he was displeased by this or not.

"That may not be true," I replied. "Perhaps we'll settle down quietly in the countryside with a gaggle of children and nothing to concern us but the state of the roads for our Sunday drive." Even as I said the words, I already dreaded them.

Sidney shook his head. "No, Ver. You and I were not meant for ordinary lives." His gaze turned tender. "And I do not regret that. Not for one moment."

"Truly?"

He lifted a hand to my chin. "Verity, I adored the woman I married. But I think I adore the fascinating, complicated woman you've become even more. Misadventures and all," he teased. But then sadness dimmed his eyes. "I only wish I'd been there to see the transformation."

My heart warmed at his words, though it was tinged with a bittersweet ache. "We both missed so much. But we have years to make it up."

He gently chucked me under the chin. "So long as neither of us has anyone else coming after us in reprisal."

"Or to silence us before we uncover their deceit," I added, not about to let him forget the reason for our last investigation.

He rested his cheek next to mine, murmuring in my ear. "Even then, I like our odds."

"So do I," I exhaled. "So do I."

Center Point Large Print
600 Brooks Road / PO Box 1
Thorndike, ME 04986-0001 USA

(207) 568-3717

US & Canada:
1 800 929-9108
www.centerpointlargeprint.com